T0070294

# The New Lovecraft Circle

**The H. P. Lovecraft editions from Del Rey Books:**

*The Best of H. P. Lovecraft:*
*Bloodcurdling Tales of Horror and the Macabre*

*The Dream Cycle of H. P. Lovecraft:*
*Dreams of Terror and Death*

*The Transition of H. P. Lovecraft:*
*The Road to Madness*

*The Horror in the Museum*

*The Watchers Out of Time*

*Waking Up Screaming*

*Shadows of Death*


**Other stories in the H. P. Lovecraftian World:**

*H. P. Lovecraft and Others:*
*Tales of the Cthulhu Mythos*

*Stories Inspired by H. P. Lovecraft:*
*Cthulhu 2000*


**Also available from The Modern Library:**

*At the Mountains of Madness*
The Definitive Edition

# The New Lovecraft Circle

Edited by
Robert M. Price

BALLANTINE BOOKS
NEW YORK

A Del Rey® Book
Published by The Random House Publishing Group
Copyright © 1996 by Robert M. Price
Illustration copyright © 1996 by Gahan Wilson
Preface copyright © 1996 by Ramsey Campbell
All rights reserved.

Published in the United States by Del Rey Books, an imprint of The Random House Publishing Group, a division of Random House, Inc., New York, and simultaneously in Canada by Random House of Canada Limited, Toronto. Originally published by Fedogan & Bremer, Minneapolis, in 1996.

"Preface" copyright © 1996 by Ramsey Campbell for this collection.

"Introduction" copyright © 1996 by Robert M. Price for this collection.

"The Plain of Sound" copyright © 1964 by J. Ramsey Campbell for *The Inhabitant of the Lake and Less Welcome Tenants,* 1964, appears here by permission of the author, Ramsey Campbell.

"The Stone on the Island" copyright © 1964 by August Derleth for *Over the Edge,* 1964, appears here by permission of the author, Ramsey Campbell.

"The Statement of One John Gibson" copyright © 1984 by Brian Lumley for *Crypt of Cthulhu* #19, Candlemas 1984, appears here by permission of the author, Brian Lumley.

"Demoniacal" copyright © 1978 by David Sutton for *Cthulhu: Tales of the Cthulhu Mythos* #3, 1978, appears here by permission of the author, David Sutton.

"The Kiss of Bugg-Shash" copyright © 1978 by Brian Lumley for *Cthulhu: Tales of the Cthulhu Mythos* #3, 1978, appears here by permission of the author, Brian Lumley.

"The Slitherer from the Slime" copyright © 1958 by Lin Carter and Dave Foley for *Inside SF* #3, September 1958, appears here by permission of Robert M. Price, agent for the estate of Lin Carter.

"The Doom of Yakthoob" copyright © 1971 by August Derleth for *The Arkham Collector* #10, September 1971, appears here by permission of Robert M. Price, agent for the estate of Lin Carter.

"The Fishers from Outside" copyright © 1988 by Cryptic Publications for *Crypt of Cthulhu* #54, Eastertide 1988, appears here by permission of Robert M. Price, agent for the estate of Lin Carter.

"The Keeper of the Flame" copyright © 1996 by Gary Myers for this collection.

"Dead Giveaway" copyright © 1976 by J. Vernon Shea for *Outre* #1, May 1976, appears here by permission of Virginia S. Burdette.

["Those Who Wait" originally appeared in an uncopyrighted fanzine. The author and his family have passed away.]

"The Keeper of Dark Point" and "The Black Mirror" (original versions) copyright © 1996 by John Glasby for this collection.

"I've Come to Talk with You Again" copyright © 1996 by the Estate of Karl Edward Wagner. In the interim between the writing of the story for this collection and its publication, it appeared in the British anthology *Dark Terrors* in a slightly modified form.

"The Howler in the Dark" copyright © 1984 by Richard L. Tierney for *Crypt of Cthulhu* #24, Lammas 1984, appears here by permission of the author, Richard L. Tierney.

"The Horror on the Beach" copyright © 1978 by Thranx, Inc.; first appeared in a limited edition from Shroud Publishers; reprinted by permission of the author and the author's agent, Virginia Kidd.

"The Whisperers" copyright © 1977 by Ultimate Publishing Company for *Fantastic,* September 1977, appears here by permission of the author, Richard A. Lupoff.

"Lights! Camera! Shub-Niggurath!" copyright © 1996 by Richard A. Lupoff for this collection.

"Saucers from Yaddith" copyright © 1984 by The Strange Company for *Etchings & Odysseys* #5, 1984, appears here by permission of the author, Robert M. Price.

"Vastarien" copyright © 1987 by Cryptic Publications for *Crypt of Cthulhu* #48, Saint John's Eve 1987, appears here by permission of the author, Thomas Ligotti.

"The Madness out of Space" copyright © 1982 by Crispin Burnham for *Eldritch Tales* numbers 8 and 9, 1982 and 1983, appears here by permission of the author, Peter H. Cannon.

"Aliah Warden" copyright © 1985 by Dracula Unlimited for *The Count Dracula Fan Club Annual,* vol. 5, no. 1, 1985, appears here by permission of the author, Roger Johnson.

"The Last Supper" copyright © 1981 by Crispin Burnham for *Eldritch Tales* #7, 1981, appears here by permission of the author, Donald R. Burleson.

"The Church at Garlock's Bend" copyright © 1987 by Davis Publications, Inc. for *Alfred Hitchcock's Mystery Magazine,* April 1987, appears here by permission of the author, David Kaufman.

"The Spheres Beyond Sound (Threnody)" copyright © 1987 by Mark Rainey for *Deathrealm* #2, Summer 1987, appears by permission of the author, Stephen Mark Rainey.

Del Rey is a registered trademark and the Del Rey colophon is a trademark of Random House, Inc.

www.delreybooks.com

Library of Congress Control Number: 2003114389

ISBN 978-0-345-44406-6

This edition published by arrangement with Fedogan & Bremer

Book design by Susan Turner

First Ballantine Books Paperback Edition: April 2004

147028622

*Dedicated to*
*my beloved Carol,*
*who shares with Asenath Waite*
*both beauty and wisdom beyond*
*her years, but with none of*
*the bad stuff!*

# Contents

# Preface

Abominable . . . detestable . . . unspeakable . . . noxious . . . noisome . . . indescribable . . . distorted . . . malformed . . . Just some of the words that come to mind as I contemplate my contributions to this book. Perhaps there's a peculiarly English charm about the way "The Plain of Sound" follows a quotation from the *Necronomicon* with the moochings of three young buggers in search of a pub, all told with an undue sobriety that must have struck me as appropriately Lovecraftian. Peculiar is certainly the term for it, and for the newsagent's unlikely dialect, but what is the word for the way the three students view another world as though it isn't much more significant than the latest development in television? Well, there's none so blasé as the young. As for "The Stone on the Island," I recall J. Vernon Shea condemning the office milieu as inappropriate to a Lovecraftian theme. Of course it was the office where I then worked, and in retrospect the notion of a character experiencing visions of supernatural terror among his fellow civil servants seems all too like idealised autobiography. Still, the story can hardly wait to finish him off, and who can blame it? Let me leave it in peace and move on to tales that are more fun.

Brian Lumley seems to have had some. As for James Wade's tale, would it be unfair to suspect it of some deadpan humour? The astounding gullibility of the narrator is almost traditional, and the way he mercifully faints, though only to revive a moment later for another sight of what did for him. But I have my doubts about an invocation that goes *"N'yah ahahah"* like a villain in a *Mad* comic, and all the business with the Guest, not least the "stupefying" spectacle of a coat, hat and scarf lying on the ground. And what about the line "For hours we droned on over northern Maine"? Surely it refers to the sound of the engine.

J. Vernon Shea seems to have felt humour wouldn't hurt his story, one of two in this anthology which I considered for *New Tales of the Cthulhu Mythos.* Despite its lightness of tone, this extravaganza does resurrect the authentic early Lovecraftian morbidity and commitment to the generation gap. And there's no question of the kind of fun Lin Carter and Dave Foley were having: they give good slither. I hope I won't be accused of blackening Lin's memory by suggesting that some of his more serious work reads like parody too—not so much "The Doom of Yakthoob," but how about the invocation in "The Fishers from Outside" to the one-legged bird-god, "Quumyagga nng'h aargh"? Still, he enjoys his lost city, and it would be unkind to suggest that his narrator should have lingered longer in Ushonga.

Alan Dean Foster revives pulp conventions with gusto, and achieves real terror in the cellar, though it seems mean to expect Cthulhu to be satisfied with nothing more than a cat. Roger Johnson exports a Lovecraftian lineage to a British landscape more appropriate than any I managed to find when I was emulating Grandpa. And Peter Cannon seems to have employed a pinch of the essential salts of the old gent himself, not to mention some sly wit. As for Don Burleson, he offers a loathsome fright which no aesthetically sensitive ghoul should miss.

Dick Tierney tells a tale worthy of the best weird pulps. Nor is he alone in returning to principles by which Lovecraft wrote. Gary Myers goes back, very effectively, to Dunsany, and David Kaufman is as delicately powerful in conveying a sense of the massive and terrible. The name of Zann is by no means betrayed by Mark Rainey. As for Tom Ligotti, he need acknowledge no imagination but his own in communicating how "the only value of this world lay in its power—at certain times—to suggest another world."

Other tales may have been added to this book since I wrote this piece to end Bob Price's anxiety about its non-appearance, and so my failure to comment on them should not be taken as expressing aversion. I look forward to reading them. I *shall* read them, I tell you—I shall be entertained! Hee, hee, hee . . . Fun's the only answer—what else is there to do but laugh if the cosmos is a joke? Chortle with Cthulhu, yuk with Yog-Sothoth, giggle with Shub-Niggurath . . . haw, haw, haw . . . But what is this cold wind which sprang to life at the very outset of that sentence? *Mercy of Heaven, what is that shape behind the parting words?* Spectral pallor . . . aquiline nose . . . elongated lower jaw . . . hands reaching out of word-processor screen . . . am dragged away from keyboard . . . hee, hee, hee . . .

Ramsey Campbell
Merseyside, England
12 May 1993

# Introduction

In his *Lovecraft: A Look Behind the Cthulhu Mythos* Lin Carter observed that August Derleth's collection, *Tales of the Cthulhu Mythos*, "marked the beginning of an era in the history of the Mythos for many reasons, and one of the most important was that it introduced an extraordinary number of new writers in the Mythos" (p. 175). These scribes Carter went on to dub "the New Lovecraft Circle." Their number included Ramsey Campbell, Brian Lumley, J. Vernon Shea (actually a friend and correspondent of Lovecraft's, but just making his Mythos fiction debut), James Wade, Colin Wilson (again, an established pro, but a new Mythos writer), Gary Myers, and Lin Carter himself. Actually, Carter and Myers began playing the game too late to make it into *Tales of the Cthulhu Mythos*, but just by a tendril.

Derleth's flagship Mythos collection followed related Arkham House volumes by Campbell *(The Inhabitant of the Lake and Less Welcome Tenants)* and Wilson *(The Mind Parasites)* and preceded collections by Myers *(The House of the Worm)*, Lumley *(The Caller of the Black, The Horror at Oakdeene, Beneath the Moors)*, and Carter *(Dreams from R'lyeh)*. Since then, Wilson has added to his Mythos canon *The Philosopher's Stone*, while several of Campbell's tales from the earlier volume were later collected, along with a few new ones, in the Scream Press collection *Cold Print* (1985).

Carter wrote several more Mythos tales, five of them forming a serial novel after the manner of Derleth's *The Trail of Cthulhu*. These he later submitted to Jim Turner at a post-Derleth Arkham House under the title *The Terror out of Time*. Turner did not take the bait, but the collection is scheduled for publication in the near future from Chaosium under the title *The Xothic Legend Cycle*.

Eventually Carter persuaded Myers, whom he judged the best among the New Circle, to pen a few more brief tales, some of which appeared in Carter's Zebra Books run of the paperback *Weird Tales*.

Others, some newly solicited by yours truly, appeared in *Crypt of Cthulhu*.

Unfortunately, Wade and Shea did not pursue Lovecraftian fiction much farther. Another tale of Wade's, "A Darker Shadow over Innsmouth," really a brief fable about nuclear weapons, did appear in the fifth issue of Derleth's *The Arkham Collector*, while the more substantial "The Silence of Erika Zann" appeared in Edward Paul Berglund's important collection *Disciples of Cthulhu* in 1976 (DAW Books). Shea's 1966 memoir of Lovecraft, "H. P. Lovecraft: The House and the Shadow" was reprinted by Necronomicon Press in 1982.

Derleth's *Tales of the Cthulhu Mythos*, then, was doing two jobs at once. It chronicled the earlier generation of the evolution of the Mythos by including important Mythos stories by Derleth himself, Henry Kuttner, Robert E. Howard, Clark Ashton Smith, Frank Belknap Long, and others. But then it went on to give the Mythos a new birth, a reincarnation in contemporary garb, even as Carter suggested.

It was significant that, while all the new stories were obviously inspired by Lovecraft, or at least by Derleth, all were unashamedly contemporary (all three of Wade's that I have mentioned, in fact, were almost too contemporary, reeking of the decade of the 60s and its various agendas, though they are so well written this does not hurt them).

Strikingly, none of them sought to locate their stories in Lovecraft's Miskatonic Valley, either. Critics of Lovecraft had scathingly pointed out the absurdity visible when one views HPL's tales synoptically: why were all these extra-terrestrial bogies so interested in one small area of New England?

Derleth had advised Campbell, and perhaps the others took the hint, not to move all his fictional luggage into Arkham and Innsmouth, since these places were already so saturated with spooks and tentacles that a fresh start might better be made elsewhere. And he was right.

So the new disciples set to work, like the pioneers driven from their familiar fatherland and impelled to carve out new frontiers elsewhere. Before long, Campbell had his Severn Valley, Lumley his

Blowne House and Oakdeene Sanitarium, Carter his Sanbourne Institute of Pacific Antiquities, etc.

But in this case a warning away from one path was the starting gun for a race down another. Imagine the fun of creating one's own Lovecraftian universe, essentially playing Lovecraft oneself! And who could stop the new writers from adding their own tomes of forbidden lore to the already voluminous canon? Campbell contributed the multivolume *Revelations of Glaaki*, which even seemed to out-arcanize itself, since there seemed to be extra apocryphal volumes of the work floating around! Carter would later think up the *Ponape Scripture* and the *Xanthu Tablets*, and Wilson decided that the mysterious Voynich Manuscript (which actually exists and puzzles researchers) was really the *Necronomicon* enciphered. Lumley added the mysterious *Cthaat Aquadingen* and Joachim Feery's *Notes upon the Necronomicon*.

This last, incidentally, might be highlighted as a perfect device for updating what had become a hackneyed prop. How rare could Alhazred's book be if every occultist had his own copy, as most of them did by the time the original generation of Lovecraft disciples were done? So leave it to Lumley to create a new book with the ring of the old. Feery, you see, was something of a medium himself and ventured to compile his own glossed edition based on no known manuscript evidence, but perhaps on Sources much closer to the horse's mouth! But all of these second-generation grimoires, it seems to me, showed quite a bit of ingenuity. None was simply another *Necronomicon* clone, like most of the books designed by the earlier group of writers.

And of course, the Lovecraftian pantheon began to bulge, too. Campbell's Daoloth and Glaaki, Lumley's Yibb-Tstll and Shudde-M'ell, and Carter's Ythogtha and Zoth-Ommog fairly forced Mythos taxonomists to add a new wing onto the zoo. In all this, in the stories of the New Lovecraft Circle, one sensed simultaneously the joys both of nostalgia and of fresh creation. Accordingly the reader, if the stories hit him right, experienced a feeling of at-home-ness (Yes, this was the Mythos, all right!) and the delight of newness. You could almost pretend it was all unfolding for the first time, and this time here you were on the ground floor.

All of which brings me to the question of pastiches, a guilty literary pleasure. Most Cthulhu Mythos fiction is either a pastiche of Love-craft and Derleth or at the very least formula fiction. Is this a bad thing? Some say it is, and this may have something to do with the un-willingness of many editors even to look at Mythos fiction. They think readers know too well what to expect: a too-familiar story in which certain things will happen, right on schedule, and in which certain code words and book titles will try, unsuccessfully, to substi-tute for atmosphere and characterization.

Prolonged exposure to fanzines has the effect of lending some credence to these suspicions. Reading many of them, one soon con-cludes that the small readership for whom they are written has a great deal in common with the seedy protagonist of Campbell's "Cold Print." The Mythos has become like pornography, and it mat-ters not whether there is any plot or characterization to speak of, any more than it does in a cheap porn paperback or skin-flick. Just as long as the proper anatomy is all there, only in this case it is tentacles rather than testicles, beasts instead of breasts.

But surely not all genre fiction, not all formula fiction, need be a poor example of its type. I will not concede that Cthulhu Mythos fic-tion is so sub-literary a genre that ipso facto there can be no good ex-amples of it, that only a bad example would be true to type. We have two important issues to address here. (Granted, if you have bought this book, you do not need to be convinced. But at least maybe we can help you win your next argument on the subject.)

I believe that we may learn much from some remarks of Lin Carter, made in his book *Imaginary Worlds*, in reply to the criticisms made by Alexei and Cory Panshin against the pulp genre of Sword-&-Sorcery fiction, damning it as "a living fossil with no apparent ability to evolve." To this Carter replied, "Well, perhaps. But what of it? The stuff is fun to read, and fun to write, and the fossilization of the genre is, I suspect, largely in the eye of the beholder . . . *Must* a school of writing evolve? I wonder why. Evolution implies change into some-thing else" (pp. 145–146).

In other words, this criticism, also aimed frequently at Cthulhu Mythos fiction, is a Catch-22: if the genre doesn't evolve, it is dead in the water. If it does evolve, it becomes something else. And in either case we are done with it.

Carter offered no contrived aesthetic defense for writing new

Sword-&-Sorcery, and I am far from ready to offer one for the continuation of the Mythos either. John Jakes, in a passage appreciatively quoted by Carter, sums it up: we don't like it because we are supposed to like it or obliged to like it by some literary conscience. We like it because we like it. Jakes: "There are just not enough of this kind of stories to go around any more; not enough, anyway, to please me" (Introduction to the author's *Brak the Barbarian*).

In other words, to put it in terms drawn from Susan Sontag's famous essay "Notes on Camp," Carter, Jakes and the rest of us enjoy this fiction precisely for the excesses that make more "serious" critics turn up their noses. In another essay ("The Pornographic Imagination"), Sontag puts down science fiction along with pornography as "sub-literary," a comparison I have borrowed just above. But she has forgotten herself when she makes such sweeping judgments. We latter-day pulpists are not to be despised, for we have acquired the sensibility of "Camp." Carter knew what qualified as great literature and what didn't and that both were enjoyable in their ways. And he was unashamed of his nostalgic, campy love for what he himself called "the gloriously fourth-rate."

But, one might persist, doesn't it get rather stale? Maybe there can be good Mythos fiction, granted, but hasn't it all been written? Does the plethora of poor Mythos imitations signal that it's been done to death? Why continue to write them?

The point is, why pastiche? Here I will appeal to the intriguing thinking of Jacques Derrida. Derrida, as part of a larger argument I dare not entertain here, contends that writing is far from the secondary fossilization of living speech most philosophers and linguists have judged it since Plato's time. Writing, so goes the complaint, is the desiccated corpse of speech. It no longer breathes with intonation, no longer allows for the possibility of clarification by the author.

But, Derrida contends, the author's "intention" for what he said or wrote was already an epiphenomenon. That is, what he thought "his" words meant was simply his own reading of a text which produced itself through him (shades of Joachim Feery!). What comes out in the writing process is the contents of the subconscious mind, which is already like a written text engraved in the neurons. It may seem new to us, but it is new like the first-time recognition of a hitherto repressed memory. It is known for the first time in remembrance, never having been seen before. This pre-written subconscious script Derrida calls *arche-ecriture*, originary writing.

You see, I think Derrida helps us grasp the fact, stated more baldly by Jakes and seconded by Carter, that when one writes a "Mythos story," one is in fact simply *reading* the Mythos story, the one written deep within by all one's years of reading and enjoying the work of Lovecraft, Derleth, et al. The second half of Derleth's *Tales of the Cthulhu Mythos* was a rewriting, and thus a rereading, of the first half. One wishes there were more of these stories, so one writes more of them, not so much for other hungry Lovecraftians to read, but for oneself to read in the very act of writing them.

All those terrible fannish Mythos yarns are so bad not because they must be, nor even because their young authors are poor writers, but rather, at the bottom of it, because they are poor readers! They have picked up nothing in Lovecraft but all the tongue-twisting names and the twisting tentacles, merely beasts and bestiaries. Mythos names, we often hear, and rightly, do not a Lovecraftian story make.

Editor Wilum Pugmire announced that his magazine *Tales of Lovecraftian Horror* would consider no Mythos fiction. An odd editorial rule, one might think, but no. Pugmire knew he had to get writers to get the names out of their heads, at least temporarily, if they were to begin to see what else made the Old Gent's tales so effective. Things like mood, style, vision. And if these elements were right, he knew he had a tale of truly Lovecraftian horror on his hands. There were only three issues, and to fill even that many he had to break his own rules more than once. The assignment wasn't easy.

But has anyone noticed that if a story festooned with *Necronomicon* passages and cries of "Iä!" does not by this token constitute a Lovecraftian tale, neither are these props needed to make a tale a Mythos tale? And it can just as well be a Mythos tale without being particularly Lovecraftian, as many by Lumley, Wilson, and Derleth demonstrate. So what is it that is integral to a story being a Mythos tale? Glad I asked!

I would venture that a "tale of the Cthulhu Mythos" is by nature (= by formula, by DNA) a strange and wondrous hybrid, a Faustian Mystery. One seeks forbidden knowledge, whether wittingly or, more likely, unwittingly, but one may not know till it is too late. This is possible because the seeking is a gradual piecing together of clues whose eventual destination one does not know. The knowledge, once gained, is too great for the mind of man. It is Promethean, Faustian knowledge. Knowledge that destroys in the moment of enlightenment, a Gnosis of damnation, not of salvation. One would never have contracted with Mephistopheles to gain it. One rather wishes it were not too late to forget it.

And usually this knowledge is such as to threaten to cancel the future, to turn it into the past, perhaps by opening oneself to replacement by Joseph Curwen, perhaps by raising up the Old Ones who will return the planet to its former domicile in alien dimensions.

As I see it, the common use of the device of such a threat, which may be clothed in as many versions as the all-purpose plot diagram of Lester Dent, need not issue in uniformity. For instance, Mythos stories may or may not end pessimistically. The threat may be turned back, or deferred, or we may be left hanging. The basic idea of a Mythos tale as I have set it forth is an interior skeleton like a mammal's, a frame on which to grow, not a hard, limiting exo-skeleton like those worn by the insects from Shaggai. It forms the base-line against which the new variations may be measured. It is not a denial of flexibility; it is something to be flexible *with*.

In my judgment we may plot the failure of both insipid fan Mythos fiction and of sophisticated New Wave Mythos fiction (some of the contents of Campbell's *New Tales of the Cthulhu Mythos* and Berglund's *Disciples of Cthulhu*) along this axis. The fan fiction tends to stick to the skeleton so closely there is no meat on the bones. Or the meat is old and rank. We've heard it all before.

The New Wave stuff, on the other hand, chucks the whole skeleton. It is either like an invertebrate shoggoth or it has simply plugged in a few familiar Mythos names here and there in an unfamiliar structure. Stories of psychological horror, for example, simply do not need Mythos touches and are not improved by them. *Psycho* would not have benefitted had Lila found a copy of the *Necronomicon* on Norman's shelf alongside *The Witch Cult in Western Europe*.

In a previous anthology, *Tales of the Lovecraft Mythos*, I sought to create a pastiche of the first half of August Derleth's *Tales of the Cthulhu Mythos*. The present collection means to ape the second half, to commemorate that dawn of a new era of Mythos fiction. I have been able to assemble several little known and seldom seen stories by most of the seven members of the New Lovecraft Circle numbered by Lin Carter and by other, more recent adepts as well, for the tradition grows. The cult will not be stamped out.

One of the ironies of a collection like this is that by now a quarter of a century has gone by since the era of the New Lovecraft Circle began. In the meantime some of the budding new Mythos writers, like some in the original Lovecraft Circle (Robert Bloch and Henry Kuttner, for example) cut their fangs on Lovecraftian fiction, then went on to other things. This is certainly true of Ramsey Campbell and Brian Lumley, with whose post-Lovecraftian works the shelves now fairly bulge. As with Bloch and Kuttner, the Mythos fiction of these two must henceforth be reckoned as "the early Lumley," "the early Campbell."

A few of the stories from Campbell's *The Inhabitant of the Lake* were axed from the Scream Press collection *Cold Print*. One of these had been one of my favorites in the earlier collection: "The Plain of Sound." I reprinted it in *Crypt of Cthulhu* #43, and now here it is again, back in hard covers where it belongs. "The Stone on the Island" appeared first in August Derleth's anthology *Over the Edge* (1964). Here one can already see the strong development of Campbell's gritty realism, the ambience of urban dreariness as the theatre of horror, the use of anti-heroic protagonists. These factors made their emergence in "Cold Print," but for my money, they are much better integrated with the Lovecraftian element here.

Brian Lumley's "The Statement of One John Gibson" first appeared in *Crypt of Cthulhu* #19 in 1984 and is resurrected here for the first time. It is related to the Lovecraft revision tale "The Diary of Alonzo Typer," which HPL wrote from a draft by William Lumley. Who better to follow up that tale than a living sequel to (though not a descendant of) that elder Lumley?

Dave Sutton's "Demoniacal" first appeared in *New Writings in Horror and the Supernatural*, Vol. II (Sphere Books) where Lumley saw it. "His tale was so obviously a Mythos story that I wrote him and said, 'Let me do a sequel!' because I had an idea for just such," Lumley recalls. "He OK'ed that and I wrote 'The Kiss of Bugg-Shash,' which definitely *was* Mythos and so brought Dave's tale firmly into the genre also." The pair appeared together in Jon Harvey's pamphlet series *Cthulhu: Tales of the Cthulhu Mythos*, 3 (Spectre Press), then in my own *Crypt of Cthulhu*.

One key feature of campiness is that it hovers just on the thin line between nostalgia and parody, half-saluting and half-satirizing. Sometimes it is not so easy to keep the balance, and so we satirize not what we scorn, but what we love. Thus did the young Lin Carter and Dave Foley in their parody, "The Slitherer from the Slime," which first appeared in *Inside SF*, #53, September, 1958, and then in *Crypt of Cthulhu* #54. The basic elements of a Mythos story need only form the skeleton and need not dictate what may grow on it, or at what *rate*. The skeleton should be able to accommodate some fun-poking, some tickling of its own ribs. Lovecraft's style, I think, may be honored almost as much in the breach as in the imitation.

In *Lovecraft: A Look Behind the Cthulhu Mythos*, Lin Carter crowned himself "the Last Disciple." I suppose he simply meant "the latest disciple," unless he was unusually pessimistic for the future of the genre. In that case perhaps he viewed himself, with typical grandioseness, as the "Seal of the Prophets." All this on the strength of a few brief cautionary tales from the *Necronomicon* he had written and mailed off to August Derleth during the preparation of the Lovecraft book. Derleth had by this time become something of a grandfatherly figure to Carter on matters Lovecraftian, and he accepted a couple of these efforts to appear in *The Arkham Collector*. One of them, "The Doom of Yakthoob," reprinted here, appeared in the 10th issue, Summer 1971. In my judgment (and I have elsewhere published all of them in the series), "Yakthoob" remains the best of these attempts to supply the autobiographical episodes Lovecraft himself had implied prefaced the darkest secrets of *Al Azif*.

In his many "excerpts" from ancient tomes Carter's command of antique translation English was never quite up to snuff. He was obviously more at ease with crisper, modern prose. Accordingly, his longer Mythos tales set in the 30s or in the 70s and 80s are more effective. "The Fishers from Outside" is one of these. In it, as in several of these stories, Lin picks up on some Lovecraftian name-dropping. In his poem "The Outpost" and his revision tale "Winged Death," HPL had referred to the mysterious Zimbabwe ruins with their enigmatic bird reliefs. What shocking significance had Lovecraft imagined as connected with them? And who or what were the "Fishers from Out-side," mentioned in both the story and the poem? It was left to Carter to solve the riddle.

From the remaining members of the original New Lovecraft Cir-cle I have managed to extract by unwholesome means best left un-specified here a set of new or at least seldom-viewed tales. Gary Myers has contributed a new story to this volume. Alas, J. Vernon Shea and James Wade both followed Lovecraft into the aether since Carter proclaimed them members of that New Circle that we may hope will someday be unbroken in the sweet Yuggothian by-and-by.

In his last years, Shea had entered Lovecraft fandom, and in the first issue of his fanzine *Outre* he published the sequel to his "The Haunter of the Graveyard," which of course had appeared in Der-leth's *Tales of the Cthulhu Mythos* (though omitted from Jim Turner's new edition). How natural, then, that "Dead Giveaway" should ap-pear in *The New Lovecraft Circle*, a sequel to Derleth's volume.

Ghoulish delvings have also retrieved the tale that represents James Wade in the present volume, "Those Who Wait." Like Shea's, this story has before now only appeared in an obscure fanzine, the second issue of the promising but abortive *Dark Brotherhood Journal* (1972). I must repeat here Wade's warning issued there that "Those Who Wait" was the story most of *us* have written: a fannish effort at aping Lovecraft, penned in the heat of early Lovecraft enthusiasm (he was only 16 when he wrote it). He said it should really have been titled "The Rover Boys at R'lyeh." Nonetheless, Wade generously al-lowed it to be published as a curiosity and to satisfy Mythos com-pletists. I am happy to include it here for the same reasons. Wade's canon of Lovecraftian stories is too small for any of the tales, even ju-venilia, to be excluded from it.

There was one more writer who had been ordained by Derleth himself to take a seat, like Randolph Carter in "Through the Gates of the Silver Key," among the ranks of the New Lovecraft Circle. But, again, like Randolph Carter, the throne was denied him. Derleth had promised to bring out an Arkham collection of Mythos stories by English weird fictioneer John Glasby. Glasby had written a huge number of tales for the English paperback magazine *Supernatural Stories*, some few of them Lovecraft-related.

The tragic death of the mastermind of Arkham House threw

many planned projects into Limbo. Sadly, Glasby's *The Brooding City* was one of these. I published all the stories in two issues of *Crypt of Cthulhu* (#s 67 and 71), and it may be that Fedogan & Bremer will yet bring them out as the hardcover they should have been. Thus I include none of them here. Rather I have chosen to reprint two much rarer Mythos tales Glasby wrote for *Supernatural Stories*, "The Keeper of Dark Point" and "The Black Mirror." In fact these tales are even rarer than that: they are the *original* versions of stories which appeared in print editorially shorn of most of their Lovecraftian associations. Here they are in all their Lovecraftian glory. Thus Glasby finds himself, years later, just where he belongs, a secure member of the New Lovecraft Circle.

The Circle has expanded in the years since it first appeared, with new writers taking the places of those who had fallen. The late Karl Edward Wagner, justly renowned as the creator of the Sword-&-Sorcery series of Kane novels and as the editor of DAW's *Year's Best Horror Stories* collections, was also an accomplished horror writer. His Lovecraftian tribute to Lee Brown Coye, *Sticks,* appeared in the new edition of *Tales of the Cthulhu Mythos.* He continued mining (or is it sucking?) that vein here in "I've Come to Talk With You Again." We have the high honor of presenting here Karl's last story, which you will find eerily prophetic.

Another Sword-&-Sorcery scribe who has not hesitated to make use of the Cthulhu Mythos is Richard L. Tierney, whose seminal essay "The Derleth Mythos" ushered in a whole era of Lovecraft interpretation that dominated the field in the 70s and 80s. Though keen-eyed and critical in his delineation of Derleth's embellishments of Lovecraft's Mythos, Tierney has always maintained that there is no reason not to continue writing Mythos fiction in the trajectory Derleth marked out. Even if it is not what the Old Gent himself had in mind, it has its own integrity and it is a lot of fun.

Tierney's object in "The Derleth Mythos" was simply to mark the difference between Lovecraft's vision and Derleth's, not to turn the clock back. As a result he has made extremely creative use of the Mythic systems of both men, combining them in intricate ways with the fictional worlds of Robert E. Howard and Clark Ashton Smith as well. (There was even one draft of a story in which Tierney's hero Simon of Gitta teamed up with Wagner's Kane, but copyright problems proved too formidable a foe for even these two stalwart barbarians! Rest assured one copy of the suppressed version rests in my archives. You may yet see it. You know how these forbidden manuscripts have a way of coming to light!) In Tierney's work we see a smoothly harmonized and integrated fictional universe that I have elsewhere dubbed "the *Weird Tales* cosmology."

His tale in this anthology, "The Howler in the Dark," first appeared in *Crypt of Cthulhu* #24, albeit with one line of text missing. That omission is corrected here.

Few readers will fail to recognize the names of Alan Dean Foster and Richard Lupoff. Both are familiar in many connections in the worlds of science fiction, fantasy, even movies and comics, realms between which most of us move rather easily. But it may come as something of a surprise to learn that both men have written quite interesting Mythos stories. Foster's "The Horror on the Beach" was published by Kenneth Krueger in an edition that was disintegrating as soon as it was published in 1978. It deserves a wider public and a more abiding incarnation.

You have no doubt seen Lupoff's excellent "Discovery of the Ghooric Zone—March, 2337" in the new version of *Tales of the Cthulhu Mythos*, where it had been reprinted from its original appearance in *Chrysalis* #1 (1977). From the pages of *Fantastic* now reappears Lupoff's "The Whisperers." His "Lights! Camera! Shub-Niggurath!" appears here for the first time. The novelette formed the basis for Lupoff's novel *The Forever City*. The original was once slated for publication, but the mag had the bad luck to fold. Note: Lupoff's sequel to "The Dunwich Horror," "The Devil's Hop Yard" (from *Chrysalis* #2) appears in my anthology *The Dunwich Cycle* (Chaosium, Inc., 1996). His sequel to "The Whisperer in Darkness," "Documents in the Case of Elizabeth Akeley" (*The Magazine of Fantasy & Science Fiction*, March 1982), appears in my anthology *The Hastur Cycle* (Chaosium, Inc., 1993).

From the crumbling pages of *Etchings & Odysseys* (#5, 1984), one of the premiere Lovecraftian magazines of the 70s Lovecraft revival, comes my own "Saucers From Yaddith." Unlike Lin Carter, who showed a similar unfortunate tendency to include his own fiction in his anthologies, I will not declare myself the Last Disciple, for the number still grows.

And one of the most interesting things about some of the newer Circle members is that they seem to be mastering the difficult art of penning tales of the kind Pugmire sought, tales not explicitly of the Cthulhu Mythos, but rather more strictly Lovecraftian in style, mood, cosmic implication, or plot structure. Thomas Ligotti's "Vastarien," which first appeared in *Crypt of Cthulhu* #48, is, I think, the perfect rendition of a theme one might by now consider fatally hackneyed, that of the forbidden book. Whether it was suggested by Lovecraft's first three "Fungi From Yuggoth" sonnets, or by their prose counterpart, the fragment "The Book," or by neither, "Vastarien" does the best job I have ever seen of unfolding the notion of "nighted worlds of ill" kept at bay between antique covers.

Peter Cannon's "The Madness out of Space" was first foisted on the Lovecraftian reading public as a tongue-in-cheek hoax in the pages of *Eldritch Tales* #s 8 (1982) and 9 (1983) where Cannon claimed to have discovered a lost Lovecraft manuscript by a series of odd chances on a trip to New England. There were clues aplenty to tell you otherwise, but Cannon had done a fine job at the difficult art of Lovecraft pastiche. *Crypt of Cthulhu* #34 featured a somewhat edited version, and still a third version appears here.

Roger Johnson's "Aliah Warden" was written on request for the special Lovecraft issue of *The Count Dracula Fan Club Annual* in 1985. Though he himself is the last to claim that it holds any surprises for the reader, I have always considered it a little gem of stylistic Lovecraft pastiche, and I am glad now to share it with a wider audience.

Donald R. Burleson, known both for his innovative horror fiction and his literary criticism of horror fiction (see his *H.P. Lovecraft: A Critical Study; Lovecraft: Disturbing the Universe* and his *Begging to Differ: Deconstructionist Readings*) is another of those with the rare gift of invoking Lovecraft the hard way, by style and theme, not with code names. Early on he wrote a small number of brief tales recalling the Lovecraft of elegant grue, the Lovecraft of "The Hound," "The Loved Dead," "The Statement of Randolph Carter." The first and best of these, "The Last Supper," which appeared first in Dirk Mosig's fan magazine *The Miskatonic* (#23, 1978), then in revised versions in *Eldritch Tales* #7, and in *Crypt of Cthulhu* #34, appears here polished a bit further.

Despite the antipathy of mainstream editors to Lovecraftian fiction, David Kaufman managed to sneak a fine example of it into the pages of *Alfred Hitchcock's Mystery Magazine* (April, 1987). I guess he was able to do it because of the fine subtlety of his writing. "The Church at Garlock's Bend" features nary a Mythos cliche, yet in its brooding atmosphere of the ominously lingering past, it seems to me perfectly Lovecraftian. What Kaufman does here, few Lovecraftians have even tried.

Stephen Mark Rainey, editor of *Deathrealm*, is another rising star in today's weird fiction field, as a look at his fine collection *The Fugue Devil* will readily verify. Like Brian Lumley he seems to have perfected the art of revivifying accustomed Lovecraftian elements by creating elusively similar variant versions of them. In "The Spheres Beyond Sound," you will discover a mysterious Maestro Zann, author of an enigmatic treatise on music. Yet, you should know, this book actually exists! One other thing you should know: an earlier version of this story appeared under the title "Threnody" in *Deathrealm* #2 (Summer, 1987), while a very different story with almost exactly the same title ("The Sphere Beyond Sound") appeared soon after in *Tales of Lovecraftian Horror* #2 (June, 1988).

At last, I must express my gratitude to several individuals for bringing some of the tales in this and my previous anthology to my attention when I would certainly never have seen them otherwise. Possessors of such sharp (three-lobed burning) eyes are Charles Garofalo, Tani Jantsang, Dan Gobbett, the late Ronald Shearer, Mike Ashley, S. T. Joshi, William Fulwiler, and Charles Gray. And thanks also to Steffan Aletti, trusty scribe, who helped me in the sanity-blasting labor of proofreading!

Robert M. Price
Bloomfield, New Jersey
July, 1996

# The New Lovecraft Circle

# The Plain of Sound

## Ramsey Campbell

*Verily do we know little of the other universes beyond the gate which YOG-SOTHOTH guards. Of those which come through the gate and make their habitation in this world none can tell; although Ibn Schacabao tells of the beings which crawl from the Gulf of S'glhuo that they may be known by their sound. In that Gulf the very worlds are of sound, and matter is known but as an odor; and the notes of our pipes in this world may create beauty or bring forth abominations in S'glhuo. For the barrier between haply grows thin, and when sourceless sounds occur we may justly look to the denizens of S'glhuo. They can do little harm to those of Earth, and fear only that shape which a certain sound may form in their universe.*

ABDUL ALHAZRED: *NECRONOMICON*

When Frank Nuttall, Tony Roles, and I reached the Inn at Severnford, we found that it was closed.

It was summer of 1958, and as we had nothing particular to do at Brichester University that day we had decided to go out walking. I had suggested a trip to Goatswood—the legends there interested me—but Tony had heard things which made him dislike that town. Then Frank had told us about an advertisement in the *Brichester Weekly News* about a year back which had referred to an inn at the center of Severnford as "one of the oldest in England." We could walk there in the morning and quench the thirst caused by the journey; afterward we could take the bus back to Brichester if we did not feel like walking.

Tony was not enthusiastic. "Why go all that way to get drunk," he inquired, "even if it is so old? Besides, that ad in the paper's old too—by now the place has probably fallen down . . ." However, Frank and I wanted to try it, and finally we overruled his protests.

We would have done better to agree with him, for we found the inn's doors and windows boarded up and a nearby sign saying: "Temporarily closed to the public." The only course was to visit the modern public house up the street. We looked round the town a little; this did not occupy us long, for Severnford has few places of interest, most of it being dockland. Before two o'clock we were searching for a bus-stop; when it eluded us, we entered a newsagent's for directions.

"Bus t' Brichester? No, only in the mornin's," the proprietor told us. "Up from the University, are you?"

"Then how do we get back?" Tony asked.

"Walk, I s'pose," suggested the newsagent. "Why'd you come up anyway—oh, t'look at the Inn? No, you won't get in there now—so many o' them bloody teenagers've been breakin' the winders an' such that Council says it'll only open t' people with special permission. Good job, too—though I'm not sayin' as it's kids like you as does it. Still, you'll be wantin' t' get back t' Brichester, an' I know the shortest way."

He began to give us complicated directions, which he repeated in detail. When we still looked uncertain he waited while Frank got out notebook and pencil and took down the route. At the end of this I was not yet sure which way to go, but, as I remarked: "If we get lost, we can always ask."

"Oh, no," protested our informant. "You won't go wrong if you follow that."

"Right, thanks," Frank said. "And I suppose there will be passers-by to ask if we *do* go wrong?"

"I wouldn't." The newsagent turned to rearrange papers in the rack. "You might ask the wrong people."

Hearing no more from him, we went out into the street and

turned right toward Brichester. Once one leaves behind the central area of Severnford where a group of archaic buildings is preserved, and comes to the surrounding red-brick houses, there is little to interest the sight-seer. Much of Severnford is dockland, and even the country beyond is not noticeably pleasant to the forced hiker. Besides, some of the roads are noticeably rough, though that may have been because we took the wrong turning—for, an hour out of Severnford, we realized we were lost.

"Turn left at the signpost about a mile out, it says here," said Frank. "But we've come more than a mile already—where's the signpost?"

"So what do we do—go back and ask?" Tony suggested.

"Too far for that. Look," Frank asked me, "have you got that compass you're always carrying, Les? Brichester is almost southeast of Severnford. If we keep on in that direction, we won't go far wrong."

The road we had been following ran east-west. Now, when we turned off into open country, we could rely only on my compass, and we soon found that we needed it. Once, when ascending a slope, we had to detour round a thickly overgrown forest, where we would certainly have become further lost. After that we crossed monotonous fields, never seeing a building or another human being. Two and a half hours out of Severnford, we reached an area of grassy hillocks, and from there descended into and clambered out of miniature valleys. About half-a-mile into this region, Tony signalled us to keep quiet.

"All I can hear is the stream," said Frank. "Am I supposed to hear something important? You hear anything, Les?"

The rushing stream we had just crossed effectively drowned most distant sounds, but I thought I heard a nearby mechanical whirring. It rose and fell like the sound of a moving vehicle, but with the loudly splashing water I could distinguish no details.

"I'm not sure," I answered. "There's something that could be a tractor, I think—"

"That's what I thought," agreed Tony. "It's ahead somewhere—maybe the driver can direct us. If, of course, he's not one of that newsagent's wrong people!"

The mechanical throbbing loudened as we crossed two hills and came onto a strip of level ground fronting a long, low ridge. I was the first to reach the ridge, climb it and stand atop it. As my head rose above the ridge, I threw myself back.

On the other side lay a roughly square plain, surrounded by four ridges. The plain was about four hundred yards square, and at the opposite side was a one-story building. Apart from this the plain was totally bare, and that was what startled me most. For from that bare stretch of land rose a deafening flood of sound. Here was the source of that mechanical whirring; it throbbed overpoweringly upward, incessantly fluctuating through three notes. Behind it were other sounds; a faint bass humming which hovered on the edge of audibility, and others—whistling and high-pitched twangs which sometimes were inaudible and sometimes as loud as the whirring.

By now Tony and Frank were beside me, staring down.

"Surely it can't be coming from that hut?" Frank said. "It's no tractor, that's certain, and a hut that size could never contain anything that'd make that row."

"I thought it was coming from underground somewhere," suggested Tony. "Mining operations, maybe."

"Whatever it is, there's that hut," I said. "We can ask the way there."

Tony looked down doubtfully. "I don't know—it might well be dangerous. You know driving over subsidence can be dangerous, and how do we know they're not working on something like that here?"

"There'd be signs if they were," I reassured him. "No, come on—there may be nowhere else we can ask, and there's no use keeping on in the wrong direction."

We descended the ridge and walked perhaps twenty yards across the plain.

It was like walking into a tidal wave. The sound was suddenly all around us; the more overpowering because though it beat on us from all sides, we could not fight back—like being engulfed in jelly. I could not have stood it for long—I put my hands over my ears and yelled "Run!" And I staggered across the plain, the sound which I could not shut out booming at me, until I reached the building on the other side.

It was a brown stone house, not a hut as we had thought. It had an arched doorway in the wall facing us, bordered by two low windows without curtains. From what we could see the room on the left was the living-room, that on the right a bedroom, but grime on the windows prevented us from seeing more, except that the rooms were unoccupied. We did not think to look in any windows at the back. The door had no bell or knocker, but Frank pounded on a panel.

There was no answer and he knocked harder. On the second knock the door swung open, revealing that it opened into the living-room. Frank looked in and called: "Anybody at home?" Still nobody answered, and he turned back to us.

"Do you think we'd better go in?" he asked. "Maybe we could wait for the owner, or there might be something in the house that'd direct us."

Tony pushed past me to look. "Hey, what—Frank, do you notice anything here? Something tells me that whoever the owner is, he isn't house-proud."

We could see what he meant. There were wooden chairs, a table, bookcases, a ragged carpet—and all thick with dust. We hesitated a minute, waiting for someone to make a decision; then Frank entered. He stopped inside the door and pointed. Looking over his shoulder we could see there were no footprints anywhere in the dust.

We looked round for some explanation. While Frank closed the door and cut off the throbbing from outside, Tony—our bibliophile—crossed to the bookcases and looked at the spines. I noticed a newspaper on the table and idly picked it up.

"The owner must be a bit peculiar . . . *La Strega,* by Pico della Mirandola," Tony read, "—*Discovery of Witches—The Red Dragon*—hey, *Revelations of Glaaki;* isn't that the book the University can't get for their restricted section? Here's a diary, big one, too, but I hadn't better touch that."

When I turned to the front page of the newspaper, I saw it was the *Camside Observer.* As I looked closer, I saw something which made me call the others. "Look at this—December 8, 1930! You're right about this man being peculiar—what sort of person keeps a newspaper for twenty-eight years?"

"I'm going to look in the bedroom," Frank declared. He knocked on the door off the living-room, and, when we came up beside him, opened it. The room was almost bare: a wardrobe, a hanging wall-

mirror, and a bed, were the only furnishings. The bed, as we had expected, was empty; but the mark of a sleeping body was clearly defined, though filled with dust. We moved closer, noting the absence of
footprints on the floor; and bending over the bed, I thought I saw
something besides dust in the hollows left by the sleeper—something
like ground glass, sparkling greenly.

"What's happened?" Tony asked in a rather frightened tone.

"Oh, probably nothing out of the ordinary," said Frank. "Maybe
there's another entrance round the back—maybe he can't stand all the
noise, whatever it is, and has a bedroom on the other side. Look, there's
a door in that wall; that may be it."

I went across and opened it, but only a very primitive lavatory
lay beyond.

"Wait a minute, I think there was a door next to the bookcase,"
recollected Tony. He returned to the living-room and opened the
door he had noticed. As we followed him, he exclaimed: "My God—
*now* what?"

The fourth room was longer than any of the others, but it was
the contents that had drawn Tony's exclamation. Nearest us on the
bare floor was something like a television screen, about two feet
across, with a blue-glass light bulb behind it, strangely distorted
and with thick wires attached. Next to it another pair of wires led
from a megaphone-shaped receiver. In between the opposite wall and
these instruments lay a strange arrangement of crystals, induction
coils, and tubes, from which wires hung at each end for possible attachment to the other appliances. The far corner of the ceiling had
recently collapsed, allowing rain to drip onto a sounding-board carrying a dozen strings, a large lever and a motor connected by cogs to
a plectrum-covered cylinder. Out of curiosity I crossed and plucked a
string; but such a discord trembled through the board that I quickly
muffled it.

"Something *very* funny is going on here," Frank said. "There's no
other room, so where can he sleep? And the dust, and the newspaper—
and now these things—I've never seen anything like them . . ."

"Why don't we look at his diary?" suggested Tony. "It doesn't
look like he'll be back, and I for one want to know what's happened
here."

So we went back into the living-room and Tony took down the

heavy volume. He opened it to its last entry: December 8, 1930. "If we all try and read it, it'll take three times as long," he said.

"You two sit down and I'll try and read you the relevant bits." He was silent for a few minutes, then:

"Professor Arnold Hird, ex-Brichester University: never heard of him—must've been before our time.

"Ah here we are—

" 'January 3, 1930: Today moved into new house (if it can be called a house!). Noises are queer—suppose it's only because there's so much superstition about them that nobody's investigated before. Intend to make full study—meteorological conditions, &c: feel that winds blowing over ridges may vibrate and cause sounds. Tomorrow to look round, take measurements, find out if anything will interrupt sounds. Peculiar that sound seems to be deafening in certain radius, relatively faint beyond—no gradual fading.'

" 'January 4: Sleep uneasy last night—unaccustomed dreams. City on great mountain—angled streets, spiraling pillars and cones. Strange inhabitants; taller than human, scaly skin, boneless fingers, yet somehow not repulsive. Were aware of me, in fact seemed to await my arrival, but each time one approached me I awoke. Repeated several times.

" 'Progress negative. Screens on top of ridges did not interrupt sound; undiminished though little wind. Measurements—northwest ridge 423 yards . . .' Well, there's a lot more like that."

"Make sure you don't miss anything important," Frank said as Tony turned pages.

" 'January 6: Dreams again. Same city, figures as though waiting. Leader approached. Seemed to be communicating with me telepathically: I caught the thought—*Do not be afraid; we are the sounds.* Whole scene faded.

" 'No progress whatever. Unable to concentrate on findings; dreams distracting.'

" 'January 7: Insane perhaps, but am off to British Museum tomorrow. In last night's dream was told: *Check Necronomicon— formula for aiding us to reach you.* Page reference given. Expect and hope this will be false alarm—dreams taking altogether too much out of me. But what if something on that page? Am not interested in that field—impossible to know in normal way . . .'

" 'January 9: Back from London. Mao rite—on page I looked up—exactly as described in dream! Don't know what it will do, but will perform it tonight to find out. Strange no dreams while away—some influence existing only here?'

" 'January 10: Didn't wake till late afternoon. Dreams began as soon as sleep after rite. Don't know what to think. Alternatives both disturbing: either brain receiving transmission, or subconsciously inventing everything—but wd. sane mind act thus?

" 'If true that transmission external, learned following:

" 'Sounds in this area *are equivalents of matter in another dimension.* Said dimension overlaps ours at this point and certain others. City and inhabitants in dream do not appear as in own sphere, but as wd. appear if consisting of matter. Different sounds here correspond to various objects in other dimension; whirring equals pillars & cones, bass throbbing is ground, other varying sounds are people of city & other moving objects. Matter on our side they sense as odors.

" 'The inhabitants can transmit whole concepts mentally. Leader asked me to try not to make sounds in radius of point of connection. Carried over to their dimension. My footsteps—huge crystals appeared on streets of city. My breathing—something living which they refused to show me. Had to be killed at once.

" 'Inhabitants interested in communication with our dimension. Not dream—transmission—frequent use of Mao rite dangerous. *Translator* to be built on this side—enables sound to be translated into visual terms on screen, as in dream, but little else. When they build counterpart link will be effected—complete passage between dimensions. Unfortunately, their translator completely different from ours and not yet successful. Leader told me: *Look in The Revelations of Glaaki for the plans.* Also gave me page reference & said where to get copy.

" 'Must get copy. If no plan, all coincidence & can return to normal research. If plan, can build machine, claim discovery of other dimension!' "

"I've been thinking," I interrupted. "Arnold Hird—there was something—wasn't he asked to leave the University because he attacked someone when they disagreed with him? Said he'd return and astonish everybody some day, but was never heard of again."

"I don't know," said Tony. "Anyway, he continues:

" 'January 12: Got *Revelations of Glaaki*. Had to take drastic measures to obtain it, too. Plan here—book 9, pp. 2057–9. Will take some time to build, but worth it. To think that besides me, only superstitious know of this—but will soon be able to prove it!'

"Hmmm—well, there don't seem to be any very interesting entries after that. Just 'not much progress today' or 'screen arrangement completed' or here 'down to Severnford today—had to order strings at music shop. Don't like idea of using it, but must keep it handy in case.' "

"So that's it," Frank said, standing up. "The man was a lunatic, and we've been sitting here listening to his ravings. No wonder he was kicked out of the University."

"I don't think so," I disagreed. "It seems far too complex—"

"Wait a minute, here's another entry," called Tony. " '—December 7.' "

Frank gave him a protesting look, but sat down again.

" 'December 7: Got through. Image faint, but contact sufficient—beings aware. Showed me unfinished translator on their side—may take some time before completion. Few more days to perfect image, then will publicize.'

" 'December 8: Must be sure about weapon I have constructed. *Revelations* give reason for use, but way of death is horrible. If unnecessary, definitely will destroy. Tonight will find out—will call Alala.' "


"Well, Frank?" I asked as Tony replaced the diary and began to search the shelves. "Crazy, maybe—but there are those sounds—and he called *something* that night where his diary ends—and there's that peculiar stuff all over the bed—"

"But how will we know either way?" Tony asked, removing a book.

"Set up all that paraphernalia, obviously, and see what comes through on the screen."

"I don't know," Tony said. "I want to look in the *Revelations of Glaaki*—that's what I've got here—but as for trying it ourselves, I think that's going a bit far. You'll notice how careful he was about it, and something happened to him."

"Come on, let's look at the book," interrupted Frank. "That can't do any harm."

Tony finally opened it and placed it on the table. On the page we examined diagrams, and learned that "the screen is attached to the central portion and viewed, while the receiver is directed toward the sounds before attachment." No power was necessary, for "the very sounds in their passing manipulate the instrument." The diagrams were crude but intelligible, and both Frank and I were ready to experiment. But Tony pointed to a passage at the end of the section:

"The intentions of the inhabitants of S'glhuo are uncertain. Those who use the translator would be wise to keep by them the stringed sounding-board, the only earthly weapon to touch S'glhuo. For when they build the translator to complete the connexion, who knows what they may bring through with them? They are adept in concealing their intentions in dream-communication, and the sounding-board should be used at the first hostile action."

"You see?" Tony said triumphantly. "These things are unfriendly—the book says so."

"Oh, no, it doesn't," contradicted Frank, "and anyway it's a load of balls—living sounds, hah! But just suppose it was true—if we got through, we could claim the discovery—after all, the book says you're safe with this 'weapon.' And there's no rush back to the University."

Arguments ensued, but finally we opened the doors and dragged the instruments outside. I returned for the sounding-board, noticing how rusted it was, and Tony brought the volume of the *Revelations*. We stood at the edge of the area of sound and placed the receiver about midway. The screen was connected to the central section, and at last we clipped the wire from the screen to the rest.

For a minute nothing happened. The screen stayed blank; the coils and wire did not respond. Tony looked at the sounding-board. The vibrations had taken on a somehow expectant quality, as if aware of our experiment. And then the blue light bulb flickered, and an image slowly formed on the screen.

It was a landscape of dream. In the background, great glaciers and crystal mountains sparkled, while at their peaks enormous stone buildings stretched up into the mist. There were translucent shapes flitting about those buildings. But the foreground was most noticeable—the slanting streets and twisted pillar-supported cones which formed a city on one of the icy mountains. We could see no life in the city brooding in a sourceless blue light; only a great machine of tubes and crystals which stood before us on the street.

When a figure rose into the screen, we recoiled. I felt a chill of terror, for this was one of the city's inhabitants—and it was not human. It was too thin and tall, with huge pupilless eyes, and a skin covered with tiny rippling scales. The fingers were boneless, and I felt a surge of revulsion as the white eyes stared unaware in my direction. But I somehow felt that this was an intelligent being, and not definitely hostile.

The being took out of its metallic robe a thin rod, which it held vertically and stroked several times. Whatever the principle, this must have been a summons, for in a few minutes a crowd had formed about the instrument in the street. What followed may only have been their method of communication, but I found it horrible; they stood in a circle and their fingers stretched fully two feet to interlace in the center. They dispersed after a short time and spread out, a small group remaining by the machine.

"Look at that thing in the street," said Tony. "Do you suppose—"

"Not now," Frank, who was watching in fascination, interrupted. "I don't know if it'd be better to switch off now and get someone down from the University—no hell, let's watch a bit longer. To think that we're watching another world!"

The group around the machine were turning it, and at that moment a set of three tubes came into view, pointing straight at us. One of the beings went to a switchboard and clutched a lever with long twining fingers. Tony began to speak, but simultaneously I realized what he was thinking.

"Frank," I shouted, "that's their translator! They're going to make the connexion!"

"Do you think I'd better switch off, then?"

"But suppose that's not enough?" yelled Tony. "Do you want them to come through without knowing what they'll do? You read the book—for God's sake use the weapon before it's too late!"

His hysteria affected us all. Frank ran to the sounding-board and grabbed the lever. I watched the being on the machine, and saw that it was nearly ready to complete the connexion.

"Why aren't you doing anything?" Tony screamed at Frank.

He called back: "The lever won't move! Must be rust in the works—quick, Les, see if you can get them unstuck."

I ran over and began to scrape at the gears with a knife. Accidentally the blade slipped and twanged across the strings.

"There's something forming, I can't quite see," Tony said—

Frank was straining so hard at the lever that I was afraid it would snap—then it jerked free, the gears moved, the plectrum cylinder spun and an atrocious sound came from the strings. It was a scraping, whining discord which clawed at our ears; it blotted out those other sounds, and I could not have stood it for long.

Then Tony screamed. We whirled to see him kick in the screen and stamp ferociously on the wires, still shrieking. Frank shouted at him—and as he turned we saw the slackness of his mouth and the saliva drooling down his chin.

We finally locked him in the back room of the house while we found our way back to Brichester. We told the doctors only that he had become separated from us, and that by the time we found him everything was as they saw it. When they removed Tony from the house, Frank took the opportunity to tear a few pages out of *The Revelations of Glaaki*. Perhaps because of this, the team of Brichester professors and others studying conditions there are making little progress. Frank and I will never go there again; the events of that afternoon have left too deep a mark.

Of course, they affected Tony far more. He is completely insane, and the doctors foresee no recovery. At his worst he is totally incoherent, and attacks anyone who cannot satisfactorily explain every sound he hears. He gives no indication in his coherent periods of what drove him mad. He imagines he saw something more on that screen, but never describes what he saw.

Occasionally he refers to the object he thinks he saw. Over the years he has mentioned details which would suggest something incredibly alien, but of course it must have been something else which unbalanced him. He speaks of "the snailhorns," "the blue crystalline lenses," "the mobility of the faces," "the living flame and water," "the bell-shaped appendages," and "the common head of many bodies."

But these periods of comparative coherency do not last long. Usually they end when a look of horror spreads over his face, he stiffens and screams something which he has not yet explained:

"I saw what it took from its victims! *I saw what it took from its victims!*"

# The Stone on the Island

## Ramsey Campbell

A rriving home that night, Michael Nash thought at first that his father was asleep.

Dr. Stanley Nash, his father, was lying back in an armchair in the living-room. On the table beside him stood an empty glass, propping up a sealed envelope, and near these lay a library book. It was all quite ordinary, and Michael only glanced at him before entering the kitchen in search of coffee. Fifteen minutes later he tried to wake his father, and realized what the contents of the glass must have been.

Nash sensed the events of the next few days with numbed nerves. While he realized that any further evidence he might give would be disbelieved, he heard the words "suicide while the balance of the mind was disturbed" with a feeling of guilt; he fingered that envelope in his pocket, but forced himself to keep it there. After that arrived those people who saw the admiration of Nash's medical ability as a pretext for taking a half-day off work; then the largely incomprehensible funeral service, the rattle of earth on wood, and the faster journey home.

Various duties prevented Michael from examining his father's papers until October 27, 1962. He might not have plunged into them even then but for the explicit injunction in his father's final note. Thus it was that as the sun flamed redly on the windows of Gladstone Place, Nash sat in the study of No. 6, with the envelope before him on the desk and the enclosed sheet spread out for reading.

"My recent research" (Michael read) "has pried into regions

whose danger I did not realize. You know enough of these hidden forces which I have attempted to destroy to see that, in certain cases, death is the only way out. Something has fastened itself upon me, but I will suicide before its highest pitch of potency is reached. It has to do with the island beyond Severnford, and my notes and diary will furnish more details than I have time to give. If you want to carry on my work, confine yourself to other powers—and take my case as a warning not to go too far."

That was all; and no doubt many people would have torn up the letter. But Michael Nash knew enough of the basis of his father's beliefs not to treat them lightly; indeed, he held the same creeds. From an early age he had read his father's secret library of rare books, and from these had acquired an awareness which the majority of people never possess. Even in the modern office building where he worked or in the crowded streets of central Brichester, he could sense things drifting invisibly whose existence the crowd never suspected, and he knew very well of the hidden forces which clustered about a house in Victoria Road, a demolished wall at the bottom of Mercy Hill, and such towns as Clotton, Temphill and Goatswood. So he did not scoff at his father's last note, but only turned to the private papers kept in the study.

In the desk drawer he found the relevant documents, inside a file cover covertly removed from his office building. The file contained a photograph of the island beyond Severnford by daylight, snapped from the Severn bank and hence undetailed; another photograph, taken by a member of the Society for Psychical Research, of the island with dim white ovals floating above it, more likely reflections on the camera lens than psychic manifestations, but inexplicable enough to be reported in the *Brichester Weekly News*; and several sheets of notepaper inscribed in vari-coloured inks. To these pages Michael turned.

The writing consisted of a description of the island and a chronology of various events connected with it. "Approx. 200 ft. across, roughly circular. Little vegetation except short grass. Ruins of Roman temple to unnamed deity at centre of island (top of slight hill). Opp. side of hill from Severnford, about 35 ft. down, artificial hollow extending back 10 ft. and containing stone.

"Island continuously site of place of worship. Poss. pre-Roman nature deity (stone predates Roman occupation); then Roman temple built. In medieval times witch supposed to live on island. In 17th cen. witchcult met there and invoked water elementals. In all cases stone avoided. Circa 1790 witchcult disbanded, but stray believers continued to visit.

"1803: Joseph Norton to island to worship. Found soon after in Severnford, mutilated and raving about 'going too near to stone.' Died same day.

"1804: Recurring stories of pale object floating over island. Vaguely globular and inexplicably disturbing.

"1826: Nevill Rayner, clergyman at Severnford, to island ('I must rid my flock of this evil'). Found in church the day after, alive but mutilated.

"1856: Attempt by unknown tramp to steal boat and spend night on island. Returns frantically to Severnford, but will only say something had 'fluttered at him' as he grounded the boat.

"1866: Prostitute strangled and dumped on island, but regains consciousness. Taken off by party of dockside workers and transported to Brichester Central Hospital. Two days later found horribly mutilated in hospital ward. Attacker never discovered.

"1870: onward: Recrudescence of rumours about pale globes on island.

"1890: Alan Thorpe, investigating local customs, visits island. Removes a stone and takes it to London. Three days later is found wounded horribly—and stone is back on island.

"1930: Brichester University students visit island. One is stranded by others as a joke. Taken off in morning in hysterical condition over something he has seen. Four days later runs screaming from Mercy Hill Hospital, and is run over. Mutilations not all accounted for by car accident.

"To date no more visits to island—generally shunned."

So much for the historical data; now Nash hunted for the diary to clarify this synopsis. But the diary was not to be found in the study, nor indeed in the house, and he had learned very little about the island. But what he had learned did not seem particularly frightening.

After all, perhaps his father had "gone too near the stone," whatever that meant, which he was not going to do; further, he would take some of the five-pointed stones from the study cupboard; and there was always the Saaamaaa Ritual if things got too dangerous. He most certainly must go, for this thing on the island had driven his father to poison himself, and might do worse if not stopped. It was dark now, and he did not intend to make a nocturnal trip; but tomorrow, Sunday, he would hire a boat and visit the island.

On the edge of the docks next day he found a small hut ("Hire a boat and see the Severn at its best!") where he paid 7/6 and was helped into a rather wet, rather unpainted motorboat. He spun the wheel and hissed through the water. Upriver the island climbed into view and rushed at him. At the top of its hill stood an isolated fragment of temple wall, but otherwise it was only a green dome round which water rippled, with faint connotations of a woman in the bath. He twisted the wheel and the island hurried to one side. The boat rounded the verdant tip; he switched off the motor, pulled the boat inshore and grounded it; he looked up, and there, glimmering faintly from the shadowy hollow, was the stone.

It was carved of some white rock, in the shape of a globe supported by a small pillar. Nash noticed at once its vaguely luminous quality; it seemed to flicker dimly, almost as if continually appearing and vanishing. And it looked very harmless and purposeless. Further up the hill he momentarily thought something pale wavered; but his sharp glance caught nothing.

His hand closed on the five-pointed star he carried, but he did not draw it out. Instead, a sudden feeling engulfed him that he could not approach that stone, that he was physically incapable of doing so. He could not move his foot—but, with a great effort, he managed to lift it and take a step forward. He forced himself toward the stone, and succeeded in pushing himself within a foot of it. However, while he might have reached it, he was unable to touch it. His hand could not reach out—but he strained it out trembling, and one finger poked the hard surface. A shiver of cold ran up his arm, and that was all.

Immediately he knew that he had done the wrong thing. The whole place seemed to grow dark and cold, and somewhere there was a faint shifting noise. Without knowing why, Nash threw himself back from the stone and stumbled down the hill to the boat. He started the motor, slammed the wheel left and cut away through the water—and not until the island had dropped out of sight did he begin to approach the bank.

"You didn't have to come back to work so soon, you know."

"I know," Nash said, "but I think I'll feel better here," and he crossed to his desk. The post had mounted up, he noted disgustedly, though there were few enough pieces to suggest that someone had tried to help him out—Gloria, probably. He began to sort the bits of paper into order; Ambrose Dickens, F. M. Donnelly, H. Dyck, Ernest Earl—and having married the post with the relevant files, he sat down again. The first one only required issue of a form, but one of which he had no stock.

"Baal," he remarked to some perverse deity, and immediately afterward discovered that Gloria also lacked the form. A search around the office gained him five or six, but these would not last long.

"I think this calls for a trip downstairs," he remarked to Gloria.

"Not today," she informed him.

"Since you've been away, they've brought in a new arrangement— everybody makes out a list of what they want, and on Wednesdays one person goes down and gets the lot. The rest of the time the storeroom is locked."

"Great," said Nash resignedly, "so we have to hang on for three days . . . What else has happened?"

"Well, you've noticed the new arrival over there—her name's Jackie—-and there's someone new on the third floor too. Don't know his name, but he likes foreign films, so John got talking to him at once of course. . . ."

"Jackie—" he mused. ". . . Oh hell, that reminds me! I'm supposed to be calling on Jack Purvis today where he works in Camside, to collect some money he owes me!"

"Well, what are you going to do?"

"Take the afternoon off, maybe—" and he began to fill in his leave sheet. He passed the new girl's desk where John was unsuccessfully attempting to discover any interest in Continental films ("No,

Ingmar") and continued to a slight argument with Mr. Faber over his projected leave, finally granted because of his recent bereavement.

That afternoon he collected the debt in Camside and caught the bus home. It was dark by the time the vehicle drew up at the bottom of Mercy Hill, and the streets were almost deserted. As he climbed the hill his footsteps clattered back from the three-story walls, and he slipped on the frost which was beginning to glisten in the pavement's pores. Lunar sickles echoed from Gladstone Place's window and slid from the panes of the front door as he opened it. He hung up his coat, gathered the envelopes from the doormat and, peeling one open, entered the living-room and switched on the light.

He saw immediately the face watching him between the curtains.

For a minute Nash considered the courses open to him. He could turn and run from the house, but the intruder would be free in the building—and besides he did not like to turn his back. The telephone was in the study, and hence inaccessible. He saw the one remaining course in detail, came out of his trance and, grabbing a poker from the fireplace, slowly approached the curtains, staring into the other's eyes.

"Come out," he said, "or I'll split your head with this. I mean that."

The eyes watched him unmoving, and there was no motion under the curtain.

"If you don't come out now—" Nash warned again.

He waited for some movement, then he swung the poker at the point behind the curtain where he judged the man's stomach to be. There was no response from the face, but a tinkle of glass sounded. Confused, Nash poised the poker again and, with his other hand, wrenched the curtains apart.

Then he screamed.

The face hung there for a moment then fluttered out through the broken pane.

Next morning, after a sleepless and hermetic night, Nash decided to go to the office.

On the bus, after a jolt of memory caused by the conductor's pale reflection, he could not avoid thoughts of last night's events. That they were connected with the island beyond Severnford he did not doubt; he had acted unwisely there, but now he knew to be

wary. He must take every precaution, and that was why he was working today; to barricade his sanity against the interloper. He carried a
five-pointed star in his pocket, and clutched it as he left the bus.

The lift caught him up and raised him to the fourth floor. He returned greetings automatically as he passed desks, but his face stiffened any attempted smile, and he was sure that everybody wondered
"What's wrong with Mike this morning?" Hanging up his coat, he
glanced at the teapot, and remembered that he and Gloria were to
make it that week.

Many of the files on his desk, he saw bitterly, related to cases
needing that elusive form. He wandered down to the third floor, borrowed a few copies, and on the way out noticed someone's back view
which seemed unfamiliar—the new arrival, he realized, and headed
for the lift.

"Well," Gloria broke in some time later, "I'd better collect the
cups."

Nash collected the teapot and followed her out. In a room at the
end of the passage water bubbled in a header, and the room's doorway gaped lightlessly. His thoughts turned to his pocket as he
switched on the light. They filled up the pot and transferred the tea to
the cups.

"I'll take our end of the office," he remarked, and balanced the
tray into the office.

Two faces were pressed against the window, staring in at him.

He managed to save the tray, but one cup toppled and inundated
Mr. Faber's desk. "Sorry—I'm sorry—here, let me mop it up, quick,"
he said hurriedly, and the faces rippled horribly in a stray breeze.
Thinking in a muddled way of the things outside the window,
the pentacle in his pocket, and the disgust of Mr. Faber's client on
receiving teastained correspondence, he splashed the tray to the
remaining desks and positioned his and Gloria's cups atop their
beermats.

He glared for a minute into the bizarrely-set eyes beyond the pane,
noticed a pigeon perched on the opposite roof, and turned to Gloria.
"What's wrong with that pigeon?" he inquired, pointing with an unsteady finger. The faces must block any view of the bird from her desk.

"What, that one over there? I don't see anything wrong with it,"
she replied, looking straight through the faces.

"Oh, I . . . thought it was injured," answered Nash, unable to frame any further remark *(Am I going mad or what?)*—and the telephone rang. Gloria glanced at him questioningly, then lifted the receiver. "Good morning, can I help you?" she asked and scribbled on a scrap of paper. "And your initials? Yes, hold on a minute, please . . . G. F. E. Dickman's one of yours, isn't it, Mike?"

"What . . . Oh, yes," and he extracted the file and, one eye on the silent watchers outside, returned to his desk. (For God's sake, they're only looking . . . not *doing* anything!) "Hello—Mr. Dickman?"

". . . My . . . married recently . . ." filtered through office murmur and client's mumble.

"Would you like to speak up, please? I'm afraid I can't hear you." The faces wavered toward the point where his gaze was resolutely fixed.

"My son Da—"

"Could you repeat your son's name, please?" The faces followed his furtive glance.

"What'd you say?"

"Could you *repeat* that please!" (Leave me alone you bastards!)

"My son *David* I said! If I'd known this was all I'd get, I'd of come round meself!"

"Well, I might suggest that the next time you call, you take a few elocution lessons first!—Hello?" . . . He let the receiver click back listlessly, and the faces were caught by the wind and flapped away over the rooftops.

Gloria said: "Oh, Mike, what did you do?"

The rest of the morning passed quickly and unpleasantly. Mr. Faber became emphatic over the correct way to treat clients, and several people stopped in passing to remark that they wished they had the courage to answer calls that way. ("Everyone seems to have forgotten about your father," said Gloria.) But one o'clock arrived at last, and Nash left for the canteen. He still looked around sharply at every reflection in a plateglass window, but managed to forget temporarily in a search around the bookshops for a new Lawrence Durrell, with the awareness of his pocket's contents comforting him.

At two o'clock he returned to the office. At three he managed to transport the tray without mishap; at four, unknown to Nash, a still enraged G. F. E. Dickman arrived, and at four-thirty left, a little mollified. A few minutes later a phone message came from Mr. Miller.

"Well, Mr. Nash," said Mr. Miller, sitting back in his chair, "I believe you had a little trouble this morning. With a Mr. Dickman, I think. I hear you got a bit impatient with him."

"I'm afraid that's true," Nash agreed. "You see, he was mumbling so much I couldn't make it out, and he got disagreeable when I asked him to speak up."

"Ah . . . yes, I know," Mr. Miller interrupted, "but I think you said a little more to him than that. Er—abusive language. Well, now I know I feel myself like saying a few things to some of the people who phone, but I feel this isn't the way . . . Is something the matter?" He followed Nash's gaze to the window and turned back to him. "Anything wrong?"

"No . . . no, nothing at all." (*Three* now? God, how many of them are there?)

"Well, as I was saying, there's a right and a wrong way to handle clients. I know 'the customer is always right' is a stock phrase—it often isn't true here anyway, as you know—but we must try and avoid any direct offence. That only leads to ill feeling, and that won't do anybody any good. Now I had Mr. Dickman around here this afternoon, and I found it quite hard to smooth him down. I hope I won't have to do it again."

"Yes, I realize how you feel," Nash answered, peering frantically at the window, "but you must understand my situation."

"What situation is that?"

"Well, since my father died. That is, the way he died—"

"Oh, of course I realize that, but really you can't make it the excuse for everything."

"Well, if that's your stupid opinion—!"

Mr. Miller looked up, but said nothing.

"All right," Nash said wearily. "I'm sorry, but—you know—"

"Of course," Mr. Miller replied coldly. "But I would ask you to use a little more tact in the future."

Something white bobbed outside the pane and disappeared in the distance.

That night, despite the strain of the day, Nash slept. He woke frequently from odd dreams of the stone and of his father with some mutilation he could never remember on waking. But when he boarded the bus the next day he felt few qualms when he remembered the haunters; he was more disturbed by the tension he was building up in the office. After all, if the faces were confining themselves to mental torture, he was growing almost used to them by now. Their alienness repulsed him, but he could bear to look at them; and if they could attack him physically, surely they would already have done so.

The lift hummed sixty feet. Nash reached his desk via the cloakroom, found the Dickman file still lying before him and slung it viciously out of his way. He started at the heap of files awaiting forms to be issued, then involuntarily glanced out of the window.

"Never mind," Gloria remarked, her back to the radiator. "You'll be able to stock up on those forms today."

At ten o'clock Mr. Faber looked up over the tea-tray; "I wonder if you'd mind going down for the stock today?"

At 10:10, after spending ten minutes over his own cup, Nash rose with a wry grin at Gloria and sank in the lift. The storeroom seemed deserted, brooding silently, but as the door was open he entered and began to search for items on the list. He dragged a stepladder into one of the aisles and climbed to reach stocks of the elusive forms. He leaned over; looked down, and saw the fourth face staring up at him from the darkness of the other aisle.

He withdrew his hand from the shelf and stared at the pale visage. For a moment there was total silence—then the thing's lips twitched and the mouth began to open.

He knew he would not be able to bear the thing's voice—and what it might say. He drew back his foot and kicked the watcher in the eye, drew it back and kicked again. The face fell out of the orifice and Nash heard a thud on the other side of the shelves.

A faint unease overtook Nash. He clattered down the ladder, turned into the next aisle and pulled the hanging light cord. For a moment he glared at the man's body lying on the floor, at the burst eyeball and the general appearance which too late he vaguely recognized, and remembered Gloria's remark: "There's somebody new on the third floor"—and then he fled. He threw open the door at the far end of the room, reeled down the backstairs and out the rear entrance, and jumped aboard the first bus out of Brichester. He should have hidden the body—he realized that as soon as he had paid his fare, for someone (please, not Gloria!) would soon go to the storeroom in search of Nash or the other, and make a discovery—but it was too late now. All he could do was get out at the terminus and hide there. He looked back as if to glimpse the situation in the office building, and saw the four faces straggling whitely after him over the metal busroofs.

The bus, he realized on reaching the terminus, went as far as Severnford.

Though it lost him all sharp outlines, he removed his spectacles and strolled with stiff facial muscles for some time. On the theory that anything in plain sight is invisible to the searcher, he explored bookshops and at twelve o'clock headed for the Harrison Hotel at the edge of dockland. Three-and-a-half hours went quickly by, broken only by a near-argument with a darts-player seeking a partner and unable to understand Nash's inability to see the board. Nash reminded himself not to draw attention in any circumstances, and left.

A cinema across the road caught his eyes, and he fumbled with his wallet. It should be safe to don his glasses now, he thought, put them on—and threw himself back out of sight of the policeman talking at the paybox.

Where was there left to hide? (And what about tomorrow . . . ?) He hurried away from the cinema and searched for another bookshop, a library even—and two streets away discovered a grimy library, entered and browsed ticketless. How long, he wondered, before the librarian approached with a "Can I be of any assistance?" and acquired an impression which he might later transmit to the police? But five-thirty arrived and no help had been offered; even though he had a grim few minutes as he passed the librarian who, seeing him leave with no book apparent might have suspected him of removing a volume under cover of his coat.

He continued his journey in the same direction, and the lampposts moved further apart, the streets narrowed and the roadways grew rougher. Nearby ships blared out of the night, and somewhere a child was crying. Nobody passed him, though occasionally someone peered languidly from a doorway or street-corner.

The houses clustered closer, more narrow arched passages appeared between them, more lampposts were twisted or lightless, and still he went on—until he realized with a start, on reaching a hill and viewing the way ahead, that the streets soon gave out. He could not bring himself to cross open country at night just yet, and turned to an alley on the left—and was confronted with red-glowing miniature fires and dull black-leather shadows. No, that was not the way. He struck off through another alley, past two high-set gas lamps and was suddenly on the bank of the Severn.

A wind blew icily over the water, rippling it and stirring the weeds. A light went out somewhere behind him, the water splashed nearby, and five faces rose from the river.

They fluttered toward him on a glacial breeze. He stood and watched as they approached, spreading in a semicircle, a circle, closing the circle, rustling pallidly. He threw out his arms to ward them off, and touched one with his left hand. It was cold and wet—the sensations of the grave. He screamed and hit out, but the faces still approached, one settling over his face, the other following, and a clammy film choked his mouth and nose so that he had no chance to scream, even to breathe until they had finished.


When the Severnford police found him, he could do nothing but scream. They did not connect him at first with the murderer for whom the Brichester constabulary were searching; and when the latter identified him he could not of course be prosecuted.

"I've never seen anything like it," said Inspector Daniels from Brichester.

"Well, we try to keep these dockside gangs under control," said Inspector Blackwood of Severnford, "but people get beaten up now and then—nothing like this though. . . . But you can be sure we'll find the attacker, even so."

They have not yet found the attacker. Inspector Blackwood suspected homicidal mania at first, but there was no similar crime. But he does not like to think that even Severnford's gangs would be capable of such a crime. It would, he contends, take a very confirmed and accomplished sadist to remove, cleanly in one piece, the skin of a man's face.

# The Statement of One John Gibson

## Brian Lumley

If only, I tell myself. If only . . .

If only James Ogilvy, of Simons, Simons and Ogilvy, had not suffered that accident upon my very doorstep. If he had not died in my arms, fumbling my father's last will and testament out of his inside pocket. And if his last words had been other than what they were, which I mistakenly took to be an adjuration that I open my father's bureau at once and study most carefully all which I might find within.

Of course I know now that old Ogilvy meant me to destroy utterly that bureau and its contents, which would have been to comply with my father's will; but at the time all was chaos, where confusion reigned. And knowing what I know, perhaps that itself is no strange thing, Ogilvy's death no mere coincidence. Forces govern this world we naively assume to be ours, in this universe we suppose to be the One Universe, which so belittle the affairs of men as to make them meaningless. What is the life of our world, of Mankind itself, but a single tick of time in the great Clock of Eternity?

I must not stray . . .

My father died of some creeping organic malfunction which aged him well before his time and withered him to death some five days ago, since when I have hardly seemed to sleep, and during which period of time I have investigated and acquainted myself with matters of cosmic—yes, cosmic—importance. With my mother in a mad-house, and myself sole heir apparent to the Gibson fortune and prop-erty, I waited upon word from my father's solicitors that all was in order and I might indeed assume that lordly rank and office.

Then . . . the telephone message from Ogilvy, saying that he was on his way to see me, and that pursuant upon one all-important di-rective I would be the legitimate Gibson heir beyond any further be-hest or requirement. Following which call, within the half-hour, there had come that crash which sent me flying from the house to Ogilvy's car, crumpled and blazing where, for no reason I could plainly see, it had crashed headlong into an old oak growing by the verge of my gravel driveway almost directly opposite the very door of the house.

Ogilvy had managed to stagger from the wreck, his jacket smoul-dering, his face badly burned, to collapse at the foot of my steps. There I found him, and cradling his upper body and head in my arms, seeing that it was all up with him, I asked if there was anything at all I could do for him.

"For . . . for your father, John . . . for him and . . . for yourself!"

"Yes, yes. What is it?"

"His . . . bureau, my boy. His bureau . . ."

"Yes, I know it. Go on—"

His eyes had by then glazed over, but still he managed to force out these final words:

"*Glub . . . glub . . .* look in . . . bureau . . . destroy . . . *glub . . .*"

And with that the old man was gone forever from the world of men.

At the time of recording this statement, of course, I know that what Ogilvy had said was "do *not* look in the bureau," that I was to destroy the bureau intact, but his voice was so quiet, so distorted by pain and the rattle of death, that I took his words to mean the opposite.

But I had time for neither will nor bureau nor anything else right then; instead I must speak to Ogilvy's office in the city, call the police, an ambulance . . . many things; so that it was some hours later when I remembered his supposed instruction that I look in the bureau.

Even at that point all might have been well, had I but taken my father's will from my pocket and read it. But no, the dying man had made a declaration of sorts—or rather, a request—and if only for his memory's sake it was one with which I would comply.

The ambulance was long gone, the police had towed away the wrecked car, and the day was drawing to its close by the time I found myself at last alone in the old and now exceedingly lonely house my family had occupied and made its seat for more than a half dozen generations; and then I went to my father's room, where in a little while I found the key to his bureau. In fact only one cupboard was locked, but since the rest of the bureau stood empty I knew that this must be the place I should look.

Actually, I felt a little annoyed with myself that I had not done so before, but my father's room had always been inviolate, "out of bounds," as it were, and I suppose that I had unconsciously kept it so even after his death.

But now . . .

The door opened easily on oiled often-used hinges, and the contents lay in dark pigeonhole recesses, neatly apportioned and labeled, dry and well preserved. They were, of course, papers, books, documents— some rolled and fastened with bands, others enveloped, the books protected by laminated covers and wholly wrapped in grease-proof papers—exactly what one would expect to find in a bureau.

If anything, I was disappointed. Plainly there was something here which my father had wanted me to read (or so I thought), but where to start?

At first I was tempted simply to close up the bureau and return to it at some more propitious time; but as I was about to close the door my eyes lighted upon an item other than the mainly paper contents—something which had a glint, perhaps of some dull metal. In the gloom of the bureau it was hard to tell. But upon drawing the thing forth I perceived it to be a medallion of sorts, of a tarnished silver or some similar metal—perhaps an alloy—on a chain of the same substance.

And now I no longer desired to close up the bureau.

There was something about this medallion that struck an inner chord. Some part of my memory was given a jolt. I felt that I had seen the thing before, and the short hairs at the back of my neck stiffened in a sort of subconscious but definite apprehension. In my hand it felt chilly, with a low, unseasonal temperature out of keeping with that of the room and bureau. And as for the thing's design . . .

I cannot say what morbid genius cut or stamped or minted the medallion except that his mind—if indeed the maker was a man, or, more to the point, human—must work along lines wholly opposed to the conventional in art or artistic impression. Shall I say it was primitive? No, for the detail seemed exquisite. Cubist? No, for despite certain peculiarities of geometry the work was not surreal. Alien . . . ?

It was not quite circular, perhaps two inches across at its widest point, one-eighth to maybe three-sixteenths of an inch thick, and bore upon one side a picture or scene and on the other a legend in some glyph with which I was not familiar . . . or should not have been. But *again* I experienced that peculiar sensation of olden affinity; so that now, against all common sense, I suddenly found myself eager to tip out the bureau's entire contents and examine each item in its turn.

I resisted the impulse. First there was the picture on the medallion, which was certainly worthy of closer examination. Since I could make neither head nor tail of the glyphs, perhaps the fine detail of the art itself might tell me something.

I fetched a magnifier. . . .

If I say that the picture graven upon that small disk had all the detail of a canvas—say, especially, a Bosch—of several square metres in area, and that even with the glass I had difficulty in discerning the very smallest figures, objects and finer points of shading and stippling, et cetera, then I should doubtless be called a liar. But it is true. Our finest craftsmen, given all their skills, ultra-modern tools and techniques of numismatic engravature, could not have duplicated this piece. And yet I knew that far from modern, the medallion was ancient beyond reckoning. How was that possible?—how can I say? Perhaps I am a liar twice over.

The scene was not of Earth, not mundane in any way. In the background there seemed a sunrise, or at least a dawning of sorts (I suspected the approach of some awesome event or Being). This was portrayed in a burst of light beyond a horizon of strangely angled architectural structures, windowless towers and turrets whose unbalanced geometry made them seem both concave and convex at one and the same time: like looking at that famous optical illusion of marching men or monks climbing the stairs of a tower without ever gaining elevation. The city on the medallion (I assume it was a city) had precisely the same effect of trapping the eye in its own visual maze. In the foreground figures fled toward me.

Now, I say *figures*. At the time I thought of them as figures, because I was uncertain of their nature. That is to say, I was not sure the artist had intended they should be seen as living creatures. They seemed rather more symbolic of life (however dreadful) than representative, perhaps in the way of elementals. But *not* the elementals of any sane Earth nature; though I must admit that Air, at least, was included. Yes, and perhaps Water, too.

These two, fleeing forward from the advent of whatever "dawning" or cataclysm I could not say, were perhaps the most clearly defined of the—"refugees"? One of them, anthropomorphic, the air elemental, strode above, his great feet hidden in the clouds, whilst the other—a vaguely octopoid shape, and yet also having features loosely manlike—slithered or flopped below. Both had faces, the expressions demoniac. Later I was to discover that the first was Ithaqua, the Thing That Walks on the Wind, and the other loathly Lord Cthulhu; but I'll get to that in its turn.

As for the others: There was a black goat shape, satanic in its bipedal, upright flight; a mass of surging bubbles; a seething *something* that boiled forward upon the earth; a spider-thing of many jointed legs; a featureless, leathery slug thing; a heaving monstrosity of tossing tentacles, claws and eyes, oh, and others quite beyond my limited powers of description. And all of them beyond any shadow of doubt evil as the pit. I knew this, that they were evil, even considering them unreal, or at best figments of some feverish imagination or images of time-lost myth.

But stranger by far than those *outré* demons or elementals viewed through my glass was my growing feeling of familiarity with them, the disturbing conviction that I should recognize what I saw and be able to place and name it. Perhaps the scene was from some obscure mythology once glimpsed in the pages of one of my father's books and till now forgotten.

I turned on the light, made myself comfortable, heaved a sigh of resignation—for I knew now that I *must* continue—and took out the papers, packages, documents and books one by one, examining them as I went. These are the things I discovered:

One: a notebook dating from about 1955 in my father's hand. Two: five bulky volumes of letters in book form, being the *Selected Letters* of H. P. Lovecraft, a macabre author I had heard to be of note, secondary only to Poe and some would say Poe's peer. Three: another book in the same format, titled *The Horror in the Museum*, being stories revised by Lovecraft from the work of other authors and published by the same house, Arkham House publishers, in 1970. Four: a sheaf of A-4 photostats. Five: a crumbling copy of *Weird Tales*, an old "pulp" magazine with a faded but still lurid cover. Six: a bundle of old letters. Seven: a number of larger photocopied sheets bearing many lines of those peculiar-looking runes I had examined upon the medallion, these rolled up and fastened with elastic bands. Eight: several family trees on similarly large sheets. Nine: A greaseproof parcel of five old books, their titles being *The Cthaat Aquadingen*, Von Junzt's *Unaussprechlichen Kulten*, Feery's *Notes on the Necronomicon* and that same author's study of the *Book of Dzyan*, and a musty, leather-jacketed volume whose spine bore the faded and conjectural legend *Ghorl Nigral*.

These latter works might have provoked a shudder in a person other than myself, but here it must be stated that my life had been one whose proximity to darkling matters had rather inured me. That is to say, my father had been a delver in obscure myths and myth-cycles, a searcher of nighted crypts and beneath desert mastabas, and a pursuer of all things esoteric and exciting to his sort of super-imaginative mind. He had not been a cultist, no (though in his time I believe he had some small dealings with the Order of The Golden Dawn); but in his personal studies—his at times all-consuming studies—he had concerned himself a great deal with all manner of Earth's elder horrors and mysteries, so that he could well be said to be an authority in such dubious and legend-shrouded matters.

Naturally, a little of his personality, his strange bent for the macabre side of existence, had rubbed off on me; though I would never have dared admit it in his presence. No indeed, for time and time over he had warned me:

"John, my boy, have nothing to do with the dark side. Avoid mediums and spiritualists, cultists and ghost-seekers. And most of all steer clear of any who aspire to demonology. Avoid 'em like the plague. They work mischief . . . have worked it since time immemorial. Oh, there are warnings enough in the Good Book—and it is a *good* book, believe me. No, they wouldn't suffer a witch or wizard to live in those days, and rightly so. Take heed, John, for I've looked deep into such things and speak from experience."

This was the sort of thing he would say if ever he found me with one of his books of strange knowledge, or poring over the astrological charts with which Mother often amused herself. At least, I thought she studied such charts for amusement. Now . . . well, now I am not so sure.

But as I grew from a small child to a tall if somewhat frail youth, it became more difficult to find such books and charts. My parents were ever more careful, and would not leave the house without first locking away anything they considered (yes, I see it now) dangerous to me. For he was right, my father, such knowledge is dangerous— and it was especially so to me. . . .

But darkling books and cosmic mysteries were not all they kept from me. In my mid-teens, when other youths were courting their first girlfriends, I was kept at my studies under an army of private tutors; and while other lads of my age were stealing their first kisses, I would be deeply immersed in Christian and other theological instruction. One would have thought (indeed I often *did* think it!) that my parents intended I should be a priest!

Priests or holy men of many religions do not marry. They are celibate . . . they do not have children. And their work is such that they shun what Father would have called "the dark side . . ." Amongst the priesthoods only exorcists—and there are few of those these days—attain to that sort of knowledge. Oh, yes, I see it all: I was to be the last of the Gibson line, and not without good reason. And the feeling grows in me, perhaps I shall be the last after all.

But now, recording this for whoever shall hear it, I realize that in my opening or introductory paragraphs this statement is incomplete; or rather, it is insufficient. I talk about the primary circumstances which have brought me to my present pass, but I have not explained . . . myself. My own genesis is still a mystery to the listener. He knows I am John Gibson, but he knows very little of my line, my beginnings. Very well, perhaps this is as good a juncture as any for a word or two of clarification. . . .

[HERE A BRIEF BREAK IN THE NARRATIVE]

My mother came from an old Dutch line, the Sleghts, formerly Van der Slaeten. And though she could accurately trace her actual English lineage back as far as 1720 or thereabouts, there was still a hint of the characteristic wide-mouth about her which is indicative of Dutch blood. The mouth and the straightness of the eyebrows were especially distinctive in her features.

As for my father: he was descended from the Boston Gibsons, who in turn came down from the Typers of New Hampshire, a family rarely found in those parts nowadays. Mother always remarked upon the hollow, sallow cast of his face by referring to the Typers in his ancestry, for apparently all of them had been known for the coarse, almost greenish cast of their features. The earliest Typers on record had been Ulster County people, but that branch is long extinct.

Now to myself:

The records show that I was born at midnight, April 30, 1957, a date few would have difficulty in recognizing as the old Walpurgis-Eve; though that is a fact which previously meant precious little or nothing to me. But to continue:

My childhood years were spent here, in this venerable, ivied, many-winged house of the Gibsons in Surrey, England, centered in a countryside of small villages and towns, secluded in a forested estate of many acres. In those years, my father's collection of books was extensive, overflowing from the official library on the first floor and extending into many smaller rooms on that level. As I grew older he would take the not unnatural precaution of locking library doors and of placing in safe-keeping those volumes which were extremely rare, old, or valuable; a measure of protection against small and careless, though never deliberately malicious, fingers. For in many ways I was just like any other boy my age. But in others . . .

It was early apparent that my mother was of an extremely nervous disposition. From snatches of conversation I had deduced that much of her trouble stemmed from my birth, which must have been difficult and later caused her to grow ill, so that she was incapable of tending me in my first year or so of life. She had developed that aversion to me which is not rare among women of brooding or excitable natures. In my advent, I had hurt her, and the wound was more in her mind than body; so that it was some time before she was able to take me to her bosom. But I was her son, after all, and so in the end blood won through. Alas, over the course of the last five years I have seen such a decline in her that I have despaired. My father, too, until in the end he was obliged to place her in that so called "refuge" for the insane.

However:

I have more than hinted that my childhood was not a normal one, and have explained something of my father's hand in this and my mother's inability to provide the stability necessary for a child's welfare. Perhaps it was this early state of affairs—a cold one at best, though not hurtful—which formed me into the chill creature that I am, not given to extremes of emotion and little caring for worldly matters or the wealth I now control; more interested in the mind than the body and spirit; more dwelling in deep wells of thought than active in the living, breathing world of men. Perhaps . . .

But be that as it may, whether or not the seclusion of my early life and the idiosyncrasies of my parents affected me, the fact remains that I was a distinctly peculiar child. A dreamer, and of no sane or healthy things.

One nightmare in particular stays with me still; or rather, its memory—that memory which this morning once more became reality! Heaven forbid that I should ever dream that *thing* again, and unthinkable that it should be with the frequency and recurrent malignancy of my early teens. It is the prime reason I will take those steps which must now be taken. And the dream was always the same:

I was trapped in a dark place. An empty, lightless, *negative* place. I knew . . . little. Bereft of memory, of mind—but not quite of will, of basic knowledge—I felt that I was prisoned, locked away in a timeless solitude. What crime I had committed against what society, I knew not. Only that this was my punishment. And I remember (how strange) that in that dream the idea of crime or criminal thought or intent had little or no meaning to me. I did not think of my misdeed—whatever it had been—as a crime but as a mistake. I had offended not by immorality but amorality. I did not know wickedness. Or would not admit of it. I had done nothing to hurt, disgust, alarm or destroy. Not deliberately. Not to achieve those specific ends. If, through actions of mine, harm had come, the harm itself was not of my design. Only the *will* to do what I had done had been deliberate.

And here I am reminded of Crowley's dictum: "Do what you will shall be the word . . ." And I shudder. However one applies it, it is a dictum of abomination, a negation of all law, order and sanity.

But the dream:

I was chained, but not in any chains wrought of iron. These were mind-chains, as if I had suffered the equivalent of a prefrontal lobotomy. And yet it was stronger than anything like that, this force which held me immobile. Then I would remember.

I was . . . enscorcelled! Yes, under a spell. Crucified undying on a cross of Science greater than Man's, mummified with my viscera intact in a place more lightless than any Pharaoh's subterranean, pyramid-capped tomb. For my "sin" I had been banished from the Universe to a place "outside," and here I must stay until Time or Entropy found and freed me, or until the olden spells broke down, or until some Other should come and speak the Words of Freedom, the Rune of Release.

The Rune of Release . . .

I myself had once known that rune, deep, deep inside, but even if I could remember it I no longer had means of utterance. My prison was like a dream from which there is no awakening. But if I strained, if I fought, if I tossed and turned and worked at my mental bonds—if I sent out mind-messages of my fate, as a shipwrecked sailor sends messages in bottles—and if somewhere someone should hear or read such a message . . . and come to find and release me.

For I knew that inside me, if only the right words were spoken, was a Power unimaginable, a burning of stars, a collision of galaxies. Oh, yes! I was—had been—a god! Or a devil.

And at this point in my dream—always at this point—I would wonder what I looked like, what shape I wore, and I would try to remember *how I had been* before my imprisonment. And it was that memory, bursting in my brain, which would wake me up shrieking—just as it woke me this morning, after all these long years of peace.

My God! My God! Or may I no longer call upon him?

For starting awake, a mere child, from this dream of utter terror, and my cries bringing parents and servants running to my room, I would find . . . I would find . . .

It is a terrible thing to imagine oneself awake, to believe one has risen up from sleep and escaped the mire of nameless nightmares, only to discover that the horror is still upon one. For the worst thing was this; that I would see, upon my pillow or twining on the covers or pulsating in the sheets where my frantic tossing and turning had disarrayed my blankets, a leprous greenish-grey tentacle thing—and I would see that this member projected from the sleeve of my pajama jacket, and I would know that this was my arm!

[HERE A BRIEF BREAK IN THE TAPE'S MESSAGE
WHERE GIBSON PAUSED]

This then was my nightmare, whose source I could never, or dared never, imagine. And now the thing has returned, and I cannot bear it. For now I know, or suspect that I know, what that forbidden source is and what I must do to confirm, one way or the other, my worst suspicions. Only one person remains who knows the truth, and she is mad. And what drove her mad, I ask myself . . . or do I already know?

To be sure I must visit her; a visit not of duty or pity but of inquisition. This I have arranged and will see her today, at noon. I will take the recorder with me. But before that I must finish, as best I can, my statement.

And where was I . . . ?

Ah, yes—the contents of my father's bureau. The books, papers, letters and documents.

For three long nights and three mornings I have pored over them, and through them finally I have come to grasp certain truths. The old, hoary books of elder magic told me this: that Man was not the first sentient dweller upon this planet, but in the beginning were others come out of strange stars and distant dimensions. These were the

Beings or demons of the Cthulhu Cycle, which Lovecraft in his wisdom cloaked in secrecy and shrouded in cryptic half-truths, so that their full horror might never be known. But because he was a writer of dark tales he could not completely ignore the monstrous and ever-reverberating call of Cthulhu. No, he must somehow tell the world, but in such a way that the world would consider the thing a fiction. In order to do this he utilized a mythology older than mankind, which is this:

That for deeds so base, for blasphemies so enormous, the Great Old Ones of that fabulous Cthulhu Mythos were banished from the lands of their previous dominion and locked away in various prisons. And some of these prisons—certainly *one* of which I knew—were too close to man's habitation and too accessible, as a result of which . . .

But I must get on.

The ageless order of benign Elder Gods of Orion took upon themselves the task of punishing the blasphemous Beings of the Mythos. Cthulhu, leader of some monstrous uprising or rebellion, was tracked down to Earth and sunken into the depths of the Pacific in R'lyeh, his house of primal stone, and Ithaqua the Wind Walker banished forever to the icy Arctic wastes. Yog-Sothoth, because of his sheer mindless bestiality and endless appetite for all things aberrant, was secured at a place where all points of time and space and dimensions beyond the ken of men come together, creating such a matrix of weird gravitation that his prison is inescapable as the funnel of a black hole. Hastur, Cthulhu's half-brother, was hurled out into the bleak emptiness of space, where some legends have it he walks the wind between the worlds, and others that he bubbles and blasphemes in the hideous depths of Hali. The Tindlosi Hounds, too, those familiars of the Great Old Ones: they were banished to the dark angles of time, a place lacking in three of the four dimensions known to man, where they exist contemporaneous with all space but never able to enter it, just as the legended Flying Dutchman may never come to rest in a port of the living. And so on. And all of these Beings and others like them held in place by the ageless spells of the Elder Gods.

But . . . the Mythos deities had a messenger, Nyarlathotep, and of all of them he alone was not prisoned. Free, his time is spent carrying word between the Great Old Ones in their various confinements, assisting in their never-ending plotting for freedom. For they would be out and ravaging again, and ever they seek a means of release. One such way would be to influence the minds of men, evolved in the time elapsed since their immemorial imprisonment, and in this they have been partly successful. Telepathic, the Great Old Ones have become masters of dreams, and are responsible for much that is nightmarish in the dreams of men. Indeed, they are responsible for a majority of the world's madness. And they have caused to come into being those secret cults and societies whose purpose—often unsuspected even by the cultists themselves, gullible fools at best—is the resurrection of Cthulhu and his star-spawn band.

And for these reasons if for no others, surely my father's warning that I avoid cultists, mediums, ghost-seekers and the like, was not idly issued. Who would know better than he? Him with his life spent in tomb-delving and far-flung discovery of olden mysteries—including that final trip which ended so disastrously.

But I go ahead of myself.

Apart from the old books and their Mythos lore, there were those charts of Mother's, the ancient family trees, and from them also I unraveled more of the mystery: that indeed the old Typer and Van der Slaeten blood is more evident in my parents and myself than ever they had admitted. Yes, and more than merely Typer and Slaeten blood.

But it was from the books of terror fiction that I learned the worst of it, from them and from my father's notebook. In the latter he speaks of Lovecraft's revision and "fictionalization" of William Lumley's work, "The Diary of Alonzo Typer," hinting that in truth the original story was based upon matters of fact. And it was his research into this thing which after many years sent him and my mother, poor Mother, on that last ill-fated trip of theirs to America—and to Attica, New York!

But this is information which will convey little to the listener unless he, too, has read "The Diary of Alonzo Typer." At which point I find myself of two minds. If I am right—and I fear that I am, horribly right—might not this recorded statement of mine send others out upon the same trail? Or will it act as a warning that they should *on no account* follow that trail? In any case, truth doubtless will out. I must say on. . . .

My parents, then, discovering this link between themselves and the doomed hero of a tale of supposed horror fiction, went out to America to track the thing down. The years had not passed idly, however, and they did not go unprepared. Not entirely. Not as Alonzo Typer had gone before them. No, the adventure was in no way lightly undertaken.

The Gibson business was handed over temporarily to my father's partners, as it had been on so many previous occasions; but since he owned a majority of shares and was little more than a figurehead where the actual work was concerned, this was hardly problematic. But that was my father's way; he was thorough in almost everything.

But I have stated that he was not unprepared, and in this I do not refer to the affairs of the Gibson business. My meaning is that he was not unprepared for what he might find . . .

My great-uncle Victor Gibson was a Professor of Anthropology, specializing in Ethnology and Mythology, at Heidelberg. That was until he retired in 1895. But prior to his position at that estimable university he was no less a wanderer and delver than my father himself. Yes, and he was one of Alonzo Typer's tutors. Typer studied at Heidelberg, and according to correspondence between my father and that venerable seat of learning, he was one of my great-uncle's favourite pupils. I can only believe, as Father obviously believed before me, that the "V_____" of William Lumley's alleged fiction was in fact Great-Uncle Victor.

But here, an apparent ambiguity. That V_____ is not mentioned (or does not appear to have been mentioned) in the original story before Lovecraft's revision. How do I know this? Simple: amongst the many photocopied sheets in the bureau, my father had procured from somewhere and reproduced not only Lumley's purported original—which now rests *sans* V_____ in the John Hay Library at Brown University—but also the *real* original, consisting of rough, handwritten, unamended notes. This was where V_____ was first mentioned, and Lovecraft, not knowing V_____ was real, left him in the story to add verisimilitude, as well as adding much additional esoteric information of his own invention. (Or perhaps, the thought dawns, he *did* know he was real; in which case his purpose must remain unfathomed.)

As for the supposed Lumley original at the John Hay Library in Rhode Island: that is either a fake . . . or Lumley subsequently saw fit to remove every mention of V____ from it. But why would he do that? Perhaps Lovecraft's death early in 1936—almost exactly one year before the first publication of the story in that crumbling old pulp, *Weird Tales*, in February 1938—prompted his action in making a final "revision". Yes, I think that this is the answer, and I think Father thought so before me. HPL's death seemed natural enough, and yet . . .

### [HERE A PAUSE IN THE NARRATIVE]

My concentrated investigation having taken me all through the night and into the next day, it was noon before I could finally tear myself from the contents of the bureau, and have cook fix me a meal; following which, armed with a large jug of coffee, I returned bleary-eyed to the task in hand.

And as the coffee began to work on me, even as I remembered my investigations, I found myself asking what drove me on? What maddening pattern or theme was there here which drew me like iron-filings to a magnet—or a moth to the candle's flame?

And then, even doubting the common sense or validity of what I was about, I came upon that which must surely be the cornerstone item of all my findings, the foundation upon which to build my final conclusion. It was a letter, from my great-uncle Victor to my father, dated 18th May 1920, which was some three months before he died, aged a sprightly eighty-five. Cause of death, apparently, a heart attack.

I have the letter before me now; it is terse, to the point, but I shall abbreviate it even more and so be done with it:

Nephew—

I'm an old man and dying, I fear, but I've lived a long life and have few regrets. One of the few I do have, however, is that I have been lured by the olden mysteries. In this you are more like me than your own father, my departed brother, and so I leave what I have to you. But as well as worldly goods, which will not amount to much, I leave you something of greater value by far: a warning!

There's that in your blood which is bad. It is in mine, too, which gives me the right to tell you of it. I have been lucky. It has not harmed me despite all I've done and seen in so many strange parts. You may not be so fortunate.

If, when you open the parcel which accompanies this letter, you feel nothing—if you feel no *affinity* for the medallion you shall discover within—then perhaps these words are unnecessary. But if you recoil from the thing, or worse still find yourself fascinated by it, then my warning is valid indeed. In which case destroy it at once if you can, and once and for all turn your eyes from the course of dark learning.

As for the medallion: I brought it back with me many years ago from Yian-Ho, whose very existence many will doubt. But it was after *that* place that I settled at last to honest work at Heidelberg. Don't think, however, that staying here has been easy; always there was the urge in me to be up and away again. The medallion is the soul-symbol of Those Who Wait and Whisper in Darkness and in Dreams, Those Who are Chained but will be Free. It has a coldness not of this Earth (which is only natural, for it is *not* of this Earth) and this is the affinity of which I have spoken.

And the thought comes to me that perhaps I err. If the blood runs true in your veins my warning will be of little use. It may well have the opposite effect. Well then, so be it. I would not keep a man from his destiny, whatever it may be.

Your Uncle Victor Gibson

And having read that letter my head whirled, even as reading it now it whirls, and I began to total up the integers in this portentous sum of cumulative facts and evidences:

Alonzo Typer would appear to have had blood of my blood in him. He died mysteriously, perhaps horrifically, under an old house in Attica in April 1908; but before that he studied under my great-uncle Victor Gibson in Heidelberg. Yes, and what did he learn from him?

As for Great-Uncle Victor, he died twelve years later in 1920. Before that he sent my father a letter and a medallion. My father patently ignored the warning, or perhaps like myself felt drawn to the medallion and lured by it. He knew of the Typer story; perhaps he had heard earlier of Typer from my great-uncle, I can't say. But in early July 1956, after many years of research into the selfsame mystery (or perhaps after reading the Typer tale in that old copy of *Weird Tales*, or maybe in another book I found mentioned in his notebook: *Beyond the Wall of Sleep*—Lovecraft again!—published in 1943), he took my mother with him and went to Attica, for a reason I can now well understand. That same reason that relative of ours, Typer himself, went there.

Then ... then ... what he found there ... and something of what transpired before he could say the Runes of Exorcism. The Thing—that monstrous, tentacled, grey-green Great Old One—was destroyed, made inert or sent outside, I know not which. But too late!

[SHORT BREAK IN THE NARRATIVE]

And there you have the facts, or sufficient of them. Oh, there is more, if you wish to delve. Hints and allusions in my father's notebook; nightmarish suggestions and whispers in the elder grimoires—all of which I have now scanned and understand as best I can. And now, too, I must do one last thing. I must drive to the asylum for my visit with Mother, who alone might explain why, in the wee hours of the morning, I dreamed again that dream ... and why upon awakening I thought I saw ... thought that I saw ...

[SHORT BREAK IN NARRATIVE]

[NOTE: From this point on the recording is divided between two voices, one being that of John Gibson, the other presumably that of his mother. This is fairly well corroborated by staff at the Hammersmith Institute for the Mentally Disturbed, where upon admittance Gibson was seen to be carrying a small portable recorder. He still had this machine with him when he was left in private with the lady, which situation was not unusual as her disorder was not by inclination violent. The tape continues.]

". . . How are you today, Mother?"

"Oh, John! I'm so *glad* you could come. But . . . why do you stare so? You look so strange, so haggard. Is his death preying upon your mind? Strange, I find only peace . . ."

"Mother, there's something I must ask you. Something very important to me."

"Important?" [Here a quickening, a quite audible gasp] "John, around your neck. You're wearing—"

"The medallion? This? Oh, yes. And I know what it is. I know where it came from and who brought it out of that place. And . . . I know where it led Father. And you . . ."

"John," [the voice gasping, alarmed now] "be careful. There's danger for you—in me! Come, forget these questions of yours. They are meaningless. Let me hold you."

"Mother, I *must* know! Don't try to put me off. Tell me what happened that night. Father's notebook hints of it, but—"

[Again the gasping, louder now] "You've read his papers? You've been in his bureau! Oh, John!"

"Then it's true. And he brought me up, allowed me to live as . . . as a man! Even knowing I wasn't his son. Was he blind—or was he simply madder than you? And my birth: nine months to the day after you found that hellish place, that awful Thing in the darkness!"

"We couldn't be sure, John. Surely you can see that?"

"No, I can't see it." [Gibson's voice harsh now, ugly]

"But as a baby you were so—"

"Normal?"

"Yes, normal! And I came to love you. And so, when finally we knew, we kept it from you. And because you were mine, and because your father held himself responsible—also because you had no harm in you—"

[A grunt] "He let me live."

[A mere whisper] "Yes. . . ."

"And you, mother, sane but locked in here. Not because you're mad, no, but because your nerves are such that they cannot bear the outside world—because you know what you brought into it! And now I know, too. . . ." [Gibson's voice now dark, sinister]

"John, don't squeeze me so. You're hurting me!"

"Hurting? Pain? Yes—but what is that to me? What is your entire human race to me? Do you think I won't hurt them, too? It is my nature, Mother, my destiny!"

"John, I love you. Don't make me—"

"Make you what?" [Gibson's voice was coarse but alert]

[His mother's voice was a choked rattle] "John . . . danger in me . . . I have the exorcism . . . words of dissolution. Don't make me . . . use them!"

[Gibson's voice, distorted almost beyond recognition] "*Gha, ngh! Hyuh, hyuh, wagl, nhing ai gha!* See, Mother, the change! So you love me, do you? Do you love *this?*"

"John!" [A mere croak] "Oh, my God!—my son . . ."

"Your son, yes—but also His son. The son of *It!*"

"John, no—the Seven Words—my God—SUAMETINE AMEVUOD FESEOD KNEOB TEHCSEJ SEIM SEID! No, no—nooo!" [The cry tapering off into a gurgle, which is lost in a simultaneous lapping or swishing sound, and a whistling scream such as steam makes in its escape from a kettle. And no more until muffled voices, a hammering at the door and the sound of splintering wood . . .]

## END NOTE:

On hearing the uproar from Room 217, which is a private ward in the trustee wing, male-nurses Franklin and Jones went to the room but had to break down the door against some internal obstruction. Inside, sprawled on the floor at the door itself, they found Mrs. Evangeline Gibson dead. Of her son there was no trace, but his recorder was there and still switched on. It had just reached the end of the tape and switched itself off automatically.

Mr. Gibson had not been seen to leave the institute's grounds but must have done so in the general confusion which followed. Since he cannot be found to voice any denial or explanation, and in light of the circumstances surrounding his disappearance, one can only assume that he murdered his mother. It would appear that he achieved her death by use of some corrosive poison, which he somehow poured liberally into her. Small pools of the black, noxious stuff—so volatile that it quickly evaporated in air, leaving only sticky stains, were seen all over the floor. Such had been her dosage that the poison was still running out Mrs. Gibson's mouth and nose when Franklin and Jones entered the room. Amidst the stains was found a half-dissolved metal disk on a badly corroded chain.

Police action in posting wanted notices in the name and description of John Gibson would seem to corroborate the institution's resolution.

A coroner's report is awaited.
Board and Trustees of the
Hammersmith Institute for
the Mentally Disturbed
Dated 11 December 1982.

* * *

Author's Note: (For the would-be investigator of malignant occurrences, in order that he be spared time and expense.)

Strange occurrences in the annals of insane asylums are legion. The Hammersmith Incident was *not* my inspiration. Indeed I do not believe such an institute exists.

The Seven Words of Dissolution have no meaning whatsoever, though it may amuse the reader to believe he can find a pattern in them or sources for them.

The fact that I was born nine months after Lovecraft's death (on 2nd December 1937, *not* 1936, as Mr. Derleth quirkily had it in *Dark Things*—though doubtless he had his reasons for that, or else it was a printer's error) is entirely coincidental.

I did have a great-uncle who emigrated to America in the mid-Nineteenth Century, but see this as being insufficient evidence upon which to link myself in any way to William Lumley. (An opinion I presented to Mr. DeCamp some years ago upon his inquiry.)

As for William Lumley the writer: I believe Lovecraft

himself somewhere points out that WL was an extremely credulous person.

There are neither Typers or Sleghts in my ancestry, which is as old a line as England itself. Indeed the present day Earl of Scarborough is a Lumley, as is Lord Hexham, but neither do I claim relationship to them.

Finally, the fact that I live in Crouch End is also entirely coincidental. Would-be visitors are, however, definitely *not* encouraged. . . .

# Demoniacal

## David Sutton

### I

"**A**nd anyway," Bart said in a hurt tone, "so what? If they want to include incantations, why shouldn't it be aesthetic?" He sipped at his lager and slumped back in the chair like an angry child. His drinking partner, Nuttall, really knew how to get him going. However, for all their arguing, they remained the best of friends.

Bart scanned the inhabitants of the lounge bar. Predominantly students, the long-haired, fashion-flaunting set, totally geared to semi-idealism, underground and folk music and frank, uninhibited chatter on any and every topic. The Windsor was a good scene, but not the most respected pub in town. At any one time Bart could see, if he looked hard enough, cannabis bought and sold, the easy pickups, the hangers-on, the erstwhile CND mob, its numbers diminishing nightly as the local group broke up through singularly nonpeaceful situations. The atmosphere was relaxed and proved the ideal place for Bart and Nuttall to go to, their politics being of a similar type to the rest of the clientele.

Nuttall decided to close the latest discussion which had reached the end of its tether, as far as Bart was concerned, and said, "I'm sorry, Alan, but it just seems to me that a progressive group like Fried Spiders needn't use gimmicks to make good music. . . ."

Bart stared at his partner. "Look, Ray, the invocations are all part of the theme in this case. They are integral and, no matter what you

say, you'll find I'm right, once you've heard the LP a couple of times."
He glanced at the empty glasses. "Another?"

He tossed back his long, brown, curly hair as he stepped up
to the bar. While he was gone, Nuttall picked up a newspaper which
had been left on the table. He slid his sunglasses upwards until they
caught in his tight, black hair. His skin was olive and smooth textured. With his dark hair and black leather jacket, he took on a sombre, aloof appearance. He had a lack of purpose about him and less
insight, or so it seemed. He resisted cult ideas and sneered openly at
the orderliness that infected most people's lives. He was also rich
enough to do so. Through dark, weak eyes, he read parts of the newspaper, his eyelids thick and heavy over the eyeballs, his mouth a con-
temptuous line of pale pink. He had the appearance of a vulture over
its prey. However, his looks belied a humour that, frequently in the
extremes of irony and sarcasm, was more often than not the basis of
his uncharacteristic friendliness.

Bart returned with the drinks, to which Nuttall nodded a "thank
you" while remaining glued to an article in the centre pages. Bart slid
a book from his pocket and began to read, combing the hair off his
face, away from his eyes. He had a more serious turn of mind than
Nuttall and looked for some purpose in life—preferably one which
would crush the present day society which ponders on the brink of
destruction with careless ease. His pale forehead was nearly always
creased in concentration, tackling a problem in his mind. As a
youngster, he had had no awareness. Having been out of school six
years, his whole character and outlook had come forward to shout
their existence in what, up until then, had been an automaton. Pale,
like candle wax, his blue eyes were orbs of azure fire set in his face; his
lips ruddy on their cadaverous background.

Nuttall took up his pint and pulled heavily on it. He looked away
from the paper and said, "Guess what? Your Fried Spiders have
caused a sensation in occult circles."

"Oh?" Bart said interestedly.

"Let me read you this." His friend paused. " 'Several occult societies and well-known experts have condemned a record released last
week by a Birmingham group known as Fried Spiders. This long-
playing record combines several lines of incantations on one of the
songs which, said Thomas Millwright, scholar of Black Magic, could

be highly dangerous. Questioned further, Mr. Millwright stated that these rituals are of a very ancient ceremony, possibly quite harmful, taken from a rare book of magic. Luckily, he continued, sections of the invocations have been omitted on the record and it is unlikely that the ordinary listener would come to any harm. A novice in the Black Arts might find the spell extremely useful and possibly dangerous, however.' How about that, Alan?"

"Hmm. You know what the papers are like, Ray. Mind you, the stuff on the LP is the real thing; the band looked it up especially. But as far as the press is concerned, it's just like those scandalised stories of rituals in graveyards, dug up graves, thorn-pierced hearts and so on."

"I thought you had a kind eye towards occultism and all that?"

"I do, though not this widely publicised and suitably glorified stuff you read about. Black Magic, and White for that matter, does go on and, I believe, with some success—behind locked and secret doors. None of it reaches the popular press."

Nuttall, however, had now become more interested in the group. "What was the title of the LP again?"

"*Ocean of Minds.* Why? Thinking of buying it?"

"No, I'll borrow yours if I want to hear it," Nuttall answered.

"Oh, yes . . ." Bart said in mock derision. "I thought you didn't like gimmick groups."

"Yes, but as you say, I have to give it a fair hearing. Why not bring it over to my flat tomorrow night and we'll see how it goes."

"All right, Ray, but don't expect too much, will you. There are only two tracks on it, *Ocean of Minds* and *Demoniacal,* which is the one with the controversial content, you might say."

"Ah, but on my hi-fi I can give it the best treatment, can't I," Ray said rhetorically. "Besides, maybe we can call up Beelzebub at the same time! See you tomorrow, then." He laughed and got up to go.

"Yes, sure," Bart said. "See you at eight. . . ." He was not at all sure that his friend was acting normally. His sudden interest in the LP made Bart wonder just what he was up to. The feeling of unease was probably just a bout of Bart's oversensitive imagination making up for the weeks of materialistic study he had just been putting in.

## II

Alan Bart slid the disc from the rack, its black cover shining, the dazzle hiding a half-seen negative photograph of a nude dancer in erotic posture. He shrugged on a tattered overcoat and left the house. As he waited for the bus, he pondered on Nuttall's strange behavior. Only a few minutes before asking to hear the record, he had argued quite bitterly on the artifices used by bands pretending to produce music. Yet it would hardly bother Nuttall since he had no strong feeling about anything. In fact, thought Bart, he argued most often just for the sake of it and would take an opposing viewpoint to keep a discussion boiling.

The bus came, screeching inevitably past the stop. Bart ran to meet the opening doors. He sat downstairs at the rear and gazed out of the window. For whatever reason Nuttall wanted to hear the record, it would be nice, he thought, to hear the macabre music on stereo equipment for a change, rather than his old record player. Nuttall was one of those hip characters who had been born with silver spoons in their mouths. It was easy for them to ignore the irrational and bizarre society in which they lived, easy to slip into a quiet, workless way of existence—tinkering with whatever took their fancy. Thus, the problems which affect the rest of working humanity did not apply to Nuttall. His flat was a lavish affair; it was really something not to miss when he held a party and that was quite frequently . . . What was it about parties . . . ? Something Bart could not quite remember. Not a party, but something else Nuttall had done at his flat . . . ?

Bart, conversely, found society at odds with him. Working through what he considered was a hateful working class society, he had achieved self-intellectualism by his own hard-earned effort. These two inseparable friends were a pair that, on the surface, did not match. They were socially at each end of the scale, but it is something a bit deeper than personal backgrounds which tie two people together.

A cold night wind bit into Bart's hands as he made his way up a litter-blown street to Nuttall's flat. He pressed the door-bell twice.

"Hullo, Alan, come on in," Nuttall cordially invited. "Coffee?"

"Yes please, Ray. It's bloody cold tonight."

"I see you've got the record. Before we play it, let me show you something."

Bart followed him into the flat, a large one with a spacious lounge. With a tastefulness which one thought Nuttall would not care to possess, the room was decorated in an unusual manner. Expensive lighting could be dimmed down at a touch of a button. The walls were painted soft brown and taking the whole length of one wall was the range of hi-fi equipment: tape, transcription unit, radio and all. The speakers were set unostentatiously near the floor on wooden stands. The furniture was soft, luxurious nut brown corduroy chairs and sofa.

The whole room, in fact, had an unnerving effect. It appeared to isolate its occupants from the world. It was quiet, as though waiting for music to bring it to life. In its way it was severe, with no ornamentation or bric-a-brac; yet the smooth, warm features opposed this idea. They suggested comfort and relaxation. Did the room have a double purpose? It was an unusual one, certainly, and not to be stayed in for any length of time without company or sound. . . .

"Take a look at this, while I make coffee," Nuttall said, handing his friend a book. It was the oldest looking tome Bart had ever seen. Bound in brown leather with metal clasps, it was extremely battered. He undid the fastenings gently and turned open the cover.

"Ugh! How old is this thing, Ray? It reeks with must," he called.

"Oh, a few hundred years." Nuttall returned from the kitchen with two steaming mugs. "So be careful with it; it's practically falling to pieces."

"I can see that!" Nuttall handed him his drink. "Thanks."

"It was written by an Englishman, name of Berkley. As you can see, he never put a title to it, though it was sometimes referred to as 'Mad Berkley's Book.'"

"But what exactly is it, Ray?"

"A book of magic, spells, and so forth. You know, there were lots of these things written by so-called magicians in those days. Sometimes they were banned by the church and burned, or driven underground. Consequently, many of these books have become very rare."

Bart sipped his coffee. It tasted slightly bitter.

Nuttall noticed his expression. "Just a little something to keep us alert," he said.

"Alert . . . ?"

He ignored the query. "Anyway, it was when I was reading you that newspaper item last night. Something struck me about that Black Magic expert they mentioned, Thomas Millwright. I'd read or heard about him somewhere before. I looked through a bunch of old magazines and, by some fluke, I came across an article on him written about a year ago. He was apparently making a study of one particular book of magic—*Mad Berkley's Book,* in fact. It's extremely rare. You know my grandfather for digging up relics; well, he gave me a pile of old books a few months back. You can imagine my surprise when—"

"Hang on a minute, Ray," Bart interrupted. "What has all this got to do with the record?"

"I was coming to that. It's quite simple. Millwright has devoted these last months to studying one book in particular, right? Now isn't it quite likely that, when he mentioned the book in the newspaper, he was talking about the very one he was studying? The one we have here. So, if I'm right, we have the *complete* text of the incantations on the LP."

Bart felt that this was too much of a coincidence. Even if it was *the* book, so what? Surely Nuttall was not thinking of practising magic? Then Bart remembered what he was trying to think of on the bus. Just vague rumours; nothing substantial. But was it not Nuttall who had been involved in that Black Magic scandal a couple of years back . . . before Bart had really got to know him? Using his home as meeting place for the rituals . . . ? No, it was too absurd.

"What's the point of the exercise, Ray?"

"Oh," he answered vaguely, "just for the research value and to see what the band make of the spells. I just thought you'd be interested. After all, we *do* have the genuine article!"

"I am, Ray," he said and took a long drink of coffee.

"Can I have a look at the record sleeve?" Bart handed it to him and he opened it out and read the notes on the music. " '*Demoniacal* contains actual invocations from an ancient ceremony used,' " Nuttall quoted, " 'for the conjuration of a demon from the netherworld.

They begin: He Who Is The Black One, The Filler Of Space, Who Is To Be Let Out Of His Place Onto The Earth . . .' Sounds typically mumbo-jumbo; but nice of them to give us the beginning of the ceremony. Now we can look it up, before playing the music."

Nuttall began carefully leafing through the pages of the untitled tome. As he did so, Bart became more interested in this authentic research and followed the painstaking work. It was a massive book and a lot of text had faded with time. Some pages had almost crumbled to powder, as if they had been exposed for a thousand years. Diagrams were dotted about here and there and marginal notes in ink still showed, however faded, the writing of a nervous hand. It was Bart who found the ritual first. "There!" He pointed to the page.

"Yes, yes." A pause. "This first bit here deals with the precautions the aspiring warlock should take before going ahead," Nuttall laughed.

"I doubt that he would be able to take any nowadays, with all that faded script. Something there about a new moon and then that whole section there is blotted out. Then it goes on about an unbroken pentagram. Anyway, Ray, we've got the text. Let's hear the music!"

Bart slipped the disc from the sleeve and Nuttall placed it on the turntable. After a preliminary cleaning, he lowered the arm and turned up the volume. He then dimmed the lights until it was only just possible to read in the darkened room. Together they sat on the sofa, with the book across their knees.

The music was heavily electronic, and the weird cosmic sounds were really effective in the darkened room. A chilling series of bubbling electronics blasted out. Then, quietly, a faint screaming began in the background; the vocalist hauntingly warbled. Both men looked at the book and followed the words with some difficulty. The music insinuated in a horrible fashion; chillingly whispering, the chant went on, given evil and frightful life with distorted voice and instrumentation. An organ intoned dreamlike, somewhere, and drums beat out a hypnotic rhythm.

The music was startling, all the more so, for whatever Nuttall had put in the coffee was now taking effect. Bart felt detached, floating free in a womb of cosmic sound. He became frightened; the drug had intensified his awareness, yet he felt he could not move of his own free will. He drifted in space, weightless, unable to control his limbs. The old book before him swam away, its pages flapping slowly, the musty smell drifting like some tangible smoke into his nostrils. He could not reach the book. He was too far away, turning hotly within a chrysalis of sticky sound.

The music came to him with full stereophonic clarity and, deeply inside his mind, the bleating chant clattered, resounding on screaming guitar pluckings. A thin, high screech dashed through the wall of sound. Hand drums came in, beating a frenzied and hypnotic pattern onto the vocalist's words. Timeless, terrible chitterings shattered in Bart's mind. It sounded like the swirling of the universe had instantaneously found voice inside his head. He spun in star-dust and nebulae and in novae of enormous sounds waves.

The booming music toned down, quiet . . . soft. Suddenly the singing stopped, but the instruments played on as he knew they would. He swam in the lush darkness as the beat developed and the sound was all there was in this huge, warm world.

Then the incantation continued. But that had not been on the record before! A sparkling, irritating and terrifying thought glanced across Bart's swimming mind. It sounded like Nuttall's voice . . .

Suddenly Nuttall screamed. Far away it seemed. Terrified now, Bart shook his head to regain some consciousness. The room was cold. He still sat on the sofa, but his companion lay sprawled on the floor. The room was immeasurably cold and black and the black filled all space. It clung wetly to him, a mire of dark, a swamp of chill night. Bart jumped up and shrieked . . . the blackness moved . . . It rolled and slithered in the now silent room. It had invisible eyes, incredibly evil eyes which looked at him.

It swam, mingling with the true dark, towards him! He felt the wetness, the horrible, filthy nauseous fingers of slime on his face . . . it was tasting his skin . . . *tasting him* . . . *licking rapturously with its invisible, quivering lips!*

He lurched up and staggered along, clutching the wall. His fingers caught something. The lights went on and the vile protoplasm of night imploded in on itself and vanished. Bart slid down the wall. He was covered in a clinging, uliginous liquid which wallowed around his eyes and drooled from his sagging mouth. He retched.

Nuttall lay groaning on the floor, trying to lift himself out of a pool of clear glutinous ooze. "Thank God for the light . . . Alan . . . Alan, we forgot the pentagram . . . The Black One . . . it's out now!"

# The Kiss of Bugg-Shash

## Brian Lumley

### I

"You let it out?" Thomas Millwright incredulously repeated Ray Nuttall's obliquely offered admission. Alan Bart, Nuttall's somewhat younger companion, nodded in eager if apprehensive agreement, shivering despite the warmth of the Londoner's city flat.

"Yes, we did, sir," he blurted, "but not intentionally, you must understand that. God, never that—and certainly not if we'd known what we were doing, but—"

"Christ, Alan, but you're gibbering!" Nuttall's disgusted exclamation cut Bart off in mid-sentence, his weak eyes peering nervously about the flat and giving the lie to his cool controlled tone of voice. "I'm sure Mr. Millwright understands everything we've told him. There's really no need to go on so."

Alan Bart's cynical-seeming friend had pulled himself together somewhat. He had accepted the horror of the thing far more readily than the younger man, since that series of events which three nights earlier had culminated when the two, albeit unwittingly, had indeed called up a demon, or demonic device, from nameless nether-gulfs into the world of men.

"Oh yes, I understand perfectly what you've told me," answered the saturnine, dark-eyed occult scholar, "though I must admit to finding some difficulty in believing that—"

"That a couple of rank amateurs, bungling about with a rather weird and esoteric gramophone record and an evocation from some old eccentric's book of spells, could actually conjure such a being?" Nuttall finished it for him.

"In a nutshell, yes . . . exactly." The occultist made no bones of it. "Mind you, I can readily enough understand how you might have convinced yourselves that it was so. Self-hypnosis is the basis of many so-called cases of demonic possession."

"We thought you might say something like that," Nuttall told him, "but we can prove our story very easily." His voice was suddenly trembling; he plainly fought to maintain a grip on himself. "However, it's not a pleasant experience . . ."

"It's horrible, horrible!" The younger man, Bart, jumped up. His normally sallow features were suddenly many shades lighter. "Don't make us prove it, Mr. Millwright! Not that again, God, not that!" his voice began to rise hysterically.

"You needn't stay for it, Alan." Nuttall took pity on the weaker man. "I can stand it on my own, I think, and anyway it will only be for a second. And I won't really be alone, as Mr. Millwright will be with me."

Millwright frowned and rose to his feet from the couch where he had been reclining. His face plainly showed his interest. "Just what would this 'proof' of yours consist of?"

"We would simply turn off the lights for a moment," Nuttall answered, reaching his hand out to the light switch on the wall.

"Wait!" Bart screamed, grabbing his companion's arm. "Wait," he gulped, his eyes wide and fearful. He turned to the occultist: "Is there a light in your bathroom?"

"Of course," Millwright answered, frowning again. He showed Bart to the bathroom door and watched bemused as the young man tremblingly entered. He noticed how Bart made sure that the light in the small room was on before he went in. Then he heard the catch go home on the inside of the door.

Suddenly Millwright began to believe. These two night visitors, with their arsenal of pocket torches and their patently psychotic fear of darkness, were not really pulling his leg. But most probably it was as he had diagnosed; the odds were all in favour of self-hypnosis. They had desired so badly that their experiment should work and they had probably been in such a state of self-induced hysteria at the time, through the music and their esoteric chantings, that they actually believed they had called up a demon from hell.

On the other hand . . . well, Millwright was not inexperienced in the darker mysteries. Black Magic, practised with a degree of discretion, and the various carefully edited works he had written in the same vein, had made life very easy for him for the past fifteen years. Now, though, he had to see for himself—or, at least, experience—this "proof" that these young men had offered him. Such proof would not be pleasant, the man called Nuttall had warned him. Well, very few magical or necromantic experiences were pleasant; but of course, Nuttall would hardly be willing to demonstrate the thing—whatever it was—if it were really dangerous . . .

They had not explained exactly what they believed they had released from its nether habitation, but possibly they did not know. They had told him, however, that they knew he was an "expert" in this sort of thing, which was why they had approached him for his help.

And now . . . there was one easy way to find out what the truth of the matter really was. Millwright returned to his study and into the presence of the olive-skinned man called Nuttall. He saw that his visitor was sweating in anticipation, though he still maintained the vestiges of self assurance.

"All right, Mr. Nuttall," Millwright said, closing the study door behind him. "Let's have your demonstration."

Nuttall's Adam's apple was visibly bobbing. "I have to stay right here," he muttered, "beside the light switch, so that I can switch it on again. And you'll need to hold my hand, I think, to really—appreciate—the thing. Are you ready?"

Despite his few remaining doubts regards the veracity of their story, the occultist nevertheless felt a thrill of unseen energies, weird forces, building in the air. He almost called a halt to the experiment there and then. Later, he wished that he had. . . .

Instead, he nodded his readiness and, at that, Nuttall switched off the light.

In the brightly lit bathroom, huddled fearfully in one corner with his face screwed up in dread expectation, Alan Bart heard Millwright's high-pitched scream and, seconds later, his sobbing accusations and vicious swearing. He knew then that Ray had "demonstrated." Weak-kneed, he let himself out of the bathroom and made his way unsteadily back to the occultist's study.

There he found what he knew he would find: the horror which he himself had experienced twice already. The two men, his friend Nuttall and the still steadily swearing, bulge-eyed occultist, were hastily removing their outer garments. All the while, they were frenziedly wiping at their faces, shaking their arms and hands and kicking their legs in a concerted effort to be rid of the viscous, clear jelly that covered them head to toe in shiny, gluey envelopes. This was the snail-trail, the residue of the Black One—the Filler of Space—He Who Comes in the Dark!—that creature or power of outer dimensions which only the purity of the light might disperse!

Nuttall sat wrapped in a towel, pale, drawn and shivering beside the warmth of a gas fire whose glowing logs looked so very nearly real. He and the occultist had showered to cleanse themselves of the obnoxious, slimy coverings and now Millwright sat, listening, while Bart explained the most intricate details of what had gone on before.

Bart narrated how he and Nuttall had stumbled across the means of drawing the horror of the jelly-substance through the fabric of alien dimensions to their own world; how they had discovered that light held this creature of darkness, this fly-the-light, at bay; and how thereafter, whenever they found themselves in darkness, the thing that lived and chittered in darkness would return to try to drown them in its exuded essence. At this mention, all eyes flickered towards that thick liquid which even now slimed the floor in stinking, drying puddles, that juice which not one of the three could as yet bring himself to touch or clear away.

"And you actually have a copy of *Mad Berkley's Book?*" the shaken occultist asked, the silver tassels of his oriental dressing-gown moving to the shudders of his body.

"Yes, it belonged to Ray's grandfather," Bart agreed. "We've brought it with us." He crossed the room to where his coat hung and tremulously removed from a large inner pocket a leather-bound volume in iron clasps. He handed the book to the occultist who opened it, studied its contents for a few moments, then snapped it decisively shut.

"Oh yes, that's *Mad Berkley's Book* all right. And, indeed, it's in better condition than my own copy. Old Berkley's believed to have combined all the worst elements of a score of esoteric volumes in this work—the *Necronomicon*, the *Cthaat Aquadingen*, the German *Unaussprechlichen Kulten*—and, by God, I can readily enough believe it now! I myself have never used the book. I knew that a lot of the stuff Old Berkley put down on paper was damnably dangerous, of course, but *this!* This is a monstrous evil!"

He paused for a moment, his hands shaking terribly; then his eyes hardened as he turned them upon Nuttall by the gas fire. "You bloody fool! You've damned me with the same hideous curse! Didn't you realise that once I had experienced that—thing—that I, too, would be subject to such visitations?"

Nuttall looked up, a shadow of his previous cynical control returning to drawn, haggard features. "I guessed it might be so, yes," he admitted, then hastily went on; "but don't you see it had to be this way? How else could I be sure you'd help us? Now that you're in the same boat, you have to help. If you can . . . exorcise . . . this horror, then we'll all be safe. At least you have an incentive . . . now!"

"Why, you damned young . . ." Millwright rose in a fury, but Bart caught at his sleeve.

"What use to fight about it, Mr. Millwright? Don't you see that there's no time for that? Sooner or later, unless we find . . . well . . . an antidote, one by one, accidentally, we'll all be caught in the dark. When that happens . . . then . . ." Bart's voice trailed ominously away as he left the sentence unfinished.

"But I don't know of any 'antidote' as you put it," the occultist rounded on him, his voice harsh.

"Then we'd better start looking for one right away," Ray Nuttall snapped, the situation finally getting the better of his nerves. "Surely you have some idea of what the thing is? I mean, you're the expert, after all. Are there no other occultists we can consult?"

"I know of three or four others in England of more than ordinary power, yes," Millwright answered, pondering their problem. Then he shook his head. "No use to contact them, however. They wouldn't help me. I might as well admit it right now—my reputation in occult circles is not good. I've used what I know of the dark powers to my own ends far too often for the liking of certain lily-livered contemporaries, I'm afraid. There are so-called 'ethics' even in matters such as these. The only men I know who might have helped—though even that is doubtful—have also fallen foul of some evil, I fear.

"You've heard of Titus Crow and Henri-Laurent de Marigny? Yes? Well, they disappeared together some months ago, when Crow's home was destroyed in a freak lightning storm. That rules them out. No, if I'm to beat this thing, then I'm to do it on my own . . . but you two will help me. Now, we've much to do. There'll be no sleep for us tonight. Personally, I doubt if I shall ever sleep again!"

## II

With all the lights of the flat ablaze, midnight found the three in various attitudes of uneasy study. Millwright had heard their story through once more in all its detail before deciding on a definite course of action. At the mention of the newspaper article that quoted Millwright and had sparked off Nuttall's interest in the progressive group, Fried Spiders, the occultist admitted that his only interest at the time had been in gaining publicity for his recent book on occult themes. In fact, he had never so much as heard the LP in question.

Millwright concluded that the two accidentally hit upon the perfect atmosphere and setting, leading up to the conjuration. Doubtless the soft drugs Nuttall had access to had helped bring about a proper connection with outside spheres, had contributed in forming a link, as it were, with alien dimensions. When the group had finished their few lines of intoned invocation, Nuttall had taken up the chant to its conclusion . . . And then came the Black One! Never guessing that any such visitation might actually occur, Nuttall had failed to take the traditional precaution of prisoning the horror in a pentagram.

And it *was* a horror! A thing with invisible, evil eyes that saw in the dark, with mouths and lips that sucked and slobbered. They had driven it off simply by switching on the light. If they had not . . . then soon they would have drowned in its hideous residual slime, the juices it exuded from alien agglutinous pores.

Having driven the thing off, they had thought that they were rid of it. However, later that night, after cleaning up, when Bart sought to leave Nuttall's place to return home, out in the dark the thing had come to him again. He had barely been able to make it back to Nuttall's door and the sanctuary of the blessed light within.

Now, unseen, the Black One waited for the summons of its beloved darkness, when it could return again with its sucking mouths to drown its liberators in loathsome slime. And now, too, it waited for Millwright . . .

The occultist was only too well aware of the horror of living with this nightmare—of never knowing when the lights might fail; the constant fear of accidentally knocking oneself unconscious and waking at night in a darkened room, or perhaps not waking at all! Now, at the midnight hour, tired as he was, he patiently turned the leaves of a great and anciently esoteric textbook, hopeful of finding some clue as to the nature of the thing his visitors had called up from the darker spheres.

Nuttall and Bart were similarly employed, albeit with lesser works of reference. Only the dry rustles of flipped pages, the occasional muttered curse as a promising stream of research went dry and the ticking of Millwright's wall-clock disturbed the silence. Their task seemed impossible; and yet by morning, through sheer diligence and hard work—engendered of a dreadful fear—they had learned much of the horror that even now stalked the dark places and awaited them hungrily. Though what they had discovered had only served to increase their terror.

This creature, being or power, had been known in the pre-dawn world to the earliest Black Magicians and Necromancers. Records had come down even from predeluge Atlantis of "The Night Thing"—"The Black One"—"The Filler of Space"—"Bugg-Shash the Terrible"—a demon whom Eibon of Mhu Thulan himself had written of as being:

One of the darkest Beings of the Netherworld, whose Trail is as that of a monstrous Snail, who hails from the blackest Pits of the most remote Spheres. Cousin to Yibb-Tstll, Bugg-Shash, too is a Drowner; His lips do suck and lick; His Kiss is

the slimy Kiss of the hideous Death. He wakes the very Dead
to His Command, and encased in the horror of His Essence
even the worm-ravaged Lich hastens to His Bidding . . .

This from that tome so carefully scrutinized and guarded from
the view of his two assistants by Millwright.

And from Feery's *Notes on the Cthaat Aquadingen*—though Millwright had warned that Feery's reconstructions and translations were
often at fault or fanciful in their treatment of the original works—
Bart had culled the following cryptic information:

> Lest any brash or inexperienced Wizard be tempted to call
> forth one of ye Drowners—be it Yibb-Tstll or Bugg-Shash
> this Warning shall guide him & inform him of his Folly. For
> ye Drowners are of a like treacherous & require even ye most
> delicate Handling & minutest Attention to thaumaturgic
> Detail. Yibb-Tstll may only be controlled by use of ye Soul-
> searing Barrier of Naach-Tith, & Bugg-Shash may only be
> contained in ye Pentagram of Power. Too, ye Drowners must
> be sent early about ye Business of them, which is Death, lest
> they find ways to turn upon ye Caller. Call NOT upon Bug-
> Shash for ye sake of mere idle curiosity; for ye Great Black
> One, neither Him nor His Cousin, will return of His own
> Accord to His Place, but will seek out by any Means a Vic-
> tim, being often that same Wizard which uttered ye Calling.
> Of ye two is Bugg-Shash most treacherous & vilely cunning,
> for should no Sacrifice or Victim be prepared for His Com-
> ing, He will not go back without He takes His Caller with
> Him, must needs He stay an hundred Years to accomplish
> His Purpose . . .

Nuttall supplied the smallest contribution towards their knowledge of the horror lurking in the darkness. This fragment was from a
heavy, handwritten tome whose title had been carefully removed
from its spine by burning with a hot iron—and it *was* a fragment. Of
the Filler of Space, the book related only this:

Bugg-Shash is unbearable! His lips suck; He knows not defeat but brings down His victim at the last; aye, even though He follows that victim unto Death and beyond to achieve His purpose. And there was a riddle known to my forefathers:

*What evil wakes that should lie dead,*
*Swathed in horror toe to head?*

"That's from the *Necronomicon!*" Millwright cried when, towards dawn, Nuttall found this piece and read it aloud in the brightly lit study. "It is Alhazred!" The occultist snatched the book from the other's hands to pore eagerly over the page—then threw it down in disgust.

"Only that," he grumbled, "nothing more. But it's a clue! This book is simply a hodge-podge of occult lore and legend, but perhaps the Mad Arab's *Necronomicon*—in which I'm sure those lines have their origin—perhaps *that* book contains more on the same subject. It's certainly worth a try. Fortunately, the blacker side of my reputation has not yet reached the authorities at the British Museum. They recognise me as an 'authority' in my own right—as a genuine scholar. Through them, I have access to archives forbidden to most others. I admit that these scraps we've found worry me . . . horribly! But we must remember that every magical conjuration has its dangers. So far in this business I have—well, I've escaped justice, so to speak. Yes, and I hope to do so again.

"If there is a way to . . . deflect . . . this horror, then I now believe I stand every chance of finding it, though that may take some time. This clue is the one I needed." He tapped the book with a fingernail. "If not . . . at least we know what we're up against. Personally, well, you will never find my home wanting for a gross of candles; I will always have a store of dry batteries and electric light bulbs; I will always carry on my person at least one cigarette lighter and a metal box of fresh, dry matches. Bugg-Shash will not find me unprepared when darkness falls . . ."

Through the morning, Bart and Nuttall slept and, even though daylight streamed in across Millwright's balcony and through his windows, still the electric lights burned while candles sank down slowly on their wicks. In mid-afternoon, when the occultist returned in cautious triumph, the two were up and about.

"I have it," he said, closing the door of the sumptuous flat behind him. "At least, I think so. It is the Third Sathlatta. There was more on Bugg-Shash in the *Necronomicon,* and that in turn led me to the *Cthaat Aquadingen,*" he shuddered. "It is a counter-spell to be invoked—as with many of the Sathlattae—at midnight. Tonight we'll free ourselves of Bugg-Shash forever . . . unless . . ." As he finished the occultist frowned. Despite his words, there was uncertainty in his tone.

"Yes?" Nuttall prompted him. "Unless what? Is something wrong?"

"No, no," Millwright shook his head angrily, tiredly. "It's just that . . . again I've come across this peculiar warning!"

"What warning is that?" Bart worriedly asked, his face twitching nervously.

"Oh, there are definite warnings, of sorts," Millwright answered, "but they're never clearly stated. Confound that damned Arab! It seems he never once wrote a word without that he wrapped it in a riddle!" He collapsed into a chair.

"Go on," prompted Nuttall, "explain. How does this 'counter-spell' of yours work . . . and what are these 'warnings' that you're so worried about?"

"As to your first question: I don't believe there's any need to explain more than I've done already. But to enlighten you, albeit briefly; the Sathlattae consist of working spells and counterspells. The third Sathlatta is of the latter order. As to what I'm frightened of, well . . ."

"Yes?" Nuttall impatiently prompted him again.

"As applicable to our present situation," Millwright finally went on, "—in this predicament we're in—the third Sathlatta is . . . incomplete!"

"You mean it won't work?" Bart demanded, his eyes wide and fearful.

"Oh, yes, it'll work all right. But—"

"For God's sake!" Nuttall cried, his usually disciplined nerves stretched now to the breaking point, evidence of which showed clearly in his high, quavering voice. "Get on, man!"

"How do I explain something which I can't readily understand myself?" Millwright snarled, rounding on the frightened man. "And you'd better not start shouting at me, my friend. Why, but for your meddling, none of us would be in this position . . . and remember that, without my help, you're stuck with it forever!"

At that, Nuttall's face went very white and he began a stuttered apology. The occultist cut him short. "Forget it. I'll tell you why I'm worried. To put it simply, the third Sathlatta carries a clause!"

"A clause?" Bart repeated the word wonderingly, plainly failing to understand.

"To quote Alhazred," Millwright ignored him, "the counterspell's protection lasts 'only unto death'!"

For a moment there was silence; then Bart gave a short, strained laugh. "Only unto death? Why, who could ask fairer than that? I really don't see . . ."

"And one other thing," the occultist continued. "The third Sathlatta is not irrevocable. Its action may be reversed simply by uttering the Sathlatta itself in reverse order."

Millwright's guest stared at him for a few moments without speaking; then Nuttall said: "Does anyone else know of our . . . problem?"

"Not unless you've told someone else," the occultist answered, a deep frown creasing his forehead. "Have you?"

"No," Nuttall answered, "we haven't . . . but you see what I mean, don't you? What is there to worry about, if it's all as simple as you say? We, certainly, will never mess about with this sort of thing again . . . and who else is there to know what's happened? Even if someone was aware that we'd conjured up a devil, it's unlikely he'd know how to reverse this process of yours. It's doubtful anyone would even want or dare to, isn't it?"

Millwright considered it and gradually his manner became more relaxed. "Yes, you're right, of course," he answered. "It's just that I don't like complications in these things. You see, I know something of the Old Adepts. They didn't issue the sort of warnings I've seen here for nothing. This Bugg-Shash—whatever he is—must be the very worst order of demons. Everything about him is . . . demoniacal!"

## III

That same evening, from copious notes copied in the rare books department of the British Museum, Millwright set up all the paraphernalia of his task. He cleared the floor of his study. Then, in what appeared to Nuttall and Bart completely random positions—which were, in fact, carefully measured, if in utterly alien tables—upon the naked floor, he placed candles, censors and curious copper bowls. When he was satisfied with the arrangement of these implements, leaving the centre of the floor clear, he chalked on the remaining surrounding floor-space strange and disturbing magical symbols in a similarly confusing and apparently illogical over-all design. Central to all these preparatory devices, he drew a plain white circle and, as the midnight hour approached, he invited his guests to enter with him into this protective ring.

During the final preparations the candles had been lit. The contents of the censors and bowls, too, now sent up to the ceiling thinly wavering columns of coloured smoke and incense. Moreover, the purely electrical lights of the room had been switched off—very much to the almost hysterical Bart's dislike—so that only the candles gave a genuine, if flickering, light while the powders and herbs in their bowls and censors merely glowed a dull red.

As the first stroke of midnight sounded from the clock on the wall, Millwright drew from his pocket a carefully folded sheet of paper. In a voice dead of emotion—devoid, almost, of all human inflection—he read the words so carefully copied earlier that day from a near-forgotten tome in the dimmer reaches of the British Museum.

It is doubtful whether Bart or Nuttall could ever have recalled the jumble of alien vowels, syllables and discordants that rolled in seemingly chaotic disorder off Millwright's tongue in that dimly lit room. Certainly, it would have been impossible for any mere mortal, unversed in those arts with which Millwright had made himself familiar, to repeat that hideously jarring, incredible sequence of sounds. To utter the thing backwards, then—"in reverse order," as Millwright had had it—must plainly be out of the question. This thought, if not the uppermost in their minds, undoubtedly occurred to the two initiates as the occultist came to the end of his performance and the echoes of his hellish liturgy died away . . . but, within the space of seconds, this and all other thoughts were driven from their minds by sheer terror!

Even Millwright believed, at first, that he had made some terrible mistake, for now there fell upon the three men in the chalked circle a tangible weight of horror and impending doom! Bart screamed and would have fled the circle and the room at once—doubtless to his death—but the occultist grabbed him and held him firmly.

Slowly but surely, the candles dimmed as their flames inexplicably lowered. Then, one by one, they began to flicker out, apparently self-extinguished. Bart's struggles and screaming became such that Nuttall, too, had to hold on to him to prevent his rushing from the circle. Suddenly, there came to the ears of the three—as if from a thousand miles away—the merest whisper at first, a susurration, as heard in a sounding shell. The rustling chitterings of what could only be . . . a presence!

Bart promptly fainted. Millwright and Nuttall lowered him to the floor and crouched beside his unconscious form, still holding him tightly in their terror, staring into the surrounding shadows. The hideously evil chitterings, madly musical in an indefinable alien manner, grew louder. And then . . . something slimy and wet moved gelatinously in the darker shadows of the room's corners!

"Millwright!" Nuttall's voice cracked on that one exclamation. The word had been an almost inarticulate utterance, such as a child might make, crying out for its mother in the middle of a particularly frightening nightmare.

"Stay still! And be quiet!" Millwright commanded, his own voice no less cracked and high-pitched.

Only two candles burned now, so low and dim that they merely pushed back the immediate shadows. As the occultist reached out a tremulous hand to draw one of these into the circle . . . so the other blinked out, leaving only a spiral of grey smoke hanging in the near-complete darkness.

At this, the abominable chittering grew louder still. It surrounded the circle completely now and, for the first time, the two conscious men clearly saw that which the single, tiny remaining flame held at

bay. Creeping up on all sides, to the very line of the chalked circle, the
Thing came; a glistening, shuddering wall of jelly-like ooze in which
many mouths gaped and just as many eyes monstrously ogled! This
was Bugg-Shash the Drowner, The Black One, The Filler of Space. Indeed, the bulk of this . . . Being? . . . did seem to fill the entire study!
All bar the blessed sanctuary of the circle.

The eyes were . . . beyond words, but worse still were those
mouths. Sucking and whistling with thickly viscous lips, the mouths
glistened and slobbered and, from out of those gluttonous orifices
poured the lunatic chitterings of alien song—the Song of Bugg-
Shash—as His substance towered up and leaned inwards to form a
slimy ceiling over their very heads!

Nuttall closed his eyes and began to pray out loud, while Millwright simply moaned and groaned in his terror, unable to voice
prayers to a God he had long forsaken; but though it seemed that all
was lost, the Third Sathlatta had not failed them. Even as the ceiling
of jelly began an apparently inexorable descent, so the remaining
candle flared up and, at that, the bulk of Bugg-Shash broke and ran
like water through a shattered dam. The wall and ceiling of quivering
protoplasm with its loathsome eyes and mouths seemed to wave and
shrink before Millwright's eyes as the awful Black One drew back to
the darker shadows.

Then, miraculously, the many extinct candles flared up, returning to life one by one and no less mysteriously than they had snuffed
themselves out. The occultist knew then that what he had seen had
merely been an immaterial visitation, a vision of what *might* have
been, but for the power of the Third Sathlatta.

Simultaneously with Bart's return to consciousness, Millwright
shouted: "We've won!"

As Nuttall ventured to open incredulous eyes the occultist
stepped out of the circle, crossed to the light switch and flooded the
room with light. The thing he and Nuttall had witnessed must indeed
have been merely a vision—a demon-inspired hallucination—for no
sign of the horror remained. The floor, the walls and bookshelves, the
pushed-aside furniture, all were clean and dry, free of the horrid
Essence of Bugg-Shash. No single trace of His visit showed in any
part of the room; no single crack or crevice of the pine floor knew
the morbid loathsomeness of His snail-trail slime . . .

## IV

"Ray!" Alan Bart cried, shouldering his way through the long-haired, tassel-jacketed patrons of The Windsor's smokeroom. Nuttall saw him, waved him in the direction of a table and ordered another drink. With a glass in each hand he then made his way from the bar, through the crush of regulars, to where Bart now sat with his back to the wall, his fist wrapped tightly around an evening newspaper.

Over a week had passed since their terrifying experience at the London flat of Thomas Millwright. Since then, they had started to grow back into their old creeds and customs. Although they still did not quite trust the dark, they had long since proved for themselves the efficacy of Millwright's Third Sathlatta. Ever the cynic, and despite the fact that he still trembled in dark places, Nuttall now insisted upon taking long walks along lone country lanes of an evening, usually ending up at The Windsor before closing time. Thus Bart had known where to find him.

"What's up?" Nuttall questioned as he took a seat beside the younger man. He noted with a slight tremor of alarm the drawn, worried texture of his friend's face.

"Millwright's dead!" Bart abruptly blurted, without preamble. "He's dead—a traffic accident—run down by a lorry not far from his flat. He was identified in the mortuary. It's all in the paper." He spread the newspaper before Nuttall who hardly glanced at it.

If the olive-skinned man was shocked, it did not show; his weak eyes had widened slightly at Bart's disclosure, nothing more. He let the news sink in, then shrugged his shoulders.

Bart was completely taken aback by his friend's negative attitude. "We did *know* him!" he protested.

"Briefly," Nuttall acknowledged; and then, to Bart's amazement, he smiled. "That's a relief," he muttered.

Bart drew away from him. "What? Did I hear you say—"

"It's a relief, yes," Nuttall snapped. "Don't you see? He was the only one we knew who could ever have brought that . . . thing . . . down on us again. And now he's gone."

For a while they sat in silence, tasting their drinks, allowing the human noises of the crowded room to close in and impinge upon their beings. Then Bart said: "Ray, do you suppose that . . . ?"

"Hmm?" Nuttall looked at him. "Do I suppose what, Alan?"

"Oh, nothing really. I was just thinking about what Millwright told us; about the protection of that spell of his lasting 'only unto death'!"

"Oh?" Nuttall answered. "Well, if I were you, I shouldn't bother. It's something I don't intend to find out about for a long time."

"And there's something else bothering me," Bart admitted, not really listening to Nuttall's perfunctory answer. "It's something I can't quite pin down—part of what we discovered that night at Mill-wright's place, when we were going through all those old books. Damned if I can remember what it is, though!"

"Then forget it!" Nuttall grinned. "And while you're at it, how about a drink? It's your round."


Against his better instincts, but not wanting Nuttall to see how desperately he feared the darkness still, Bart allowed himself to be talked into walking home. Nuttall lived in a flat in one of the rather more "flash" areas of the city, but walking they would have to pass Bart's place first. Bart did not mind the dark so much—he said—so long as he was not alone.

Low, scudding clouds obscured the stars as they walked and a chill autumn wind blew discarded wrappers, the occasional leaf and loose, eerily-flapping sheets of evening "racing specials" against their legs.

Nuttall's flat was city-side of a suburban estate, while Bart's place lay more on the outskirts of the city proper. The whole area, though, was still quite new, so that soon the distances between welcome lamp-posts increased; there was no need for a lot of light way out here. With the resultant closing-in of darkness, Bart shuddered and pressed closer to his apparently fearless friend. He did not know it, but Nuttall was deep in worried thought. Bart's words in the smoke-room of The Windsor had brought niggling doubts flooding to the forefront of his consciousness; he could quite clearly recall all that they had uncovered at Millwright's home—including that which Bart had forgotten . . .

At the city end of Bart's road, almost half-way to Nuttall's flat and within half a mile of Bart's door, they saw a man atop a ladder attending to an apparently malfunctioning street lamp. The light flickered, flared, then died as they approached the lamp-post and the base of the ladder.

"These people," Bart asserted with a little shudder, "are the grafters. Out here all hours of the night—just to make sure that we have . . . light."

Without a breath of warning, simultaneous with Bart's shivery uttering of the word "light," the great bowl of the street lamp crashed down from above to shatter into a million glass fragments at their feet.

"My God!" Nuttall shouted up at the black silhouette clambering unsteadily down the ladder. "Take it easy, old chap. You bloody near dropped that thing right on our heads!"

The two men stopped in the dark street to steady the precarious-looking ladder and, as they did so, a splattering of liquid droplets fell from above, striking their hands and upturned faces. In the darkness they could not see those liquid droplets . . . but they could feel the clinging sliminess of them! Frozen in spontaneous horror, they stared at each other through the shrouding night as the figure on the ladder stepped down between them.

Bart's pocket torch cut a jerky swath of light across Nuttall's frozen features until it played upon the face of the man from the ladder. That face—stickily wet and hideously vacant, dripping nightmare slime as it was—*was nevertheless the face of Millwright!*

Millwright, the pawn of the Black One, fled from the mortuary—where Bugg-Shash had found his body in the dark—to accomplish that Being's purpose, the purpose He *must* pursue before He could return to His own hellish dimension!

Only blind instinct, the instinct of self-preservation, had caused Bart to reach for his torch; but the sight revealed by its beam had completely unnerved him. His torch fell from uselessly twitching fingers, clattering on the pavement, and the dead man's heel came down upon it with shattering force. Again the darkness closed in.

Then the slimy figure between the two men moved and they felt fingers like bands of iron enclosing their wrists. The zombie that was Millwright exerted fantastic strength to hold them—or rather, Bugg-Shash exerted His strength through the occultist's corpse—as dead lips opened to utter the ghastly, soul-destroying strains of the *reversed* Third Sathlatta!

In the near-distant darkness faint, delighted chitterings commenced; and the weird trio thrashed about across the road, to and fro in a leaping, twisting, screaming tug-o'-war of death as, at last, the thing that Bart had forgotten came back to his collapsing, nightmare-blasted mind:

> He wakes the very Dead to His Command, and encased in the horror of his Essence even the worm-ravaged Lich hastens to His bidding . . .

The hellish dance lasted, as did the screaming, until they felt the lips of Bugg-Shash and his monstrous kisses . . .

# The Slitherer from the Slime

## H. P. Lowcraft*

*It is my firm belief that we are but the puppets of some evil, malignant Thing, beyond all mortal comprehension, that torments man and has done so since the very Dawn of Time; and that the foul worship of Incarnate Darkness still goes on in the far corners of the globe.*

LOUISA MAE ALCOTT

Had I but received some occult premonition of the ghastly horrors that awaited me that fateful evening, I have no doubt but that I would have turned my coach about and gone back to Arkham forthwith. However, no such warning from the Beyond was mine, and my mind was at ease as I drove my lathered horses up the storm-swept, treacherous road to the mouldering, incredibly ancient castle that crowned Gallows Hill. It was a night of unbelievable hideousness; the lightning flamed and flared in the sky like a burning iron held in the hand of a slavering demon with which to torture a helpless, chain-bound god; the wind shrieked and bellowed like a frenzied horde of shambling ghouls, mad with unmentionable hungers, and the rain poured down to sweep a sin-drunk mankind from this

---

*This curious manuscript, believed by prominent Lowcraft authority August September to be authentic, and perhaps the last thing Lowcraft wrote, is published here for the first time, with the permission of the owners of the manuscript, Lin Carter and Dave Foley.

cosmic globe of fecund slime. In the goblin-flickering of the levin-bolts that racked the tortured welkin with their demoniac fires, I caught intermittent glimpses of crumbling, ivy-covered Castle Drumgool where it crouched, rotting with the centuries, atop the barren hill like some waiting monster. The leering cornices, the blind windows, the crumbling cupolas, the tottering turrets, the slimy por-ticos, all cast a pall of unutterable desolation within the hidden adyts of my shuddering heart.

As thunder (or *was* it thunder?) whooped and gobbled down the inky skies like the babblings of an insane god, I drove my curiously unwilling steeds through the tottering arch, over-grown with pecu-liarly unwholesome fungoids of obscene shapes and eldritch colours, and into the mouldering courtyard. A sodden groom appeared from the darkness to seize the reins, and as he led my mares off to the sta-bles, I found myself speculating oddly on his shambling, loping gait, and the scaly batrachian appearance of his bloated, grayish face with its leering, disturbingly mocking eyes.

My unknown host was not at the crumbling portal to greet me, so I pushed open the ancient, decaying, oaken-panelled door, and entered the gloom-shrouded, dust-mantled, dark and fetid vault of the castle vestibule. Black unseen horrors seemed to flutter back into the shadows at my approach, and I watched with growing un-ease as the faint and ghostly shaft of light from the outside narrowed and was gone. The rotting oaken door boomed shut behind me and I found myself alone in the hellish, stygian hall of the cursed and be-nighted Castle Drumgool.

A foul and decaying foetor rose from deep within the dark halls, and as it enveloped me, I felt my heart shudder and quail. I backed toward the door, involuntarily, and at length, unable to bear for a sec-ond longer the nauseous miasma that assaulted my nostrils, turned to leave. But on the instant, from deep within the gloomy depths of the ghostly halls, there issued a sound of crusted metal squealing as an inner door swung open. My fingers froze on the latch, and I could do nothing but stare in growing horror as the bent and sham-bling figure of a man (or *was* it a man?) made its way toward me across the echoing chamber. There sounded a voice from this twisted travesty of a human, and as he approached my unwilling eyes beheld his corpse-like pallor, and the subtly rotted aspect of his dress. His eyes fixed me with a stare, and repeated that phrase which I had not before heard, or perhaps had refused to hear—"*Welcome to Castle Drumgool!*"

My frame quaked as the full import of these words struck me, and I staggered back a pace in order to protect myself from the aura of evil that sprang up almost tangibly around the ebon apparition. My heart sank in my breast as, from a fold of his decaying robe, he produced a taper, and I was for the first time subjected to the sight of the face of the master of Castle Drumgool of Gallows Hill (or *was* it a hill?). The wavering flame of the candle, that was, my shuddering mind conjectured, fashioned perhaps of corpse-fat, revealed—ah, imagine, if you but can, the rotund, worm-soft, slug-like, unwholesomely bloated figure that met my cringing gaze; a swollen-cheeked visage whose pallid flesh seemed acrawl with pulpy maggots; and eyes, half buried within the folds of flaccid flesh, glinting hellishly with a diabolical counterfeit of friendly welcome. Hastily I muttered some conventional acknowledgement of his greeting, while my fear-frozen gaze took in, with what inward quaking my reader is at liberty to surmise, the unutterable loathsomeness of his robe (which I now perceived to be a smoking jacket), his obscene felt slippers, the hideous travesty of jollity in his smirking face. My host ushered me into a large, dimly-lit cavern of a room, and showed me to a seat, while he rung, ostensibly to summon a servitor, although my terror-fraught mind visioned all too clearly the ghastly creatures his alarm was meant to rouse, a bell. The room, my paralyzed senses gradually perceived, was a library, and, in an effort to calm my leaping pulse, I tore my eyes away from his gruesomely rubicund visage, and fixed them upon the tomes that crowded his shelves.

A thrill of pure horror pierced my innermost soul, as I glimpsed the titles lettered in gold (or *was* it gold?) upon the bindings. The books, if such they could be called, exuded an almost palpable odour of foulness and decay, a grave stench before whose unnerving assault my nostrils crinkled involuntarily. There I glimpsed that hellish text which celebrates the splendours of the Elder Dark, that monstrous volume of demon-worship, *Black Beauty*; next to it rested a copy of that unholy and blasphemous history of a necromancer famed in eldrich legend, *The Wizard of Oz;* beside that, bound in the rotting, ophidian hide of some loathsome serpent, was that foul tome which the ancient pagan deities of the woods hold sacred, *Peter Pan;* and next to it, that chaotic and monstrous volume, that incredibly ancient compilation of eldritch lore, that vast anthology of demoniac wisdom culled from forgotten ages, *The Pickwick Papers!*

Though I, as the reader of these tortured words might well perceive, found my soul reeling in revulsion as each new title defiled my eyes, still I was not able to tear them from the continuing shelves of literary horrors which sprawled around the walls of the darkened chamber. My unwilling eyes pressed on into the dark corners of that damned and benighted library, and each turn of the shelf brought some new terror, some more monstrous and perverted blasphemy.

My shuddering gaze fell upon a copy of that black and nefarious tale of alien life on Earth, that hellish chronicle of that dweller in the dark and sinister depths of haunted woodlands, *Winnie the Pooh.* Resting next to it, I beheld a volume of the foul and ghastly legends and lore which are known to the horrors of the night; that fiendish compilation of eldrich terrors, that awful and soul-searing tome, *Aesop's Fables.* And at last, though my brain reeled in rejection of this crowning horror, I forced myself to gaze upon the volume which inhabited the last space on the worm-eaten shelves—a work of unspeakable loathesomeness and terrific monstrosity, a tome of ghastly and consuming hellishness, that foul and blasphemous atrocity, which no one may name aloud, and at the writing of whose title my pen recoils from the paper, *The Power of Positive Thinking!*

I struggled with my tortured mind, attempting to regain some semblance of composure, so that my host would not perceive that I had discerned his devilish nature, but no sooner had I suppressed the expression of loathing and fear which threatened to contort my face, when a new and more frightful horror became apparent. A thrill of terror shot across my brain, as I saw the latch of the library door (or *was* it a door?) slowly lifting—*without any visible hand to raise it!*

I shrank back into the cushions of the unspeakably loathsome chair in which I was seated, in a transport of horror. My frozen brain searched frantically for some explanation of the ghastly phenomenon which was taking place before my very eyes—some sane, rational *physical* force which could raise a door latch without making itself apparent in any other fashion. My mind boggled, however, and I could only watch numbly as the latch was raised to its limit, and the door was slowly opened.

A thing stood in the doorway, half in shadow, and for the first time in that dark and grim evening I was struck with the diabolical cleverness of my eldritch host. The phantoms which no doubt occupied the chamber had not, after all, made themselves known. No, my host was far too clever. The raising of the latch had been done by the dark creature which stood now in the doorway, deliberately calculated to convince me that the chamber was indeed the abode of spirits from hell, and to then dispel the illusion and convince me of the opposite. But I was far too clever—I was now more firmly convinced than ever!

The creature on the threshold entered, and I saw at once that he was dressed in the attire of a manservant. His costume, however, was of such a material and aspect as to present an impression of naked, rotting flesh, seeming, in the firelight, to be acrawl with maggots. His face was a fiendishly clever imitation of a human countenance, but, apprehending his hidden nature, it was not difficult to see beneath this mask to the lurking monster beneath. His eyes burned like twin coals dying in a cup of hemlock, and his mouth was like some rotted wound as he opened it to shape this grotesque phrase—"*The brandy, sir.*"

The very walls of Castle Drumgool rocked about me as his words fell upon my ears. I wanted to shout, to cry for help, to beseech someone from the world of light to come and rescue me from the cloud of evil that held me in its crushing clutch. Through a haze of palpitating disconcert, I watched the man-servant-thing cross the room, and set a tray of beverage upon a table. My hellish host, who had been, with a fiendish counterfeit of composure, lighting what seemed to be a briar pipe, as I had gazed at his servitor, now cleared his throat (of what unmentionable phlegm I could but conjecture), and said, in his diabolical travesty of a voice, "The night is cold. Would you care for a warming beverage, sir?"

The very Universe seemed to shatter, as before the mad pummelings of some idiot-god, and crumble about my frozen mind, as the true hidden meaning lurking behind the obvious hidden meaning behind his *apparently* ordinary invitation dawned within my panic-riven brain. What could I do but accept his ghoulish invitation? Were I to refuse his offer, then he would know, beyond any wan phantom of a doubt, that I was *aware* of his true, indescribably nauseating identity. Forcing my visage, with a colossal effort of will, to show no sign of my revulsion, I murmured acceptance, and watched with congealing blood as he poured a gelid, incarnadined fluid into a gruesomely-carven goblet of what may, *or may not,* have been crystal. I received the goblet he handed me (writhing inwardly as his rotting talons touched my flesh), and sat numbly, my mind a chaos of boiling shadows, gazing at the squamous liquid of which I must imbibe.

With a vulpine leer, my host uttered these damnable words, which burned, as a smoking iron in the claws of a tittering fiend, into my quaking brain—*"There, old man, drink up now!"*

My time had come.

With a supra-human effort, I lifted the noisome goblet to my cracked, parched lips, and *drank down* the slimy brew, conjecturing (as the reader might well imagine) in blind perturbation upon what necromantic potion, what nightmare philtre, what unutterably un-mentionable ingredients comprised the devilish draught. The room spun about me—the evil, ghoulish leer on my host's bloated counte-nance, the zombie-blank face of the servant-thing, the rotting row of demoniac tomes—all loomed madly as the insidious poison bubbled through my veins. Space and time seemed to crack; the world crum-bled from beneath my feet; I went careening off into a chaos of spin-ning stars. . . .

And then, with a flash like that of an entire universe of planets exploding at the command of a blood-mad, satanic god, the full im-port of the incredible truth burst upon my brain. *Nothing what-ever had been in the brandy!* My host, from whatever pit of hell he hailed, had been clever enough *not* to poison the brandy. Then what, my shuddering soul asked, unthought-of torment had he planned for me?

As my mind sought desperately to answer this question, the fell servant moved the goblet from my clutch and left the room, ominously closing the great door behind him. We sat alone, my monstrous host and I, as, outside, thunder gibbered and rolled; a nightmare wind shrieked cacophonically and clawed with icy talons at the window panes. A numbing chill, as from grave-soil, soaked into the room, unrelieved by the eerie red and yellow flames that coiled and wavered in the great fireplace, flames that fed (doubtlessly) upon the fang-picked bones and splintered coffin of a nearby tomb.

I felt the forces of hell gather around the crumbling walls of Castle Drumgool as the night shrieked on, and their insane voices roared as if in answer to the thunder, as if in challenge to the elements, with every flash (lighting up the fetid land surrounding the high and hellish castle in a deadly and corpse-like pallor) of lightning, while the wind howled through the overgrown turrets and down the chimney, blowing the fire in the grate into mad, phantasmagorial shapes, the significance of which I could not bring myself to imagine. I could only attempt to converse with my host in what must seem a normal fashion, never once allowing my mask to slip, never once allowing to fall from my lips any word, from my hands any gesture, that would suggest to him that I knew his true and hideous nature, knew him to be, not a simple mortal, but a creature of the nameless pit, a being of the black and awesome region which, thankfully, lies beyond the ken of mortal-kind and invades the world of daylight only in abysmal dreams and nightmarish fancies.

In a few minutes he spoke again, inviting me, ostensibly, to partake of his hospitality for the night. My mind shuddered, its very fabric ineffably soiled, at the hellish implications of his apparently harmless words; however, I allowed him to precede me (again with that hellish taper of corpse-fat, whose sickly coil of filthy vapour tainted my quivering nostrils) out of the library and into the darkness of the outer hall; thereupon, he led me up a rickety staircase fashioned (by *whose* fingers my frozen brain could not imagine) of some unutterably hideous wood (or *was* it wood?), which teetered over the yawning edge of an ink-black pit, above which we wound our slow and tortuous way, at every step my mind quailing at the thought of what might await me above; we proceeded upward, however, while the wind screamed and whooped outside and the thunder rocked and rolled like the mad laughter of an insane deity, while darkness closed about us, clammy, noisome darkness tainted with the charnel-stench of things long dead and better left unnamed; then my eldritch host, reaching the worm-rotted landing of the hideous staircase, gestured to a scarred and slime encrusted door, which, as I watched with growing horror, began slowly to open, its hinges groaning, as the sound of a damned soul crying for succor from the depths of hell's blackest pit, revealing behind it a stygian chamber whose infernal darkness the oily taper could not penetrate, and with a thrill of terror I realized that this foul cell was intended by my host to be my resting place; feeling then his gnarled talon gripping my arm, and hearing these perverted syllables escape his fusty lips—"Here's the guest room; hope you'll be comfortable."—I felt myself drawn irresistibly into the dark and fearful maw, upon entering into which my fractured senses perceived the great iron-bound portal closing behind me, perhaps, my careening imagination led me to surmise, although every fiber of my consciousness rebelled at this most ghastly of fates, forever; and all the while my mind revolved on a line from the Crazy Arab who had once described just such a horrible scene, just such an indescribably hideous, unmentionably blasphemous, incomparably disgusting, unnameably nauseating, overpoweringly ugly, chaotically loathsome, blood-chillingly, unsettling, sickening, soul-searing, sight-defiling—sight—*sight*—NOT SIGHT! I see with a *new sense—lightning flashes, but—UGUG! YIG! BLAH! YOO-HOO have mercy—I . . . UNIFY THE FORCES . . . Yubbleglub and Cobble-nobbin—gods of night, WOW! . . . HELL FIRE AND TITANIC FOOF . . . FARB SAVE ME . . . THE EIGHT-NODED FLAMING EYE—OR IS IT AN EYE? OOOO aaaa ee*

NOTE:

The curious manuscript which trails off above was found beside the body of Hirum Phineas Lowcraft, who had apparently died of something resembling a stroke while spending the night at Pleasant-Acres-by-the-Thames, the country estate of Sir Rodney Happie-Happie, famous author of children's books. Sir Rodney, when questioned about the odd circumstances surrounding Lowcraft's sudden death, commented:

*Demmed peculiar; couldn't make anything out of the fellah; seemed to be always jumping or looking about for something. Must have been from writing too much of that irregular horror stuff—you know, all that* heldritch *bosh, and that sort of thing. Well, I certainly wouldn't have invited him out again. . . .*

# The Doom of Yakthoob
## from *The Necronomicon*

## Lin Carter

(Most editions of *The Necronomicon* omit for some reason which I shudder to conjecture, the little-known "First Narrative," going straight from the so-called "Introitus"—the opening paragraph which, in Dee, reads: "The Book of the Laws of the Dead, which was written by the poet Abdul Alhazred of Sanaa, in Damascus, the Year of the Hejira 113, so that all Mankind might know of the Horrors of the Tomb and of those greater Horrors which await Beyond"—to the famous "Second Narrative," that of the City of Pillars. My own copy of Alhazred—a virtually priceless manuscript in Dee's own hand—luckily contains this rare episode, which I have transcribed here for the use of the serious student.)

A s a youth I was apprenticed to the notorious Saracen wizard, Yakthoob, among many others, of whom the languid and dissolute Ibn Ghazoul became my closest friend, despite his voluptuous and immoral habits. At the behest of the Master we learned the summoning-up of Evil Things and conversed with ghouls in the rock tombs of Neb and even partook of the unnamed Feasts of Nitocris in loathsome crypts beneath the Great Pyramid. We went down the Secret Stair to worship That which dwelleth in the black catacombs below the crumbling ruins of elder and ghoulhaunted Memphis, and in the noxious caverns of Nephren-Ka in the sealed and unknown

Valley of Hadoth by the Nile we performed such Blasphemous Rites that even now my soul shuddereth to contemplate.

Ever we begged of the Master that he instruct us in the calling up of the Great Princes of the Pit, the which he was fearful to do, saying that the Lesser Demons be easily satisfied with the Red Offering alone, having a horrid thirst for the Blood of Men, but that the Great Ones demand naught less than the offering up of a Living Soul, save that ye have a certain Elixir, compounded according to the Forbidden Books from the ichor of holy angels, the secret of which is known but to a certain great Necromancer who dwelleth amongst the dead tombs of accursed and immemorial Babylon.

For a time the Master sated our lust for daemonic knowledge with Rites and Horrors terrible to think upon, but ever and again we did beseech for that Great Secret whereof I have spoken, and at length he was persuaded and dispatched the youth Ibn Ghazoul to crumbling and antique Babylon with much gold to purchase from the Necromancer the terrible Elixir. In time the youth returned therefrom and bore with him, in a flask of precious orichalc from dead Atlantis, the Elixir, and we thus repaired to sealed and hidden Hadoth where the Master did That of which I dare not speak, and Lo! a great Thing rose up tall and terrible against the stars. Scarlet and wet and glistening was It, like a flayed tormented thing, with eyes like Black Stars. About it hovered a burning cold like the dark wind that blows between the Stars, and it stunk of the foetor of the Pit.

In a slobbering voice the Abomination demanded its price, and bore the flacon of orichalc to its snout in one scarlet Claw, and snuffled thereat, and then to our immeasurable Horror howled forth a braying Laughter and hurled the Flask from it, and caught up the Master in one Claw of horrible cold and plucked and tore at him, all the while making the Night hideous with terrible laughter. For a time the hapless Yakthoob squealed and flopped in the clutches of the Claw, but then lay still, and dangled therefrom, black and shrivelled, as the laughing Thing ripped at it until it raped forth the Spirit of Yakthoob, which it Devoured in a Certain Manner which made my dreams hideous with Nightmares for twenty years . . .

We screamed and fled from the accursed gloom of Hadoth where a Scarlet Thing howled and fed abominably under the shuddering stars, all but the vile and horrid Ibn Ghazoul, that wretched voluptuary, who had squandered the Master's gold on the lusts of his flesh during his travels to Babylon, and had substituted *naught but wine* in place of the rare Ichor . . . Him we saw never again, and to this day I quake with nameless terror at the thought of summoning forth the Great Ones from the Pit, mindful of the horrible Doom of the wizard Yakthoob.

# The Fishers from Outside

## Lin Carter

### STATEMENT OF HARLOW SLOAN

When Mayhew found the Black Stone beneath the ruins of Zimbabwe, it was the culmination of many long and weary years of work. His quest had begun twenty years before, when as a young student at Miskatonic he had first heard of the "Fishers from Outside" in the unpublished journals of the explorer Slauenwite. That odd and curious term was the name by which the Gallas of Uganda referred to a mysterious race that had ruled Central Uganda—according to the legend—before the first mammals were.

Intrigued, Mayhew read on with growing excitement as Slauenwite told of certain hellishly old stone ruins which the local tribes dread and avoid, of jungle-grown megaliths believed to be "older than man," and of a certain stone city somewhere in the south which their witch-doctors whispered was an abandoned outpost of creatures "flown down from the stars when the world was young."

I suppose it is hard for a scholar or a scientist to exactly pin down what first impelled him in the direction of his future work. But Mayhew always said it was the native stories Slauenwite recorded in 1932 in his journals. At any rate, he embarked on a search for more information about the Fishers from Outside. He found fragments of lore concerning the mystery-race in such old books as the dubious *Unaussprechlichen Kulten* of Von Junzt, the notorious *Book of Eibon*, Dostmann's questionable *Remnants of Lost Empires*, *De Vermis*

*Mysteriis* by the Flemish wizard, Ludvig Prinn, and the frightful *Ponape Scripture* that Abner Exekiel Hoag had found in the Pacific islands. In the fervor of his growing obsession, Mayhew even dared to look into the nightmarish pages of the *Necronomicon* of Abdul Alhazred, the Arabian demonologist.

According to Alhazred's account, the Fishers were the minions or servants of the demon Golgoroth, who had anciently been worshipped on Bal-Sagoth, which some rather questionable authorities claim to have been the last foundering remnant of the mythical Atlantis. On Bal-Sagoth he was worshipped both as the "god of darkness," and in his "bird-god" avatar, wrote the Arab. Most scholars would dismiss the legend as idle tales, but Mayhew knew there was independent corroboration for at least part of the account, for Norse voyagers during the early Crusades had seen Bal-Sagoth, recording something of its strange gods in their sagas.

After completing his doctorate, Mayhew obtained a grant and went to Africa. He followed the footsteps of Slauenwite, exploring Central Uganda, studying native myths and stories. Tales came to his ears of an ancient stone city buried in the southern jungles of the Dark Continent, which some thought the ruins of the legendary King Solomon's mines but which others ascribed to the handiwork of Portuguese slavers or traders. Mayhew knew that the Egyptian geographer, Ptolemy, had written many centuries ago of "Agysimba" the stone city in the jungle. Doubtless the Ugandan myth and the old Egyptian story referred to the same ruin . . . and that could hardly be anything else than old Zimbabwe itself, that immemorial and mysterious stone city deep in the jungled heart of Rhodesia . . . Zimbabwe, whereof so much is whispered and so very little known for certain.

I joined him at the site of Zimbabwe in 1946. I had been studying at the University of Capetown, and one of his papers—a monograph on Ugandan petroglyphs, still undecipherable—caught my eye. I wrote, applying for a job, and was promptly accepted.

I knew little of Zimbabwe. I knew it was the focal point of a vast system of mighty towers and ramparts spread out over something like three hundred thousand square miles of trackless jungle. The ruins are found in Mashonaland, the mining areas of Gwelo,

Que-Que and Selukwe. At the center, deep in Southern Rhodesia, about two hundred and eighty miles from the sea in the valley of the Upper Metetkwe lie the colossal fortifications of enigmatic Zimbabwe—greatest and most fabulous of the roughly five hundred stone structures found in this wide zone, which seem the work of a race unknown to history, and whose puzzling architecture has no parallel elsewhere on this planet, save in certain fearfully ancient ruins in Peru.

This little I had gleaned from that tantalizing book, Hall's *Great Zimbabwe*, which raises so many disturbing questions and settles so very few—if any—of them. And soon I was to see the fantastic city myself!

My first sight of mysterious Zimbabwe came at dusk. The sky was one supernal blaze of carmine and vermilion flame, against which the titanic walls of the enclosure soared impressively, composed of massive blocks weighing each many tons, the wall extending hundreds of feet, enclosing the weird, uncanny "topless towers" of which I had heard. Mayhew's workmen had cleared away the vines and undergrowth which for ages had encumbered the gigantic rampart, but the jungle, I somehow knew, had not surrendered, but had merely retreated before superior force, and was biding its time, waiting for the puny, ephemeral children of men to leave that it might inexorably regain its antique dominion over the mighty walls and towers.

A shudder, as of eerie premonition, ran through me as I first gazed upon lost Zimbabwe drowsing the ages away. But then I forced a shaky laugh, and put such trepidations from me; after all, night had nearly fallen, and the breeze was dank and wet . . .

Mayhew I found a devoted, even fanatic, scientist. His peculiar fixation on the legend of the "Fishers from Outside" set by, he was a learned and scholarly man. He told me something of the Golgoroth myth, and discussed what scraps of knowledge had been accumulated as to the history of the stupendous ruin before us. The Portuguese had first glimpsed it about 1550, he told me, but the first explorer did not reach these parts until 1868.

"I understand no inscriptions have ever been found," I murmured. He nodded, his lean, ascetic face serious and troubled.

"Yes, and that's another mystery! A race that can build a stone wall fourteen feet thick, in an elliptical enclosure eight hundred feet in circumference, should surely have some form of writing, if only for the required mathematics," he mused.

"And no artifacts have ever been found?" I hazarded.

"Only these," he said somberly, holding out a wooden tray. Within I saw a number of small, oddly-shaped objects of baked clay and carven stone. They resembled curiously stylized birds, but not like any birds I knew . . . there was something misshapen, deformed, even—*monstrous*, about them. I repressed a shiver of distaste.

"Do you know what they represent?" I asked faintly.

For a long moment he peered down at the tray of tiny artifacts, peering at them through his eyeglasses, a pair of pince-nez spectacles he wore always, looped about his throat on a long ribbon of black silk. These pince-nez were his most famous affectation, and I knew of them long before I ever came to know the man himself.

Then he turned and looked at me.

"Perhaps the Fishers from Outside," he said, his voice dropping to a faint, hoarse whisper. "Or, perhaps their mighty Master . . . *Golgoroth.*"

Something in the uncouth, harsh gutterals of that strange name made me wish, obscurely, that he had not spoken it aloud. Not here, amidst the immemorial ruins of elder Zimbabwe. . . .


I shall not bore you with any extended account of the many weeks it took to complete our excavations. First, we investigated the weird topless towers, which were devoid of any interior structure, save for thick stone piers jutting at intervals into the hollow, chimney-like interior. They were uncannily reminiscent of the pegs in an aviary, the perches in a birdcage, it seemed to me; but I said nothing, leaving the Professor to his own conjectures.

Within a month I was sent upriver to obtain supplies. I was rather glad of this, for I would miss our work in the Plain of Megaliths. There was something about this vast and level field, covered with row on row of mammoth stone cubes, that made me think of hundreds of Druidic sacrificial altars, and as the date of their excavation approached, my sleep was disturbed by dark dreams in which I seemed to see hundreds of squirming naked blacks bound to row after row of the altar-stones . . . while weirdly bird-masked shamans raised an eerie, cawing chant beneath the peering Moon whose cold eye was obscured by drifts of reeking smoke from many fires . . .

Terrible dreams they were!

Upriver, I found the trading post and loitered there long enough for the excavations to be completed on the Plain of Megaliths. My host was a local tradesman of Boer descent, who questioned me intently about our work, and eyed me furtively from time to time, as if there were questions he did not quite dare ask.

"Ever heard of the 'Great Old Ones'?" he blurted one night, his courage bolstered by rum. I shook my head.

"I don't think so," I said. "What are they, some native legend?"

"Yes . . . but, *mein Gott!* . . . native to what world, I could not say!"

I stared at him, baffled; but before I could ask another question, he abruptly changed the subject and began to talk lewdly and disgustingly about the local native women. I left downriver the next day with the supplies.

It seems I had lingered at the Ushonga trading-post longer than had been needful; the Plain of Megaliths had been excavated, and the diggers had turned up nothing more interesting than hundreds of the little birdlike stone images. Mayhew had therefore turned his attention to the great Acropolis, and beneath the foundations of the huge center-stone a remarkable discovery had been made.

He showed it to me by the wavering light of a hissing kerosene lamp, tenderly unwrapping the odd-shaped thing with hands that shook with excitement. I stared at it in awe and amazement . . . yes, even as I had stared at Zimbabwe itself that first night . . . and with a cold inward shudder of ghastly premonition, too.

## THE BLACK STONE.

It was a decahedron, a ten-sided mass of flinty, almost crystalline black stone which I could not at once identify. From the weight of it, I guessed it to be some sort of metal . . .

"Meteoric iron," Mayhew whispered, eyes alive with feral enthusiasm, behind the glinting lenses of his pince-nez, for once askew. "Cut from the heart of a fallen star . . . *and look at the inscriptions!*"

I peered more closely: each of the ten angled sides was a sleek plane of glistening black, covered with column on column of minute characters or hieroglyphs in a language unknown to me, though naggingly familiar. They in no slightest way resembled hieratic or demotic Egyptian, or any other form of writing I could remember having ever seen. I later copied some of them down in my notebook and can reproduce a few specimens here:

The Professor reverently turned the metallic block over. "This side in particular," he said in a low voice.

I stared at the weird, stylized profile figure of a monstrous thing like a hideous bird with staring eyes and a gaping beak filled with fangs. There was a stark ugliness to the depiction that was quite unsettling.

I looked up at him, a mute question in my eyes.

". . . *Golgoroth,*" he breathed.


Within the week we departed for the States. Nor was I at all loath to go, for all the excitement of our excavations and the discoveries they had unearthed. To tell the truth, ever since that night I had first set eyes on the Black Stone, I had not been sleeping at all well. A touch of jungle fever, perhaps, but night after night I tossed and turned, my dreams a mad turmoil of frightful nightmares . . .

One night in particular, after I saw the Stone, I again dreamed of Zimbabwe as it might have looked at its height, the sacrificial smokes staining the sky and obscuring behind lucent veils the white face of the leering Moon as it gloated down on scores of writhing blacks bound to the stone altars, grotesquely masked priests leaping in a wild and savage dance . . .

I knew that they were trying to call down from the stars some monstrous horror-god, but how this knowledge came to me I cannot really say. But then the moon was hidden by black, flapping shapes that circled and swooped like enormous fishing-birds, darting down to the altars to pluck and tear at the wriggling bodies bound there . . . and one of the huge, queerly deformed-looking bird-things emerged into the moonlight, and I stared with unbelieving horror at its hulking, horribly apterous, quasi-avian form, clothed with scales not feathers . . . one glimpse of the repulsive thing with its one leg and one glaring Cyclopean eye and hideous, hooked, fang-lined beak—

I woke screaming, with a bewildered Mayhew shaking me by the shoulders, demanding to know what was the matter.

No, I wasn't unhappy to be going home: I had had more than my fill of the sinister brooding silence of that thick, fetid jungle, crowding so ominously close to the ruins as if waiting, waiting . . . of that horribly old stone city, whose mysterious past contains hideous secrets I did not wish to plumb . . .

The reason for our abrupt departure was quite easily explained. It would seem that Professor Mayhew had found what he had been looking for. The discovery of the Black Stone from Zimbabwe would make him very famous—and his fame would be all the greater, of course, were he able to decipher the inscriptions.

For he, as well, had half-recognized them. My vague, teasing recollection of having somewhere once seen something very much like those queer glyphs tormented me; I could neither pin it down nor could I get it out of my mind.

It was Mayhew, however, who remembered where he had seen symbols very much like them, and the moment he spoke of it I felt certain that he was right. The *Ponape Scripture*! I must have seen the glyphs reproduced in some Sunday supplement article about the cryptic old book. But the Professor, of course, had studied the actual *Ponape Scripture* itself, in its repository at the Kester Library in

Salem, Massachusetts. He had examined the actual book, written in an unknown tongue, and had compared it against the debatable English version prepared by Abner Exekiel Hoag's body-servant, a Polynesian halfbreed from the isle of Ponape.

Mayhew hoped to find, somewhere, somehow, the key to the unknown language. On the boat he fretted over that, sending radio-telegraph messages.

"Churchward would know, if he were alive, I'm sure of that," he muttered. "His *Naacal Key* has never been published, but I have seen his speculative work on Tsath-yo and R'lyehian. Somewhere among his notes there might be data on this Ponapian glyph-system, whatever it is called . . ."

One night, as we neared the coastline, he burst into my cabin, triumphantly waving a piece of yellow paper.

"Churchward's widow has given me permission to borrow his unpublished notebooks and papers!" he crowed, face unhealthily flushed, eyes bright with excitement. "A chance, at last!"

Privately, I doubted it. But I kept my reservations to myself.

We disembarked, and went immediately to Salem, where the Professor had reserved rooms for us at the University Club. The next morning, leaving me to unpack our notes, records and sample artifacts, he was off to await the arrival of Churchward's papers. For days he pored through them in growing exasperation, for the author of *The Lost Continent of Mu* and other dubious works of pseudo-scientific speculation had known nothing of the unknown language, it seemed.

"What about Hoag's papers?" I suggested. "Perhaps his servant left a glossary or something; I know it was back in the seventeen hundreds, but still, since the *Scripture* is right here at the Kester, perhaps they hold the remainder of his library, as well."

His eyes flashed and he smote his brow with a groan, dislodging his pince-nez from their perch. "A splendid idea, young fellow!" he cried. "My intuition on hiring you was right."

The next day, I accompanied the Professor to the Library, where his scholarly credentials quickly gained us access to a private reading-cubicle and to the strange old book itself. While he pored over it eagerly, I regarded the volume with thinly disguised repugnance. I recalled what little was known of its curious history: the famous

"Yankee trader," Abner Exekiel Hoag of the Hoags of Arkham, had discovered the ancient book on one of his rum-and-copra trading ventures in the South Seas, back in 1734.

It was a weird document of many pages, inscribed with metallic inks of several colors on palm-leaf parchment sheets, which were bound between boards of archaic wood, carven with grotesque designs . . . the very reek of the ages rose from it, millennia made almost palpable, like the miasma of age-old rottenness . . .

I had read what the famous Pacific archaeologist, Harold Hadley Copeland, had written of the book in his own shocking and controversial *The Prehistoric Pacific in the Light of the 'Ponape Scripture,'* which only increased my repugnance. Poor Professor Copeland, that once-brilliant and pioneering scholar, had developed an uncanny fixation regarding the so-called "lost continent of Mu" which some occultists and pseudo-scholars, like Colonel Churchward, consider to have been the original birthplace of humanity—the "Atlantis of the Pacific."

Suddenly I became aware that Mayhew had turned upon me a glittering eye, bright with excitement.

"What is it, Professor?"

"Sloan, my boy, it's here . . . many of the identical symbols we traced and copied from the Black Stone! See—" he indicated several of the symbols on the crumbling, half-decayed sheets of leather-tough native parchment, "—here—and here, and—here!"

"Odd that you didn't recognize them at once, when you first began making your tracings from the Stone," I murmured inanely, searching for something to say. He shrugged, restlessly.

"I only glanced over the original codex," he explained, "as I was more interested in the English version . . . but look: I have tried as best I could to match the hieroglyph to the English text, with the following conjectural result—"

I glanced at the sheet of scribbled note-paper he brandished before me. I do not recall all of the symbols or their meanings, but of the three symbols I drew earlier in this statement, the first stood for the name or word "Yig," the second for "Mnomquah," and the third for . . .

"*Golgoroth!*" Mayhew breathed, almost reverently.

For some reason, I shuddered as if an icy wind was blowing upon my naked soul.

The Curator of Manuscripts at the Kester Library was Professor Edwin Winslow Arnold, a chubby-faced man with a cherubic smile and piercing blue eyes. He had obviously heard of my employer and I knew somewhat of his academic reputation, for we found no obstacle in our path which would prevent us from examining the miscellaneous diaries and papers of Abner Exekiel Hoag. A large number of these were in the Massachusetts Historical Archives, of course, but these could hardly be expected to contain the information Professor Mayhew desired. The documents which related to the *Ponape Scripture* were in the "sealed" files, and were made available only to reputable scholars.

Within a day or two, Mayhew found what he was looking for, in the form of a battered, water-stained notebook obviously kept by Hoag's man, Yogash. This Yogash was the bodyservant Hoag had "adopted" in the Pacific islands, a Polynesian/Oriental halfbreed of some kind (weirdly there filtered into my memory a bit of nonsense poor mad Copeland had recorded in his book, *The Prehistoric Pacific,* in which he conjectured that this mysterious Yogash person might be, in his inexplicable phrase, "a human/Deep One hybrid," whatever *that* might mean).

Yogash had kept a workbook in which the English equivalents, often marked with an interrogation-point in the margin, perhaps to indicate that the equivalency was dubious or uncertain, were aligned with columns of minutely-inked glyphs. This was the key to the language of the *Scripture,* by perusal of which Mayhew hoped to be able to translate the secrets of the Black Stone.

"They are all here," gloated Mayhew, peering enthusiastically over the blurred, stained pages of the old notebook. "Nug, and Yeb, and their mother, Shub-Niggurath . . . Yig and Mnomquah and Golgoroth, himself . . ."

"Are these the gods of some Pacific mythology?" I hazarded.

"So they would appear to be, from their prominence in the *Scripture,*" he murmured abstractedly.

"But—if that *is* true, then, how do you explain their recurrence on the other side of the globe, in the depths of South Africa?" I cried.

The Professor peered at me over his pince-nez.

"I cannot explain it," he said finally, after a moment's silence. "Any more than I can explain how virtually the same characters found on the *Easter Island Tablets*, whereof Churchward wrote, appear in the Mohenjo-Daro inscriptions, found in the northerly parts of India."

"Churchward was an occultist of sorts," I protested. "His reputation as a scientist has never been taken seriously!"

"Nevertheless, the *Easter Island Tablets* exist—you can find excellent photographs of them in backfiles of *National Geographic*, without needing to search more deeply into the scholarly periodicals. And I trust you are aware of the veracity, if not of the significance, of the inscriptions found at the site of Mohenjo-Daro?"

I nodded, my resistance to his arguments subsiding. But—how could this mystery be explained, save by postulating some worldwide prehistoric race or network of religious cults which have hitherto eluded the attention of scholars?

Baffled, I turned to other tasks, abandoning speculation.


With the help of the amiable Dr. Arnold, Professor Mayhew and I had clear and distinct photographic copies of the notebook made for further study and comparison with the inscriptions on the Black Stone, since obviously the Kester Library could not permit Yogash's notebook to leave the premises, as it was a part of the Hoag Papers.

For days and weeks we compared the symbols, jotting down a rough rendering into English. The grammar and punctuation, of course, had to be supplied by the Professor and myself, as it was not possible to deduce from the notes of Yogash what equivalents of these were in the unknown language of the *Scripture*. From a study of the notebook, many bits of data came to light which meant little to me at the time, but which excited the Professor tremendously.

"So!" he exclaimed one evening, "the language is neither any known form of Naacal, neither is it R'lyehian or even Tsath-yo . . . I had rather conjectured it might be a form of Tsath-yo . . . but, no, Yogash refers to it in six places as 'the Elder Tongue' and in two places as 'the Elder Script' . . ."

"I've heard you mention that word 'Tsath-yo' before," I interjected. "What exactly does it refer to?"

"It was the language of ancient Hyperborea in prehistoric times," he muttered off-handedly.

"Hyperborea?" I exclaimed, skeptically. "The polar paradise of Greek mythology? I believe Pindar refers to it in—"

"The conjectural name—lacking a better one!—for a polar civilization which was the presumed link between elder Mu and the more recent civilizations of Atlantis, Valusia, Mnar and so on. Although Cyron of Varaad, in his brief *Life of Eibon*, does indeed suggest that the first humans migrated from foundering Mu to Valusia and the Seven Empires, and Atlantis as well, then in its barbaric period, before traveling north to Hyperborea . . ."

I could make little or nothing of these rambling explanations, but filed them away for future reference. My concepts of ancient history, I perceived, were going to require some extensive revisions, if I must include therein, as true and veritable cultures, such fairy-tales as Mu and Hyperborea and Atlantis.

That night my bad dreams bothered me again, and I awoke soaked in cold sweat, and shivering like a leaf in a gale. Across the room I saw the white moonlight bathing the eerily-inscribed facets of the Black Stone, and suddenly I felt an uncanny and inexplicable fear. Or was it—*foreboding?*

Before many weeks had passed, Professor Mayhew gradually came to understand the purpose and nature of the mysterious inscriptions on the Black Stone from Zimbabwe.

They were nothing less than litanies and ceremonials for the summoning—the "calling down," to employ the ominous phrase of the Stone's language—of the Fishers from Outside which were the minions and servitors of the dark demon-god, Golgoroth. Odd, how my weird dreams had seemed to predict this very discovery, for those horrible nightmares which had plagued me from the first day I laid eyes on the accursed Stone had been of rituals whereby the hideously masked priests had seemed to call down from the nighted skies those horrible bird-things (the Professor had discovered, in deciphering the Stone, that they were properly termed "Shantaks")! But here I caught myself beginning to take almost for granted that one's dreams can actually presage the future.

As for the dark divinity they served, Golgoroth—at least in his bird-avatar form—was presumed by mythology to dwell beneath the "black cone" of Antarktos, a mountain in Antarctica, at or very near to the South Pole. (Of course, I am translating these concepts: the actual text calls it "the ante-boreal Pole," and the name "Antarktos" was supplied by the Professor himself.)

When he had gotten to that portion of the translation, he seemed to hesitate, to become lost in dreams. I asked him if all was well, if he felt ill; he roused himself with an effort, and gave me a shadowed smile.

"It is nothing; a momentary qualm. No, Sloan ... I called to mind a scrap of verse I have somewhere read—I cannot think just where—but the name *Antarktos* was attached to it—"

And in a low, throbbing voice, he recited these strange lines:

*Deep in my dream the great bird whispered queerly*
*Of the black cone amid the polar waste;*
*Pushing above the ice-sheet, lone and drearly*
*By storm-crazed aeons battered and defaced ...*

Something in his hushed, hoarse voice—or was it in those grim and ominous lines of verse?—made me shudder uncontrollably. And I thought again of my weird dreams of that Plain of Megaliths, of those naked bodies bound for sacrifice, and of the semi-avian, semi-apterous bird-monstrosities as they swooped, and plunged, and clutched and clawed, ripping and tearing the naked, writhing meat staked out for them. And again that night I had ... unwholesome dreams.

Two days after this incident—and fear not, officers, my story is very nearly done—the Professor seemed to have concluded the major portion of his researches. That is, as far as I could tell he had finished deciphering the last of the summoning-rituals of the Shantaks cut deep on the slick metallic planes of the Black Stone.

"Sloan, I want you to go to the Kester today," he told me that afternoon, just when I had assumed our day's toil was done. "I will need the text of this part of the *Book of Eibon*—" and here he handed me a scrap of paper torn from his pocket-notebook, with page numerals scribbled down. I gave him a surprised look.

"But surely the Library is closed by this time, Professor, and I could make the trip tomorrow morning—?"

He shook his head. "I need the text of that passage tonight, and the Library, while it may be closed to the public, will still be open in that the staff are on hand and qualified scholars with passes signed by Dr. Arnold should be able to gain entry without difficulty. Take care of this at once, please."

Well, there was no refusing such a request—Professor Mayhew was my employer, after all—so I left the University Club and caught the streetcar on Banks Street to the Library. The sky was lowering and gray; a fitful, uneasy wind, chill and dank as a breath from the very grave prowled amidst the dry leaves of early fall as I hurried between the granite pillars and into the bronze gateway.

I found no difficulty in securing the *Book of Eibon* from the files and began copying down the passage which the Professor required. It consisted of certain matter from the sixth chapter of Part III of the *Eibon,* a lengthy mythological or cosmogonical treatise called 'Papyrus of the Dark Wisdom.' The passage read as follows:

> . . . but great Mnomquah came not down to this Earth but chose for the place of His abiding the Black Lake of Ubboth which lieth deep in the impenetrable glooms of Nug-yaa beneath the Moon's crust; but, as for Golgoroth, that brother of Mnomquah, He descended to this Earth in the regions circumambient to the Austral Pole, where to this day He abideth the passage of the ages beneath the black cone of Mount Antarktos, aye, and all the hideous host of Shantaks that serve Him in His prisonment, they and their sire, Quumyagga, that is the first among the minions of Golgoroth, and that dwelleth either in the nighted chasms beneath black Antarktos or in the less inaccessible of peaks of frightful Leng; where also did great Ithaqua, the Walker Upon the Wind, take for His earth-place the icy Arctic barrens, and mighty Chaugnar Faugn dwelleth thereabout as well, and fearsome Aphoom Zhah, who haunteth the black bowels of Yaanek, the ice-mountain at the Boreal Pole, and all they

that serve Him, even the Ylidheem, the Cold Ones, and their master, Rlim Shaikorth—

It was with a distinct shock that I realized suddenly that there was nothing—*nothing at all*—in this Eibonic material that the Professor and I did not already have recorded in our notes, and that the only explanation for my being sent on this false errand was to get me out of the way while the Professor did—what?

Seized by a nameless premonition, I snatched up the papers in which I had copied the passages from *Eibon*, returned the old book to the clerk, and left the grounds of the Library. Dark clouds had come boiling up over the horizon, drowning the long narrow streets in gloom. The wind blew from the north, cold and dank as the panting breath of some predatory beast.

Abandoning the notion of waiting for the streetcar, I hailed a passing taxi and drove back to the University Club. I had the horrible feeling that every moment might count against life or death; and yet I could not have told you what it was that I feared. There are certain times in our lives when knowledge comes to us by unknown paths, and woe unto him who ignores the warnings explicit in that fore-knowing!

Tossing a crumpled bill at the driver, I sprang from the cab and raced into the building. Plunging up the staircase, I entered the rooms assigned to us, only to find no sign of the Professor.

But even as I turned to descend the stair and to seek for Mayhew in the Club library, there came to my ears a weird, ragged, chanting ulullation from the roof directly above our rooms, and among the weird vocables I recognized certain words—

*Iä! Iä! Golgoroth! Golgoroth*
*Antarktos! Yaa-haa*
*Quumyagga! Quumyagga!*
*Quumyagga nng'h aargh—*

These were the opening words of one of the summoning-litanies to the Shantaks, for I clearly recalled them from the manuscript of Professor Mayhew's tentative translation of what he called the "Zimbabwe Rituals." And then I knew, with a surge of cold fear that closed like a vise about my heart, that the Professor had employed a mere subterfuge to get me out of the way while he went up to the roof and tried out the summoning-litany . . . and I cried out, and I cursed the unholy curiosity of the scholar that would dare such an enormity.

Up to the roof I ran, stumbling over the stairs, and burst out upon the rooftop to see before me a scene of horror!

A dome of leaden clouds hid the sky, as if some immense lid of gray metal had been clamped down upon the world, from horizon to horizon. The wan luminance that filtered through the roiling vapors was lurid, unnatural, phosphoric, sulphurous yellow. For a fleeting instant I was reminded of the skies over Zimbabwe in my dreams—the flaring bale-fires, the drifting smokes, the bird-masked priests, the leering Moon—then I shrieked and saw—*and saw*—

Down they came, the apterous, semi-avian hurtling shapes, all slimy scales where feathers ought by rights to be, hippocephalic clubbed heads hideously grinning . . . and hovered on scaly, translucent wings: hovered and swooped and dipped, to tear and tear at the shrieking scarlet-splattered thing that jerked and jiggled prone on the rooftop, wallowing in a bath of blood—that shrieking thing that I could never have distinguished as having once been human, had it not been for the one detail to which my shuddering gaze clung with unbelieving terror . . . *the blood-spattered pince-nez on their sodden ribbon of black silk, about the crimson ruin of what had once been a man's head.*

# The Keeper of the Flame

## Gary Myers

The great stone face of the temple of Kish looks out over the broad plain of Shand from the lofty precipice that rises above it. Out of the precipice it looks indeed, for its makers carved it from the living rock, and the rubbish of its carving can still be seen heaped against the bottom of the cliff. The shaded archway of its wide front door, through which three elephants might easily pass, is on clear days visible even as far as the gates of Shand itself. Not so visible is the little path that winds its way down the face of the cliff, the only road between the temple and the plain.

It is hard to imagine how the temple can exist in a place so little accessible to the city it serves. It is no less hard to imagine how faith alone can sustain a regular traffic between them. Yet the day seldom passes that has not seen its little band of pilgrims climbing the path from the plain below, to say its prayers on the temple's steps, and to leave its offerings of wine and meal and oil on the porch before the temple's threshold. Before the threshold the offerings are always left, for it is the law of the temple that no pilgrim may advance beyond it. Only the priest of Kish may cross the threshold. Only he may enter the holy of holies and the presence of the living god.

But upon a time there came to the temple one who cared nothing for its law. At that period the priest of Kish was a man whose exceeding holiness was matched only by his exceeding age. For more than half a century he had performed faithfully the duties of his office, greeting the pilgrims when they came, giving them words of hope and comfort, hearing their prayers and accepting their offerings all in the name of the god. But on the morning of the day of which I tell, he was sitting in the sun on the temple's porch when a lone pilgrim came to stand at the foot of the temple's steps.

The old priest had greeted many pilgrims in more than half a century, but the young man now standing before him was like no other pilgrim he had ever seen. For one thing, he lacked the pilgrim's wonted humility. He bore himself as proudly as an emperor, though there was little in his worn tunic and broken sandals to justify such bearing. For another, he had not brought the customary offering. But the strangest thing about him was the answer he gave when the old priest asked him who he was and why he had come. For he answered in a loud clear voice that must have been heard in the heart of the temple itself: "I am Nod, and I have come to seek an audience with Kish."

Even to conceive of such a purpose was a violation of the temple's law, yet the old priest did not denounce the young man who had expressed it. For he hoped that he had spoken thus out of ignorance or misunderstanding. He therefore proceeded to explain to him that the privilege he sought was reserved to the priest of Kish alone, and that any prayer intended for the god must be entrusted to the priest. For it was the function of the priest of Kish to be the messenger between his worshippers and the god. But Nod denied that he had spoken out of ignorance. He needed no messenger to go between him and Kish. For the freedom to worship was the right from birth of every man, and access to his god could no more justly be denied him than access to wind and sun.

Then the old priest knew beyond any doubt that this was no common pilgrim. Yet he still had hopes of recalling him to reason. If he did not admit the arguments of law, he might admit those of tradition. For it was the glory of the worshippers of Kish that they had worshipped their god in this way and no other for as long as his worship had been. By following these traditions the worshipper of today could partake of the timelessness of the god himself, and quench his thirst at the same cool stream that had soothed the parched throats of generations. But Nod only mocked at the metaphor. For an old thing was not necessarily good simply because it was old. And when tradition came to choke the stream it should have let flow freely, it was every man's duty to break it.

The old priest was still undaunted. The young man might fail to see the timeless beauty of tradition, but even he could not be blind to the eternal truths of philosophy. For the gods, being as it were the embodiments of the sacred, could not be approached by the profane. Only their priests who had undergone a rigorous course of purification and enlightenment, only they could approach the gods with impunity. But Nod denied these truths as well. For how could the gods be offended by honest worship? And so far were they above men that for them the distinction between priest and layman could hardly be said to exist. That distinction had been invented by the priests themselves to enlarge their importance among men, and to divert the blessings of the gods toward their own selfish ends.

The old priest sat in silence after that, considering how to proceed. He felt no animosity toward this young man, in spite of his heretical words and their thinly veiled personal attack. He could only admire this fiery zealot who would let nothing stand between him and his god. He wondered if in his own forgotten youth he had ever been as passionate in his faith. He had hoped to send the young man away with his faith intact. But now that law, tradition and philosophy had failed to turn him from his purpose, the old priest was forced to admit that the time had come for stronger measures. So, "Come with me," he said, and rose and turned toward the temple door.

Just inside the door the priest took up the small clay lamp which he had left burning there against his return. And by its light Nod saw for the first time what lay within the temple walls. It may be that he had expected to find a rich display of gold and jewels, a shining monument to mere worldly splendor. If so, he must have been surprised at the truth. For the interior of the temple was only a tunnel cut in the stone, a tunnel continuing the colossal scale of the entrance, but no less dark and depressing for that. The few doorways that opened in the walls on either side showed only dark and comfortless cells more befitting a prison than a temple. But maybe Nod was not surprised: For what need had they of worldly splendor who could bask in the glory of a god?

Proceeding down the tunnel, they came presently to a gate of iron bars that spanned it from wall to wall and from floor to ceiling. The gate was too large for the men to move, but there was a smaller gate framed within the larger, and this the old priest unlocked and opened to let Nod and himself pass through. Beyond the gate the tunnel continued as before. But by the time they reached the second gate, they might have seen a greenish light glowing faintly in the distance. This light grew brighter the farther they advanced, until the little flame of the small clay lamp seemed to extinguish itself for shame. And when they arrived before the third and final gate, the light had become a luminous green mist that filled all the tunnel before them, a luminous green mist that rolled like the sea along its shore, and grew now brighter, now dimmer as it rose and fell.

Here the old priest turned to reason with Nod for the last time. He had brought him here, where none but a priest of Kish had ever been, in a final attempt to turn his feet from the ruinous path they were set upon. What did Nod really know of the nature of the gods? How could he be sure that the priests had set themselves between men and gods to deprive them of their blessing and not to defend them from their curse? Nod thought of his god as a comforting flame whereat he might warm his spirit. But what if the reality was a fiery furnace that might burn his spirit to ashes? Let him heed therefore the old priest's warning. Let him abandon the dangerous quest for truth, and take refuge in the comforting lies of faith. For there alone was any hope for man.

So said the old priest, speaking with the eloquence of desperation. But his eloquence only stirred Nod to anger. For this was blasphemy and rank atheism. Nod would not have his ears polluted with such filth. If the priest again profaned the name of the gods within his hearing, he would drag him from the temple, and cast him down the precipice to his death on the stones below. So spoke Nod in his anger. But his words did not trouble the old priest half as much as the look in his eyes when he spoke them. For they never turned from the greenish vapor, and they responded to its unearthly glow with a more than answering fire. It was this more than anything else that finally persuaded the old priest to unlock and open the gate.

Finding the last obstacle gone from his path, the young man began to move forward, slowly at first, but with gathering speed as the green vapor rose to engulf him. His figure dissolved in its misty radiance, so that only the sound of his sandals on the stone remained to tell of his further progress. And soon even this was lost in the distance. The stillness that followed was complete. Even the mist had ceased its heaving. And then, suddenly and without warning, the greenish light began to strengthen in intensity. Brighter it grew and brighter, feeding its power from some hidden source, until it reached a level of blinding brilliance. Then, the source of its power exhausted, it began to die back down again, and to return by slow degrees to its old sullen glow.

Only then did the old man close and lock the gate, clumsily with shaking hands. Only then did he grope his way back to the clean white light of the sun.

# Dead Giveaway

## J. Vernon Shea

### I

Miss Mary Peabody (you can give her surname the New England pronunciation! Peb'-uh-dee) turned as was her wont into the street that led to Old Dethshill Cemetery. It was almost a daily ritual with her, barring abominable weather. Her progress down the sharply sloping street did not go unobserved! The few people outside (it was a blustery day, with tall trees bent low as if trying to send more roots into the ground) turned to stare at her, and people inside pushed aside curtains for a better look.

For Miss Peabody had become somewhat of an institution upon the street. It always looked as if she had picked the clothes that were closest to hand, and her wardrobe must have bulged with bizarre items. People were curious (and even made bets) as to what the next day's outfit would be like. Today's ensemble was a conglomeration of clothing of various periods, all completely out of fashion.

Tonight would be Hallowe'en, but she wore a summery flowered hat; although the flowers were artificial, they somehow looked wilted and dusty. Her red velvet dress was of 1910 length, and in the rear it was stuck in the crack of her behind, exposing a great expanse of petticoat. Over it she had put on a button-down man's sweater which may have belonged to her brother, and upon her feet she wore black high-button shoes. She carried an unraised pink parasol which the wind sought, ruffling its silk furiously.

She was walking into the wind, and its sharp sting brought an unaccustomed rosiness to her withered cheeks.

And then the calls came:

*Crazy Mary, won't you go home,*
*Crazy Mary, won't you go home.*

It was the children, sprung up magically everywhere. A few of the bolder ones would approach her closely, recite their lines, then dart giggling around the corners of houses. Miss Peabody did not mind them, having become accustomed to them, but as usual she passed her hand across her brow in bewilderment, wondering who "Crazy Mary" might be.

The children followed her at a distance down the street, chanting. And now she was approaching the old Elmer Harrod house. Usually deserted, for the city had boarded it up and shut off the utilities after Harrod's mysterious and horrifying death, it now thronged with life; a group of teenagers were upon the porch, watching her.

One of them, whose name she had never known, but whom she recognized as one of her principal tormentors, came from the porch over to her.

He recited some just-coined lines:

*Dress up your ass,*
*High-button shoes.*
*Want something else up your ass?*
*It's time to choose.*

She caught her breath in shock at the foulness of the language. Just then the teenager seized the parasol and gave it a twirl. Still clinging to it, Miss Mary Peabody was spun around, and she almost fell to the sidewalk in dizziness.

"Oh, you want to dance?" the teenager said, and he pushed her backwards in a parody of the waltz.

"Let her alone, God damn it!" someone said.

It was old Emil Weiskopf, who lived two doors away, Old Emil Weiskopf, who kept to himself and never bothered much with children.

The teenager let Miss Peabody loose in astonishment. Old Emil picked up the parasol, which had fallen to the sidewalk, and handed it ceremoniously to Miss Peabody.

"Would you come to my house and rest awhile?" he asked her.

"Oh, no, no," she said. "I must get to the cemetery."

"But why today? It's cold and windy out there."

"I must get to the cemetery," she said, as if by rote. And she wore the bewildered look again.

*Why* must she get to the cemetery? She couldn't remember. Oh, yes, it was to find Benjy, her little brother. She had lost Benjy somewhere, and she could never remember just where. She had a hazy recollection that it had something to do with Old Dethshill Cemetery, and that was why she made her daily trips there, in the hope that someday she would remember *exactly*. She wanted Benjy back. She needed him. It was so lonely in her apartment without him. He had always known what to do. A man knows such things; a woman doesn't. (Had Benjy grown to *manhood*, or was she thinking of someone else? She wished she could remember.)

The wind died down strangely as she entered Old Dethshill Cemetery. The death of Elmer Harrod, the TV horror film host, had received national publicity, and the cemetery was now somewhat of a tourist attraction (tourists came *once*, and never returned); so the city officials had been compelled to cut a road through the back section into which the street debouched, and had even razed some rundown houses of a nearby slum area to make room for a new section of the cemetery, as some of the city residents had expressed a perverse desire to be buried there. But even with the changes, Old Dethshill Cemetery remained much the same. It was still a place which did not welcome intruders.

She shivered with sudden cold. Despite the frequency of her visits, Miss Peabody still felt herself an intruder. The cemetery gave her a feeling of guilt, as if she had done something very wrong there years before. But she could never remember just *what*. Her visits were, in a measure, an atonement.

As she made her way into the cemetery grounds, she could hear the old scuttering sounds with which the place abounded. *Something* was lurking behind that tree over there; if she remained quite still, she might catch a glimpse of its face. Could it be little Benjy, playing tricks upon her?

"Benjy!" she called out with a sudden impulse. "Where are you? It's your sister Mary. You called me Mamie, don't you remember?"

There was no response, but the scuttering sounds seemed to be intensified. And down the hillside, thick now with once splendid leaves, the figure with the red velvet dress and pink parasol strolled, calling out "Benjy!" time and again, the sunlight muted and without warmth as it struggled to penetrate the maze of trees overhead.

Miss Peabody was seeking one particular grave, her own discovery. Now that the city provided caretakers, who mowed the grass occasionally, but with the greatest reluctance (caretakers never stayed on their jobs very long), graves were easier to find; she had merely to brush the dead grass away from the markers with her foot. She was engaged in doing so when she noticed a very curious thing.

She had frequently passed the grave of Obediah Carter in her trips here, one of the oldest graves in the cemetery, one whose marker bore almost obliterated dates: 179_–18_7. But today all the grass and weeds surrounding it were cleared away, and the marker looked freshly washed—and, much more disturbing, the marker did not quite meet the packed earth around it; it looked for all the world like a *fresh* grave.

The Carter grave had always seemed to Miss Peabody much too close to the place which Elmer Harrod had called "Witches' Hollow"—a place she always skirted—for her liking, and she hurried on. (Not that she had ever met a witch there; she always was afraid that if she *did* meet something there, it would be something far worse than a witch.) She reached the object of her search almost too soon, almost unexpectedly.

It was another very old grave, probably even older than Carter's, for the time had done even more damage to the carving. Only BEN-JAMIN was decipherable, the eroded surname defying identification. The little she could make out certainly didn't look like PEABODY, but it *might* be. One part of her brain told her that this *couldn't* be Benjy's grave, for Benjy wasn't that old, but it was the only Benjamin she had ever been able to discover in the cemetery, and she felt for it a sense of proprietorship. Sometimes she even brought flowers to strew upon it (which someone had always removed by the next day). The grave was always the end point of her journey and, as was her wont, she stretched herself tiredly upon its marker.

But the cold air and the cold marble soon penetrated her dress and thin sweater, and she had to rise. She thought she would return by a different route, and she chose to go by way of the new section. Perhaps she might even find Benjy there.

She didn't much like the new section, for, as today, it usually had a few visitors. It had an air of modernity not in keeping with Old Dethshill Cemetery. The graves were packed much too closely together, and the grass looked freshly watered and manicured. The newest grave, which bore the name RUSSELL CARMODY, was blazing with flowers, cut ones and potted ones.

"This fellow has too many flowers," Miss Peabody said to herself, "while this poor soul doesn't have any." So, putting her parasol down, she picked armfuls of flowers from the Carmody grave and placed them upon the grave of his neighbor, distributing them equally.

It was becoming dark as she approached the new shaft which had become the tallest thing in the cemetery, a focal point. As always, she felt a touch of chill as she gazed up at it. It was made of some curious black polished stone, and it stretched up much higher than Miss Peabody could reach, and it rested upon a thick circular platform composed of the same black stone.

Both sides of the shaft (it was really an obelisk, but Miss Peabody didn't know that) were covered with some very weird and outre drawings and sentences (presumably) in a great many languages, none of which Miss Peabody understood. For instance, the top lines were in Assyrian cuneiform symbols which an amateur linguist amongst the city officials had transliterated as *kutullu, shub,* and *nagarra.* The sounds of these symbols had so disturbed him (he had the eerie sensation that something close by had stopped to listen) that he had refused to continue his research. And the drawings were of a nature which Miss Peabody refused to contemplate steadily. There were faces there which reminded her of the statues of Easter Island; and there was something which looked like a horrendous goat; and there was something much worse which had a great many tentacles; there were depictions of actions which were obviously obscene, and, even more nauseating, depictions of people being devoured by nameless monsters.

It must have taken the stonecutter (or stonecutters) tremendous time and effort to perform so horrifying a task.

"Beautiful, isn't it?" a voice behind her said, and turning, Miss Peabody saw that the speaker had a profile which reminded her of a frog or toad. He was obviously some inhabitant of nearby Innsmouth. But there was no longer an Innsmouth. Trembling, Miss Peabody hurried away as fast as she could, her parasol bounding ahead of her like a jackrabbit.

## II

At the approach of twilight Mrs. Charlotte Carmody seated herself in the chair by the window which commanded the best view of the street. The strong winds had not yet subsided, and she was conscious of a draught from the window. The furnace was on, but she felt cold, and she rose and got herself a sweater. She had not felt really warm since the moment last week when she had seen the casket of her son Russell being lowered into the new grave in Old Dethshill Cemetery. She shivered at the memory, and she dabbed with her handkerchief at her red, swollen eyelids.

The house was cold, cold, old and empty like herself. Why had she picked such sombre furniture? She needed bright, warm colors. Russell cold in his grave and she here all alone . . . the bleak years without Russell stretched interminably ahead. She was not really old, and she knew she was going to live for a long, long time. . . .

And now the street was becoming dark, and already people were beginning to welcome the Hallowe'eners. She pursed her lips. The good, generous people. What an easy way to buy friendship, with just a few bags of penny candy! "Trick or treat" indeed! It was really a kind of blackmail. Nobody had ever given *her* anything when she was a girl in St. Louis. Children then were content just to dress up in costume and parade up and down the streets. But the kids today were spoiled, spoiled rotten. Look at the way they went through her garden after a ball and trampled her roses! And daring to ride up and down her sidewalk on their bikes! "Oh, mother, they don't mean anything!" Russell used to remonstrate. But Russell was too easy-going. One had to assert one's rights. And so she had had to yell at them, "If you don't get out of my garden, I'm going to call the police!" And she had meant it. *Let* them call her "the mean old lady"!

Well, she had no intention of turning on *her* porchlight. She never had before, and she wasn't going to set a precedent tonight. The children on this street knew her too well; they'd never dream of ringing *her* doorbell. She'd never let them in if they did. She saw now a car being driven slowly down the street and coming to a halt, and a mother letting her small children, just wee tots, out and waiting while they rang doorbells and came back to the car loaded with gifts. And then came a mother walking with her children and bending over them and tying their scarves tighter, bundling them against the cold. They bulged so with clothing that their skeleton costumes were incongruous.

Well, Mrs. Carmody thought, the city streets were so dangerous nowadays it was no wonder that parents were afraid to let children venture out after dark.

Blaring sounds came suddenly from further down the street, from Elmer Harrod's old place. It wasn't Harrod making all that racket, that was sure.

And now it was really dark out, and time for her to repair to the back of the house. On Hallowe'en night she always turned off the lights in front to make the children think she wasn't home.

She sat down at her kitchen table and began to read the evening paper. But it was even chillier facing the north with its cold wind, and she had to turn on the stove to get more heat. She rubbed her hands together over the gas flame. How prominent the veins on the backs of her hands were getting to be—and there were even a couple of horrid brown spots. Oh, she was getting old, getting old. . . .

She was in the midst of reading her paper when the doorbell rang. It must be some mistake: Some child new to the neighborhood who didn't know her reputation. But the ringing persisted for long minutes, and at last Mrs. Carmody went to her seat by the window and pushed aside her curtain. A group of masqueraders was on her porch, carrying shopping bags already almost filled; mostly small children, but they were accompanied by some larger boys. The leader seemed to be the rowdy red-haired teenager who used to be her paper boy. He must have sensed her presence by the window, for he called out suddenly, "Trick or treat! Trick or treat!" And after a moment he added the grim line: "Treat or you'll be tricked!"

*You can stay there all night if you want to,* Mrs. Carmody thought;

*I'm not going to open the door.* Where was Russell when she needed him? Oh, yes, oh, yes . . . She started to cry again and returned to the kitchen. She had barely begun to read again when there came a tapping at her high side window and, looking up, she saw a blazing orange face leering down at her.

Pains shot sharply across her heart, but after a moment she recognized it for what it was: *It's just a jack o' lantern.* "Come out, Charlotte," a voice came, "we know you're in there."

"If you children don't go away," she screamed then, "I'm going to call the police."

"Hush, hush, sweet Charlotte," the voice said mockingly, and she heard feet running away. And silence held—for a little while.

### III

Old Emil Weiskopf was the first person upon the street to switch on his porch light. The porch was decorated with Hallowe'en *motifs*: pumpkins and Indian corn and cornhusks upon the railings, cutouts of black cats in the windows, and upon the porch a witch (driven by an electric motor) who rocked back and forth upon her broomstick, tittering evilly. He went back to the kitchen and removed the last tray of candy molds from the refrigerator. The tray contained chocolates which he had been preparing lovingly all day.

He touched one of the chocolates tentatively: yes, it was sufficiently hard. He sat down at the kitchen table and began to wrap the chocolates in the expensive-looking wrappers he had carefully saved all year. He had quite an accumulation of them, for, like his dear Fuehrer before him, he indulged his craving for sweets.

The table was piled high with his day's handiwork: hand-dipped chocolates. He hadn't the slightest desire, of course, to nibble upon one of them, for he knew what they contained. Things carefully preserved for just this day, things selected just for the children of his street. Things like used razor blades and ground glass and dead insects and rat excrement.

Oh, they would serve the little bastards right! Scarcely a day passed that they didn't disturb him with their noise and their tricks. Almost every day some youngster—he could never catch him at it, or he'd box his ears—twisted the outside rear-view mirror around so that he could no longer see if a car was approaching, and this was dangerous, especially in the winter months when his rear window was steamed up or thick with ice. You'd think the youngster would eventually tire of his little game, but he never did. And once he had found the mirror with its cracked glass hanging by shreds: it looked as if someone had deliberately struck it with a hammer—or possibly it had been shattered by a ball thrown in a game. And sometimes the children stole the cover of his gasoline tank, or filled the tank with dirt, and once they had removed his hubcaps and filled them with stones and replaced them, and such a dreadful racket had developed when he started out that he had thought his muffler was dragging along the street. In the summer months the children were always darting out into the street unexpectedly to retrieve a ball or riding their bicycles in the middle of the street, and when he returned from work they would be out in the street playing baseball, that stupid American game, and practically dared him to run over them. Or they would ask him not to park in just that spot, as it was first base, but to park further up the street! (They would not soap or damage his car *tonight*: he had it stored away in a safe place.)

And the racket they created was even worse: The calls and the screams and the off-key singing. His sense of hearing had always been extremely acute, and age had dimmed it only a little. It had been an asset in the grand old days of the fatherland, when he had served as concertmaster with the leading orchestras. The proudest day of his life, of course, had come—and he shivered in ecstasy at the memory—when the Fuehrer had attended a Wagnerian matinee and had come backstage and personally shaken his hand.


Oh, the fools, the swine-dogs, the poor, benighted fools! Germany was no longer a fit place to live; they had thrown him into prison and carefully "de-Nazified" him (as if anyone could erase those glorious years!) and no longer wanted him in their orchestras, so now he was a "DP" in this boobland, where he could not play his Stradivarius because of his arthritic fingers, but instead served as a . . . as a . . . (he could not force himself to complete the thought).

The doorbell rang just then, and old Emil Weiskopf began to

hum triumphantly the opening bars of the Beethoven Fifth (the Fate knocking at the door theme) as he hurried to answer it.

It was much later, and old Emil had disposed of almost all his chocolates. He went to his front window and peered out. The wind had died down, and the trees and the few flowers which had survived the cold were barely quivering. The street was deserted except for one figure, a tall and very emaciated one, dressed very fittingly in a skeleton costume, which leaned against Emil's gatepost, as if too weary or too shy to enter the yard.

Emil gathered up the rest of his chocolates and put them in a bag and opened his door.

"Come here, lad," he called. "I have a nice treat for you."

The figure with the skeleton mask looked up and shook its head. It raised a bony finger and beckoned to Emil.

*OK, if you want to play games,* thought Emil, a trifle annoyed.

He hurried over to the figure.

And now he could see the figure more clearly.

The skeleton face was not a mask.

## IV

"Cut it down a bit, guys," said Ronnie Sears, "or old Charlotte will be calling the pigs."

Still in Hallowe'en costume, they were sprawled comfortably—upon the floor or upon sofas, feet over the sides—in the room Elmer Harrod had used as a recording studio. A few of the younger ones were puffing upon reefers (which they didn't really like but felt that they should) but most of them stuck to cigarettes adulterated only by their natural poisons.

Ronnie's parents were away for the evening, not willing to cope with the Hallowe'eners, and as usual upon such occasions, Ronnie had run a cable from his house next door to the Harrod house for lights and had turned on the water from the street main. The Harrod house served effectively as a clubhouse for the neighborhood children, although usually they just played Harrod's old tapes or leafed through his books (they didn't know how to operate his movie projector).

"Aw, don't be a candy ass, Ron," one of them said. "This music is cool."

"Right on, brother."

"Yeah," said Ronnie Sears, "but what we need now is some real creepy music, you know, like Dr. Phibes played on the organ. What we have here is a failure of communication: we're supposed to be scaring the hell out of the old bastards."

"Right on, man. Creepy music for the creeps. Like old Emil Wisehead. Did you notice how sweetly he handed out his candy? I'll bet it's full of bugs."

"Shit, man, I'm not going through all these tapes just for spook music. Say, here's something we haven't played yet," and he picked up a small tape recorder from Elmer Harrod's writing desk.

It was the tape recorder which had been found upon Harrod's corpse. The police had played it back repeatedly for a possible clue to his death, but the words didn't make sense. They were just gibberish.

"Well, play it, man."

Night. The sighing of the wind in the trees. Little odd scuttering sounds.

"Say, that sounds just like the cemetery."

"Aw, turn it off. It don't say nothin'. "

As if to refute him, words suddenly tumbled forth, in Harrod's recognizable voice.

*Iä! Iä! Cthulhu fhtagn! Ph'nglui mglw'nafh Cthulhu R'lyeh wgah-nagl fhtagn.*

"What in the hell is that?"

"Great, man, great! It's just what we needed! Turn it up louder. This'll frighten 'em out of their fright wigs."

"No, don't! I don't like it. It's s-scary."

"Listen to the candy ass! Why don't you go home to mama?"

The volume was increased, and they played the recording endlessly. There was something oddly fascinating about the uncouth sounds, something that seemed to evoke memories. They thought of nearby Innsmouth, now destroyed, and of the great reef out in its harbor, and of the fish-faces and the frog-faces who had dwelled there, who had practiced unseemly rites.

*Iä! Iä! Cthulhu fhtagn! Ph'nglui mglw'nafh Cthulhu R'lyeh wagh-nagl fhtagn.*

They heard the sounds again, but this time they seemed to be coming from a great distance. They couldn't seem to pinpoint the direction; some claimed that they came from the cemetery, while others insisted that they were in the house itself, at a point beneath them, possibly the basement.

The sounds were clearer now, clearer and *closer*. They were changing into a chanting, at a faster tempo, and words were being added, words not to be found upon the tape recorder:

*Iä! Shub-Niggurath! The Black Goat of the Woods with a Thousand Young!*

" 'The Black Goat of the Woods with a Thousand Young!' Man, is this far out!"

"I'm getting out of here!" one small boy said, and he departed to derisive cries.

*Nyarlathotep . . . N'gah-Kthun . . . Hastur! . . . Yig, Father of Serpents . . . Tsathoggua . . . Yog-Sothoth . . . Yian . . . Azathoth . . . Iä! Iä! Great Cthulhu . . . L'mur-Kathulos . . . He Who Is Not To Be Named.*

"You think it could be the old creeps, trying to play tricks upon *us*?"

"You're out of your ever-lovin' mind!"

For some time, unconsciously they had been aware of sounds, sounds odious, inexplicable, and they seemed to denote movement of some kind, for they were obviously coming *nearer*. They were accompanied always by the chanting of the gibberish words: gibberish to the boys, but obviously not gibberish to whomever was making them. They had a perceptible rhythm, and were apparently an incantation, an evocation of some kind. A calling forth of *what*?

"They must be coming from the cellar," said Ronnie Sears. "Agreed?" There was a murmur of assent. "Let's take a look-see."

"Aw, do we *have* to?"

"Don't be a candy ass *all* your life."

But there was nothing in the cellar, a dank and cobwebbed place where Elmer Harrod had stored things which must have spoiled by now, for there was quite a perceptible stench.

But they were obviously closer to the source of the sounds and of the chanting; when they pressed their ears against one wall, the sounds were magnified.

"Say, didn't Harrod say something about a secret passageway down here in one of his broadcasts?"

"No, he said he had a *dream* about a secret passageway."

"Well, there must be one somewhere. Let's try pressing on the bricks or looking for a switch."

The switch was soon discovered. A section of the wall moved back with a squeaking protest from unoiled fixtures, and a surprisingly wide and high tunnel was revealed. The air from the tunnel was musty and foul, hinting of things long dead, strong enough to make them recoil involuntarily.

And at the tunnel entrance the sounds and the chanting could be heard with considerable clarity. Somewhere there was a splashing sound, like that of a hippopotamus dropping into water.

"Man, I'm not going in there!"

"Oh, yes, you are—" and he was pushed into the tunnel.

Nothing came along to gobble him up.

None of the boys really wanted to enter the tunnel, but none of them wanted to be accused of cowardice either. The longer they looked at the tunnel the more their curiosity grew—and with it the fascination which tunnels and secret passageways have always exerted upon mankind.

"Well, let's go, men," Ronnie Sears said, and he took the initiative.

The tunnel dipped sharply into the burrows of the earth, a tunnel which many people had passed through before, for there were fixtures to hold torches and little recesses cut into the walls which, so far as Ronnie's flashlight could discover, were quite unoccupied now. Nothing disturbed their progress, not even a rat.

Progress—for, for some odd reason, they found themselves hurrying. None of the boys wanted to be at the tail of the procession, so they were all bunched together as closely as the width of the tunnel would permit. The tunnel took weird twists and turns: sometimes the sound of the chanting seemed to be *above* them, sometimes even *beneath* them—and such was the subtle insistence of the rhythm that one or more of the boys would find themselves chanting along with it; they had picked up the words very quickly.

*Bethmoora . . . Leng . . . Bran . . . Innsmouth . . . The Lake of Hali . . . The Stalker Among The Stars . . . Iä! Shub-Niggurath . . .*

It was very much later that they detected illumination toward the tunnel's end, and the chanting that assailed their eardrums increased now many-fold, and the foolhardiness of their venture struck them all at once, and they stopped in their tracks.

But the sounds and the chanting continued without pause. And presently they could see in the distance the flaring of torches borne aloft, torches which lit up a noisome black lake into which water from the roof of the tunnel constantly dripped, and the torches were being carried by a number of people with monstrous frog faces, the people formerly of Innsmouth.

It was time then to retreat, and they started to do so, but just then one of the boys cried, "Look!" and pointed to the tunnel ahead.

An entire block of the flooring was being raised slowly, and from it an overpowering sea-stench was emanating, and an ever-lengthening coil of tentacle came probing across the floor toward them.

## V

Miss Mary Peabody had been wandering dazedly through the cemetery for hours. She couldn't seem to be able to find the way out. She had never been in the cemetery at night before, and everything looked different—different and much more malign. The little scuttering sounds were much louder now, and once and again she could hear the cry of something apparently in mortal agony.

She leaned against the bole of a tree and shivered, for her thin sweater afforded scant warmth and it was very much colder now. From quite a distance away she could hear dogs barking, and she felt a moment of relief, for the sound denoted the street by which she had entered, and people there.

Oh, she had been seeing people—of a kind—all night; she seemed perpetually to be turning into the Witches' Hollow, where were gathered the fish-faces and the frog-faces performing some strange ritual or other and chanting the most frightening sounds.

But she preferred even *them* to the sight of the tall shaft in the new part of the cemetery. Whenever she passed by it, it seemed to be slowly revolving upon its platform, and she grew quite dizzy at the sight.

"Ma-mie!"

The call came from not far away. Miss Peabody listened intently.

"Mamie, where are you? I'm cold and I'm lonely."

"Benjy? Benjy? Is that you, Benjy?"

There was no immediate answer. Miss Peabody hastened in the direction of the voice, almost tripping over her parasol.

"Oh, there you are, Benjy." She hurried to what seemed to be Benjy as she remembered him, a small boy in a cap and old-fashioned knickers, but which turned into a tree trunk when she got there.

It was so dark in here under the trees. She would never find Benjy now.

She turned away in disappointment—and almost ran into something in her path, something very tall and very dark and quite distinguishable.

It blocked her path again and wrapped itself around her.

"Let me go! You're not Benjy!"

"Oh, yes, I am—or used to be. Did you really want to find Benjy—Benjy, remember, whom you hit over the head with a rock and buried here? I was not quite dead then."

"Let me go! You're hurting me!"

"Yes, I'm Benjy. I'm so cold and so lonely and so very, very hungry."

## VI

The night wore on, so full of horrors that Mrs. Carmody felt that she would never be able to sleep. The wind rose again and rattled the windows of her bedroom, and it moaned occasionally like a banshee. A dog kept barking and then the sound became a duo and then a trio and then a quartet, a contagious thing, but there was nothing joyous about it; they seemed to share, mutually, a misery. The dogs seemed disturbed by the presence of some stranger or strangers upon the street. But presently their sounds were transmuted oddly; they became whines and moans and whimpers to be let in. Then one of them yelped out in agony, and the other three became panicky and Mrs. Carmody could mentally visualize their straining at their leashes.

The sounds from Elmer Harrod's old house frightened her even more. She had heard Harrod's familiar sardonic voice repeatedly, and her heart had pounded wildly, but then she had realized that these must be playbacks from old broadcasts. Playbacks—for she recognized the music and some of the lines from years ago.

But then, still in Harrod's voice, came some new words. Words they must be, but they didn't make sense, yet they were curiously—detestable. Words like Biblical lines read backwards at a black sabbath. Words that seemed to evoke some ancestral horror. She felt that she had heard these words somewhere before, and she didn't want to remember *where*.

Then, from the direction of the *cemetery*, the words were repeated. Repeated, and then new words were added, in the same kind of abominable gibberish. Words that were like the names of forbidden places. The words increased in volume, and Mrs. Carmody had the chilling sensation that whoever was uttering them was coming *nearer*, was approaching her street. Not *whoever*, for there was more than one voice, there were many voices.

Then, abruptly, the sounds from the Harrod house ceased. But there still sounded as if there were a great deal of activity in the cemetery—once she thought she heard a woman screaming, and the voices repeating their sinister doggerel did not die down, but came ever closer.

And now it was *her* house that was being besieged. She had heard the trundle of heavy wheels from the cemetery—there had been a cart upon her street before—and the whinnying of horses, and the group of people driving the cart speaking minimally among themselves. They were stopping at each house in turn, like garbage collectors making their rounds, and they moved quite slowly, as if their burdens were heavy. The dogs were frantic at their approach. And now they were in front of her house.

Ice seemed to engulf her in her bed. Her curiosity had quite forsaken her; she had absolutely no desire to see whom or *what* was out there. She was a woman who had rarely experienced terror, but she was afraid now as she had never been afraid before in her life.

There came the sound of someone or something laboriously climbing her steps, dragging himself or itself across the porch, trying the door, rattling the doorhandle, scrabbling as with claws at the door and windows. She listened in an agony of suspense. Then, getting no repose the visitant reversed his or its procedure, and retreated from her steps. But then she could hear the unwelcome visitor coming with what seemed like infinite slowness down her sidewalk and stopping under her bedroom window.

"Mother," the voice came, "let me in. Please let me in."

She felt an excess of fury. It must be the teenage redhead coming back to pester her. How could anyone be so cruel as to torment a bereaved mother in the middle of the night, even going so far as to imitate the voice of her dead son? Well, she would get on her 'phone in the morning and make him wish he hadn't!

Her feeling of fury quite supplanted her terror, and in a few minutes she was sleeping quite soundly.

## VII

Morning broke sharp and clear. There was little wind, and the sun promised to break through its bondage of clouds at any moment. It was going to be a fine day.

The people who lived upon the street rose reluctantly from bed, some to get ready for work. Most of them had gone without sleep, awake the night through because of the fearsome sounds. For some obscure reason they all postponed looking outside for as long as possible.

When they did, they were aghast at what they saw, and most of them called the police immediately. The police cars came presently with sirens shrieking, a number of them, and almost the first act of the policemen was to barricade the street against traffic. Passersby and people from the neighboring streets, drawn by the sirens, came hurrying up and gazing down the sharp slope of the street which led to Old Dethshill Cemetery. The crowds increased greatly, and before long there were people there hawking balloons and roasted chestnuts and hot dogs. And downtown the city editors left their front pages open for photographs.

There was really quite a lot to photograph, although later most of the pictures were "killed" as being too gruesome. For the night's visitors had been quite generous, bestowing upon each house in turn—either upon their lawns or propped up on steps or against trees of the trim lawns—a corpse from the cemetery. Some of the corpses were in an advanced state of putrefaction and stank quite dreadfully, while others had been stripped clean of flesh and were only skeletons, like the one which had a death-lock upon the throat of old Emil Weiskopf, who stared up at the sky in a perpetual look of disbelieving horror.

The very first stop the visitors had made was to Elmer Harrod's old home, and they had left Elmer himself, or rather his skeleton, for he was recognizable only by his clothing. Elmer's body had lain long unclaimed in the city morgue, and it was the first one to be buried in the new section of the cemetery, dubbed Harrod Place in his honor. What no one could quite understand was why it was wrapped now in a cocoon of tapes.

The street's inhabitants had a considerable problem with their pets. Some of the dogs came up sniffing at the corpses and stole back to their doghouses and lay there quivering in terror, while others worried the bones and had to be driven off by their owners. Inexplicably, there was the body of a dog there also, its body contorted quite oddly. There was one cat which had retrieved the liver from a corpse and sat there devouring it, and which spat out with blazing eyes when its owner approached it.

Mrs. Charlotte Carmody had had to be removed to the hospital suffering from shock. When she had come out early that morning to sweep her sidewalk, she had found on the sidewalk beneath her bedroom window, scrabbling at the stucco, a corpse. Its face was already too decomposed to permit identification, but she had recognized the suit it wore as the suit in which she had buried her son Russell.

The police had found the old Harrod house still blazing with lights, and in one room a tape recorder which was still turned on. Leaving it on all night must have ruined it, for the words upon replay were quite indecipherable, just outlandish gibberish. But of the children of the neighborhood who had occupied the house the night before there was no trace. The police had searched the house thoroughly, and in the cellar had eventually come upon the secret tunnel, but in the tunnel itself there was nothing but a fearful odor, mostly compounded of the sea. The tunnel led up to the freshly washed grave of Obediah Carter, elegant in the sun.

The new section of Old Dethshill must have been visited by vandals during the night, for each of the graves had been torn up and its contents removed. The caskets had been smashed and piled up like so much kindling wood. The police were inclined to attribute the damage to the neighborhood children, who, tiring of the Harrod house, had sought more mischief elsewhere. An intensive search for the children was instituted and their descriptions broadcast to neighboring cities.

But the police didn't know what to make of the death of Miss Mary Peabody. Her pink parasol had been raised and tossed up into the limbs of a tree, and its handle pointed mockingly toward her corpse. Whatever it was which had eaten her had been quite selective, scooping out just the torso and leaving her head and thin, scrawny arms and legs attached precariously to her spine; when the police had carefully lifted the corpse, it had bounced up and down upon its spinebone like a jumping jack.

Nor could the police quite understand why, of all the things in the new section of the cemetery, the only thing which had been left undisturbed was the tall obelisk. It stood there triumphantly and the sunlight which fell upon its black stone seemed to linger longest upon the carved letters CTHULHU.

# Those Who Wait

## James Wade

Fortunate indeed is he whose range of experience never exceeds that tiny segment of Infinity which it is meant that Man should explore and subdue. He who steps beyond these borders walks in dreadful danger of life, sanity, and soul. Even if he escapes the peril, life can never be the same again—for he cannot escape his memories.

It is now seven months since I came to the archaic Massachusetts town of Arkham, to attend the small but widely-known Miskatonic University. Since then, my knowledge has increased in an unprecedented manner, but not in the ways I had expected. For me, new worlds have been opened—new worlds containing fascinating vistas of wisdom, and also undreamable abysses of horror, in which I learned the fatal weakness of the human mind in dealing with forces beyond its comprehension.

The first few weeks of my attendance at the university were occupied with settling myself in the new surroundings and becoming accustomed to my classes. My room-mate, Bill Tracy, I instinctively liked. A tall, blonde, self-effacing fellow, he was one of those utterly frank and compatible individuals one meets all too seldom. He was a sophomore, and helped my absorption into the school's routine by answering my innumerable questions as to the location of rooms, the dispositions of instructors, and the thousand other things about which the beginner at a school is ever curious.

Almost a month elapsed thus when the event occurred which was to set in motion a train of events unparalleled, so far as we know, in the history of the Earth. It began, however, prosaically enough.

One evening, rather late, I suddenly remembered some quotations from Shelley I would be expected to know by the next day for my literature class. Apprehensively I asked Bill Tracy, "Do you suppose the campus library is still open?"

"Probably," he replied, "but better hurry. They close at ten. You should have gone earlier." He grinned at my negligence.

I hurried from the dormitory and took the gravel path across the campus toward the large brick library building. On nearing it, I was relieved to notice that faint lights were still burning on the ground floor. Inside, I procured the needed book, and, passing the busy librarian, I suddenly turned on an impulse and made my way into the rare books room, which was then completely empty, as was the rest of the library. Seating myself at one of the tables, I prepared to delve into Shelley's odes, when suddenly I saw it—the thing which was to change my very life.

It was nothing but a sheet of paper lying on the table near me, written part of the way down one side. Out of idle curiosity I picked it up. It seemed but a series of notes, such as students might jot down when sitting together rather than disturb the quiet of the reading-room by speaking aloud. There were short sentences in two alternating hands. I was about to toss the paper aside, when something caught my eye, and I read it with ever-mounting interest and mystification. As nearly as I can remember, this is what the written conversation said:

> "What time is it?"
> "9:15."
> "I wish they'd leave."
> "There are only two. They will leave soon."
> "Hope they hurry. I'd like to let Ithaqua get the—"

(Here the script was hurriedly broken off, and there had been an only partially successful attempt to cross out the cryptic word. After which:)

"Fool! I have told you—never write those names!"

"All right.—Can we finish tonight?"

"I can copy the chant."

"We can open the Gate by—"

(Here again the writing was interrupted)

"They're leaving. Bring the key."

This completed the contents of the paper. I was baffled. What were these two planning—a robbery? But what about the cryptic reference to a "chant" and "opening the gate"? Who was "Ithaqua" and why shouldn't that name be written?

I was interrupted in these speculations by the opening of a nearby door marked "Private," and the emergence of two men. I caught a momentary glimpse of the rows of books within the room, and then a piercing gaze was directed upon me and the paper before me.

The gazer was tall, beetle-browed, and excessively dark, and had the appearance of being too adult for a student, but both he and his companion—a shorter, stouter, and younger-looking fellow who carried a brief-case—wore school sweaters. The younger man, apparently quite agitated at seeing me, quickly closed and locked the door, and then stood waiting for his older companion to act, which he immediately did. Striding forward, he addressed me in low, fierce tones with a hint of fear in his voice.

"Pardon me, sir, this paper is mine." And without further ado, he snatched it up and turned away.

"Just a moment!" I exclaimed angrily, "What are you up to? Have you two been stealing rare books from in there? What's in that brief-case?"

Seeing he could not get away without an explanation, he stopped and became immediately suavely polite.

"Pardon my haste," he said, smiling blandly. "My companion and I are engaged in no untoward activities. It is true: We were using the so rare books within that room, but we were merely copying portions of them, for a—thesis; yes, a thesis on demonolatry." Something in the inflection and wording suggested that he was a foreigner. "You will excuse us now." Grasping the arm of his companion, he turned once more.

"Do you think he understood—?" began the smaller man, but he was hushed by a gesture from the other, who looked guardedly back at me. The two quickly left the library, leaving me to muse on what I had witnessed.

My work was soon finished, but as I walked across the campus, thoughts of the two strange men obsessed me. If they had been engaged in authorized reference work, why had the note hinted that they wished to be left alone before entering the locked room? Too, parts of the dark, moody note seemed curiously irreconcilable to that explanation.

Over the thickly clustered, shadowy grove to the east hung a waning moon. Stars, those bright specks of light from distances incomprehensible, held dominion over the more subdued hues of darkness at the zenith. Ahead of me stretched the half-lit dormitory. Within was Bill Tracy. Perhaps he could shed some light on this matter.

I hurried to our room. Bill greeted me with a cheery, "Hi! Get your work done?"

"Yes," I answered abstractedly; then: "Have you ever seen a tall, dark, foreign, older-looking fellow in the student body?—Maybe tagged by a stoutish, younger fellow?"

"I think I know who you mean. His name is Renaunt. He *is* older. Taking a post-graduate course in Ancient Literature and Folklore."

"What do you know about him?"

"Oh, nothing in particular. Rather reserved chap. You meet him?"

"In a way." I told him what had occurred. He seemed peculiarly disturbed when I mentioned the strange name Ithaqua and the locked room.

"He's up to no good," muttered Bill, more to himself than to me.

"What do you know about it?"

"It's more than you can imagine. I was born and raised here. There are legends. . . ."

He told me then: fantastic tales of ancient books on malignant evil come down from ages immemorial, kept in Miskatonic Library's locked room. Sane or not, the dark beliefs and rituals contained in these books have been practiced even down to the present. The thick woods bordering the Miskatonic River had seen hideous, illogical rites celebrated within ancient circles of standing stones, and the forgotten hamlet of Dunwich, surrounded by altar-crowned hills, degenerated year by year from more cause than mere isolation. There were those, especially among the oldsters of Arkham, who averred that dark things *could* be called from the hills or the sky, if one was willing to pay the price. It was universally admitted that at certain seasons the sky lit up disturbingly over the hills, and queer rumbling earth-noises were heard. Scientists mumbled about seismographic shocks and Aurora Borealis, but few dared to investigate. In the old days, it had been quite generally believed that indescribable legions of demons were served there by wicked cults. Strange disappearances of those who lived or ventured too near the woods at night were invariably laid to the cult or its hideous deities, especially when the bodies would be found months later far away, only a few days dead.

Here my informer paused.

"Surely," I prompted, "you don't believe that!"

"Believe it? I wouldn't believe that *Renaunt* believed it if it wasn't for that note you told me about. They sound in earnest."

"Couple of crackpots!"

"If you really want to know something about this crazy business, just ask tomorrow to examine some of the books in that room. They'll let you. But as for copying wholesale from them, there'd be suspicions. That's why your two playmates made their own key and nosed in on the books secretly."

That night I had little rest. Indeed, my loss of sleep was not the result of vague and later definite fears which would soon beset me, but was rather caused by excitement: I thought perhaps I had discovered a new myth-pattern (new to me, at least), as my hobby had for years been the gathering of native legends from my home state, Wisconsin.

Suddenly in the middle of the night, I remembered where I had heard that cryptic name, Ithaqua. During my explorations of Wisconsin's north woods in search of lore for my collection, I had met an old Indian who had told me vague legends of the Wendigo, sometimes called "Wind-Walker" or *Ithaqua*—a titanic and repulsive monster, haunter of the great unfrequented snow-forests—a being who took men with him high and above the woods to the far corners of the Earth, but who never relinquished his victims until they had been frozen to death.

Such, then, was the thing which these unusual collegians spoke of as a reality, or—?

The next day passed slowly for me, but at last my classes terminated and I went quickly to the great library. Rather timorously I approached the aged librarian, and asked whether I might examine the rare occult books contained in the locked room. He eyed me oddly but assented, and, giving me a key from the ring at his side, bade me lock the door carefully when I finished.

With queer misgivings I approached the fated door and applied the key. Inside, I was confronted with several rows of books held in wall-shelves. The immense antiquity of the rotting tomes greatly impressed me. Many were incomplete or mutilated; others merely bound manuscripts. I saw such titles as the *Necronomicon* of Abdul Alhazred, *Unaussprechlichen Kulten* by Von Junzt, *Liber Ivonis,* and *De Vermis Mysteriis* by Ludwig Prinn. I was blissfully ignorant of the hellish evil around me, but was not long to remain so.

To open the *Necronomicon* (one of the largest and best preserved of the lot) was the work of the moment. Thumbing through it, I learned for the first time of Great Cthulhu; of Azathoth, the Lord of All Things, of Yog-Sothoth and Shub-Niggurath, of Nyarlathotep and Tsathoggua, and of other horrors the nature of which I could grasp no better. Had I believed what I read then, I should inevitably have gone mad at once, but thinking it merely a particularly malignant myth-pattern or a devilishly clever hoax, I read on with only a curious interest.

There were many hundreds of pages of rambling, disconnected essays in Latin, containing charms, counter-charms, spells and incantations (which latter seemed to be entirely in a laboriously spelled phonetic language). Frequently there was a crude diagram of complicated signs, such as a pattern of intersecting lines and concentric circles, as well as a fire-outlined star designated as "The Elder Sign."

From the particularly lucid passages, I gleaned a strange story. It seems, according to the crazed Arab author that, billions of aeons before Man, great cosmic entities "from the stars" had come to Earth.

These Things (possessing the queer names that had so puzzled me) were extra-dimensional and beyond the ties of Time and Space. They were the personifications of universal Evil and had fled from cosmoses beyond human ken the wrath of the benign Elder Gods, against whom They had rebelled. These evil Great Old Ones built cyclopean cities according to non-Euclidean geometric principles, and from Earth planned to renew their fight against the Elder Gods. But before They were fully prepared, "the stars went wrong" as the author put it, and these Great Old Ones could not live. Neither could They ever die, but being preserved by the black magic of Their high priest Great Cthulhu, slept within Their monster cities to await a coming time. Some were banished into caverns in the bowels of the Earth; others, imprisoned beyond the known universe.

In the course of an unbelievable passage of time, Man had arrived and the Great Old Ones had communicated with some individuals telepathically, telling them of the great awakening that was to come, and instructing them in the chants and rituals which, together with proper sacrifices and worship, could bring the gigantic Things temporarily to great circles of stone monoliths set up in abandoned places, and further hinting that Man would be instrumental in the permanent release of the Old Ones, as They could not yet move under Their own volition.

These secrets had been learned and passed on by wicked groups of men even after R'lyeh, the nightmare-city of Cthulhu, had sunk into the sea in the same cataclysm that spelled doom for Atlantis and Mu. The cults would go on until "the stars again became right" and the release of the blasphemous elder monsters would be accomplished as the culmination of its supreme purpose.

In addition to these wild historical notes, the book held hundreds of stories of various strange happenings, authenticated by long-forgotten witnesses and inexplicable save in the light of the lore the book expounded. Concerning the physical aspect of these extra-terrestrials and Their minions, the book was distressingly hazy. Once it alluded to Them as "of no substance"; other times mentioning a hideous plasticity and the capability of becoming invisible.

Being so completely absorbed in the book, I failed to notice light steps approaching the door, but I dropped the *Necronomicon* in fright as a menacingly familiar voice sounded behind me.

"Are you perhaps looking for something?"

It was Renaunt, of course, not far preceding his pudgy accomplice with the eternal brief-case. In strange agitation I tried to reply lightly.

"I was just checking up to see what interested you so much last evening."

"I thought you perhaps might do so," he returned narrowly. "Have you found anything of interest?"

"Yes, indeed! Here seems to be a myth-pattern of great antiquity upon which I have never before stumbled."

"You are interested in the ancient religions?"

"Very much."

"So are we. You must pardon me. I am Jacques Renaunt—that is my so good friend Peterson."

We shook hands. I did not enjoy the experience.

"I have something you might like to see," said Renaunt in a disarmingly friendly manner. "Perhaps last night you thought us devil-worshippers, to copy from these old books, but this is uncorrect."

"Incorrect." Peterson spoke his first word in the conversation. "You mustn't forget your English."

"Quite right. Thank you. As I was saying, we are merely amateur archaeologists, but we have discovered, not far from here, some very unique ruins, which, if we are not mistaken, were once used in connection with rites given in this books."

"These books," put in Peterson.

"No matter. The point is, we have been perusing—these books to gain further information. We planned to visit these ruins toni—this afternoon. We would be glad for a—companion." The two exchanged glances.

Did I let my instinctive aversion to these men cause me to refuse their bland offer? No; logic conquered instinct, and I made myself see only a new and fascinating experience in a venture against which my every dormant intuition cried out loud.

"I would be delighted. First let me tell my room-mate . . ."

"Peterson will do that when he gets the car. Hurry, Peterson."

The stout man scuttled away, while Renaunt let me rather furtively out a side exit. In a surprisingly short time Peterson drove up in the car. Renaunt opened the back door for me and then climbed in beside Peterson. For a few minutes, silence prevailed as the car swept swiftly across the leaf-strewn campus grounds and through the autumn-tinted, rolling Massachusetts hills. Then Renaunt turned and addressed me politely.

"You must pardon me while I converse with Mr. Peterson in my native language. It is tiring for me to constantly formulate my thoughts into the English."

They immediately began talking in some foreign dialect. Listening idly, I could not trace any Romance language or Greek or even Slavic in what they said; it seemed a kind of guttural Oriental tongue, but as I sat listening to it, mile after mile in that stuffy car, I could take no pleasure in the beauties of the wooded hills, or of the forest-cradled Miskatonic River, now tinted a flaming orange by the rays of the descending sun.

Much further than I had expected we drove. The sun was hidden behind the tall pines of the mountains ahead when we turned from the main road. The eastern sky was dusky behind us as the car jogged along a narrow, rough dirt trail. Several times it branched off again on bypaths leading through quiet forest glades of the greatest sylvan beauty. The trail became barely wide enough to permit passage to the sedan. Few were the farms we passed, and these few were always in a deplorably run-down condition. It was a poor district, ruled by Nature and not Man.

Long after losing sight of the last farmhouse among the thickening trees, Peterson brought the auto to a lurching halt.

"This is as far as we can go by the car," said Renaunt, opening the door.

Within a few minutes we were plunging through thick undergrowth among the huge boles of an amazing cluster of trees. This, I thought, must be one of the few out-of-the-way virgin forests in the state. Another thought occurred to me and I asked Renaunt, "Why were these ruins not discovered before? They are reasonably near human habitation."

"The natives around here fear these woods," answered my guide cryptically, "and few others have occasion to visit them."

In silence we covered the distance of perhaps a mile. The ground gradually became damp and spongy until it was apparent that we were nearing a swamp.

"The ruins are on a kind of island in the midst of a marshy crescent lake near the Miskatonic," explained Renaunt in response to my query.

A deep dusk, enhanced by the somber shade of the forest, had now indeed fallen.

"How can we see when we arrive? We have started too late," I commented.

I received no reply, save the pulsing croak of frogs which now reached us from somewhere ahead in the leafy labyrinth.

Little by little the trees thinned and I saw stretched before me, surrounded by woods like those from which we were emerging, a low, open, marshy spot in the shape of a giant crescent moon. Reeds and rushes grew at the margin, while near the middle the water was clear and deep, albeit rather stagnant. Near the center of the lake rose a small island, almost covered with the sprawling ruin of a strange, irregular grey stone platform surrounded by a crumbling parapet, much in need of repair. Low stone columns rose at intervals from it. The last reflected rays of the setting sun shone behind it, outlining the skeletal remains of a once-great and still imposing structure. I was astounded to find such a complex piece of architecture in apparently unexplored wilds.

"The lake of Y'ha-nthlei," breathed Peterson, "Iä! Cthulhu!"

"What did you say?" I exclaimed, "I—"

But Renaunt interrupted me with a terse command to Peterson.

"Now is the time!" he snapped. "Concentrate!"—and I felt all suddenly go black around me. My last conscious impression was one of the two grasping my arms to keep from falling as I slipped into the black trough of insensibility.


When I awoke, the deepest night had fallen. My first sensation was of lying uncomfortably on a very hard substance; my second was of bewilderment: I could not realize the significance of the bonds around my wrists and ankles. I knew now that I was a prisoner. Then, suddenly, the meaning of my situation came back to me. I remembered the strange trek through the shadowy woods with my queer companions; the marsh lake, the ruins. I remembered too my faint (for such I then deemed it) at the edge of the woods. Then I began to struggle, for, gazing around, I discovered that I was lying on the rough stone flags comprising the floor of the island ruin. My companions must have brought me here, I thought; but why bound?

The extent of Renaunt's treachery was soon to be made clear to me, however. I heard voices approaching and soon, from behind a pile of crumbling stones, two robed figures appeared. They were Renaunt and Peterson, hooded and encased in black garments. With a shudder of unbelievable terror, I realized that they planned to stage a ceremony, of which I might be a part. *That* was why I had been enticed on this devilish trip!

Renaunt approached me, more than human wrath and contempt glowing in his eyes.

"Ah, my so curious young friend, you will not let well enough alone, and now see what it has got you!"

"Let me go!" I stormed, with more courage in my voice than in my heart. "What is the meaning of this?"

"It means you shall be a living sacrifice to Those Who Wait!"

"Madman! You plan—to sacrifice me in some idiotic ritual? Are you going to kill me?"

"Our hands will be clean, I assure you—you will leave this island alive."

"Then you—?"

"But you will never be seen so again!"

"Nonsense!"

"You will see!" he cried in a fit of anger. "We are come from the Supreme One of Irem to open the Gate for the Great Old Ones! The stars are almost right again! Tonight, we will tell Great Cthulhu so He may prepare. Soon shall They do battle with Those of Betelgeuze, and—!—But light the torches, Monog!"

The one I knew as Peterson, with a long flambeau, fired masses of dry wood atop the pillars of the parapet. "You," said Renaunt, "will be the bait to draw Great Cthulhu here, as is written in the Old Books."

Peterson, or Monog, had by then completed his task, and he and Renaunt lifted my bound body, tossing me roughly upon a high pile of crumbling stones.

The ceaseless piping of frogs, which all the while had formed a weird background to the words of my captor, now seemed to increase in intensity and to fill the night air. Beneath me, Renaunt and Peterson were stooping to chalk diagrams drawn from papers they held (doubtlessly copies from the *Necronomicon* and the other books) on the stone flags. Renaunt then began a weird chant, while Peterson cowered beneath an outcropping of stone. What would these lunatics do, I wondered, when they realized that their mad activities brought no result? Then all speculation was swept away and I abandoned my soul to terror!

For something *was* happening—not only below me but all around; on the lake, on the rampart—as the meaningless mouthing continued. The landscape seemed to change subtly under the pale rays of the dying moon; a blur dimmed the horizon; angles shifted and solid stone swayed formlessly. The waters of the lake were wildly stirring, though there was no wind. *From all sides,* great waves broke over the low parapet, threatening to douse the frantically flickering fires. A stench as of all the dead and rotting water life of the world nauseated me. A strange wind now stirred, moaning, through the tumbled stones, and above the chorus of frogs, Renaunt's voice was lifted in a primal incantation:

"*Iä! Iä! N'gah-hah! N'yah ahahah! Cthulhu fhtaghn! Phn'glui vulgmm R'lyeh! Ai! N'gaii! Ithaqua vulgmm! N'gaaga—aaa-fhtaghn! Iä! Cthulhu!*"

The leaping flames of the great torches now revealed to my horror-stricken eyes a thin, wavering line across the sky. More appeared, traversing the space above my head. A low, thunderous roar competed with the truly cacophonous chant of the frogs and the incantation shouted by Renaunt, while greenish flashes from over the horizon lit the scene fitfully. A great blast of cold air swept over the lake, followed immediately by a foetid warm draft, as with a hideous stench, and an uncouth bubbling sound, a giant shape sprang seemingly from the lake itself and hovered over us without visible means of levitation! Mercifully, I fainted.

When I regained my senses (it must have been but a moment later) the Thing was still there. It is beyond the power of any pen to hint adequately at the aspect of It. An alien, undimensioned entity from beyond the known Universe, It seemed by turns to be a great, green, monstrous tentacled squid; a boiling, changing, flowing mass of protoplasm, constantly altering yet ever the same, having malevolent red eyes opening from every part of its non-terrestrial body, and a swollen, empurpled maw from which issued an idiotic, frantic, bubbling ululation, so low in timbre that it struck one as a physical vibration rather than a true sound.

*Great Cthulhu! High Priest of the Old Ones! Carried from His crypt in sunken R'lyeh by Ithaqua the Wind-Walker; summoned by the evil man in whose hands I was prisoner!* Great God! *I believed; I saw!* But I could not die; I could not even faint again. Even now my hand trembles when I think of my hideous captivity as the helpless prey of that hellish daemon!

Below, Renaunt was conversing with It, in the same unholy dialect with which he had summoned It (the same, indeed, in which he had talked with Peterson in the car), mentioning such names as Azathoth, Betelgeuze, R'lyeh, the Hyades, as well as the names of the other weird monsters. As his monologue progressed, Cthulhu became greatly excited, quivering in agitation as His great body overshadowed the entire lake, and later uttering a few ghastly mouthing sounds which thrilled my soul with a new fear when I had thought I had reached the extremity of terror.

Abruptly, the awful communication ended. Renaunt fell on his knees below the Thing and extended his hand toward the pile of debris on which I lay bound. It flowed toward me, extending from Its plastic self a tentacle or trunk which groped downward at me. Directly above me, the savage opening of what It used as a mouth yawned wide, disclosing a hollow body cavity striated with red bands. In another moment I would have known a thing far worse than merciful death; but at that instant, something intervened to save me.

Bill Tracy—what tributes are due his courage!—appeared at the top of the sacrificial mound, approaching from the side opposite that of Renaunt. Sickening horror showed in every line of his face, but he nevertheless sprang to my side and slashed my bonds with a ready knife. As I leapt up, he extended his right hand towards the excrescence of Cthulhu, which had almost reached us. It recoiled, and the massive bulk overhead lumbered away.

"Run!" shouted Tracy. "Swim the lake! Get to the car!"

We were off, racing madly over the shattered flags and plunging into the stagnant lake. Behind us, Renaunt was imploring Cthulhu, and as we swam frantically for shore, we heard him racing in pursuit.

He and Peterson dragged a small rowboat to the margin of the lake and pulled after us. Overhead, the great bulk of the monstrous entity Cthulhu flowed along, lashing the affrighted air with thousands of loathsome tentacles. Fortunately, Tracy and I were both good swimmers, and the surprise instituted by Tracy's daring move gave us a head start.

Upon reaching the shore, we plunged into the pitch-dark forest. The sounds of frantic shouts and the ululant mouthings of Cthulhu (who had evidently joined the chase) goaded us to frenzied exertions.

"We must separate," gasped Bill. "They know these woods. I'll go this way, but if I don't get through, remember: don't go to the police. It won't do any good. Go to Professor Sterns."

Thus saying, he plunged off to the left, attempting to cross a clearing whose edge I was skirting. As he reached its center, Renaunt and Peterson broke from the woods on the opposite side. Behind them, over the tops of the trees, Cthulhu rapidly neared. Renaunt, with amazing speed, sought to grapple with Tracy, but again extending his right arm, on which I saw something gleam, my deliverer caused my former captor to fall. In doing so, he clutched Tracy's knees. The latter, after a desperate struggle to retain his balance, plunged heavily to the ground. As they rolled free, Renaunt half-rose, extending one arm toward Tracy, the other toward the blasphemous monstrosity hovering overhead. He shrieked a flaming command, and immediately the Thing put forth dozens of squamous tentacles which entangled the struggling body of my rescuer. He was lifted, screaming hideously toward the frothing maw of the monster.

Cold with icy terror, I ran on through the clutching undergrowth of those haunted woods. After what seemed an almost interminable interval, the trees thinned and I emerged on the highway less than a quarter of a mile from the cars. Tracy's vehicle was parked near Renaunt's. He had obviously suspiciously trailed us, perhaps becoming lost in the forest, and arriving only in time to save my life at the cost of his own.

With a prayer of thanks, I saw that the keys were still in the ignition. Moments later, I was speeding recklessly over the deserted highways, caring only to get far from that awful spot. Through the blackest hours of the night I was lost, but at dawn I found myself approaching Arkham. What had poor Bill said? "See Professor Sterns." A short consultation with the telephone directory in a small confectionery told me his address. As I was leaving the store, I shuddered to see blatant headlines on a cheap astrology periodical proclaiming, "Portentous Events in the Stars—Something Unprecedented!"

I drove slowly along pleasant, tree-lined residential streets, hazy in the early morning sunlight, and stopped at a decaying mid-Victorian mansion bearing the number I had memorized. And so, shaken in body, mind and spirit, with an indelible memory fomenting in my consciousness and a gnawing fear tormenting me, I lifted the knocker beside the ancient nameplate with the legend, "Professor Arlin Sterns, Ph.D."

A mellow-faced, white-bearded elderly man opened the door and in response to my agitated query introduced himself as Professor Sterns. Upon learning my name, he grew pale, but civilly invited me in.

"How much do you know," I began hurriedly, "of Bill Tracy and me and what goes on in that—"

"I know," he said laboredly, "that a young man came to me this morning and told me of two college students he believed to be engaged in very nasty business. He expressed fear that you, his friend, might be drawn into it. I advised him to keep a watch on you, and I gave him a certain bracelet which I felt would give him protection. What has happened?"

I thereupon told him my full story, ending on an almost hysterical note as I recounted my mad flight through the forest and the endless race along tree-lined highways. As I spoke, the savant stroked his stubby goatee, but when I told of Bill Tracy's gruesome fate, he stopped abruptly and muttered, "I told him the grey stone from Mnar wouldn't stop the Old Ones Themselves."

"Do you believe what I say?" I asked. "I can hardly believe it myself!"

"Unfortunately, yes," replied Professor Sterns. "Before my retirement as Professor of Anthropology at Miskatonic, I had occasion to be convinced in a most horrible manner. But that's neither here nor there. The point is,"—his face showed worried lines—"the world, the whole universe as we know it, is in danger of being obliterated in a terrible way in a coming battle between extra-dimensional entities whose nature we cannot even begin to grasp. That is the purpose and purport, veiled, garbled and cloaked in mysticism, of all religions and cults, and, more directly, of the evil books now found in only a few scattered libraries and manuscript fragments in private possession." He turned. "But I must not keep you waiting out here. Please come into my study."

He led the way through a dark, narrow hall into a large room, lined with bookcases and strewn with the odds and ends of a long and varied career. With a serious demeanor he unlocked one of the lower drawers of his desk, and drew forth a folio of manuscript. After bidding me seat myself on a chair near the desk, he addressed me in this fashion:

"These are the extracts I copied from the *Necronomicon* and other books while I was at Miskatonic. Allow me to point out to you some pertinent passages." He passed over to me one of the sheets. I took it and read,

*Nor is it to be thought that Man is either the oldest or last of the Masters of Earth; nay, nor that the greater part of Life and Substance walks alone. The Old Ones were, the Old Ones are, and the Old Ones shall be. Not in the spaces known to us, but between them, They walk calm and primal, of no dimensions, and to us unseen . . . They walk foul in lonely places where the Words have been spoken and the Rites howled through at their Seasons . . . The winds gibber with Their voices; the Earth mutters with Their consciousness. They bend the forest. They raise up the wave; They crush the city—yet not forest nor ocean nor city beholds the hand that smites. They ruled; soon shall They rule again where man rules now. After Summer is Winter and after Winter is Summer. They wait patient and potent for here shall They reign again, and at Their coming again, none shall dispute them. Those who know of the Gates shall be impelled to open the way for Them and shall serve Them as They desire, but those who open the way unwitting shall know but a brief while thereafter.*

"Now this," said the professor, handing me another sheet.
I read,

*Then shall They return and on this great returning shall Great Cthulhu [—I shuddered at the name—] be freed from R'lyeh beneath the sea, and Him Who Is Not To Be Named shall come from His City, which Carcosa near the Lake of Hali, and Shub-Niggurath shall come forth and multiply in His hideousness, and Nyarlathotep shall carry the word to all the Great Old Ones and Their minions, and Cthugha shall lay his hand on all that oppose Him and Destroy, and the blind Idiot, the noxious Azathoth, shall rise from the Middle of the World where all is Chaos and destruction, where he hath bubbled and blasphemed at the Centre which is of All Things, which is to say, Infinity, and Yog-Sothoth who is the All-in-One and the One-in-All shall bring His globes and Ithaqua shall walk again, and from the black-litten caverns within the Earth shall come Tsathoggua and together shall take possession of Earth and all things that live upon it and shall prepare to do battle with the Elder Gods. When the Lord of the Great Abyss is apprised of Their returning, He shall come forth with His Brothers to disperse the Evil.*

"You mean," I exclaimed, "that this book—written a thousand years ago—actually foretells what is happening now?"

"I'm sure of it!" said the professor forcefully. "Look: astrologers proclaim that something unprecedented is in the stars. The writer of this mythology claims that 'when the stars are right' those who know 'shall be impelled to open the Gates.' These men come, frantically study the books, and conjure up a monster beyond the wildest dreams of a hashish-eater. They admit their purposes. What could be plainer?"

I was convinced for once and all of the absolute veracity of the Arab necromancer.

"But," I inquired, "Renaunt mentioned something about being sent 'by the Supreme One of Irem.' What does that mean?"

"Let me read you what Alhazred says; here—

*But the first Gate was that which I caused to be opened, namely, in Irem, the city of pillars, the city under the desert.*

"Irem is the headquarters of this hellish thing. There, the entire purpose of the Old Ones is known, or at least as much as Man can know of it, and there are some things in Irem that are not even human, unless I miss my guess. Renaunt and Peterson, or whatever their names are in Irem, must be high up, if they were sent on this crowning mission. The island must be a vital spot if it was chosen for Cthulhu's awakening. We must prevent this, my boy! It is bound to come some day, but if we can stop them now, it will be thousands of years before the stars are right again!"

"But how?" I gasped. "Aren't the Old Ones already loosed? How about last night?"

"That was just a warning to Great Cthulhu," said Professor Sterns. "The real awakening can only be scheduled for All-Hallows' Eve; a month yet."

"How can you know?"

"There are certain times when these ceremonies grow more potent; stronger; intenser. The times are May Eve, Walpurgis night; Candlemas; Roodmass; and All-Hallow's Eve. The opening of the Gate will be a difficult thing. It will shake the Earth, and its consequences will destroy mankind. It is infinitely important to—Them."

"How can we hope to stop these invincible monstrosities?"

"It will be hard; hard! But Their weak points are Their minions. They must be there to perform the ceremonies. And though all the powers of Irem and the Old Ones Themselves protect them, they're only human. Not *much* more than human, anyway—I hope."

During the following month, both Professor Sterns and myself were feverishly busy. I was able to continue my classes at the university, but every day after their termination I hurried to the ancient savant's crumbling brownstone house, which I had come to look upon as not only a second home, but as a sort of mecca for all the world's hopes. It was fantastic: a world of beings living in complete ignorance of a ghastly and unspeakable fate which was inexorably approaching and threatening their very souls, while two men struggled to avert the catastrophe with all the knowledge and skill, human and inhuman, in their possession.

Or, rather, not just two, for I found that there was a considerable band of learned men, all over the world, united in a common knowledge of and belief in the nightmare myth, and a desire to thwart the Great Old Ones and Their minions. There was a steady stream of strange visitors to the weathered old house on Harper Street, and an equally strange flow of outlandish letters and parcels. Professor Sterns' large desk in the library became heaped with neat folios of papers and small packages. What were they? All manner of charms, spells and diagrams helpful against the malignant monsters and Their worshippers. Professor Sterns was particularly excited over the arrival of a large crate from a Buddhist priest in Tibet. This, the professor informed me, contained the Elder Gods' benign sign, carved by Their Very Selves on a stone brought from another world and spirited away from the ancient and accursed Plateau of Leng expressly to aid us in our mission.

Weeks went by; Bill Tracy, whose disappearance had caused a wide stir, was not found, alive or dead. The beings known to us as Renaunt and Peterson had also vanished.

On a pale, sombre October evening late in the month, Professor Sterns telephoned me and asked me to visit him for final instructions. I left for his house, feeling acutely the nervous apprehension under which I had so long labored.


A near-full moon, rising above the trees surrounding Professor Sterns' house shot feeble rays glinting along the ridgepole of the roof, along the old tin spouting, along the banisters of the wide front porch. A queer chill gripped me as I approached along the gravel walk; the house was lightless. Half formed fears stirred uneasily in my mind as I plied the knocker, but after a short, suspenseful interval I recognized the slow tread of my aged friend approaching the panel from within. It opened slowly and I discerned the kindly, bearded face peering narrowly through the gloom. Almost instantly a look of relief and welcome swept over it.

"Ah! You!" muttered the professor. "I am glad to see you. You came sooner than I had anticipated. Step into the hall."

Inside, he spoke quietly but rapidly.

"There has been a change in plans. I—we have a guest. He is to help us. He's—strange. Doesn't speak English, but he's on our side. Do you remember how you lost consciousness at the edge of the lake after Renaunt told Peterson to concentrate? That was instantaneous hypnotism, showing a great development of mind-power. Well, our guest has just such mind-power, and more. He will be an immeasurable aid to us."

Professor Sterns led the way into the study, switched on the light, and there, standing by the desk, was the Guest. Little could be seen of him, for he wore a long, tightly-buttoned overcoat which dragged on the floor. It had been thrown over his shoulders, so that the arms dangled uselessly at his sides. On his head he wore a large hat pulled far down, and (strange to tell!), over his face he wore a grey scarf, knotted firmly at the back of his head. Thus not an inch of his person was visible. Only once did I see him without all this paraphernalia intact.

"This is the young man I was telling you about," the professor was saying. He seemed highly respectful, almost reverential, toward the muffled figure. But what was it he had said?—"He doesn't speak English!" He must understand it, though, I thought.

The figure made a movement which might be construed as a bow, and I murmured conventional words of greeting to it. I noticed that the top of the desk had been cleared, and that three suitcases lay in the shadows. I flashed a questioning look to Professor Sterns.

"We are leaving," the savant spoke nervously. "I have discovered where the Great Awakening is to take place. The information is hidden by a clever code in the *Seven Cryptical Books of Hsan*, but I haven't deciphered it. In fact, we are leaving immediately. You won't need to pack anything. It will all be over—one way or the other—soon. You see, tomorrow night is *All-Hallows' Eve!*"

The street was dark, the walk was long, the suitcases heavy. I carried two; Professor Sterns carried the remaining one. Our Guest followed us in a peculiar quiet and gliding manner, unburdened. He seemed shorter than when I had first seen him, but I put this down to a trick of light and shadow.

It may have been half an hour later when we arrived at the field. Under the rays of the moon, dry stubble took on a beautiful yellow sheen, and the airplane shone with a pale silver glow. For there *was* an airplane on the field, and in it the professor placed his suitcase, instructing me to do the same with mine.

"But," I stammered, "where are we going? Who is taking us?!"

"We are going," replied the aged man grimly, "to the north woods of Maine; to a place which I will not name and for a purpose you know too well. Get in, my boy."

Inside the tiny cabin Professor Sterns settled himself at the controls, with me beside him, while the Guest sat on the suitcases behind.

"I learned to fly," explained the professor, "from Professor Peaslee, the man whose father had such a dreadful experience when those singularly ancient ruins were discovered in Australia that he committed suicide."

With a whine and a growl that deepened to a roar, the motor awoke and in a few moments we were bouncing swiftly down the field. At its extreme end our pilot lifted the plane's nose and we were airborne, climbing sharply to gain altitude and leveling off to streak swiftly northward.

Looking down, I could see the thin line of light that was the Miskatonic River fade into the distance. Silence and darkness (save for the monotone of the motor and the illuminating instruments) closed in on us, wrapping us in a pall of almost sentient gloom as we sped on for hours over northern Massachusetts and the southeastern corner of New Hampshire.

Midnight found us over Maine. Professor Sterns was explaining to me more in detail about both our mission and our adversaries. Some of what he said I cannot bring myself to repeat, for the world is better off without it, but other parts of his information were vital and pertinent.

"As you know, the Great Old Ones are elementals; that is, each is identified with and has dominion over one of the ancient so-called elements. Cthulhu is the deity of water, Cthugha of fire, while Nyarlathotep, Tsathoggua, Azathoth and Shub-Niggurath seem associated with Earth. The air-beings are Hastur, Zhar, Ithaqua, and Lloigor. Yog-Sothoth, who is spoken of as the 'All-in-One and the One-in-All,' seems not to be associated with an element.

"From hints in the *Necronomicon*, I can guess at some of the things that will happen at the Great Awakening. First of all, there will be the celebration of rites for days in advance. Of their nature, there is no need to speak. Then, on All-Hallows' Eve (tomorrow night) there will be a long ritual beginning at sunset. Then, at midnight, the book says,

> . . . shall the sky be torn away and from Their dimensions on Outside shall the Old Ones be seen upon the Earth. And the Earth shall tremble at Their aspect, and the Old Ones shall descend and inhabit and ravage.

"What we must do is to stop that ritual, to which there are two parts. The first 'Opens the Gate' and the second frees the Old Ones to move. If we can stop it before the end, then the fleeting moment in which the stars are in the right position for it to take effect will pass, and Earth will be saved."

"How can we stop the ritual?" I asked. "Murder?"

"That is neither necessary nor would it be effective. There will be far too many there. Renaunt and Peterson may or may not be there. What we must do is to counteract their spells and charms with our own, and, finally, destroy their lair of cosmic evil by sealing it with the Elder Sign on that stone block from Tibet. But there are many risks. We may be apprehended before we can do any of those things. For that reason, I have wrist-bands for us to wear. None of the minions of the Old Ones can bear to touch these stones with the Elder sign on them, but only on the Tibetan enchanted stone is it potent enough to stop *all* evil. Remember, Bill Tracy found the weakness of the bracelets his undoing."

For hours we droned on over northern Maine. The hands of the clock on the instrument panel pointed to 4 a.m. when suddenly I noticed something.

"Look!" I murmured to the professor, "There ahead!"

Shifting his gaze slightly, he too saw what had attracted my attention. *Miles ahead of us, a titanic shadow had blotted out the stars, a shadow whose blurred outlines seemed a hideous caricature of the human form, and from the space where the head appeared to be, there shimmered with an unholy light what seemed to be two great green stars!*

*And the Thing was moving,* rushing to meet us; a giant shape, miles high, whose colossal bulk filled the horizon and stretched to the zenith! Simultaneously, a howling wind sprang up, bearing on its wings the sound of shrill, terrible music, as of great flutes or reed pipes being played all around us in the air.

"One of the Old Ones sent to destroy us!" shouted Professor Sterns. "An air-elemental. It is Ithaqua the Wind-Walker!" Black terror gripped me. . . .

The shadow-like Being neared rapidly, yet our pilot held his course, flying straight at the mound-like, neckless head and the star-eyes.

"We must flee!" I exclaimed.

"No use," said the professor, "this is the only way."

Louder sounded the demoniac music, nearer rushed the monster. For a moment Its flaming eyes shone directly before us, and then I closed my own. When I opened them, the sky ahead was clear.

"We have cut across another dimension and passed directly through His body," breathed the professor. "He cannot touch us because of the grey stone. We are safe!" But just then a tremendous gust of wind threw the plane into a dangerous spin. "He is sending His winds to wreck us!"

Through the black night tore howling, whistling blasts of air, throwing us off our course despite everything the professor could do. For minutes he fought valiantly with the controls, but at last a seething vortex of cyclonic strength seized the machine like a huge black fist and seemed about to hurl it to destruction on the earth below. But at the last moment, the winds subsided and the plane righted itself.

"What . . . ?" I began, when Professor Sterns interrupted me with a whispered, "*Look!*"

On the horizon a pale, opalescent glow broadened imperceptibly, reflecting thin rays upon the mists above.

"Dawn!" The first night of terror had passed safely, but the Great Adventure was just beginning.

Less than half an hour later, our plane landed near the village of Chesuncook. There, the professor loaded our luggage into a car which was somehow waiting for us, and, with the Guest in the back seat, we embarked on a trip very similar (and yet how different from) one I had taken a month before.

The day was damp, foggy and uncomfortable. The pine forests on either side of the road stood dark and expectant, unwarmed by the cloud-obscured sun. About noon, the professor extracted a box lunch from one of the suitcases, but the Guest did not partake, nor did the professor offer him any of the food.

It was long past noon when the car stopped. The grey clouds in the sky were still unrelieved, save for a dull glow between zenith and horizon which was all that was visible of the sun.

Professor Sterns then opened another suitcase and extracted a queer apparatus consisting of a square board with a circular hole in the center. In the hole was fastened a shallow metal tray of the same shape, with a curved glass over it which prevented the spilling of the liquid in the tray. In this clear fluid floated an oblong piece of dark wood several inches long, whittled to a point at one end. On the outside board, queer designs were carven.

Holding this odd contraption level, the professor gazed intently at the wooden pointer. It seemed to turn slowly counter-clockwise, but suddenly it reversed its direction and jerked quickly three-quarters of the way around, there remaining immovable.

"This is our guide," remarked the professor. "It's a kind of compass, but it doesn't point north!"

We set off into the woods, following the direction set by this compass that was not a compass. I took the two remaining suitcases (one was very heavy), and the aged savant went ahead with the direction-finder. The Guest moved unobtrusively along in the rear.

The undergrowth was very thick, and the pines seemed to grow abnormally close together, so our progress was slow and none too steady. I called frequent halts for rest when I noticed that the professor was staggering from fatigue.

Imperceptibly, the shades of the forest deepened and it was night. I began to feel an indefinable aura of evil surrounding these black woods; a sense of cosmic dread and alien purpose, so that I did not like to let my mind dwell on our mission.

Quite abruptly, we came to the clearing. It was about a quarter of a mile across, and in the center was a stone structure resembling a well, bathed in rays of a ghostly full moon which shone from a rift between two clouds. This, the professor informed me, was the only entrance to the most unholy and accursed temple on earth; a place where dark things dwelt with degenerate men, and the site of the All-Hallows' Great Awakening.

A flickering light as of torches came from the mouth of the open cylinder-shaft, and a faint murmur also reached us from it.

The following events which occurred on that hellish night I must be very careful in describing.

We scuttled across the clearing and crouched by the lip of the round shaft, which rose perhaps a yard from the ground.

"The ceremony has started," whispered Professor Sterns. "Watch the sky and do what I say." He unlocked both suitcases, took from one a folio of papers from amongst many more, and from the other eased the great grey Tibetan stone, with its queer carving, laying it between himself and the Guest.

For a long time, the only thing audible from below was the murmur of chanting men's voices, occasionally broken by a strange, deep, ecstatic moan. Then, syllables in English floated up to us.

"Oh, Raythore, the time has come. Begin, thou!"

I started wildly as another voice began in chant-like speech. For the second voice was that of Jacques Renaunt!

"*Death-Walker! God of the Winds! Thou Who walkest on the Winds—adoramus te!*"

The sky slowly faded to a dark grayish-green, and the wind stirred.

"*Oh, Thou Who pass above the Earth; Thou Who hast vanquished the sky—adoramus te!*"

The wind grew in a few seconds to a cyclonic pitch, and high in the sky the clouds rushed back with breath-taking speed, as if its force up there were thousands of times greater than we felt below.

"*Ithaqua! Thou Who hast vanquished the sky—-vanquish it yet*

*again that the Supreme Purpose may be fulfilled. Iä! Iä! Ithaqua! Ai! Ai!*
*Ithaqua cf'ayak vulgtmm vugtlagln vulgtmm. Ithaqua fhtaghn! Ugh!*
*Iä! Iä! Iä!!*

Thunder rumbled and crashed around us, adding yet another voice to the insane canticle of chant and wind. The chorus of men's voices welled up deep and strong as a climax approached in the indescribable chaos of the elements.

"*Iä! Azathoth! Iä! Yog-Sothoth! Iä! Cthulhu! Iä! Cthugha!*"

Flashes of light showed the straining sky flecked with lines of glowing green.

"*Iä! Hastur! Iä! Ithaqua! Iä! Zhar! Iä! Lloigor!*"

A loud buzzing sound seemed borne on the shrieking blasts of wind.

"*Iä! Shub-Niggurath! Iä! Tsathoggua! Iä! Nyarlathotep! Ai!*"

On the last word, a fiendish shout of expectancy echoed up from below. Why didn't the professor do something? I wondered shudderingly. Glancing at him, I saw him worriedly watching the passive Guest. But all thought was extinguished as, with a noise unequalled since the birth of the world, *the sky cracked!*

There is no other way to express it. The darkness split, shrivelled and rolled up, and, from Outside, a hideous and unknown light bathed the Universe, as the Great Old Ones once more looked upon Earth.

Of what I saw beyond the ragged shreds of the borders of our Space-Time continuum as new, final chants rose from the temple below, I can only begin to hint. I had the simultaneous impression of stupendous, amorphous entities; of fluid hyper-intelligences of dominating universal Evil; of an undimensioned chaos of impossible angular curves and curved angles; of a boiling, changing cauldron of moving, massing monstrosities *approaching*; then, being a mere human being, I fell backward to the ground and turned my face away. What I saw on the ground was almost as stupefying as the sky's ghastly change.

For there in the dirt was an overcoat, a hat, and a gray scarf, lying in crumpled disarray, while in the shadows of the wood a black form was disappearing!

Seconds later, a titanic column of flame exploded from the forest and shot upward, sending showers of sparks flying everywhere. Its base left the Earth and it expanded swiftly, while moving upward at a rate inconceivable. Simultaneously, from the four points of the compass, four similar pillars of fire were propelled to the zenith, where they were superimposed on one another in the form of a colossal pentagram, or five-pointed star, silhouetted against the torn sky and the amorphous shapes streaming across it. I cowered in abject terror!

"Come!" whispered Professor Sterns. "We have work to do!" He began copying strange designs, from the papers he held, onto the ancient stones of the shaft with a queer paste-like substance from a metal tube.

"Now!" he exclaimed, throwing the implement aside, "help me with this stone!"

We lifted the heavy Tibetan mystical stone, which had begun to glow with a curious russet light, to the lip of the shaft and cast it over. It fell inside with a crash, and immediately the shaft caved in amid cries of agony from below, which superseded the former chanting. The professor murmured a few indistinguishable words and made a curious sign with his right hand.

"Our job is finished," he said in a trembling voice. "We must escape the forest-fire." For the woods from whence the Flame-Being had risen were indeed burning fiercely.

We fled swiftly the way we had come, but not too swiftly for me to glance back and catch a glimpse of the fiery star vanquishing the beings from Outside, the hellish vision fading away, and the heavens returning to normal.

But the rest of that flight through the fear-haunted forest is to me even more nightmarish than what had preceded it, and I shall never again know peace of mind, even though the newspapers babble reassuringly about a volcanic disturbance in Maine and its strange effect on the skies. For the answer which Professor Arlin Sterns gave in a shuddering whisper to my question about the identity of our mysterious Guest is forever burned into my brain. As we plunged through the nighted woods, he gasped to me,

"It came to my door one night . . . It was black and as plastic as jelly . . . It sent a message into my mind telling me what I had to do tonight . . . telling me It would go with me . . . I got it to form into a piece about the shape of a man, and put those clothes on It to disguise It . . . It told me in my mind that It had come from the star

Betelgeuze, 200 light years away with Its Brothers to combat the Great Old Ones!"

And as we ran toward the car and the safety of civilization, there came back to me half-forgotten passages from the abhorred *Necronomicon* which caused me to tremble in a new ecstasy of fear and agony of remembrance, even though the Earth had been saved for a time. . . .

> *Ubbo-Sathla is that unforgotten source whence came the Great Old Ones Who dare oppose the Elder Gods being the Ones Who are of a black fluid shape. And Those Ones who came in the shape of Towers of Fire hurled the Old Ones into banishment . . . but they shall return; Those Who Wait shall be satisfied . . . And together shall take possession of Earth and all things that lived upon it and shall prepare to do battle with the Elder Gods . . .*

WHEN THE LORD OF THE GREAT ABYSS IS APPRIS'D OF THEIR RETURNING, HE SHALL COME WITH HIS BROTHERS AS TOWERS OF FIRE AND DISPERSE THE EVIL!

# The Keeper of Dark Point

## John Glasby

The strange disappearance of Stephen Delmore Ashton during the summer of 1936 evoked little interest either in the local or national press. Almost certainly this was due to his earlier unannounced, and often unexpected, trips to various parts of the world. Indeed, it may truthfully be said that since the age of eighteen he had resided at the ancestral home, Trewallen Manor, for less than a total of three years.

On this occasion, however, there was a solitary witness to the bizarre events which led up to his disappearance; one able to testify that Stephen Ashton will never be seen on Earth again.

While it is against my better judgment to make these facts widely known, and knowing there is little chance of such wildly monstrous and controversial evidence being accepted except by those few, like Ashton and myself, who understand something of the true nature of mankind's existence in the universe, it is vital that some warning should be given of that which lies just beyond the rim of our present knowledge.

Those in authority will doubtless maintain that while it is an undisputed fact that Ashton's family, on his maternal side, can trace their lineage back almost two thousand years in an unbroken line, the grotesque myths and legends surrounding them are nothing more than idle gossip and hearsay. The incredibly ancient book we found will be dismissed as a comparatively modern fake and the note inserted between the pages nothing more than the ramblings of an unsound mind.

Even the utter destruction of Dark Point Light, standing on its rocky promontory off the Cornish coast will be put down to the violence of that unprecedented storm shattering an already decaying structure which had lain untenanted and unmaintained for more than fifty years.

In the end I must rely upon those who can correlate the facts as I relate them and see that they point in a different, and far more terrible, direction from the more commonplace and rational theories.

When I first met Ashton, during my years at university, his passion for obscure folklore had immediately drawn me to him. His intense fascination with strange myth-cycles which pointed to some underlying race memory of a far-distant past parallelled my own. We would spend hours discussing the possibility of remote, pre-human civilizations stretching back to the very youth of this planet; of strange, alien ruins buried in remote places, built by unhuman hands long before the coming of mankind. Even after gaining our degrees and going our separate ways, we kept up a close correspondence. Whereas I remained in England earning my living as a writer of books on ancient and medieval history, he took himself off on numerous trips to weird and exotic places, searching at first-hand for the origin of these myths.

On no occasion did he announce the date of his return, and his unexpected appearance on my doorsteps that summer evening came as no little surprise. I had recently taken a small cottage on the outskirts of Riveton, a picturesque little village near the Yorkshire moors, requiring the peace and solitude to complete my volume on medieval witchcraft. Nevertheless, his arrival was welcome since it provided me with an excuse to cease my literary labours for a while.

I must admit, however, that his general appearance and demeanour shocked me more than a little. He had always been an inordinately tall individual, thin almost to the point of gauntness. But now he seemed thinner than I remembered him and the only part of his features which appeared really alive were his eyes, black and oddly piercing.

After letting him in, I showed him into the front parlour where he deliberately seated himself near the window where he could see clearly along the lane running through the village. Offering him a drink, I sat down at the table and waited for him to explain his visit, wondering how he had managed to find me since my last letter had been written from London.

Apologizing for his unheralded arrival, he continued, "I've come to ask a favour of you, Martin." He gestured towards the typewriter and papers on the table. "I can see you're in the middle of another of your books and you probably have a deadline to meet, but I need your help desperately."

"Go on," I said.

"There's a certain book I must find and once I lay my hands on it, I'll need your help in deciphering it."

"You seem quite certain you'll find it," I remarked. Knowing his predilection for visiting strange and distant places, I inwardly hoped he did not intend to drag me on some journey halfway across the world.

He did not reply for a few moments, staring down at his drink, and I noticed that his hands were trembling visibly. Watching him closely, I could scarcely believe this was the same person I had known at university. Then, he had always been so sure of himself, brimming with self-confidence. I also took note of the furtive way he kept glancing out of the window as if expecting to see someone—or something—lurking outside.

Finally, he fixed his piercing gaze on me and when he spoke there was a curious intensity in his voice which made me shiver.

"If it still exists, I know exactly where to find it. Unfortunately, these ancient writings are of such a nature I daren't show them to anyone else. Not only for fear of being ridiculed but because I believe the knowledge this book contains could be highly dangerous in the wrong hands."

"I see. But why come to me?"

"Because I understand you can read archaic English and I know you don't dismiss the old myths and legends out of hand like so many so-called scientists who're only prepared to believe what they can see and measure with their instruments. I need someone like yourself who isn't afraid to delve into such things."

"And where is this book supposed to be?" I asked, speaking a little more sharply than I had intended.

"I'm afraid I can't tell you that at the moment, except that it's in Cornwall."

Seeing my hesitation, he immediately launched into a rambling monologue of what had happened to him since our university days and it soon became abundantly clear his researches had taken a far different path from mine in his search for the truth behind the age-old stories that dated from the pre-dawn of mankind. His vague circumlocution touched upon highly controversial things of which I had no previous knowledge.

In low, hushed tones he spoke of certain ancient tomes which were reputed to have been in his family's possession for centuries, volumes which were kept securely hidden from the outside world. If such books ever existed and had come to the notice of the authorities centuries ago, there seemed little doubt his ancestors would have been burned at the stake as witches and warlocks.

It was evident he was in a highly emotional state and yet there was a note of utter sincerity in his manner which intrigued me to the point where I finally, albeit reluctantly, agreed to accompany him to Cornwall, offering to put him up for the night so that we might travel down early the next day.

During the long train journey, I learned more of Ashton's family history. Now that I was an accomplice in his investigations, he was more open and forthright although most of what he told me was fantastic in the extreme. It was only on his mother's side of the family, the Trewallens, that there were these vague hints of horror, spoken of in weird tales going back almost two thousand years. How he had succeeded in tracing his lineage back so far in time, he didn't divulge, yet it seemed strange that such a long record could exist unbroken. That his investigations had been extremely thorough, I could not doubt. His recent visit to America, he said, he had undertaken with the express purpose of seeking out old records concerning a branch of the family which had emigrated to New England in the seventeenth century where there were certain references to the witchcraft trials held in Old Salem and other towns along the eastern seaboard.

This, however, proved to be only a small, divergent stream of the main family line. The Trewallens had, in the main, settled in Cornwall in the face of the advancing Roman armies where they had remained until the deaths of his parents a few years previously.

I listened to this account with a growing sense of apprehension and disbelief for there was something in his words which filled me with a nameless foreboding so that, at times, I doubted his sanity. What strange and terrible events had shaped the destiny of his maternal forebears I could only guess at for it was clear that the hints he gave concealed something more sinister and frightening. I must admit there were moments during our journey when I wished I hadn't submitted to his urgent entreaties and had remained in the sane vales of Yorkshire.

It was still light when we arrived in Penzance where we found Ashton's car still parked outside the railway station where he had left it the previous day. The sun had set almost half an hour earlier but it was still sufficiently light for me to make out details of the surrounding countryside as we drove along narrow, twisting roads beside the rugged coast. After leaving the town I had expected the general aspect of the country to be similar to that of my more northern county. Yet, scanning the low, humped hills and wild moorland on the one side and the sheer drop of the cliffs on the other, I sensed a subtle difference.

Taken individually, the moorland, hills and ocean seemed normal enough. Yet it was the way in which the three combined in the fading colors of the sunset which disturbed me in some odd way. There seemed to be a curious disharmony about the amalgamation which grated on my nerves. The hills on the skyline crowded too closely together as if striving to conceal dark secrets from some far-distant past.

From what he had told me earlier, I had expected Ashton to live in some large, isolated manor, well away from any other human habitation. But just as it was growing dark, we drove through a small, picturesque village where he stopped the car outside a two-storey house at the end of a narrow lane leading off the main road. As I took my case from the back seat and followed my host along the garden path, I noticed that his furtive manner was now even more pronounced. In particular, his gaze kept flicking towards some point on the horizon which clearly evoked some queer restlessness in him. I was on the point of mentioning it but forbore to do so, some instinct warning me that this might affect him further. That he was afraid of something out there in the deepening twilight was obvious. Yet I could see nothing out of the ordinary to account for his odd behaviour.

Unlocking the door, he ushered me inside, closing the door quickly behind him and turning the key in the lock. Switching on the light in the front room, he motioned me to a chair and while he busied himself lighting a fire in the wide, stone hearth, I surveyed the room, noticing in particular the long bookshelf along one wall. Most of the titles I could make out were clearly related to Ashton's interests as a historian and antiquarian. Indeed, many of them reposed on my own shelves. But there were others which were either completely unknown to me or of whose existence I had heard only vague and frightening rumours.

Once the fire was going to his satisfaction, Ashton seated himself in the chair opposite me, his features peculiarly flushed but whether from the heat of the fire or from some inner excitement, it was impossible to tell.

"I see you're admiring my collection," he said. "Believe me, it's taken years and a lot of travelling and searching to acquire some of those volumes."

I got up and perused the books more closely, aware all the time of his intense gaze on my back, watching my every move. Here and there, I came across volumes which, if they were originals, were incredibly rare and ancient. Many were written in faded Latin or Greek, others in Arabic, on yellowed parchment so brittle I was afraid to turn the pages for fear they might disintegrate into dust beneath my fingers. Yet, oddly, I could find none written in archaic English.

When I pointed this out to my companion, he gave a quick, jerky nod. "As I said, the book in question isn't here."

"Then where is it?" I asked, returning to my chair.

Ashton made an odd motion with his left hand, then pointed towards the window. "It's out there, hidden where no one else can find it. Tomorrow, I'll take you there."

For a moment, sitting there, I experienced a sharp surge of anger. Clearly, he desperately needed my help but although he had told me much on the train, I had the feeling he was hiding far more and once again, I was beginning to regret I had acquiesced to his request to accompany him.

As he rose to his feet, I said abruptly, "Perhaps you'd better explain yourself, Stephen. So far, I've heard little more than odd rumours concerning your family history. None of which appear to have any bearing on the reason you asked me to come here. Indeed, much of what you've told me makes very little sense."

"Please don't misunderstand or misjudge me, Martin." The expression on his gaunt features was one I couldn't analyze. Fear, perhaps, or some strange inner excitement. He leaned forward, fingers gripping the back of his chair tightly. "I can assure you that my hesitation in acquainting you with all the facts is simply that there is so much to explain and I find it extremely difficult to put these matters into words which even you might understand."

With a sudden abruptness, he changed the subject. "We're both hungry. I'll prepare something to eat and then we can talk."

Refusing my offer of help, he busied himself in the kitchen and we ate our meal in a strained silence. Inwardly, I felt concerned about his mental condition and more than a little disturbed by the fact that no one knew I was in this house, hundreds of miles from Yorkshire.

Not until the table had been cleared did my host continue with his explanations. He still appeared tense and nervous but evidently he had regained some of his composure and had himself under tight control as he seated himself in front of the blazing fire.

"Much of what I'm going to tell you may seem like the ravings of a madman but I must assure you that everything is true. The spectral tales concerning my maternal ancestors are a matter of record although initially I put them down to exaggeration and the writings of superstitious men down the ages. Now, however, I'm quite certain they are nothing more or less than the literal truth."

"I'm quite prepared to accept that such records were made, especially during the Middle Ages," I told him. "And that those who wrote them believed them to be true. But it seems to me you're talking about something more than mere superstition."

"I am." He leaned forward, a vibrant intensity in his voice. He waved a hand towards the bookshelf. "I've gone far beyond these comparatively recent writings, back for more centuries and millennia than you can possibly imagine. We talk glibly of the first great civilizations of Egypt and Sumer as if there was nothing before them. Good God, Martin, this planet has been capable of sustaining intelligent life a thousand times longer than the period between now and the First Dynasty of Egypt. *Mankind isn't the first race to have inhabited the Earth—we're simply the latest in a long line!*"

"There's no proof of that whatsoever," I told him firmly.

"I believe there is. That's what I want to tell you so that you, too, can understand all I've discovered."

I listened to him for the next hour, immersed in a growing sense of disbelief. Yet in spite of my natural skepticism, and doubt as to his sanity, there was an odd conviction in his tone which held me entranced.

Much of his discourse was curiously disjointed and interspersed by long periods of contemplative silence as if he was unsure how to put his beliefs into words. At times, he seemed mortally afraid, while at others his mood was one of elated anticipation, like a man on the verge of some tremendous discovery.

Most of his narrative concerned periods of time so incredibly remote that my mind had difficulty in accepting them fully. He spoke in low, measured tones of ages before mankind's existence, of races which had populated the Earth long before the first Ice Age that had covered much of the northern hemisphere; of other beings which came to Earth from outer gulfs of space, leaving behind few tangible records of their presence.

There were, he averred solemnly, certain stone fragments which bore symbols having no counterpart among any languages now known, indecipherable remnants of aeon-old writings whose existence was known only to a few. Gradually, during the course of his seemingly irrational outpourings, he brought in the Trewallen family and its part in such cosmic matters. Throughout the ages, he maintained, certain sects, scattered around the world, continued the worship of the Old Gods, claiming these beings never died but lived on in unbroken slumber in out-of-the-way places until the time was right for them to rise again, sweeping away the newer gods that had replaced them with the emergence of mankind.

Almost whispering now, as if afraid of being overheard, Ashton spoke of how the Trewallen family had been the custodians of secret, arcane knowledge from pre-Celtic times. Shuddering visibly, he told of how they had been persecuted by the Druids in those far-off days, for even these people who carried out human sacrifices and the most hideous rites amid circles of standing stones older than memory had revolted against the secret ceremonies enacted in the name of gods more ancient and fearful than their own.

That these rites had continued, virtually to the present day, seemed clear from the hints which Ashton dropped. There had always been animosity against his family from the local populace and this had culminated, ten years earlier, in a shrieking mob from the village, roused by a small number of hot-headed individuals, advancing on the manor one November night and putting the ancient building to the torch. Both of his parents, together with three servants, had perished in the holocaust.

Throughout this extraordinary tale, my feeling grew that over the years Ashton had become obsessed with this monstrous superstition and that his mind was in grave danger of becoming unhinged. Certainly from what I had heard he seemed scarcely capable of rational thought. Something of my feelings must have shown in my face for he stopped abruptly and forced himself to sit back more calmly in his chair before continuing in a marked change of tone. "I'm afraid all of this must strike you as the ravings of a lunatic, Martin. And you must be wondering what I've brought you into. All I ask is that you bear with me until tomorrow. Then, I'm sure, you'll have all the proof you need that I'm as sane as you are."

After that he said no more on the subject for by now the hour had grown late and we were both tired by the long journey. Inwardly, I was glad when he showed me to my room and had retired to his own. Some instinct prompted me to lock my door before going across to the window, taking off my jacket and placing it across the back of the chair beside the bed.

It was a warm, sultry night and I opened the window slightly to let some air into the room. Outside, it was still not completely dark although it was past midnight. Capella lay low towards the north where a pale blue glow lit the horizon. The room was situated at the rear of the house, overlooking a wild stretch of moorland and in the distance I could just make out the ocean. Physically, I felt drained and exhausted, yet my mind was curiously alert, filled with the odd things which Ashton had revealed.

How much truth could be contained in those strange ramblings? That his family had been involved in certain queer rites down the centuries I could accept. The old pagan religion had maintained its insidious grip on this part of England long after the coming of Christianity, persisting down the years well into the Middle Ages.

But all that fantastic talk of pre-human civilizations, of Old Gods from outside the Earth still living on in remote and inaccessible places, waiting to rise again, communing with their adherents by means of dreams and age-old ceremonies. All of that was nothing more than the result of an over-active imagination. Yet why had the inhabitants of this area suddenly descended in a frenzied mob upon the old manor and deliberately set it ablaze, knowing that five people were inside with literally no hope of escape? I tried to recall any mention of it in the newspapers of that time but nothing came to mind. If it had actually happened as Ashton had described, either I had missed any reference to it—or the authorities here had hushed it up so that no news of the deed had reached beyond the confines of this tiny region.

I was on the point of turning away from the window when something caught and held my attention. Over to my right, a bright light flicked on and off, long and short flashes following each other in a rapid, and seemingly random, sequence. Puzzled, I stood rigid, trying to ascertain its origin and nature. My first impression was that someone was signalling across the moors. But I dismissed this almost at once when the realization came that the source of the light must have been at least four miles away for it clearly originated from somewhere beyond the rim of the cliffs where the land fell precipitously towards the sea.

Swiftly, however, logic and common sense asserted themselves. Possibly colored by what I had heard, my mind had insisted on seeing something sinister behind those flashes whereas there was, of course, a logical explanation. Out there, that stretch of coast was almost certainly marked by hidden shoals and rocks and what I was seeing was nothing more than the warning light sent out by a lighthouse, acting as a beacon for vessels in the vicinity.

At breakfast the next morning, I casually mentioned what I had seen. While Ashton affirmed that there was, indeed, an old lighthouse on a rocky promontory four miles distant, he insisted it had not been in operation for more years than he could remember. He argued that it could not have been a beam from the old lighthouse I had seen, if I had seen anything at all, and it must have been from some vessel passing along that stretch of coast. There was clearly no point in pursuing this subject any further in his present state of mind and when he suggested I accompany him to the ruins of the manor I readily agreed.

The weather was again warm and sunny as we left the house and struck off across the moors towards a dense copse of trees perhaps two miles away. There had once been a number of tracks across the moors but most were now overgrown with thick strands of briar which virtually obliterated them in places. By the time we reached the trees we were both perspiring freely and, looking about me, I saw that the wood was more dense and overpopulated than I had imagined from a distance. Enormous oaks grew so close together it seemed impossible that anyone could squeeze between them. As we paused to get our breath back, I noticed Ashton had turned and was surveying the ground behind us. He appeared oddly ill at ease and I glanced back along the path we had travelled to see what was troubling him. Certainly there was no one in sight on the moors and there were no places where anyone might conceal themselves. But then, sweeping my gaze along the horizon, I glimpsed an odd structure which could only have been the lighthouse. Its outlines were indistinct, partially obscured by a haze which lay over the sea. Yet even from that shadowy glimpse, I realized there was something peculiar about that sky-rearing shape. It rose, squat and ugly, from its rocky base, unlike the slender towers of most other similar structures I had seen, and the lamp room at the top was of a curiously bulbous configuration.

Ashton continued to stare at it as though mesmerized, totally oblivious of his surroundings for several moments. Then, with an effort, he pulled himself together and without a word led the way into the trees. Here, out of sight of the sun, for the grotesquely thick, gnarled branches shut out all view of the outside world, the brooding trunks crowded in on us from every side. Utter silence hung thick and heavy in the unmoving air and the thick layer of dead and decaying vegetation deadened the sound of our footsteps.

How Ashton managed to orientate himself and gauge his direction, I could not guess, for he thrust his way through the dense undergrowth without once deviating from his path. Then, suddenly, we came out into a wide clearing. Here, the ground was devoid of all vegetation while in the center stood the fire-blackened ruins of Trewallen Manor.

It was immediately obvious that the fire had done its work well. Gaunt stone walls rose desolately towards the heavens. Twisted, splintered beams hung lopsidedly within the interior where the piles of debris lay in mouldering heaps open to the sky. Glassless windows leered at us like hungry eyes watching our approach with a loathsome malevolence that sent a shiver through me in spite of the warmth of the day.

Ashton paused while still a little distance away and stared at the ruins with the same expression on his face as that which I had noticed on the outskirts of the wood.

Coming alongside him, I said softly, "Surely you don't expect to find anything still intact in there?"

For a few seconds it was as if he had not heard me, then he turned his head quickly in my direction. "I'll find it," he muttered thickly. "I must. Otherwise everything may be lost. Make no mistake about that."

Clutching me by the arm, he hustled me towards the ruins. A thick layer of grey dust and ash lay over everything so that we were forced to tread carefully. Broken and cracked slabs lay concealed beneath the ash and the twisted remnants of scorched wooden beams criss-crossed the floor. Even a cursory glance was sufficient to tell me that nothing could possibly have survived the inferno which had destroyed this place.

I made to point this out to my companion but he had moved away to a far corner of what had once been a large banqueting hall. There, the remains of a wide stairway thrust up towards the shell of the upper floors.

Ashton went down on one knee beside the unsupported stairs and peered intently at the stone floor, scraping away the ash and debris with his hands. I inched my way past the tattered shreds of once-rich tapestries which had once adorned the walls.

"It has to be here somewhere," Ashton muttered and I had the impression he was speaking more to reassure himself than to me. "I seem to remember—" He broke off abruptly as his questing fingers found what he was seeking. Beneath the stairs, flat against the floor, was a large iron ring which he grasped firmly in both hands. Straightening up, he pulled with all his strength. The heavy trapdoor lifted slowly and I bent forward to help him. The next second we were both reeling and gasping in the blast of noxious air that swept up from the gaping hole in the floor. With a sudden surge of frantic strength, Ashton hurled the door back on its hinges and staggered away from the opening, covering his mouth and nostrils with his hands.

After a few minutes we were both sufficiently recovered to peer down into the abyssal blackness using a powerful torch which Ashton had brought with him. Shining the beam downward, my companion illuminated the narrow steps which led into unknown depths beneath the ruins. If whatever he was seeking still existed, and he clearly expected to find it somewhere in the cellar, there was undeniably a possibility it had escaped the effects of the flames and smoke which had destroyed the rest of the manor. The thick stone floor would have afforded a great deal of protection, even from the tremendous heat.

Yet in spite of the importance he attached to finding this book, Ashton seemed oddly reluctant to descend those steps.

"What are you hoping to find in this book if it's down there?" I asked, wincing a little at the way my voice echoed eerily from the shattered walls.

"The key to all I've been searching for all these years," he replied in a hoarse whisper. "Ever since I can remember, I've been told of the duty laid on the Trewallens. I learned certain things from my mother and perhaps she foresaw there might come a time when the villagers would take things into their own hands for there was no doubt they both hated and feared us. She always said that if anything did happen, I was to search down here."

"Then we'd better go down and take a look."

Still hesitant, Ashton finally nodded and lowered himself gingerly into the aperture, directing the torchlight between his feet so that he might see where he was going. I stood quite still, watching his slow descent, the wavering beam sending his shadow dancing grotesquely over the ancient stone walls.

The steps led far deeper into the foundations than I had anticipated and it was a full five minutes before I heard his voice calling on me to follow. In the same instant, he directed the torchlight up the shaft in order to delineate the stone steps for me.

Cautiously, I eased my way over the edge and commenced feeling my way down the steps, steadying myself against the confining walls which gradually became more slippery and slimy under my fingers. By the time I reached the bottom, my hands were smeared with a ghastly green mold and there was a queer musty smell in my nostrils, a stench compounded of decay and certain chemical odours which I couldn't place.

I straightened up slowly, expecting my head to touch the ceiling but instead, I found we were standing in a lofty passage which stretched away in both directions and with no visible end either way.

My companion shone his torch around the dripping walls as we edged away from the steps, the light picking out details of the rough surface. At intervals, metal brackets had been affixed to the stone and in one we found the burnt remains of a rushlight, adding further evidence to the antiquity of the place for these lights had obviously been placed there to provide illumination of a sort in bygone ages. I had no means of knowing how old this building was but from what I saw in that vast cellar, I reckoned it must have dated back not less than four or five centuries. Indeed, I suspected the manor had been erected on an even earlier site and this subterrene passage had been carved from the solid rock more than two thousand years before.

At one point we encountered a narrow passage leading off to our right but although we probed it with the light of the torch we could see no end to it and it seemed too incredibly narrow for a normal passage. Whatever purpose it had once served, it was clearly not intended for men to walk along.

Some thirty yards further on, the tunnel widened abruptly, leading into a huge chamber whose furthermost limits were only just touched by the torchlight as Ashton swung the beam around.

Scattered across the stone floor were several crumbling wooden cases. Some had been bound with iron straps and for the most part these metal bindings were all that was left of them, the wood having totally disintegrated over the years.

Ashton gave these only a cursory examination. Evidently what he sought was not to be found there. Then I heard him utter a sharp exclamation as the wavering torchlight touched upon something against the far wall. The next moment, he was rushing forward, kicking aside the rotting boxes in his haste. I followed as quickly as I dared.

Jutting from the wall was a thick stone shelf about three feet in width and on it stood a large metal chest whose lid bore a number of hideous ideoglyphs moulded in low relief. Thrusting the torch at me, Ashton directed me to shine the light upon the chest, pulling hard on the lid only to find it securely locked.

"See if you can find anything with which to prise this open," he commanded tersely.

Casting about, I spied a short metal bar on the floor which had obviously been used at one time to open the long wooden cases. Seizing it from me, he thrust the end savagely under the lid, forcing it up with all his strength. There was a harsh rending screech of metal and the lid flew open with an explosive crack, slamming hard against the wall. Dropping the bar, Ashton thrust his hands inside and withdrew a voluminous tome which he held up to the light, his features oddly elated. He uttered a sudden cry that echoed through the chamber.

"Is that it?" I asked. My voice trembled slightly, not from the excitement of this discovery, but because in that same instant, a strange aura seemed to have pervaded the chamber. The silent walls seemed to ooze menace and I had the unshakable impression there had been a sound somewhere along the wide passage we had recently traversed; a sound which had come in answer to Ashton's sudden cry. The noise was extremely faint, it is true, yet it was one which sent a shiver of nameless dread through me and I felt an irresistible impulse to turn and flee from that subterrene chamber with its age-old secrets.

Ashton must have heard the sound too, for he lifted his head from his perusal of the tome and stared at me with an ashen face, his dark eyes glinting strangely in the torchlight.

I could only nod mutely in affirmation. Whether his interpretation of the noise was similar to mine, I could not say. To me, the impression I had was one of something huge and monstrous slithering across the stone floor; a dragging, nauseous sound which had faded swiftly into the distance.

In the utter silence of that cellar, it had seemed unnaturally sharp and alien. Had it come towards us, instead of receding into the distance, both of us would have been trapped with no way of escape. Standing there, staring wildly at each other, we were both frantically seeking some natural explanation, some logical explanation of that shocking echo, straining our ears for any repetition. Finally, Ashton laid a shaking hand on my arm and motioned towards the passage leading back to the outside world.

Clutching the ancient book under one arm, he hurried beside me as I used the torch to light our way back. The thought of being trapped in that underground tunnel impelled us to hurry in spite of the treacherous, slippery unevenness of the rocky floor. Not until we reached the nitre-covered steps leading up through the foundations of the manor did we pause. Here, where the tunnel continued in the opposite direction, I shone the torchlight along it, striving to pick out anything which might account for what we had heard, certain that whatever it had been, the originator of that sound had moved away in that direction.

In a low, shaky whisper, I asked, "Do you know where that tunnel leads?"

"Out under the moors, I suppose." Ashton's voice was pitched equally low. "But as to where it emerges, I've no idea. And I'm not inclined to find out." He cast a quick, apprehensive glance along the passage where the beam of the torch picked out nothing more substantial than shadows. "Let's get out of here. I've got what I came for."

One after the other, we clambered up the slimy steps, finally pulling ourselves through the exit, dropping the heavy trapdoor back into place.

Hastening from the blackened ruins, we thrust our way through the surrounding trees, back over the moorland track to the village.

In the bright noon sunlight streaming through the windows, we examined Ashton's find. It was impossible to put any date on the book although the condition of the yellowed pages pointed to great antiquity. The writing, in places faded almost into illegibility, was in a spidery script, undoubtedly old English as Ashton had intimated two days earlier.

But it was as my companion turned the brittle pages that something else fell onto the floor at our feet. Picking it up, Ashton turned it over in his hands before laying it flat on the table. It was something far more modern than the tome—an ordinary sheet of common paper, folded carelessly as if the message it bore had been hurriedly scribbled and thrust between the pages. Staring down over Ashton's shoulder, I read through it with a growing sense of perplexity and horror.

My Dearest Son,

If you ever read this letter, it will mean that both your father and myself no longer exist in this world. By now, you know a little of your dark heritage; that bondage which was forged countless centuries ago and has continued, unbroken, throughout the ages. Yet now the signs are ominous. Too many events are conspiring against us and those around us are mortally afraid of that which they cannot understand and I fear they now intend to bring about the end of the Trewallen line.

Whatever happens, I urge you to heed my instructions and follow them to the letter. Believe me when I say it was no wish of mine to bring this doom upon your father and yourself. Yet my own fate is more terrible still and my final peace rests in your hands alone. The Old Ones cannot be denied. They demand their sacrifices in return for that which we receive. We, the Keepers of Dark Point Light, are among the foremost of their minions on Earth while They sleep through the eternal cycles until the time of Their coming again.

Unless you wish my fate to fall upon you, heed my words well. The book gives you the two formulae; that for the zenith which is the opener of the way for Those outside—and the other for the nadir. It is the second you must use but only at midnight when Capella lies directly beneath the star of the boreal pole. Above all, fear not that which lies beneath the manor.

Your loving mother.

What were we to make of that? The letter seemed full of vague portents and hints of doom and disaster and yet the instructions given made little, if any, sense. The reference to the Old Ones evidently alluded to those ancient beings mentioned by Ashton the previous day. But what were we to take from that final, enigmatic sentence? To what was she referring when she intimated that her son had no need to fear what lay beneath the manor?

During the long afternoon, Ashton and I pondered long over the puzzling contents of the letter. Certain points seemed clear and unambiguous. Dark Point Light clearly referred to that ancient lighthouse out on the distant promontory and Ashton readily agreed that the Old Ones were those aeon-old gods whose worship dated back far beyond Christianity or any other religion and which was still carried on to this day in various parts of the world.

As he spoke, he grew more and more agitated and behind all that he said was the urgency for me to help him by translating the archaic English in the book. This, he insisted, was essential for otherwise the consequences could be utterly catastrophic. There was no doubt that the contents of that letter had shocked and disturbed him and from the manner in which he continually paced the floor and glanced through the window, I wondered if he suspected the inhabitants of the village were coming to burn down the house as they had the manor.

As his talk grew progressively wilder and more fantastic, I realized that if I was to be of any help to him, I needed answers to the riot of questions which plagued me. By degrees, I succeeded in calming him down, forcing him to take his time in answering me.

It was not easy to piece together a complete and coherent picture since Ashton kept jumping from one subject, or from one period of history, to another. Yet from what he told me, I gathered that it was his firm belief that among those secret cults which existed in many countries to continue the worship of the Old Ones, the Trewallens were among the oldest. They knew many of the secrets which had been handed down from time immemorial, knew the locations of hidden places that lay close to those outside realms where only madness and terror lurked.

Ashton accepted as a matter of faith that Dark Point Light was one of these locations, believing it possibly from tales handed down from generation to generation by his forebears. Though when, and in what manner, the members of his maternal family became Keepers of the tower, he did not know. Certainly, he was puzzled by his mother's reference to something under the manor and could only surmise that this was the dread knowledge contained in the ancient tome which now reposed on the table in front of us.

Although we had not eaten since breakfast, neither of us had any thought for food. Ashton's initial agitation had now become a mood of desperate urgency. Checking his almanac, we determined that, as near as we could estimate, Capella would lie directly beneath Polaris at midnight three days hence. Now, the one thought uppermost in his mind was to decipher as much as possible of the archaic English and, in particular, to determine the two formulae mentioned in his mother's letter.

The book was voluminous and the script was, in many places, scarcely legible as we pored over it in the growing darkness. Although it was the normal script of an early Saxon age and one which I had encountered on several previous occasions, there was something in those archaic symbols which made me shudder inwardly as I painfully transcribed them, reading aloud while Ashton wrote down every word.

From the shape of the pointed characters, I dated the book to around the third or fourth century A.D., at a time when any Christian influence was extremely tenuous and more ancient beliefs still seethed and simmered strongly beneath a thin veneer of civilization.

The story which unfolded from our reading of the tome confirmed many of the things which Ashton had spoken of. But whereas he had merely scratched the surface of the lurking horror which had infested this tiny region of Cornwall, this account embellished it with hideous detail, revealing seemingly endless vistas of alien time and space that our minds refused to accept completely.

There were references to long aeons of time before the first cities of men were raised from the clay; of monstrous beings that stalked the black, matterless spaces between the stars; of cataclysmic battles which resulted in certain of the Old Ones being imprisoned on young, newly-formed planets of which Earth was but one. Moreover, the unknown author claimed such imprisonment did not imply death. Even with the passing of millions of years, during which many races inhabited the Earth, only one of which was human, they remained in a sorcerous slumber in hidden and inaccessible places, awaiting the time when they might rise again.

Furthermore, in addition to these beings, there was mention of others, nameless entities which dwelt outside of normal space-time continua but which could enter the known universe through a number of secret portals provided the correct incantations and rituals were performed.

Towards the end of the book, there was an abrupt change in the writing where some unknown, and more modern, hand had penned what appeared to be an addendum. While the individual letters were a more recent form of English, the words themselves were in the style of a period of at least two hundred years earlier. These few pages detailed the erection of Dark Point Light which had evidently replaced a much older stone tower on the same site. Whether the structure was ever intended as a conventional lighthouse was unclear although from the narrative we were reluctantly forced to the conclusion that its primary purpose was something far more alien and sinister. There were peculiar alignments drawn into its design and location which suggested that the building stood at the focal point of one of the portals mentioned in the earlier text. For centuries, it seemed, the Trewallens had been guardians of the ancient knowledge and, in more modern times, Keepers of Dark Point Light. Just what that entailed was far from clear for the writer assumed that any reader of the manuscript would be familiar with the details of this post.

By the time we had finished, it was almost dawn. We had worked on the tome throughout the entire night, unaware of the passage of time, totally enmeshed in a growing web of horror and bafflement. We had read of things almost beyond human belief, of secret pacts between the Trewallens and both the Old Ones and those other beings who dwelt outside the time and space of the normal universe. Small wonder that the frightened inhabitants of the village had stormed the manor that November night ten years before and burned everything and everyone in it.

How it had survived the Middle Ages when hatred against witches and warlocks was at its height, I could not imagine. Yet there still remained one mystery. Even though we had gone through the transcription meticulously, we had found no reference to the two formulae mentioned in that hastily scrawled letter. Certainly there were long passages so faded or stained as to be virtually unreadable, yet this did not appear to be the reason for this strange omission. Had Ashton's mother been mistaken? Somehow, we doubted that. She had given sufficient detail to insinuate their importance in averting some terrible catastrophe and it was unlikely she would have stressed where they were to be found if she had not been absolutely certain.

Yet what other explanation was there? At my companion's urgent insistence, I went through the volume slowly once more, page by page, in the event that the one in question had been deliberately removed.

Then, almost halfway through the volume, I came across a page which seemed slightly thicker than the others. Running my finger carefully along the edge I found, as I was beginning to suspect, that two pages had been stuck together. Separating them required extreme care owing to the general brittleness of the parchment and it was the work of several minutes to gently prise the two sheets apart with the edge of a sharp knife.

I think we were both expecting to find what was written there to be in the same hand and archaic English as the rest of the main text. In this, we were frustratingly disappointed. The symbols on each of these pages bore no resemblance to English. The odd cursive script was unknown to me. The minuscules were boldly delineated, clearly formed, as if the writer intended there should be absolutely no dubiety as to the symbols he had written. Yet, in spite of the alienness of the characters, Ashton declared shudderingly that there was something familiar about them, something he had seen before.

Clearly, although time was now desperately short, there was little to be gained by attempting to solve these cryptic formulae just then. We were both at the point of utter exhaustion and knew that to go on without rest would inevitably lead to fatal errors. It now being after eight-thirty, Ashton made something to eat and we both retired.

When I woke, some six hours later, it was to find Ashton already up, searching diligently through the volumes on his bookshelves. He glanced up quickly as I entered. There were dark circles under his eyes and it was evident he had had very little sleep. There was now only one thing driving him on, pushing him relentlessly to the utmost limits of his physical and mental resources.

"It has to be here somewhere," he said hoarsely, indicating the rows of books with a sweep of his arm. "It must be. I'm sure I'm not mistaken."

"Then let's go at this problem logically and methodically," I told him. "We still have two days left to find the answer."

We were able to disregard most of the volumes since those in his collection written in Latin, Arabic and Greek were clearly of no concern. Then, late that morning, my companion uttered a sharp exclamation and, glancing up from my own searching, I saw he had a slim, tattered volume in his hands and was riffling through it in a frenzy of excitement, flicking the pages in rapid succession. There was a strange expression on his drawn features as he leaned across the table to compare the writing with that of the volume we had brought from the cellar beneath the manor.

Glancing over his shoulder I saw there was, indeed, a very close resemblance between the two sets of characters.

"This is it," he declared elatedly. "I knew I'd seen that script before."

I forbore to inquire the title of the book. From its condition, I knew it to be one of the oldest in his collection.

"Can you translate these formulae into some kind of phonetic rendering?" I asked tensely.

Ashton hesitated, then nodded. "I think so. It won't be easy. Evidently they're similar to the Naacal language but there appear to be subtle differences and, whatever happens, I have to make absolutely sure. If I'm to carry out my mother's instructions, everything has to be exact. The smallest error and—" He broke off in mid-sentence but I could guess at the meaning behind his words.

Leaving him to the task of deciphering the strange formulae, I made myself something to eat, then asked if I might take the car since there seemed little I could do to help him at the moment. After only a momentary hesitation, he agreed and handed me the keys.

Outside, the air was still warm and the mid-afternoon was bright and sunny. I had taken the precaution of bringing a map of the local area with me and before switching on the ignition, I studied it carefully, having already made up my mind where I wanted to go. I had not mentioned my intended destination to Ashton for fear that he might refuse the car and do his utmost to dissuade me.

Putting the car into gear, I drove slowly out of the village and took the narrow track which the map indicated led towards the coast, terminating at a point only a short distance north of the promontory on which Dark Point Light stood. There were few people about although those I passed gave me strange looks.

The track I was following was undeveloped and full of potholes, evidently seldom used. Around me, the terrain grew perceptibly wilder as I neared the cliffs, the richer vegetation giving way to sparse tufts of grass and stunted bushes. Topping a low rise, I made out the curiously shaped lighthouse clearly for the first time and even that initial glimpse was enough to tell me that I had not been mistaken the previous day when I had noted its odd silhouette. Yet, on that occasion, distance and the haze had obscured most of the abnormalities associated with its shape. In addition to the peculiar nature of the lamproom at the top, I noticed several bizarre bulbous projections around the sides which seemed to serve no ordinary purpose that I could determine. All in all, it held an air of indefinable mystery that grew more pronounced as I manoeuvered the car down a steep, rocky incline towards the beach.

Presently I was forced to stop the car where the track petered out completely. In front of me was bare shingle, still wet from the now receding tide. The long, rocky tongue which thrust out from the shore stood out several feet above the water although judging by the long strands of seaweed which festooned its length, I reckoned it would lie completely submerged at high tide.

Even as I walked cautiously towards it, picking my way carefully over the slippery rocks, I could see that the stone tower was in a state of great decrepitude. Parts of the upper structure had decayed over the years and fallen. Desolation and decay hung over it like a dark cloud in stark contrast to those other similar buildings I had sometimes seen around the English coast. At the top, the brilliant sunlight glinted off the glass which, unlike the stonework, appeared to be intact. I had expected to see a massive door on the side facing the land but the curved stone wall continued in an unbroken line as far as I could see.

Not until I had approached to within a few yards of the base did I see there was a narrow raised platform which clearly ran around the entire circumference with a short flight of steps leading up to it. There had once been a metal rail there but it had long since vanished, whether by the action of the pounding waves or vandalism it was impossible to tell. Now only a few rusted iron stumps projected from the stonework.

Clambering up the steps, I worked my way around the tower before encountering a large, iron-banded door on the far side looking out over the ocean. In spite of the sinister aura which surrounded the tower and the odd tales I had heard concerning it, I pushed open the door on its creaking hinges and peered inside. Piles of debris and fallen blocks of stone met my gaze in the dimness. Stepping inside, I examined the immediate area minutely, aware of the curious atmosphere which pervaded the place. It was not simply the musty smell which comes of long years of emptiness and neglect although there was certainly a surfeit of greyish dust in places and a forest of cobwebs around the walls. Rather it was an odd electric tension which tingled unpleasantly along my nerves as if every inch of the building held an intense electrostatic charge.

There was also a further odd fact which I noticed at once. The floor and lower steps were covered with the same species of seaweed I had seen on the promontory outside. Yet how those strands had got there was beyond me, for they were still damp. The massive door looked capable of withstanding the incessant pounding of the ocean and there was no other means of ingress.

Bracing myself mentally, I crossed the smooth floor, edging around the fallen blocks, and approached the stairs. Curiously, there was no furniture, nor any sign there had ever been any as I would have expected if the lighthouse had been used in the past. Yet there were odd markings on the floor but in the dim light it was almost impossible to make them out. Only when I had climbed a dozen stairs and looked down from that height was I able to discern anything of the overall design with any clarity.

Even then, I found it difficult to take it in for there were curiously curved lines in faded red which intersected and crossed at abnormal angles and at various points around the design were other geometrical symbols in black. While my mind persisted in suggesting significant mathematical relationships in these cryptograms, I also noticed that in several places they had been almost completely obliterated. Not, I felt certain, by some natural ageing process but by some deliberate effacement.

The ascent to the top of the tower took me several minutes for the stairs wound spirally around the inner circumference and, in one or two places, were so broken I feared it might prove impossible to attain the top. As I ascended, I became aware of a further strange thing. While the bottommost steps and much of the floor were literally covered with debris and seaweed, the rest of the way was clear as if someone, in the very recent past, had swept the stairs completely free of dust and dirt.

Finally, I came to a stout wooden door which opened creakingly at my touch and stepping through I stared about me in bewildered amazement. The sunlight shone fiercely through the glass, highlighting every detail in the room. In the center was the lamp, set on its axis, and beside it stood a number of levers whose purpose I could not, at first, determine for they appeared to be connected internally with the lamp mechanism.

It was not until I glanced up at the curved dome over my head that a glimmer of understanding came. I had expected the roof to be of solid metal. Instead, there were two iron shutters which were clearly capable of being opened for they rested on a set of well-oiled runners. Just why they took my attention I could not tell but something about them evoked a sudden thought in my mind. The implications of this strange set-up were now clear. Experimentally, I pulled hard on the nearest lever. For several seconds, nothing happened although the lever moved easily under my hand. Then, with a noiseless movement, the twin shutters slid aside revealing a section of sky directly above the lamp. I had thought the aperture would lie open to the atmosphere but instead, I saw the shutters had concealed a clear crystal lens, perhaps three feet in diameter. As I watched, a cloud drifted slowly across the scene, its outlines oddly magnified and distorted by the lens.

What engineer had constructed this mechanism I could not even guess. It seemed scarcely credible that it had been installed when this tower had been erected for it was immediately apparent that exceptionally specialized knowledge and equipment would have been necessary for its manufacture and installation. Yet what was its purpose? To send a highly focussed beam of light directly into the heavens? That seemed absurd, yet on looking closer at the internal mechanism of the lamp, I saw that it could be aligned to do exactly this, possibly by manipulation of the other, smaller levers.

What in God's name was this place? Ashton had claimed it had been abandoned for many years and yet everything pointed to it having been used during recent times. The smooth sheen of oil on the shutter bearings; the undoubted intricacy of the lamp mechanism; the cleanliness of the upper stairs and the incredible mechanical engineering which had gone into its design and construction, all suggested some very modern origin. If it was so closely associated with the hated Trewallens, I felt sure none of the villagers would venture out here and, apart from my companion, the last of his line had perished in flames ten years before.

The longer I stood there, staring around me, the more my imagination worked until I began to fancy strange things. I seemed to sense some alien, formless presence close by, watching me with a fearsome intentness. I felt entwined with something—something which was not of this world—but which encircled me with an alien malevolence.

Swiftly, almost of its own volition, my hand moved and thrust the lever back into its former position and it was as the shutters slid shut over my head that I heard a soft, muffled sound from far below me. The thought that something was making its way stealthily up the stairs, trapping me in that curious lamproom, held me petrified. Then, all at once, the spell was broken. Thrusting my way through the door, I plunged down the stone stairs, slipping and sliding precariously where they had all but crumbled away. Somehow, I reached the bottom, my breath harsh and raw in my throat. The furtive, slithering sound which had so panicked me was still audible. But it was fainter now and with a further shock of superstitious horror I realized it came from still further below me, from beneath the foundations of the tower, deep within the solid rock.

Somehow, I managed to push myself through the heavy door, running headlong over the slippery rocks towards the waiting car. Reversing it quickly, heedless of spinning the wheels into the muddy shingle, I drove as rapidly as I dared back along the narrow track towards the comparative safety of the village.

By now, my chaotic thoughts had shaped themselves into some kind of order. Approaching the village, I had been turning over in my mind what to tell Ashton of my visit to Dark Point Light. By the time I drew up outside the house I had already reached the decision, rightly or wrongly, to say nothing of it. After all, what had really happened? I had seen nothing which did not admit to a reasonable explanation. I had certainly heard that oddly frightening sound far below the rocks. Yet it had been almost identical to that which we had both heard in the cellar of the manor and could, quite readily, be attributed to the ingress of the sea along subterranean tunnels.

As for the odd mechanism in the lamproom, there had been nothing supernatural about it. Certainly it had appeared extraordinarily complex. Yet it was a well-established fact that the Victorians had produced similar machinery, such as the camera obscura, in their scientific heyday.

I discovered Ashton in a highly elated mood, having almost completed his phonetic rendering of the twin formulae. Much of his former apprehension seemed to have evaporated although I noticed he still glanced occasionally through the window as if to assure himself he was not being kept under surveillance.

"I must confess I thought it might be beyond me," he admitted excitedly, waving the piece of paper in his hand. "Until I discovered these characters are simply a variant of Naacal which was used by certain cults of antiquity."

"And you're absolutely certain you have everything right?"

"I'll have to check it again, of course. But now it's simply a matter of ascertaining the exact pronunciation. Anyway, I'm confident I'll be able to use the correct formula when the time comes."

With that, I had to be content. But during the next two days, I watched him intently, troubled a little by his attitude and general appearance. His face appeared more drawn than before and there was a haunted, frightened look in his eyes which suggested he knew more than he was telling me of what he had to do in order to carry out his dead mother's implicit instructions.

Then, shortly before eleven o' clock on the second night we made our final arrangements. In addition to the phonetic rendering of the Nadir Formula, Ashton carried a powerful torch and, against my better judgement, a revolver. Not knowing what to expect, I took along a pair of binoculars.

Even at that hour, the sky was not fully dark. To the north was a pale blue glow where Capella gleamed yellowly above the horizon, a spectral beacon slightly to the west of north.

Starting the car, Ashton drove slowly out of the village, the headlight beams rising and falling as we bumped over the numerous potholes. Neither of us spoke during the journey for there was something about the utter stillness of the countryside which militated against conversation.

About half a mile from the coast, my companion stopped the car and switched off the lights. Even in the darkness, it was possible to make out the spectral tower of Dark Point Light with an amazing clarity but several seconds passed before I recognized the reason. The ocean that frothed around the lighthouse possessed a peculiar luminescence; a greenish, phosphorescent glow which highlighted the watery background. I pointed this out to Ashton but he merely put it down to the presence of certain algae which he maintained were known to produce this effect.

Whether he believed this or not, there was no way of telling but I had the impression he had given this explanation simply to allay my natural fears.

Taking my arm, he gestured towards the lighthouse, then swung his gaze back to where Capella shone unwinkingly towards the north.

"Come," he said curtly. "There's very little time left. I want to take a look inside that lighthouse before I use the formula."

"Is that wise?" I asked, recalling what I had seen on my previous visit.

"There's something I have to know." His tone was now one of oddly heightened fascination. "If you're afraid, you can remain here in the car."

I shook my head, got out, and fell into step beside him. The narrow track down to the beach seemed longer than I remembered but finally we stood on the long tongue of rock which jutted out into the sea. This time, the tide was coming in and near the tower the water was already lapping over the rocks. Splashing ankle-deep through the foam we worked our way cautiously to the great door on the seaward side where Ashton produced his torch before thrusting it open and going inside.

Somehow, recalling the sound I had heard on the previous occasion, I half expected to find something changed but at first sight I could see nothing to indicate that anyone had been there since my exploratory search.

I thought my companion intended to mount the stairs but instead, he walked forward towards the middle of the room, sweeping the torchlight across the floor, ignoring the strands of seaweed which littered the place. It was then I saw something which sent a shudder of loathsome horror through me. Previously, the floor had been virtually covered by that thick layer of greyish-white dust. Now, in the torchlight, I saw that this had been swept clear in a long, wide swathe from a point near the center of the weird, cabalistic design daubed on the floor!

And in the very center was revealed a large trapdoor with an iron ring which had earlier been concealed. Someone—or something—had entered the tower from below since my departure and my whirling mind instantly connected it with that frightening slithering, bumping sound I had faintly heard beneath the foundations.

Shaken by what I saw and its gruesome implications, I started forward as Ashton bent towards the iron ring, hooking his fingers around it. Before I could stop him, however, he had heaved the trapdoor up and was shining the torchlight directly downward into the yawning aperture. A mephitic stench rose from the gaping hole and we both reeled back, hands over our mouths and nostrils.

I had expected to see a flight of steps leading down into the Stygian blackness but the light picked out smooth stone walls that went straight down as far as the beam could reach. Unwilling to imagine how anything could possibly have climbed that shaft without visible hand or footholds, I pulled Ashton away.

We were both trembling uncontrollably now for, in spite of the unscalable nature of that tunnel, it was abundantly clear that something had come up from those unplumbed depths and I saw, on my companion's ashen face, that he had guessed the same thing as I. This opening had another exit, one which we had seen for ourselves, deep beneath the fire-blackened ruins of Trewallen Manor!

What monstrous creature inhabited that four-mile-long tunnel beneath the moors which connected these two places, I had no wish to know. Yet in that instant, there came a flash of memory. Did that enigmatic sentence in Ashton's mother's letter refer to something alive which haunted those night-ridden depths? And if that was what it signified, why had she maintained he had no cause to fear it?

For a moment I think we both felt an uncontrollable urge to flee that eldrich tower with its strange, hidden secrets. Indeed, I would have done so had not Ashton seized my arm, pointing towards the stairs. Moving ahead of me, he continually flashed his light around our feet as we climbed, helping me over the places where the stairs had crumbled, until we eventually reached the door at the top. Whether my companion had any prior knowledge of what lay beyond, I could not tell, nor did I ask him for scarcely had we paused before the door than a sound reached us from just beyond that entrance into the lamproom.

It was a diabolical sound; a low keening moan that undulated up and down a saw-edged scale. To call it a wail like that of a soul in torment would be to ignore the quintessence of loathsome nauseousness it possessed. Yet, faint as it was, it almost masked the other sound which accompanied it; a squelching, sucking noise, as if something huge and ponderous was moving around inside the room.

Whatever else Ashton may have lacked, it was certainly not courage. Perhaps he believed that, armed with the knowledge of the Nadir Formula, he was protected against anything he might encounter. Whatever the reason, he reached out and twisted the handle of the door, throwing all of his weight against it as it refused to budge. I tried to hold him back, for I sensed, with some strange instinct, that whatever lay behind the door was something not of this Earth. For an instant, the door gave slightly under his frenzied push and a horrible fishy odour swept out. Only for a second did the torchlight show something scaly and of a hideous green color filling the entire aperture.

Then Ashton staggered back, thrusting at me to get away. Somehow, we made it safely down the treacherous steps to the bottom. Here, Ashton halted and even though I urged him to leave that terror-haunted tower, he shook his head in adamant refusal.

"You must go—quickly," he commanded harshly. "It's almost midnight and the Nadir Formula must be recited at the focal point if this portal is to be destroyed for ever. Have no worry on my account. Now go!"

In the face of his perverse obduracy, there was no other course open to me. Leaving him alone in that lower chamber, I splashed through the knee-high tide, slipping and sliding on the treacherous rocks until I reached the top of the cliffs where I stopped, staring back at the lighthouse.

Acting on a sudden impulse, I lifted the powerful binoculars to my eyes and swiftly focussed them on the top of the tower. Through the glass which surrounded the lamproom, I could make out very little. A great, shapeless mass obscured much of the interior but the outlines continually blurred and wavered so that no definite shape emerged before my eyes.

Then, even across that distance, I heard Ashton's voice and knew he was beginning the chant, mouthing archaic syllables which were not meant for human speech. The words boomed and echoed from within the lighthouse as if the walls were an amplifier, reaching out across the shingle, evoking strange antiphonal reverberations that shivered in the still air.

Even as the first dread syllables rang out, my eyes were suddenly seared by a brilliant light which sprang into being at the top of the tower. In that split second, I saw everything. Not only the nature of that thing which lurked inside that unholy room but the hideous truth behind the long, pagan centuries during which the Trewallens had been Keepers of Dark Point Light, the meaning behind that cryptic letter, and the identity of that burrower beneath the moors.

A chill wind sprang up almost in the same instant from the sea, swiftly increasing in ferocity, whipping at my coat. With an effort, I tore my gaze from the tower as something prompted me to look upward. There, near the zenith, directly above Dark Point Light, was a swirling of blackness, obscuring the stars.

At the same time, the air trembled with a vibration which added to the berserk fury of the wind. The great spreading blur of midnight blackness swooped down from the stars and the next moment a vicious lightning stroke speared downward, striking the bulbous lamproom atop the tower.

Across the intervening distance I heard Ashton's voice uttering the final word of the incantation, and scarcely had the booming echoes died away than a beam of bluish light soared upward from the top of the tower toward the inky, formless nebulosity. I had a fragmentary glimpse of something else which shot skyward, trapped within that cyanic glow; two dark shapes that writhed and twisted and spiralled towards infinite distances. The impression which seared into my brain in that horror-filled moment was of a gigantic octopoid body with tentacle-like appendages that threshed helplessly in the few seconds before it vanished utterly, followed by a more human form which I knew to be Stephen Delmore Ashton.

In the ensuing darkness and silence I was only just aware that the howling gale had died away completely. When I could see clearly again, it was to find that the lightning bolt had riven the rearing tower in twain and all that remained of it was a pile of tumbled, shattered stone at the end of the promontory, the incoming tide washing over it.

By his invocation, his reciting of the Nadir Formula, Ashton had indeed closed that aeon-old portal into those outer realms beyond normal space and time. Yet the crowning horror of that night was not the fact that he had been somehow drawn into it, vanishing utterly from the Earth—but what I had witnessed through the binoculars during that brief moment when the lamp in the tower had abruptly illuminated that huge room with its bizarre machinery designed, as I now knew, for sending that beam *upward* towards unguessable regions beyond all human imagination.

The monstrous shape of the last Keeper of Dark Point Light, its grotesque bulk filling the room with a horrid plasticity. Everything about that frightful outline had been oddly indistinct with but one exception. The head perched distortedly on that bloated body had been that of a woman *and I knew, with a loathsome certainty, it had been that of Ashton's mother!*

# The Black Mirror

## John Glasby

The plain fact that Philip Ashmore Smith was somehow burned alive is disputed by no one, particularly by those in authority who investigated his death at first hand. Yet there are a number of disturbing features which prompt others to see more deeply into the strange circumstances surrounding his demise and suggest more terrible connotations. They point significantly to certain unexplained counter-evidence such as the unscorched carpet on which his charred remains were found; the complete absence of any fire in the room or traces of flammable material on the burnt clothing, and that no one witnessed any flames or smoke issuing from the open window beneath which his body lay.

The curious entries in his diary have been taken as the jottings of an over-imaginative mind for it was well known in the small community that the victim was given to the study of occult and bizarre lore, often frequenting old bookshops and other premises in Exeter in search of fabulous and ancient volumes and seeking out rare items which, if genuine, were of equal antiquity.

It was one of these items, a strangely ornamented black mirror, which was removed from Smith's room without the prior knowledge or permission of the police and thrown down one of the old mine shafts five miles from Torpoint where it was doubtless smashed into countless fragments. The perpetrator of this deed, Doctor Alexander Morton, later maintained that his act of vandalism had saved mankind from something far more evil than could ever be conceived.

Certainly the doctor was the only person to have had more than a passing acquaintance with Smith and had visited the old farmhouse on a few occasions although it was noticed that, towards the end, his visits grew more and more infrequent as if there was something there of which he felt mortally afraid. Although he never confided in anyone concerning what transpired at the house, it became progressively clear to those who knew him that something had touched him palpably, frightening him more than he would ever admit.

Whether Smith's death was due to spontaneous combustion as the police doctor once tentatively suggested in private, or to something which came from ultramundane realms as a number of scholars insist, must be left for the reader to decide, for the only tangible evidence left by Smith is his diary and all that can be done is to attempt to draw together the dark strands of this disjointed account and trace the mysterious chain of events to some conclusion.

Philip Smith had clearly been interested in ancient myths and legends from an early age for he already possessed a vast store of arcane knowledge by the time he came to Torpoint in the early autumn of 1937. Although still only in his mid-twenties he was in possession of independent means and had travelled widely to various parts of the world although it must be admitted that, in keeping with his outlandish researches, these excursions were invariably to the more out-of-the-way places, untouched by ordinary tourists. He had apparently spent several months in a strange stone monastery situated on a high plateau in central Tibet where he had been instructed in the secrets of a rare drug distilled from the flowers of the purple poppy grown only in that region. Travelling south into India, he had sought out a strange Hindoo who, according to Smith's diary, told him odd tales of other realms, exterior to our own universe of space-time, and how such realms may touch, or even overlap, at certain points. Here, he also learned the truth behind the legends of various ancient cults whose members worshipped the Old Ones, mentioned by the American writer Lovecraft, with whom Smith had had some correspondence several years earlier.

On leaving India, in the spring of 1937, Smith had stopped off in Transylvania where he had journeyed deep into the mountains to the ruins of an ancient castle in whose deepest crypts he had discovered a number of mouldering tomes reputedly written in a language never previously deciphered. According to local legends whispered around blazing fires in the dead of winter, these inscriptions had been faithfully copied centuries earlier, shortly after the Romans had deserted the area in A.D. 271, from chiselled characters found in a tunnel deep within the Transylvanian Alps.

Immediately on his return to England, Smith had purchased an old farmhouse on the outskirts of Torpoint which had lain untenanted and abandoned for almost fifty years. His arrival there aroused much curiosity and eventually became the source of several queer rumours, mainly concerning the contents of four large packing cases which accompanied him.

Smith's attempts to get any of the villagers to help him clean the place and carry out essential repairs proving futile, he engaged three men from Exeter to perform the work. Situated as it was more than a mile from Torpoint, the farmhouse stood in an isolated region surrounded by thick woodland with only a narrow dirt track leading up to it from the road. It was thus well concealed from travellers to and from the village and for the first few days little attention was paid to this newcomer. It was not until the workmen began talking in the village inn that the rumours began to escalate and take on a more sinister and puzzling aspect.

While the men confessed to seeing nothing really frightening at the old house, they maintained that certain of the books which Smith had collected were odd in the extreme. One of the workmen, William Sheridan, who possessed some slight scientific leanings, spoke with Doctor Morton, the village practitioner, describing some of these volumes which apparently covered a wide range of cabalistic and alchemical lore dating back over many centuries.

Also mentioned during these discussions was the fact that Smith had set aside a small outbuilding a little way from the house as an astronomical observatory, carefully siting a large telescope which he was positioning according to certain specific alignments so that he could view a particular area of the southern sky.

This news prompted the doctor to pay a call on Smith on the pretext of introducing himself and, although he was received cordially enough, it was apparent from Smith's attitude that he desired absolute solitude and would not welcome the attentions of his neighbours. It was during this visit that the doctor casually mentioned his own passing interest in astronomy and, on being shown the observatory, expressed his admiration of the optical instrument which was almost completely assembled.

Although obviously an amateur, Morton saw at once that Smith had spent a great deal of money converting the building and purchasing the instrument. Even though only a novice in this branch of science, Morton was struck by the peculiar aspect of the observatory. As Sheridan had claimed, the layout was such that, while it would prove extremely difficult for Smith to observe the heavens towards the zenith and the north, the telescope had an excellent and unhindered coverage of the heavens low down along the southern horizon. On pointing this out to his host, he received only evasive answers. The question had clearly put Smith on the defensive and he merely mumbled that his primary interest was in certain stars which lay too far south to be observable from the more northern counties of England. Morton forbore to interrogate him further along these lines since it was apparent that Smith was becoming extremely agitated at this line of questioning and, although not wishing to show any lack of manners, his attitude indicated he would prefer Morton to leave.

It was as he was following his host to the door that the doctor noticed the book lying on a small table. The volume was evidently incredibly old and lay open so that he was able to read part of the script which had been heavily underlined. Since it appeared to have some bearing on what he had just seen, the doctor recalled it from memory immediately on his return home, jotting it down in a small notebook. In essence, it read:

> In the Zegrembi Manuscript it is written that Cthugha who is great among the Old Ones lies bound within the raging fiery chaos Korvaz, which is a small star lying close in the heavens to Fomalhaut, brightest star of Piscis Australis, the Southern Fish. While his minions, the Jinnee, may be called up through the black mirror, take care lest you also call Him before his time, for He cannot be put down.
>
> Above all, keep close watch on the sky near Fomalhaut,

for the time will soon come when Korvaz shall brighten in the heavens to rival brilliant Fomalhaut. Then shall Cthugha come in fire and flame to claim that which has rightfully been His from the beginning of time.

Perplexed by what he had read, Morton attempted to make some sense out of these enigmatic paragraphs. Evidently, Smith had so arranged the layout of the observatory so that he might keep a constant watch on the sky around Fomalhaut. Yet what was he to make of the rest? Who were Cthugha and the Old Ones? And that strange statement that He and his minions might be called up through the black mirror—what mad kind of nonsense was that?

Inwardly, he shuddered as he struggled to formulate some rational meaning behind the words. As a doctor, Morton was a scientific man, yet he could form no reasonable conclusion. Something—some presence—which existed inside a star, could be drawn across the black interstellar void to Earth and manifest itself by means of a mirror? Had this been the Middle Ages, even the possession of that book would have resulted in young Smith being tried and hanged as a warlock.

There was, of course, the equally disturbing possibility that Smith's mind had become, to a certain extent, deranged. To Morton's keen eye there had been something about the young man which he had felt, rather than seen, during his brief talk with him. He had given the impression of being on the verge of some tremendous discovery, yet one which had such frightening overtones that he could not bring himself even to hint at it to an outsider. At that time, Morton was unaware of the travels which Smith had embarked upon prior to coming to Torpoint. He had, however, received the impression that the young man was searching desperately for something of vital importance; that he had deliberately chosen this place in which to live for some reason other than the astronomical one of observing parts of the sky which could not be seen from any position much further north.

After all, if Smith merely wished to pursue his hobby of watching the southern skies, would it not have made more sense to have settled in some other country closer to the equator? The more he tried to puzzle things out, the more convinced Morton became that, whatever it was that Smith was looking for, he had reason to believe it was somewhere in the vicinity of Torpoint.

Although he tried to dismiss the idea as too fantastic for belief, Morton was reluctantly forced to the conclusion that Smith actually believed in the literal truth of those words in that ancient book which he had somehow acquired. However insane it might seem, Smith had obtained some ancient arcane knowledge by means of which he was hoping to call up some contravention of nature which he was certain existed near Fomalhaut and to do this it was necessary he should gain possession of one thing—the black mirror mentioned in that outlandish text.

That this was a similar kind of fantasy which had afflicted the early philosophers in their futile search for the Elixir of Life and the Philosopher's Stone, Morton recognized at once. He recalled that Sheridan had mentioned that certain of the books Smith had collected dealt with alchemy. The logical explanation of all this, if there was one, was simply that Smith had a fanatical interest in this ancient wisdom and had taken this belief to an extreme. While such an outlook was definitely unhealthy if taken too far, it was not a case in which he could interfere directly as a doctor. However, he felt it was his duty to keep the young man under discreet scrutiny for there was no telling what effect this obsession might have on his mind if it was allowed to take over his personality completely.

Within the space of three weeks, most of the repairs and renovations to the farmhouse had been completed to Smith's satisfaction and the workmen were handsomely rewarded for their handiwork. As his study, Smith had chosen a large room on the top floor at the rear which overlooked the solitary opening in the tall trees which ringed the house in an almost complete circle, shutting it off from the surrounding fields and hills. It commanded an unimpeded view of the horizon almost due south with only the low outbuilding sited on a small knoll dominating the nearer landscape.

The distant horizon in this direction was reasonably flat with most of the humped hills showing above the ring of trees towards the west. Beyond them, he knew, the precipitous slopes plunged sheer towards the ocean. For much of the day he would sit at the large oak desk, poring over the musty tomes he had brought with him, working feverishly on his attempts to decipher those which he had discovered in Transylvania.

Initially, he assumed that the writing was in cipher for it was well known that the ancient alchemists and necromancers used such complex codes, either to protect their secrets from rival researchers or to hide them from the prying eyes of the church authorities. When success continued to elude him, he soon saw that his original deduction was incorrect. These writings had to be copies derived from much earlier sources and his conviction that he might soon stumble upon the key became severely shaken. Evidently he would have to resort to other books, ones which he didn't have in his possession, if he was to make any headway.

Accordingly, early one warm day in late September, he drove into Exeter, parking his car near the center of town. There was no possibility, of course, that any of the modern, fashionable bookshops would stock the volumes he was seeking and he deliberately struck off the main streets, wandering the maze of narrow roads where innumerable alleys led off in all directions. Here, he sought out the older and lesser-known shops which seemed to tuck themselves away, out of sight, as if not wanting to be frequented by the tourists.

In one of these he inquired of the shopkeeper about any books dealing with the Zegrembi Manuscript but the man merely looked oddly frightened and shook his head and when Smith pressed him for an answer, he feigned ignorance and maintained he had never heard the name.

There seemed no point in asking further, for it was clear that the man knew something but would never tell what he knew. Acting on impulse, Smith left the shop hurriedly and concealed himself in a narrow alley a few yards from the shop entrance. He had only been there a couple of minutes when the shop owner emerged and, after throwing a wary glance along the street, looking in both directions, hurried off across the small, cobbled square, vanishing around a corner immediately opposite Smith's vantage point. Fortunately there were few people about and Smith was able to follow the man, keeping him in sight without the other being aware of his presence.

The man did not go far. Halfway along a narrow alley, he paused and then darted into an even narrower passage between two tall Victorian houses, turning left at the far end. Swiftly, Smith went after him and was just in time to see him entering a small, dingy-looking shop on the opposite side of the street. The interior was dim and Smith could only just make out the two figures through the dust-smeared glass of the window. But it was evident the man he had followed was talking animatedly with his colleague behind the long counter. Even though he could hear nothing, Smith did not doubt they were discussing him and his request.

While Smith pondered his next move, the first man came out, hesitated a moment, then hurried back along the street. After he had gone, Smith stood staring at the dingy shop. It somehow excited him to find that his few words in the last shop had elicited this reaction for it seemed to confirm he was now on the track of discovering something important.

Acting almost without conscious initiative, he made his way across the street and inside the shop. For a moment, he had the impression it was completely empty. Then he noticed the shadowy figure behind the counter and was aware of eyes watching him shrewdly as he approached.

"So you're the one who's inquiring about the Zegrembi Manuscript," the man said. His voice was little more than a hoarse whisper and there was a curious metallic quality to it which surprised Smith.

Seeing no reason to deny that this was so, Smith nodded. His eyes had now grown accustomed to the gloom inside the shop and he saw that the owner was a small, wizened man of indeterminate age although, to Smith's startled gaze, he could not have been less than ninety years old. And his eyes, in the dimly shadowed features, were strangely upsetting—oddly slanted like those of a Chinese and in their black, seemingly irisless, depths twin flames seemed to flicker redly.

"I must admit I didn't expect you so soon. Evidently you must have discovered a great deal in your travels."

Despite the abrupt shock evoked by this statement from a complete stranger, Smith somehow managed to keep his composure. Perhaps it was the fact that in his short lifetime, he had been witness to so many strange and inexplicable things which allowed him to keep his voice normal as he asked, "How do you know where I've been?"

"Ah, but I happen to know a lot about you, Mister Smith. I know why you came to Torpoint, even though you may not know the real reason yourself. I know all of the places you've visited and what you heard and found there. And above all, I know what it is you're searching for so urgently. The black mirror of Zegrembi."

Gripping the edge of the counter with white-knuckled hands, Smith experienced a mounting tide of insidious horror and apprehension surging through him. He could not recall having ever seen this man before and knew he would certainly have remembered such features if he had ever done so. Then he recalled the three workmen he had engaged and it occurred to him that, in spite of all the care he had taken, one of them might have gone through his books and, on returning to Exeter, spoken with this man concerning his travels and recent activities. With an effort, he forced himself to relax slightly, assuring himself that this was the logical explanation.

"Then if you know so much about me," he said harshly, "you may be of some help. I need to decipher a certain script which is clearly written in some language unknown at the present time."

"Of course." The wrinkled head nodded grotesquely on the shopkeeper's scrawny shoulders. "The volumes you found in Transylvania."

"Why, yes."

"I thought so. But you must understand that those volumes are only copies of a much earlier work and were themselves copies of copies. The original was written on stone long before there were any men on this planet. Some say the stone was taken into some other realm, beyond our own universe of angled time and space, millions of years ago. The Zegrembi Manuscript is, however, a faithful reproduction."

"But how—?"

"How did Zegrembi, the necromancer, gain possession of it and succeed in deciphering it?" The flickering flames within the old man's eyes seemed to brighten and Smith found that, no matter how hard he tried, he was unable to tear his gaze from this mesmeric stare. He seemed to hear the wheezing voice echoing strangely from a great distance. "Zegrembi had discovered the meaning behind certain planes and angles, how these could be enmeshed together so that passage from one realm to another became possible. This arcane knowledge enabled him to enter that particular sphere within which the graven stone was concealed and he brought it back with him to his garret in London in the year 1663.

"How long it took him to decipher it no one else knows, but that he had succeeded three years later is obvious from subsequent events. You see, he also brought back something else with him from the outer realms—the black mirror which, as you have already guessed, is the portal through which those who serve great Cthugha may pass."

In spite of his natural revulsion at the other's appearance, Smith felt a sudden surge of excitement at the owner's revelations. "And you know where this mirror is now?" he asked.

"I can only tell you that Zegrembi is said to have taken it with him, together with other documents, when he fled London in 1666. I said there were other events which prove this beyond all shadow of doubt. Perhaps you recall what happened on September the second, 1666."

Smith thought for a moment, then nodded. "The Great Fire of London."

"Just so. And Cthugha is the Old One associated with fire, just as Cthulhu is Lord of the Waters and Ithaqua rules the winds."

"Are you saying that Zegrembi called up Cthugha through the black mirror?"

"No. Not Cthugha, otherwise the entire Earth would have been reduced to a blackened cinder. But he did call up one, or more, of the *Jinnee*, the servants of Cthugha, those beings who dwell in the outer realms."

The old man paused, the blazing eyes still fixed hypnotically on Smith. "I know that you have followed the trail of Cthugha for many years and perhaps it is only right I should aid a believer in his search."

Turning suddenly, he moved towards the rear of the darkened shop and when he came back there was something in his hand which he placed carefully on the counter. "Take this. It is the only copy in existence. Look upon it if you wish as your Rosetta Stone in translating the aeon-old writings which were graven upon Earth's rocks long before even the dinosaurs roamed this planet."

Almost before he was aware of it, Smith found himself standing in the narrow street, blinking his eyes against the bright sunlight. He had no knowledge of how he had got there; certainly he could not recall having passed through the shop door, and for several moments he stood there, swaying slightly at the sudden transition.

It was not until he turned to glance behind him that the full horror burst upon him. Where he had imagined the bookshop to be was a hardware shop sandwiched between two dilapidated buildings, their windows boarded up and clearly untenanted. In a daze, he wandered the whole length of the street, scarcely sure of his own sanity, for there was no sign of the bookshop he had just visited.

Either he had dreamed the entire episode while still walking through these narrow streets, or he had suffered a temporary lapse of memory and had walked some considerable distance without being aware of it before regaining his senses here in this street which, although it looked like that where the old bookshop was located, might be some distance away. Yet even as he struggled to orientate himself, aware that some of the passersby were eyeing him curiously, his hand went to the inner pocket of his coat, withdrawing a rolled-up parchment which he recognized at once as the long-lost Zegrembi Manuscript.

This discovery sent him hastening back through the twisting alleys to where he had parked his car. All the way back to Torpoint he attempted to rationalize what had happened. His possession of the parchment was concrete proof that he had neither dreamed nor imagined everything. Someone—or something—had wanted him to obtain the Zegrembi Manuscript, for what obscure motive he could not even guess. Gradually, however, his initial feeling of dark apprehension and awe gave way to one of intense elation.

Now he felt certain he had the means of deciphering that prehuman language of the Transylvanian volumes and also of discovering the whereabouts of the black mirror.

Back at the farmhouse, Smith wasted no time in perusing the parchment. As the old man had claimed, it was indeed a Rosetta Stone, written in three languages. The first was undoubtedly identical with the weird hieroglyphs given in the ancient tomes he had found in that subterranean crypt in Eastern Europe; the second was a script he could not identify although the linear characters appeared allied to the Nordic runes. The third portion of the text was in Latin.

At once, he recognized that if the two lower scripts were an exact translation of the first, the decipherment of the terribly ancient volumes lay within his grasp. That it would not be easy, he realized, and it would undoubtedly take some time. But when he retired that night, he felt like a man on the verge of a great discovery. In spite of his physical tiredness, his brain was still active, going over what had happened again and again so that it was two full hours before he fell asleep, listening to the creaks and groans of the old house.

For the first time since he had moved into the farmhouse, he dreamed. In his dream he found himself plunged into a vortex of cyclopean horror. He hung motionless in a black, forbidding sky and at first thought he was suspended somewhere in the intrasolar deeps much closer to the Sun than on Earth. But then he realized that the dully gleaming orb which floated before his dreaming vision was not the Sun. Ugly dark blotches mottled the dull orange surface and great columns of spinning flame arced around the rim.

For an immeasurable period of time, he floated there, his entire attention focussed on the strange star, watching the titan sunspots drift slowly across the hideous disc, at times growing larger and merging into great gaping chasms in the fiery atmosphere, while at others dwindling almost to nothingness.

Then he noticed that the black abyss around the star was not entirely vacant. Swinging around from behind the sun came a smaller body which he immediately concluded was a solitary planet previously hidden by that blotched, fiery sphere. As it swung closer in, towards his vantage point, he glimpsed the meteor-pocked surface, crowded with indescribably angled stone monuments which clustered in alien-shaped groups, sprouting from the ground like monstrous fungi. Titan columns reared up into the star-strewn heavens and everything he saw held a touch of unspeakable menace and horror; and then, as the black planet swung past him he almost screamed aloud as he glimpsed the fearsome denizens of that midnight world. Alien-hued creatures which swarmed across the undulant surface, their crazy outlines surrounded by what appeared to be flickering flames.

In that same instant, he became aware, for the first time, of a sound; a roaring, shrieking confusion of noise which permeated the dark void, rising and falling in some abnormal rhythm which, somehow, seemed to be synchronous with the motion of that seething mass of inhuman life.

The sound reached a soul-shuddering pattern of aural violence and then diminished slowly as the gigantic orb floated past him in its erratic orbit around the star. Even though some strange inner sense told him he was simply dreaming and he struggled desperately to waken, there came one final episode which crowded insanely into his whirling mind. His gaze suddenly switched from the black planet back to the central star. At first, it seemed just as it had been before but then he noticed it was not only growing larger but seemed to be spinning more rapidly on its crazily-tilted axis. The umbrous spots on its surface swept across it with an increasing acceleration, the leaping flames soared swiftly into the surrounding void, curved and fell back as spinning magnetic fields twisted and warped. Something was stirring deep within that fiery atmosphere; something monstrous that roared an insatiable anger against the chains of the Elder Gods which had bound it there for an eternity.

And Smith knew that he was being drawn irresistibly towards it. Unable to resist, utterly powerless to control his movements, he was diving headlong towards that ravening chaos, that age-old intelligence which was Cthugha. Then, even as the horrendous disc expanded swiftly before him, he jerked upright in his bed, a shriek of utter horror bursting from his shaking lips, perspiration boiling from every pore of his body. He was trembling uncontrollably, staring into the darkness, that final dreaming image still strong in his mind. For the rest of the night he lay in the dark, fighting against sleep until the first grey glimmer of dawn showed through the windows when he went down into the kitchen and prepared himself a strong coffee in an attempt to calm his taut nerves.

That morning, with ominous thunderheads piling up towards the south-east, Smith could scarcely bring himself to tackle the task of beginning the translation of that ancient text which had intrigued him for so long. His mind was still reeling under the impact of that nightmarish dream which had assailed him during the night. No longer could he doubt that what he had witnessed during that dreaming state had been the lair of great Cthugha; that faint star which lay close in the heavens to the more brilliant Fomalhaut.

And that night-black planet on which had crawled those loathsome creatures—was that the abode of the Jinnee, those who had worshipped Cthugha throughout the aeons since that titanic battle which had resulted in the defeat and subsequent imprisonment of the Old Ones? Shuddering at the memory, he seated himself at his desk where he unrolled the parchment bearing the three inscriptions, keeping it flat with a quartet of paperweights as he puzzled over the weird characters of that earliest language, striving to correlate it with the Latin text.

He knew he was inevitably making a number of assumptions and there was a strong possibility that one, or perhaps all of these, might be incorrect. Yet he would gain nothing by merely looking at them. Evidently the old necromancer, Zegrembi, had somehow found the means of transcribing the pre-human script into Latin and now Smith attempted to do likewise with the tattered, mouldy tomes, painfully decoding the fabulous characters into their Latin equivalent. Progress was inevitably slow and he was still struggling with the text when the gathering storm broke. Vicious lightning strokes and rolling thunder crashed across the heavens, accompanied by torrential rain which battered incessantly at the windows.

Smith did his best to ignore the sound, concentrating on the task before him but ten minutes later there came another sound which jerked him upright in his chair, a surge of anger going through him. The loud knocking on the door downstairs was repeated. Tossing his pen angrily onto the desk, he went downstairs and opened the door, recoiling slightly as a savage blast of air struck him. Doctor Morton stood there, the rain dripping from his hat and overcoat.

Apologizing for his unexpected appearance on Smith's doorstep, the doctor explained that while returning from visiting a patient, he had been caught in the sudden downpour on his way back to the village and asked if he might shelter until the storm abated. Although annoyed by this unwanted intrusion, and anxious to get back to his work, Smith could not very well refuse this request since this would not only arouse suspicion in the doctor's mind but might do the same where the villagers were concerned should the doctor let it be known he had been denied shelter.

Wordlessly, he took his visitor into the parlour and motioned him to a chair after taking his wet hat and overcoat, draping the latter over the back of a chair in front of the fire.

While studying his host minutely from beneath lowered lids, Morton inquired how his astronomical observations were progressing, remarking that the recent nights had been extraordinarily clear with excellent conditions for viewing the heavens.

Smith waved this question aside quite summarily, merely saying that, unfortunately, pressure of other work had meant he had been forced to postpone such observations for the time being. This statement, Doctor Morton found difficult to believe. After all, Smith had evidently paid a great deal of money buying the telescope and setting it up in the outhouse. If his earlier statement, given when they had first met, had been true, whatever it was that Smith intended to observe so closely, it had to lie in a region of the sky very low on the southern horizon. And although the doctor had only a passing interest in astronomy, his knowledge of the subject was sufficient for him to know that any stellar object so low down near the southern horizon would only remain visible for a short period during the year. What also worried him was Smith's general demeanour. The young man was clearly ill at ease, fidgeting nervously in his chair, and it was abundantly clear that all he really wanted was for the rain to cease and his guest to depart.

Something, Morton felt, was wrong; and he wondered what other activity Smith was engaged upon which had prompted him to shut himself away like this. Astronomical observation was, he felt sure, only a small part of Smith's reason for being there. And whatever it was, he evidently did not wish anyone to know of it.

He recalled those curious books which Sheridan had mentioned and wondered whether they played any part in Smith's researches and, in the hope of drawing his host out, he mentioned something of the history of the farmhouse, hoping to evoke some kind of response. At first, Smith listened in a desultory fashion as if totally disinterested in what the doctor was saying and it was clear he was no antiquarian. It was not until Morton mentioned that, according to local superstition, the farmhouse had once been the home of the reputed necromancer, Nicholas Zegrembi who had resided there for several years after the Great Fire of London in 1666, that Smith's expression changed dramatically. His initial look of startled surprise, which he tried vainly to hide, was quickly replaced by something else; an air of heightened interest.

"You've heard the name?" Morton asked.

Smith shrugged. "I've come across it once or twice," he said, striving to sound calm and casual. "Wasn't he supposed to be some kind of warlock in the Middle Ages?"

"If you were to listen to some of the tales they still tell in the village, you'd realize he was something more than that. I suppose you know that your arrival here, particularly when it became known you were buying this place, caused quite a lot of talk in Torpoint. Not that I set much store by such myths and legends myself. But you won't get any of the villagers entering this place, nor coming near it, especially after dark.

"It's a fact, though, that several queer happenings occurred in these parts at that time, all well documented in the records of the library in Exeter."

"What sort of happenings?" Smith demanded. For a moment, there seemed such alarm in the young man's voice that Morton felt a momentary fear for himself. Then Smith abruptly changed his tone, forcing himself to relax in his chair although he never once removed his gaze from the doctor's face. "Forgive me," he continued harshly, "the trouble is I had quite a traumatic experience while abroad and it affected my disposition, making me far more nervous than I used to be."

"Perhaps I might be able to prescribe something which would help you," Morton suggested.

"No, thank you. I'll be all right, I assure you. It's just that I came here for peace and quiet and this talk of strange occurrences makes me feel a little queer. But please continue; if there's anything strange about this place, it's better I should know."

By now, Morton was convinced there was something more to Smith's questions than a mere interest in a man who had been dead for more than three centuries. His sudden start at the name Zegrembi, and his feeble excuse, indicated that there was more to this matter than he was willing to tell.

In the hope of obtaining some further reaction from his host, Morton enlarged upon his story. "According to the reports of the time quite a number of people from the village vanished around that time and there were vague rumours of strange, flickering lights seen moving among the trees yonder and curious scorch marks found at various places. Whether there is any truth in what some of the villagers discovered, that these marks all bore an odd resemblance to the shape of a human body, I wouldn't like to speculate upon.

"But there seems no doubt that the local people shunned this place and its strange occupant like the plague. After a time, when more folk disappeared, the authorities were called in but nothing definite was ever proved."

"And Zegrembi?" Smith demanded hoarsely. "What happened to him?"

"According to the stories which have been handed down over the centuries, the villagers finally decided they'd get no real help from the church or the authorities, so they got together and took matters into their own hands. Led by three worthy clergymen, they came out here with the intention of burning him at the stake. However, when they arrived and stormed the farmhouse, they could find no trace of him. Some said he'd been warned of their coming and had fled, while others reckoned he'd been taken back to his master—Satan."

"And what's your opinion, doctor?" There was an odd intensity in Smith's voice, his tone so insistent that for a moment the doctor was unsure how to reply.

At that instant, Morton was absolutely certain that the youth was dabbling in something far more sinister than he had previously imagined. What it was exactly, he couldn't be sure. But suddenly he felt afraid. Forcing evenness into his tone, he answered, "I wouldn't care to form any opinion. It all happened a long time ago and it's impossible to say how much credence can be placed upon these records of the time."

Anxious now to leave this place, he rose swiftly to his feet, remarking that the rain had now ceased and he had overstayed his welcome.

Smith saw him to the door and watched the stooped figure until the doctor had disappeared among the trees, heading back towards Torpoint. Returning to his study, he stood for several minutes staring down at the scribbled notes he had already made, struggling to absorb this new information concerning Zegrembi. Was it possible that his terrifying nightmare of the previous night had been occasioned by the fact that this was the house which had harboured the old wizard following his precipitous flight from London all those years ago?

That this ancient house had had some subtle influence upon him ever since he had moved in, he could not deny. And there had been certain passages in the old volumes which had suggested that the black mirror he was seeking was concealed somewhere in the neighbourhood of Torpoint. And now, with the Zegrembi Manuscript in his possession, he hoped he might soon discover its exact whereabouts.

Still pondering on these things, he crossed to the window. Now the storm had passed over, the clouds were beginning to break up and pallid rays of sunlight filtered through the grey overcast. For a few moments, he watched the play of sunlight over the fields in the far distance, then lowered his gaze in the direction of the trees. Something moved suddenly at the edge of his vision; a dimly seen figure that seemed to flit among the trees, giving only a tantalizingly brief glimpse of its outlines.

Smith's first intuitive conclusion was that one of the villagers was spying on him, keeping him under surveillance from a safe distance. Then the man stepped out from among the trees, walking slowly but deliberately towards the observatory and Smith saw him clearly for the first time. Even from that distance, recognition was immediate. It was the old man from the bookshop!

Running down the stairs, Smith thrust open the back door and sprinted towards the low building. There was no sign of the old man by the time he reached it but, on trying the door, he found it open though he could have sworn he had locked it securely the last time he had been in. Pushing his way inside, he flicked on the light, staring around him. The place was just as he had left it. Nothing seemed out of place and a swift check assured him there was no one there. Yet where could that stooped figure have gone? And, more to the point, why was he here?

Smith was now beginning to believe strange things about that ancient shopkeeper and all sorts of weird conjectures entered his mind as he walked slowly back to the house. The logical explanation was that the doctor's revelations had so colored his thoughts that he had simply imagined he had seen him. Perhaps this place was getting to him more than he realized. As soon as possible, he would have to go back into Exeter and try to find those old records, check for himself just what had happened here in 1666.

The next day dawned bright and sunny and as he drove along the winding country road into Exeter, Smith felt, more strongly than ever, that he was on the brink of unravelling this mystery. He located the main library with little difficulty. Finding a seat in the reading room, he soon located the volume he needed, scanning the yellowed pages for references to Zegrembi and Torpoint.

Apparently, the necromancer had arrived in the village on September 8, 1666 and had taken up residence at the old farmhouse two days later. Several reliable witnesses had testified to the enormous amount of luggage he had brought with him; wooden boxes bound with thick metal strips, three massive trunks and more than a dozen packages of various shapes and sizes. There was much local talk of weird bluish lights and deep-toned rumblings emanating from inside the house, particularly after dark.

Gradually, however, more sinister occurrences took place. Nocturnal travellers on the road between Exeter and Torpoint spoke of witnessing screaming figures fleeing across the open moorland pursued by flaming demons; of search parties finding curious marks in the grassy fields or even scorched out of the solid rock, marks which bore an uncanny resemblance to a human outline. Since all of these events began with Zegrembi's arrival in the area, it was inevitable that they became connected with his sorcerous activities.

The account of the storming of the farmhouse and the subsequent discovery that the necromancer had mysteriously disappeared was far more brief than Smith had hoped. There was, of course, speculation as to his whereabouts and a bewildering description of the many books and pieces of alchemical apparatus found in the house, the latter being smashed by the mob, while the former were all taken into the yard and burned under the watchful eyes of the clergymen who maintained that all of these blasphemous volumes were written in some heathen language which no one could understand.

All in all, the account told Smith little more than he had already learned from the doctor and it was with a feeling of intense disappointment and frustration that he made to close the book. It was then that he noticed that the final blank page had been sealed by its edges to the hard back cover. Glancing round to see that he was not being observed, he took out his penknife and, inserting the tip of the blade carefully near the binding, he slit the paper all the way around.

The two concealed pages fell open and he stared at them with a shock of horror and disbelief. On the first some unknown writer had scrawled a hidden message, now barely legible where the ink had faded over the years. The crude symbols were obviously similar to those in the terribly old volumes he had taken from the crypt in Transylvania, and beneath the words, but here written in English, were the words: *Ye copy of that which is written on ye wall in ye attick.*

But it was not this which evoked the spasm of horror that shook Smith to the core. It was what appeared on the facing page which made him shiver uncontrollably as he sat at the library table, struggling desperately to think coherently. Even though faded, like the writing, the pen and ink drawing, captioned Nicholas Zegrembi, was instantly recognizable as the old man in the bookshop!

How such a thing could possibly be, he could not tell. From the page, the wizard's features stared at him with a malevolence that seared into his brain so that he dropped the book onto the table with a loud clatter. Wildly, he glanced around, aware that one or two of the other readers in the room were eyeing him curiously. It was only with a supreme effort that he succeeded in controlling the tremoring in his limbs, rising shakily from his seat and replacing the volume on the shelf before walking unsteadily from the library.

Once in the open air, he stood quite still on the library steps. He had hoped to discover something which might help him in his search for the black mirror—but certainly not this. Even though common sense and logic told him he must be mistaken, that the interior of the bookshop had been very dim and he had only been there for a few minutes, he knew, deep inside, that there had been no mistake. Scarcely aware of the streaming traffic and the pedestrians who passed him in the streets, he made his way back to the car. Yet shaken though he was with horror, his sense of grim determination was still uppermost in his mind, making him even more intent on leaving no stone unturned in his search for the mirror.

By the time he was safely back in his study, he had examined several possibilities without coming to any firm conclusion. That the man in the bookshop and Nicholas Zegrembi were one and the same he was forced to accept. So what did this signify? That Zegrembi had not fled the farmhouse in the normal sense when those villagers had come to burn him at the stake? Calling upon all of his arcane knowledge, the youth slowly began to piece together the scattered bits of the mystery, rejecting no idea, however fantastic, in an attempt to form a coherent picture.

Zegrembi had disappeared, it was true, but he had not taken to his heels for some other part of the country; he had used his sorcerous knowledge to enter some other realm of existence. And now, possibly by the same means, he had returned, though for what purpose, Smith could not imagine. That the ancient necromancer wished him to successfully decipher the old Transylvanian tomes and learn their dread secrets was obvious since he had supplied the only means of doing so. Whether this was part of some diabolical plan evolved down the ages, or some means of wreaking revenge upon the descendants of those who had forced him to cease his practices three centuries earlier, it was impossible to tell.

With an effort, Smith pulled himself together and began working again on the manuscript. A strange compulsion seemed to have seized him, urging him to complete this task as soon as possible. Gradually, he was able to make some sense of the pre-human script. While Smith's diary gives only a brief outline of what he discovered, whether because of difficulties in translation or because he was mortally afraid of what he discovered, he was clearly troubled and disturbed by what he did manage to decipher.

The black mirror was mentioned on numerous occasions as also was the name Zegrembi. If his own transcription could be trusted, it became clear to Smith that the necromancer must have plied his sorcerous trade far back through the ages, long before the most recent occasion in 1666. Awed and shocked by these revelations, Smith sat at his table, reading through this disjointed Latin translation again and again, struggling to adjust his mind to the notion of long ages stretching far back into the past when the cult of Cthugha had flourished in antediluvian times.

Yet in spite of his efforts, there was one thing missing. One vital piece of information he desperately needed was not there. As far as he could determine, the text gave no clue as to the present whereabouts of the black mirror which he was now convinced was the secret portal through which the Jinnee, those servants of great Cthugha, could pass from one dimension to another and by means of which Zegrembi had escaped the retribution of the superstitious villagers three centuries before.

By now the hour had grown late. He had been sitting at the table throughout the whole of the long afternoon and evening without thought of food or rest while the sun had set and the shadows out-side had lengthened. Going down into the kitchen, he made himself a hasty meal, washing it down with black coffee. It was then, in the deepening twilight, that he realized there was something he had failed to remember when that odd compulsion had come over him. That cryptic message he had come across in the library that morning.

*A message written on ye wall in ye attick.*

Since the book had been a compilation of the events which had occurred when Nicholas Zegrembi had lived in this very house, it was possible that the attic referred to was that beneath the sagging roof of the farmhouse.

Acting on a sudden impulse, he lit a lantern for he doubted if there was any electricity laid on to that part of the building and made his way up the stairs to the long storeroom at the front of the dwelling where he had previously noticed a trapdoor in the ceiling. Here, he saw that the entrance into the attic had been boarded up with long strips of thick wood and nails. The nails had long since rusted and, finding a heavy hammer, it was the work of only a few minutes to strip away the wood from the opening. The door was not hard to lift, swinging back with a crash on squealing hinges, reveal-ing a dark opening through which he hauled himself, half choking on the dust.

Holding the lantern high over his head, he stared about him. The attic seemed far larger than he had imagined and he soon saw that his first impression, that it was roughly circular in shape, was incorrect. The lanternlight showed it to be seven-sided, and one corner, where the roof angled downward from two directions, he judged to be per-haps thirty feet away. Yet when he walked towards it, lowering his head where the roof dipped down, he discovered it to be less than twelve feet from where he had been standing. Clearly there was something peculiar about the angles and distances in that particular part which produced an extremely realistic illusory effect.

The dust-covered floor was completely bare but, as his shoes scuffed away some of the grey dust, he noticed faded markings which showed up dimly in the light. Placing the lantern on the floor, he knelt and cleared away as much of the dust as possible to reveal a large pentagram surrounded by a wide circle with what seemed to be an arrow pointing directly towards the oddly-angled corner. In places, the marks were especially faint as if some attempt had been made to erase the figures with only partial success.

Getting to his feet, Smith now turned his attention to the walls. At first, it appeared that all of them were of bare stone with no adornment, but then he noticed that the lowest, next to the far corner, had been daubed with some kind of limestone wash. That this had been done hurriedly and a long time before was clear from the way this covering was flaking and peeling from the stone. Holding the lantern closer, he made out the faint markings in those places where the wash had cracked and come away from the underlying stone.

Certain now that he was on the right track, he took out his knife and commenced scraping away the whitish-grey coating, taking care not to disturb the daubing underneath. Finally, the entire section of wall was uncovered and in the lanternlight he could make out the rows of glyphs which, as far as he could recall, were identical to those given on that concealed page.

In the dim yellow light, Smith made an exact copy of the ideoglyphs whose strange cursive characters spoke shudderingly of blasphemous gods and long-dead aeons. Whoever had tried to obliterate this writing had either had some knowledge of its terrible meaning or, associating it with the old necromancer had attempted to erase all evidence and memory of his stay there.

Before leaving the attic, Smith paused near the trapdoor and looked once again towards the furthest corner of the room, wishing to verify what he had seen earlier. There was no doubt that the alien manner in which the roof and walls met at that point did produce this weird optical illusion, giving the unshakable impression of seeing into an infinite distance. For almost a minute he found he could not tear his gaze from it and, as he looked, that small region of the room appeared to extend further and further from him and he fancied it grew pellucid with moving, half-formed shapes drifting beyond it in an infinite void. Crazy configurations seemed to impose themselves upon his stultified vision so that it was only with a supreme mental effort of will that he succeeded in eventually tearing his gaze away. Lowering himself quickly through the aperture, he dropped to the floor below, then pulled the trapdoor shut.

Returning to his study, he laboriously transcribed those weird symbols from the attic wall. In spite of the feeling of terror he had experienced in that crazily-angled room upstairs, he felt a growing sense of excitement and elation as the Latin phrases began to emerge. These, when roughly translated, read: "To him who comes after me, that which you seek lies within the circle where the oaks are seven."

The implications of this message were clear and to Smith there could be no doubt that it had been Zegrembi himself who had scrawled that message on the wall, giving the location of the black mirror. Sighing, he straightened in his chair. Clearly there was no point in searching in the dark. In the morning, he would explore the surrounding wood in a determined attempt to locate it.

Smith woke just as the dawn was breaking. Yet even though he had fallen asleep before midnight, he felt little rested. As before, his sleep had been plagued by strange dreams but although he tried to recall them, on this occasion he could remember only brief snatches. There had been a place of titan stone cliffs, atop which long columns of graven figures stretched away in either direction as far as the eye could see. A nightmarish landscape of jagged rocks and midnight-black chasms across which he ran and ran, knowing that he had to outrun the sunrise on this alien planet for, once the dawn brightened into day, that which rose above the serrated horizon would be too horrible even to contemplate.

And finally, the supreme horror. Unable to run any further he had stood on that hideously-distorted surface, watching as the sun rose, lifting into the umbrous heavens; a sun no longer dim and mottled with sunspots as in his previous dream but an eye-searing, tentacled mass of fire that writhed and bubbled and twisted with an evil intelligence.

Shivering a little, even though the room was warm, he dressed quickly, trying vainly to shrug his unease away. Were these dreams a warning that he was meddling in things which were best left alone? Or were they an indication of something more—that he was on the point of making the most important discovery in all his long years of searching for the truth behind these ancient myths and legends?

The sun was well clear of the eastern horizon when he left the farmhouse, carrying a spade with him. Nonetheless, the wood around the house held no more assurance in broad daylight than it did after dark. The thick, malignly-gnarled oaks crowded closely together as if seeking some protection from an age-old evil that had once dwelt there, leaving lingering traces behind. Since he had no idea where the spot given in that cryptic message might lie, he had already decided to work his way through the wood in a clockwise direction from the observatory. Once within the trees, his progress was slowed considerably for the ancient trunks grew so close to the narrow path running between them that he was forced to thrust his way forward against the impeding undergrowth, ignoring the thorny branches and tough, wiry grass that whipped and lashed at his body. There was an oppressive air of age and decay hanging like a miasmic shroud over everything.

The deeper he progressed among the trees, the more absolute was the silence. Nothing rustled through the abnormally dense undergrowth; no birds twittered in the overhanging boughs. Here and there, he came across huge rings of whitish fungi which seemed larger and more grotesquely-shaped than normal growths and these he avoided where he could. Once, in a small clearing, he came upon a place where no vegetation grew in the area and there was something about its outlines which made him turn hurriedly away and push on with a renewed vigour.

Then, suddenly, he came to where the half-seen path angled close to the perimeter of the wood and glancing through the trees he noticed a small knoll, perhaps a quarter of a mile away, crowned with a ring of seven trees. Without hesitation, he left the wood and strode rapidly across the open fields.

Clambering up the knoll which proved steeper than he had expected, he entered the open space among the trees. At first, he could see no outward sign to indicate where Zegrembi's mirror might be concealed. Huge tufts of creeping vegetation covered the ground, snaking tendrils of an obnoxious grey that strove to impede his progress with an almost sentient malevolence. Thrusting forward, he explored the nearer rim of the knoll, then almost fell as he stumbled over something completely hidden in the rank growth. Bending, he tore at the creepers, hacking them down with the edge of the spade. Set deep in the hard ground was a large square stone some three feet along each side.

Scraping away the dirt, he saw that the rough surface was crudely incised with figurings of a truly horrific nature. Whatever creatures they were supposed to represent it was clear they had never originated on Earth. What hand had chiselled those symbols, Smith could not even guess. Yet interspersed with these hideous figures were others, somewhat more modern in style—the devices used in alchemy—the sun, moon and planets. For an instant, Smith recoiled in indeterminate panic. It was not merely the sight of what was inscribed upon the stone which brought about this feeling of superstitious awe. There was also the sudden overpowering feeling that he was not alone; that there was some invisible presence close by, watching him with a dark intentness.

Clearly, this place was beginning to get on his nerves, as well it might in the light of what he had just discovered. Nevertheless, he did not intend to allow such feelings to interfere with his task. Thrusting the end of the spade deep into the earth beneath one edge of the slab, he heaved with all his strength. Slowly, the heavy stone lifted and by twisting the spade he was able to prop the slab up on the steel blade.

Hooking his fingers beneath the edge, he pulled mightily, so that the slab fell over onto its side. Beneath was a square of sandy soil into which the sharp-edged spade sank easily as Smith dug rapidly, still keenly aware of that unseen presence watching his every move. Some three feet down, the spade struck something solid and, going down on his hands and knees, he wiped the soil away. It was a large object, wrapped in a thick red cloth, still remarkably intact owing to the dry nature of the soil. Carefully, he eased it out of the hole and unwrapped it with trembling hands.

That the object was a mirror of some kind was clear but it was not what Smith had been expecting. It had a curiously asymmetric shape, made up of odd-angled and weirdly curved sides. Around the circumference were the pictographs of that ancient text he had been so laboriously translating and he shuddered inwardly as he recognized the name Cthugha. Of the rest, he could decipher nothing from memory although he did not doubt he could translate it from the Zegrembi Manuscript.

But it was not this that shocked him in a most alarming fashion. He had expected to see glass or crystal with his own half-scared reflection staring out at him. Instead, there was only blackness; an ebon sheet which seemed to absorb all light. Kneeling there, peering into that inky nothingness, he had the unnerving impression he was falling forward into infinite depths, into an abyss of midnight emptiness which was as limitless as the universe itself.

Sickening vertigo twisted the muscles of his stomach into a painful knot as he fought desperately to turn his head and look away. How long he knelt there, unable to move, it was impossible to tell. Then, all at once, the eldrich spell was broken. Jerking his head around with a painful wrenching of neck muscles, he staggered upright, still holding tightly to the mirror. Without looking down, he succeeded in wrapping the thick cloth around it, clutching it tightly under one arm as he hurried back to the house.

Into his mind flashed incongruous memories of those ancient heroes who had looked directly upon the face of the Gorgon and been turned to stone. What exactly was this relic of age-old cosmic evil? Where had it originated and by whom had it been fashioned? These were questions he found difficult, if not impossible, to answer. As to its purpose, this he had already guessed from his earlier readings of the ancient tomes. He shook inwardly as he recalled those events chronicled around the time of Zegrembi's disappearance. Those fiery demons that had pursued their hapless victims across the moors—had they been Jinnee, raised by the necromancer by means of this hideous artifact? The fact that immediately following Zegrembi's vanishment there had been no further reported disappearances in the neighbourhood pointed to the fact that, somehow, the sorcerer had known of the action intended by the irate, yet terrified, villagers and before he had so cleverly concealed the mirror, he had possessed the means of sending those creatures back to their own plane.

Clearly, until he had completely translated the cryptic script around the mirror and perfected his own protection against what might be called up, he would have to proceed with the utmost caution.

His return to the house took him longer than he had anticipated. Twice, he lost his way among the trees and was forced to retrace his steps before stumbling upon the right path. Finally, however, breathing a soundless sigh of relief, he came out into the opening where the observatory stood. Once inside the house, he carried his find to his study and placed it carefully against the wall, leaving it covered.

At the moment, he had no wish to peer again into those night-black depths wherein, he felt certain, lurked something unutterably terrible and evil, biding its time with an insatiable hunger, hovering just on the threshold between his own reality and the blasphemous terrors of the outer spheres.

The next three days he spent checking and rechecking the transcriptions he had made. The nights he spent at the telescope, anxiously watching that spot in the southern heavens close to Fomal-haut, fixing his unwavering attention on an extremely faint star which he had tentatively identified as that around which the black planet rolled in its eccentric orbit, shrouded in elder mystery and horror. At times, he fancied it would brighten and then fade in a curi-ously irregular manner and his fright and anxiety would increase a hundredfold as he strained his vision to keep it in view.

On the second day, he received a further unwelcome visit from Doctor Morton, who expressed his grave concern at the youth's hag-gard and drawn appearance. Smith listened with an ill-concealed im-patience as the worthy gentleman attempted to persuade him to ease up on whatever he was doing, insisting that he was pushing himself to the utmost limits. Smith explained that the astronomical side of his work would soon be coming to an end and he would then be able to relax at nights.

Although the doctor was clearly not satisfied with this explana-tion there was nothing further he could do since the youth was obdu-rate in his insistence that his work was of such importance it had to be completed without delay. From the scribbled statements in Smith's diary it would thus appear that once the doctor had left, no other living person saw Stephen Ashmore Smith alive.

From this point onward, Smith's entries in his diary lapse into an untidy scrawl, evidently written in great haste and under extreme mental pressure. In places, they are scarcely legible; in others there is a curious substitution of Latin phrases and archaic English. While the coroner recorded an open verdict on the case and the manner in which Smith died, and the police surgeon virtually ignored these odd changes in language, putting them down to some form of mental breakdown on the part of the victim, a number of other investigators have reached a much different conclusion.

They point to Smith's travels prior to settling in Torpoint, to his undoubted obsession with the occult and weird myth cycles and to the fact that the strange hieroglyphs in the attic and the curiously graven stone on the knoll do indeed exist. Above all, they take note of the fact that the day after Smith's charred body was removed from the farmhouse, Doctor Morton gained entry and left with a heavy, flat object, carefully swathed in a thick red cloth which he threw into the old mine shaft.

That Smith succeeded in translating the script graven around the circumference of the mirror appears certain from his diary and certain scribbled notes he left. From the jottings, it would seem he continued writing almost to the end of his life. There were such statements, only barely intelligible, as:

"Have memorized the descending formula and now intend to recite that which will call up Those from the outer sphere."

"Nothing happening . . . perhaps Fomalhaut too close to the horizon . . . may have to try again although . . ."

"Another voice in the room . . . cannot see clearly but . . . small stooping figure near door . . . dear God—Zegrembi!"

"Must write what I see. Mirror no longer black . . . brightening! Something in the sky outside . . . coming closer . . . glowing trail like a meteorite . . . tendrils of fire from the mirror . . . must get away but Zegrembi blocking the doorway . . . only the window left now . . ."

# I've Come to Talk with You Again

## Karl Edward Wagner

They were all in The Swan. The music box was moaning something about "everybody hurts sometime" or was it "everybody
hurts something." Jon Holsten couldn't decide. He wondered why the
country-western sound in London. Maybe it was "everybody hurts
somebody." Where were The Beatles when you needed them? One
Beatle short, to begin with. Well, yeah, two Beatles. And Pete Best.
Whatever.

"Wish they'd turn that bloody thing down." Jon Holsten scowled
at the offending speakers. Coins and sound effects clattered from the
fruit machine, along with bonks and flippers from the Fish Tales pinball machine. The pub was musty with mildew from the pissing rain
of the past week and the penetrating stench of stale tobacco smoke.
Holsten hated the ersatz stuffed trout atop the pinball machine.

Mannering was opening a packet of crisps, offering them around.
Foster declined: he had to watch his salt. Carter crunched a hand-
ful, then wandered across to the long wooden bar to examine the
two chalk-on-slate menus: Quality Fayre was promised. He ordered
prime pork sausages with chips and baked beans, not remembering
to watch his weight. Stein limped down the treacherous stairs to the
Gent's. Insulin time. Crosley helped himself to the crisps and worried
that his round was coming up. He'd have to duck it. Ten quid left
from his dole check, and a week till the next.

There were six of them tonight, where once eight or ten might have forgathered. Over twenty years, it had become an annual tradition: Jon Holsten over from the States for his holiday in London, the usual crowd around for pints and jolly times. Cancer of the kidneys had taken McFerran last year; he who always must have his steak and kidney pie. Hiles had decamped to the Kentish coast, where he hoped the sea air would improve his chest. Marlin was somewhere in France, but no one knew where, nor whether he had kicked his drug dependence.

So it went.

"To absent friends," said Holsten, raising his pint. The toast was well received, but added to the gloom of the weather with its memories of those who should have been here.

Jon Holsten was an American writer of modest means but respectable reputation. He got by with a little help from his friends, as it were. Holsten was generally considered to be the finest of the later generation of writers in the Lovecraftian school—a genre mainly out of fashion in these days of chainsaws and flesh-eating zombies, but revered by sufficient devotees to provide for Holsten's annual excursion to London.

Holsten tipped back his pint glass. Over its rim he saw the yellow-robed figure enter the doorway. He continued drinking without hesitation, swallowing perhaps faster now. The pallid mask regarded him as impassively as ever. An American couple entered the pub, walking past. They were arguing in loud New York accents about whether to eat here. For an instant the blue-haired woman shivered as she brushed through the tattered cloak.

Holsten had fine blond hair, brushed straight back. His eyes were blue and troubled. He stood just under six feet, was compactly muscled beneath his blue three-piece suit. Holsten was past the age of sixty.

"Bloody shame about McFerran," said Mannering, finishing the crisps. Carter returned from the bar with his plate. Crosley looked on hungrily. Foster looked at his empty glass. Stein returned from the Gent's.

Stein: "What were you saying?"

Mannering: "About McFerran."

"Bloody shame." Stein sat down.

"My round," said Holsten. "Give us a hand, will you, Ted?"

The figure in tattered yellow watched Holsten as he arose. Holsten had already paid for *his* round.

Ted Crosley was a failed writer of horror fiction: some forty stories in twenty years, mostly for nonpaying markets. He was forty and balding and worried about his hacking cough.

Dave Mannering and Steve Carter ran a book shop and lived above it. Confirmed bachelors adrift from Victorian times. Mannering was thin, dark, well-dressed, scholarly. Carter was red-haired, Irish, rather large, fond of wearing Rugby shirts. They were both about forty.

Charles Stein was a book collector and lived in Crouch End. He was showing much grey and was very concerned about his diabetes. He was about forty.

Mike Foster was a tall, rangy book collector from Liverpool. He was wearing a leather jacket and denim jeans. He was concerned about his blood pressure after a near-fatal heart attack last year. He was fading and about forty.

The figure in the pallid mask was seated at their table when Holsten and Crosley returned from the bar with full pints. No need for a seventh pint. Holsten sat down, trying to avoid the eyes that shone from behind the pallid mask. He wasn't quick enough.

The lake was black. The towers were somehow behind the moon. The moons. Beneath the black water. Something rising. A shape. Tentacled. Terror now. The figure in tattered yellow pulling him forward. The pallid mask. Lifted.

"Are you all right?" Mannering was shaking him.

"Sorry?" They were all looking at Holsten. "Jet lag, I suppose."

"You've been over here for a fortnight," Stein pointed out.

"Tired from it all," said Holsten. He took a deep swallow from his pint, smiled reassuringly. "Getting too old for this, I imagine."

"You're in better health than most of us," said Foster. The tattered cloak was trailing over his shoulders. His next heart attack would not be near-fatal. The figure in the pallid mask brushed past, moving on.

Mannering sipped his pint. The next one would have to be a half: he'd been warned about his liver. "You will be sixty-four on November 18." Mannering had a memory for dates and had recently written a long essay on Jon Holsten for a horror magazine. "How do you manage to stay so fit?"

"I have this portrait in my attic." Holsten had used the joke too many times before, but it always drew a laugh. And he was not going on sixty-four, despite the dates given in his books.

"No. Seriously." Stein would be drinking a Pils next round, worrying about alcohol and insulin.

The tentacles were not really tentacles—only something with which to grasp and feed. To reach out. To gather in those who had foolishly been drawn into its reach. Had deliberately chosen to pass into its reach. The promises. The vows. The laughter from behind the pallid mask. Was the price worth the gain? Too late.

"Jon? You sure you're feeling all right?" Stein was oblivious to the pallid mask peering over his shoulder.

"Exercise and vitamins," said Holsten. He gave Stein perhaps another two years.

"It must work for you, then," Mannering persisted. "You hardly look any older than when we first met you here in London some ages ago. The rest of us are rapidly crumbling apart."

"Try jogging and only the occasional pint," Holsten improvised.

"I'd rather just jog," said Carter, getting up for another round. He passed by the tattered yellow cloak. Carter would never jog.

"Bought a rather good copy of *The Outsider*," said Foster, to change the subject. "Somewhat foxed, and in the reprint dust jacket, but at a good price." It had been Crosley's copy, sold cheaply to another dealer.

Holsten remembered the afternoon. Too many years ago. New York. Downstairs book shop. Noise of the subway. Cheap shelf. *The King in Yellow*, stuffed with pages from some older book. A bargain. Not cheap, as it turned out. He had never believed in any of this.

The figure in the pallid mask was studying Crosley, knowing he would soon throw himself in front of a tube train. Drained and discarded.

"Well," said Holsten. "I'd best be getting back after this one."

"This early in the day?" said Mannering, who was beginning to feel his pints. "Must be showing your age."

"Not if I can help it." Holsten sank his pint. "It's just that I said I'd meet someone in the hotel residents' bar at half three. He wants to do one of those interviews, or I'd ask you along. Boring, of course. But . . ."

"Then come round after," Mannering invited. "We'll all be here."

But not for very much longer, thought Holsten; but he said: "See you shortly, then."

Crosley was again coughing badly, a stained handkerchief to his mouth.

Jon Holsten fled.


The kid was named Dave Harvis, he was from Battersea, and he'd been waiting in the hotel lobby of the Bloomsbury Park for an hour in order not to be late. He wore a blue anorak and was clutching a blue nylon bag with a cassette recorder and some books to be signed, and he was just past twenty-one. Holsten picked him out as he entered the lobby, but the kid stared cluelessly.

"Hello. I'm Jon Holsten." He extended his hand, as on so many such meetings.

"Dave Harvis." He jumped from his seat. "It's a privilege to meet you, sir. Actually, I was expecting a much older . . . that is . . ."

"I get by with a little help from my friends." Holsten gave him a firm American handshake. "Delighted to meet you."

The tentacled mouths stroked and fed, promising whatever you wanted to hear. The figure in its tattered yellow cloak lifted its pallid mask. What is said is said. What is done is done. No turning back. Some promises can't be broken.

"Are you all right, sir?" Harvis had heard that Holsten must be up in his years.

"Jet lag, that's all," said Holsten. "Let's go into the bar, and you can buy me a pint for the interview. It's quiet there, I think."

Holsten sat down, troubled.

Harvis carried over two lagers. He worked on his cassette recorder. The residents' bar was deserted but for the barman.

"If you don't mind, sir." Harvis took a gulp of his lager. "I've invited a few mates round this evening to meet up at The Swan. They're great fans of your work. If you wouldn't mind. . . ."

"My pleasure," said Holsten.

The figure in tattered yellow now entered the residents' bar. The pallid mask regarded Harvis and Holsten, as Harvis fumbled with a microcassette tape.

Holsten felt a rush of strength.

Holsten mumbled into his pint: "I didn't mean for this to happen this way, but I can't stop it."

Harvis was still fumbling with the tape and didn't hear.

Neither did any gods who cared.

# The Howler in the Dark

## Richard L. Tierney

### I

Irving Hamilton pulled the collar of his topcoat closely about his throat as a gust of icy wind lashed his face with tiny snow crystals. Far below he could hear the thunder of the waves dashing in wind-lashed fury against the base of the cliff. Carefully he followed in the footsteps of his companion, keeping close behind him and occasionally glancing out over the storm-tossed sea. He wished the narrow footpath was not so near the edge of the precipice and that it did not wind so obscurely among the jagged boulders and protruding rock formations.

As they topped a rise, Hamilton's companion stopped and pointed away toward the next jagged ridge of the clifftop. Hamilton thrilled as he saw the irregular outlines of an old castle silhouetted against the gray northern sky.

"There it is," said his guide. "Duncaster Abbey—or what's left of it."

Hamilton eyed the dark pile with careful interest. Much of the ancient edifice had crumbled into ruin, and only one dark tower now protruded intact above the ragged battlements to stand, like a symbol of mystery, against the lowering sky. The entire structure seemed almost part of the cliff—a pinnacled outcropping balanced high and precariously above the roaring sea. To the east, wooded hills rolled away to form a panorama of wild beauty—frozen, snow-clad and desolate.

"How delightfully Gothic," exclaimed Hamilton. "And you say, Clyde, that it's supposed to be haunted?"

Clyde Mayfield, turning his back on the chilling wind, answered his friend with a gesture of derogatory amusement.

"Not haunted," he laughed; "just inhabited. The townspeople like to dramatize this place."

"I can see why! It's so picturesque and colorful . . ."

"Not so very colorful today, I'm afraid," said Mayfield, shivering. "We should have picked a better day to come out."

"I suppose we'd better start back, then—though I *would* like a closer look. Perhaps we can come back another day when it's not so cold."

They threaded their way carefully back along the wind-swept footpath and, ten minutes later, after reaching the road and Mayfield's parked car, were speeding back to the town of Duncaster.

"Sorry I coaxed you into bringing me out here on a day like this," said Hamilton, "but I didn't realize the weather would be so nasty."

"Quite all right—I wanted to show you the place sometime during your visit, and Sunday's the only day I can leave the pharmacy for long. Besides, I find the walk and the view invigorating."

Hamilton settled back contentedly and watched the countryside flow past. There was something strange and awesome about these desolate hills—something about the way the black, gnarled oaks clung to their craggy, snow-covered flanks that suggested fleeting visions of olden times. He turned once more to Mayfield.

"Why do the townspeople dislike the castle so much?"

Mayfield laughed. "They don't—they love it. You'll learn to take what they say with a grain of salt if you stay here awhile. That castle is Duncaster's only claim to fame, and it's kept the gossips hereabouts entertained for centuries, ever since it was finally abandoned around 1700 . . ."

"But I thought you said it was inhabited," protested Hamilton.

"Ah, so I did. This year two fellows have been living there. Come to think of it, they're Americans—fellow-countrymen of yours. Since you're so interested in the place, perhaps you could strike up an acquaintance with them and get them to show you around."

Hamilton, an architect by trade and possessing a passionate interest in antiquarian architecture, leaned forward eagerly and asked: "Do you think they would?"

"I don't see why not. Still . . ."

Mayfield pursed his lips thoughtfully. "It's hard to say. I've seen them only the few times they've come to my pharmacy. They're not at all talkative. I think they're engaged in some kind of scientific research."

"Maybe they want privacy."

Hamilton laughed. "You're too unimaginative! Don't you see what we have here? Two mysterious strangers living in the remains of an ancient castle, procuring strange chemicals from the local pharmacist for some nameless purpose—ha! All we need is a distressed damsel in a white nightgown and we have all the elements for a first-rate Gothic horror story."

"Now you're beginning to sound like the townspeople . . ."

"Aha!" cried Hamilton triumphantly.

"Furthermore," Mayfield continued, "the men have never ordered any 'strange' chemicals from me—merely a variety of common pharmaceutical and medical supplies."

"Simply no imagination," grinned Hamilton.

Mayfield shrugged. "Maybe not, but imagination nets me no profits. I don't care if they're building Frankenstein monsters if it keeps them as good customers of mine as they have been."

Now, as the car topped a rise in the road, the lights of the village of Duncaster hove into view, softly brilliant beneath the mantle of dark creeping out from the westward hills. Those lights, gaily-colored amid the quaint decorations in the house-windows, reminded the pair that Christmas was only a week away, and their conversation turned involuntarily to brighter things.

As Hamilton shared a cheerful Sunday dinner with Mayfield and his family, the topic of the afternoon's discussion was far from his mind. Later, however, as he retired to the Mayfields' comfortable guest room and lay listening to the winter wind before drifting off to sleep, he could not help but recall his visit to the old castle by the sea—that bleak, age-haunted pile of masonry standing above the angry, pounding sea—and wondered about the two strange men who chose to live in such lonely isolation.

## II

When Hamilton woke next morning it was late; Mayfield had already left for the pharmacy. Accordingly, after partaking of a breakfast Mrs. Mayfield had accommodatingly kept warm for him, he set out on a solitary jaunt through the streets of Duncaster.

The sky was clear and blue. A crisp wintriness sparked the air. Hamilton breathed deeply, enjoying the quaint atmosphere of the old village and watching the townspeople bustling about in their preparations for Christmas. Though he had been here only a week, many of the people hailed him by name as they passed him on the street, and he began to feel a sense of easiness and belonging steal over him.

Entering a small bookshop which he had begun to frequent almost daily, he closed the oaken door with its diamond-paned windows and stamped the snow from his boots.

"And how be you today, Mr. Hamilton?" asked old Mr. Scott, the white-mustached proprietor, his blue eyes twinkling from behind thick, square spectacles.

"As chipper as you look to me, Eric—or so I hope," said Hamilton. "I'm wondering if you can show me any books recording the history of this region."

"I think so." Eric Scott fumbled around on his bookshelves and presently withdrew a dark, worn volume. He thumbed through it rapidly, peering intently at the yellowed pages.

"Here it is," he said finally, pointing to a chapter heading. "This covers it all from the Roman times to the Nineteenth Century. Please handle it gently, Mr. Hamilton—that book is over one hundred and fifty years old."

"I certainly will. May I read it here?"

"Of course. Use the table by the window. It's a pleasure for me to see a man of your age enjoying the old things that so many have forgotten how to enjoy."

Hamilton sat down and opened the old book. He felt again the comfortable sense of belonging. It was a privilege, he knew, even to be allowed in old Eric Scott's bookshop, let alone to be free to browse amid his fascinating, antiquated tomes. Scott's stock was entirely of rare, old items and all his business was done by mail-order, so that profane hands never touched a book without a prior reimbursement sizable enough to indicate that the book would receive shelf-space in a loving home. Only Mayfield's assurances, plus Hamilton's obvious enthusiasm toward ancient architecture and all writings pertaining thereto, had relaxed the old man's guard and finally endeared the American to him.

Hamilton soon lost himself in the old book. The chapter he was reading dealt with the history of Duncaster and the larger, nearby community of Burntshire. Presently he was gratified to find a fairly lengthy description of Duncaster Abbey itself. The conquering Romans had found ancient rings of stones there and, after abolishing the Pagan rites which the natives had practiced, had built a fine, colonnaded temple of their own—which was, in turn, destroyed centuries later by bands of Vikings who for a time overran northern England.

It was during the Twelfth Century that the Norman-French Baron, Hugo de Taran, returned from the Crusades and built the first castle on the site that was later to be Duncaster Abbey. Baron de Taran ruled his serfs with no more than the usual harshness of the time, but was reputed to practice non-Christian rites which generated a great deal of gossip and repugnance—rites which, it was said, included even human sacrifice. Baron de Taran's Frankish mother was of the d'Erlettes of Averoigne, a lineage and a region both long associated with sorcerous practices; moreover, it was said that the Baron, during his campaigns against the Paynim in the Holy Land, had acquired for spoil certain ancient documents written by the magi of Arabia and Egypt. However, Church rule was weak on the frontiers of what passed for civilization in those Dark Ages, and the heads of Baron de Taran's accusers were soon skewered on pikes to dry in the sun.

The descendants of Hugo de Taran, according to legend, used their position of lordship to carry on the blasphemous tradition their sire had begun. Some even claimed the ancient Roman and Celtic rites had been revived. Lights and sounds were seen and heard about the castle on certain nights of the year, while people who mysteriously vanished on those same nights were never seen again.

These sinister activities began to decline during the Fourteenth Century as Catholicism became ever stronger in England. By the

1600s, perhaps because of the iron rule of the Calvinistic Church of Scotland, the activities had ceased altogether. But then, in 1690, when the problem of Witchcraft was also being confronted in the American colonies, the village of Duncaster was smitten with a strange terror which might have been a plague. The cause of the widespread deaths, however, was unanimously believed to be connected with the last members of the declining de Taran line, and the Church of Scotland was called upon to take action. There followed the witch-burnings of 1690, which apparently ended the reign of the hated lords who had ruled for so long with such superstition-inspiring terrorism.

The clergymen chronicling these events were vague, and only hinted at the things which were dragged to light from the towers and dungeons of the ancient castle. Signs of paganistic ritual were abundant, and there were remains of bloodstained altars inscribed with primal symbols of forgotten meaning. Of the volumes of accursed elder lore alleged to have been collected down the centuries by the wicked barons, not a trace could be found, and it was assumed that they had been carefully secreted in some inaccessible nether crypt. On these grounds, the Church ordered that the entire castle be burned, so that the frightful knowledge of the de Taran's might never be brought to light and spread abroad.

Though the castle was not destroyed utterly, its charred remains lay abandoned for over a century. Then an attempt was made by the Anglican Church to use the edifice, and it was partly rebuilt and given the name of "Duncaster Abbey." For some reason, however, the building was used as a monastery for only a few months, after which it was abandoned once more. This time it lay vacant until the present day—or rather, Hamilton reflected as he finished reading the account, until the two Americans had established themselves in it nearly a year ago.

"Did you find what you wanted?" asked the old bookseller as Hamilton closed and laid aside the aged volume.

Hamilton nodded. "Fascinating! What do you know about the two men now living in the castle? I'm hoping to get their permission to look it over."

Eric Scott brushed back his thinning hair thoughtfully, and Hamilton sensed a slight uneasiness in the expression of his watery blue eyes.

"Those two are an odd pair," he said. "I'm not sure I'd care to know them better. Just my own impression, of course—but you'll find most people hereabouts will say the same."

"Why?" asked Hamilton

"It's nothing anyone can lay a solid finger on—but let me tell you something . . ."

The old man launched himself into an account of what he knew and what local gossip had to say about the strangers, and Hamilton leaned forward on his elbows and listened attentively . . .

It was during the previous February that the strangers had first appeared in Duncaster, residing in old Mrs. Knapp's rooming house near the sea-road and having nothing to do with the townsfolk. Here they lived for more than a month, making occasional trips to the deserted castle by the sea. Their brief appearances on the streets of Duncaster, sporting their brown beards, wide-brimmed hats and long, dark overcoats, soon earned them the reputation of ludicrous, albeit somewhat sinister, eccentrics.

Old Mrs. Knapp talked a great deal about the pair, and about the many crates of electrical apparatus, glassware and books they had lugged from their station-wagon to the upstairs rooms they had rented. The men gave their names as Pitts and Taggart, though for some reason Mrs. Knapp preferred to think these were not their true appellations. Indeed, the landlady, gossip that she was, took a certain pride in her mysterious tenants and no doubt often exaggerated their peculiarities. Their main trait, however—outstanding in such a small community—was their extreme taciturn reticence. Their accent proclaimed them Americans, but other than this bit of information nothing factual could be deduced.

Next to old Mrs. Knapp, however, Eric Scott himself was probably the foremost authority on the men. They had actually written to him shortly before their arrival, professing an interest in certain rare old books, and had subsequently visited him several times in his musty old book-shop. Scott had been vaguely disturbed at some of the titles they had mentioned, for he had heard terrible things of the blasphemous *Necronomicon* of the mad Arab Abdul Alhazred, and he associated monstrous legends of evil with certain odd names inscribed on the yellowed papyri of the fragmentary *Book of Thoth-Ammon.* He was somehow glad that he was almost entirely unable to aid the strangers in their quest, and hoped they would not be inclined to seek further for the information they desired.

Besides Eric Scott's old book-shop, the strangers also began to frequent Mayfield's Pharmacy and Howell's Medical Supply store. Occasionally they would drive over to Burntshire to make use of the library there and, as the gossip soon had it, to request from the librarians anything pertaining to the ruins of Duncaster Abbey.

Then, during March, the strangers journeyed to London and apparently made some transactions with those who owned the castle, for on their return to Duncaster they immediately began to transport all their belongings to the ancient edifice. After finally completing their change of residence, Pitts and Taggart had paid off old Mrs. Knapp, thus breaking all ties with the world. Many of the townsfolk had been shocked at all this, for to the religiously orthodox the castle was symbolic of evil from time immemorial.

For several months the two continued to dwell in their strange abode, virtually cut off from the outside world, for the nearest road was more than half a mile from the castle. Infrequently they would pick their way over the old footpath along the ragged seacliffs and drive into town to purchase large quantities of food and other supplies. Finally they sold their station-wagon to a man in Burntshire, retired to the castle and vanished into utter seclusion. The town gossips, of course, speculated wildly but futilely on the activities of the two Americans.

Toward summer, however, events took a darker and more sinister turn with the disappearance of little Tommy McCallister, who vanished mysteriously one afternoon while playing with several friends near the bluffs by the sea. According to the other children, Tommy, who was known as a rather aggressive youth, boasted that he was not afraid to approach the forbidding castle and attempt to spy on its two mysterious inhabitants. Against the advice of his companions, the lad had set out to prove good his boast, charging the rest to wait for his return. They had seen Tommy walk off toward the northern horizon and vanish into the dark woods which surrounded the castle on its three landward sides; but, though they waited for nearly three hours, the boy did not return. At last, seeing that dusk was near, the youngsters turned reluctantly homeward.

At first the children said nothing to their elders about Tommy, for their parents had sternly warned them not to play near the sea; but next day, when the frantic McCallisters began to inquire about their missing boy, the youngsters finally broke down and confessed what had happened. Immediately a search party set out to scour the wooded hills near the sea. Yet, though the searchers persisted throughout the day and part of the night, they found no trace of the missing child.

The townspeople, however, were not totally surprised at this failure, for many had already begun to hint sullenly that the boy had met with foul play. It was Constable Dunlap, the town's single law-enforcement officer, who suggested this possibility most strongly, pointing out that the boy had been last seen actually approaching the old castle with the intention of spying on its inhabitants. Was it not possible that these reclusive eccentrics might be madmen who would not hesitate to inflict harm on any they considered trespassers?

On hearing Constable Dunlap's opinions, the villagers immediately accepted them as fact and displayed a great deal of emotional indignation. They loudly demanded that Dunlap go forth and arrest the pair—though none volunteered to accompany him—and the very next morning the constable set out to question the dwellers in Duncaster Abbey.

He did not return. When it was learned that the constable had vanished as mysteriously as Tommy McCallister, a great furor ensued. Officials in Burntshire were informed, and the Sheriff and several of his local constabulary were sent immediately to check up on the inhabitants of the castle. This they did, but the results of their investigation fell far short of satisfying the citizens of Duncaster.

According to the Sheriff, the two Americans had received him and his men openly and even hospitably. They were very accommodating, offering no resistance to a search of the premises and answering all questions with seeming frankness while expressing a desire to help in any way they could. The Sheriff was not convinced of their sincerity, of course, but search as they might, his men could find not the slightest trace of anything even remotely suspicious. Judging by the furnishings and books about the castle, the Americans were merely a pair of scholarly bachelors engaged in antiquarian pursuits.

After several hours the Sheriff and his men left, annoyed at having no evidence on which to base an arrest.

It appeared, however, that the townspeople might have been wrong about Pitts and Taggart; for the very next day, when a group of fishermen found the body of Tommy McCallister washed up on the seashore, just south of Duncaster, there were no indications whatsoever that the boy had met death by violence. The autopsy performed by the mortician in Burntshire revealed no indications of murder, and it was officially assumed that the thirteen-year-old boy had fallen from the cliff into the sea while returning from the castle by way of the narrow footpath.

Constable Dunlap's fate, however, was more perplexing. No trace of him was ever found. For many weeks the Sheriff continued his investigation, several times questioning Pitts and Taggart and searching their Gothic residence for some clue. Each visit was met by the same lack of either resistance or evidence, and the Sheriff was at last reluctantly compelled to admit—officially, at least—that the curious pair probably had nothing to do with the disappearances. Possibly Constable Dunlap had fallen into one of the fairly numerous pits or crevices which were known to be a hazard in the hilly woodlands along that seacoast.

The case was brought to a final close early in the fall by the Sheriff's untimely death, and the official who replaced him filed the report of the affair and soon forgot about it. Having no personal interest in the case, the new Sheriff was content to regard it as largely a sensationalistic uproar. The people of Duncaster, however, held to their opinions and continued to regard the castle and its inhabitants with distaste. Dark speculation continued to flit from mouth to mouth—whispers not only of possible murder, but of wilder things like torture, witchcraft and human sacrifice. There were even those who maintained that the old Sheriff's death might not have been as simple as it seemed—that Dr. Bannister's diagnosis of some "strange, epileptic-like seizure" may have been only a cover-up for his own ignorance. Certainly there had been something disturbing about the way the Sheriff had screamed out in the night just before he was found dead in his room, his eyes fixed wide as if in horror—but then, all this was idle gossip by rustics whose only traditions were handed down from superstitious peasants of the Dark Ages.

Twice more the strangers visited Duncaster, hiking to town on foot, but now they were regarded with revulsion rather than amused curiosity. Only a few local tradesmen, whose shops they patronized lavishly, would look upon the pair with anything less than aversion. Both times they visited the old book-shop of Eric Scott, purchasing various odd volumes of ancient religious and Rosicrucian lore. Scott remembered that these books dwelt largely on subjects such as hypnotism, astral projection and hidden powers of the mind, and that the man had referred to older and darker texts dealing with half-forgotten secrets that had barely managed to struggle down the ages from times of unguessed antiquity. What these men sought to achieve through the acquisition of such long-suppressed knowledge, Scott did not like to guess.

For the rest of the autumn, Pitts and Taggart were seen no more except by a few early fishermen who, from the distant vantage of their boats, claimed to have noticed the pair combing the beach beneath their crag-perched castle, gathering objects washed up by the Atlantic tides. However, the citizens of Duncaster did not forget, and the gossips whispered of dim lights and wild cries which had issued from the castle on the night of All Hallows Eve; while thereafter, some claimed, one could hear an eerie, mournful howling if one stood in certain places at the base of the castle-crowned precipice. Few ventured to prove these things for themselves, however, most preferring to accept the testimony of the local story-tellers. And so it was that, after nearly an entire year, the mystery of the dark strangers of Duncaster Abbey was as baffling as—perhaps even more baffling than—it had been on the day of their arrival.

## III

At first Hamilton did not realize that Eric Scott had finished speaking; the old man's story had held him enthralled. Feeling vaguely uneasy, he tried to bring his mind to focus on the present.

"That's quite a story," he said. "Just what do *you* believe about the Americans?"

Scott shrugged. "I'm not ready to believe everything I hear, Mr.

Hamilton, but at the same time I'll not go out of my way to scoff at everything that seems strange. It's my opinion that those men are up to something they shouldn't be. I know too much about the books they've sought to doubt that."

Hamilton's uneasiness increased. There were many points in common between Scott's story and the account he had read of the de Taran line of olden days—mysterious disappearances, forbidden books of dark lore, hints of witchcraft and fearful rites practiced within the castle's black precincts ... He rose from his chair and, thanking the old bookseller, set out rather hurriedly into the open air of the street. Somehow he was glad to leave the bookshop with its dry atmosphere of age and stuffiness, glad to feel the winter wind blowing cold against his face.

Later, however, as he chatted with Mayfield at the pharmacy, he found himself actually chuckling over the odd notions of the aged bookseller.

"Yes, old Scott is quite a storyteller," said Mayfield. "He's full of odd notions—especially when it comes to the subject of Duncaster Abbey."

"He certainly has excited my curiosity," grinned Hamilton. "I simply can't leave without seeing that old castle now—and meeting its inhabitants!"

Mayfield glanced at his watch. "Look, I'll be busy for the rest of the afternoon, so why don't you take my car and drive out there yourself? The weather is fairly decent now, and you know the way."

"You mean it? You're sure you won't be needing the car?"

"Not at all." Mayfield handed over his car keys. "Just be back in time for supper or my wife will throw fits. There's an extra tire under the back seat if you should need it. Good luck!"

A few moments later Hamilton was motoring rapidly out of Duncaster, enjoying the wild beauty of the wooded hills and feeling a bit uneasy about driving upon the left side of the road. During the solitude of the drive his mind returned to the things he had read and heard in the quaint old bookshop, and he pondered again over the odd coincidences between the past and the present. Probably Scott and the rest of the townspeople, knowing the legends concerning the bygone de Taran line, had projected similar characteristics on the two strangers now residing in the Abbey.

At length Hamilton pulled over to a short turnoff and parked the car. Doubtless this was where the Americans used to park their vehicle, also. As he stepped out, he could hear the pounding of the nearby surf. It was but a short walk to the footpath along the cliff edge, and thence to the ridge from which the castle could be seen.

The place seemed less foreboding under blue sky and sunlight, but the wind still blew in from the sea with considerable gustiness, causing angry waves to crash loudly upon the rocks below. Carefully Hamilton picked his way along the footpath, remembering suddenly that the young McCallister boy must have fallen from the ledge somewhere nearby. The thought was not pleasant, and he found himself wondering again about the fate of Constable Dunlap and the odd things people had hinted concerning the Sheriff's death.

Presently the path turned away from the cliff and entered the thick grove surrounding the castle. Hamilton lost sight of the building as he picked his way among the dark boles of gnarled oaks whose branches twisted weirdly above him. His uneasiness grew as he realized how completely isolated the castle was. Yet, at the same time, he was enjoying his adventure, anticipating what his friends back home would say when he told them of the old "haunted castle" he had visited in England. . . .

Emerging from the wood, Hamilton saw that the castle was quite near, looming above him on its rocky crag with imposing grandeur, its ruined battlements dark against the sky. He stopped to gaze at it for a moment, wishing he had thought to bring a camera; and, as he looked, he heard a strange, drawn-out wail that seemed to emerge from the base of the cliff. It was obviously, he decided, a trick of the wind as it howled among the jagged rock spires of the cliffside—and yet, it seemed at times so like the cry of a person in anguish, as though someone were actually trapped in some dark crevice or cavern within the rock, that Hamilton could easily see how the imaginations of the locals had conjured up voices from nowhere.

He climbed the remaining distance up the footpath and picked his way among the tumbled, frost-covered blocks of the shattered walls. The path ended at a door of solid oak set in a massive wall. Overcoming a momentary hesitation, Hamilton raised the heavy iron knocker and let it fall noisily against the door.

Several times Hamilton knocked, but no one answered. Perhaps, he thought, the inhabitants were ignoring would-be visitors. He had about decided to leave when he heard a clanking of heavy bolts being shot back, and the next instant the door swung open on grating hinges.

Hamilton glanced quickly over the figure that stood in the doorway, wondering what to say for an opening. The man confronting him was slightly shorter than himself, slender, and sporting a trim brown goatee and mustache which merged together. He wore a dark cloak, of a type fashionable in the early Nineteenth Century; it hung about his form like raven wings. His alert brown eyes gazed suspiciously at Hamilton from behind dark-rimmed spectacles.

"Sorry to trouble you," began Hamilton, "but I'm interested in the construction of this castle, and was hoping you might allow me to examine it more closely. You seen, I'm an architect by trade and an antiquarian at heart. . . ."

The man suddenly grinned and his eyes lost their suspicious glare. "Ah, of course—an antiquarian! There aren't many of us left, I fear. Do come in."

Hamilton, pleased at being accepted so readily, stepped quickly inside. His host immediately closed and bolted the door once more.

"I hope you don't mind my intrusion," said Hamilton, "but I fear my curiosity concerning ancient architecture is often more than good manners can hold in check. . . ."

"Please don't apologize. I sympathize with your interest—which is one of the reasons I chose to live here, Mister. . . ."

"Hamilton. Irving Hamilton."

"Mr. Hamilton. And I am John Taggart." The man wrung his guest's hand, then motioned him to follow. They walked through several vaulted stone corridors, which Hamilton admired with great interest, and presently entered a large room sparsely but comfortably furnished with articles of Nineteenth Century manufacture. Two plush easy chairs and a large mahogany table occupied the center of the room, the table being littered with books, papers and a few glass containers of assorted sizes and shapes. Heavy, thick drapes flanked the single arched window of the chamber, hanging limply from the ceiling to the stone floor, while on either side of this narrow casement rested massive bookcases, their many shelves filled with books both ancient and modern.

"Our living room and library," said Taggart. "The table is rather cluttered, but we weren't expecting company." He began somewhat hurriedly to clear the table of its volumes and papers, placing them in various niches in the bookcases. "I judge by your accent that you're a New-Englander."

"That's right. And judging by *your* speech, I'd say you're originally from the upper Midwest. . . ."

"You are perceptive," said Taggart briefly. "But, come—I'll show you around the castle. It isn't often I meet anyone with interests similar to my own, and it does me good to know there are still those who find joy in the antiquated things of the world."

So saying, Taggart conducted Hamilton through several halls and chambers on the main floor, then gradually worked upward to higher suites of rooms. Hamilton became deeply absorbed in everything around him and in his host's comments on the history of this aged Gothic structure. He reveled in the imagined glories of ages past, and speculated a bit uneasily about those who had dwelt in the castle so many centuries ago. Taggart was quite attentive to his questions and insisted on accompanying him as a guide; the man obviously took a certain pride in his strange home, and commented with great knowledge on every detail of the antiquated architecture about them. Almost it seemed that he was conducting a guided tour which he had been over many times before.

At length, after ascending a long, narrow stairway of worn stone, they emerged onto a small circular area beneath the open sky. Here the wind blustered cold and strong, but Hamilton forgot the chill as he gazed over the massive battlements of the tower and beheld the landscape of dark wooded hills stretching away on all sides, save to the west where the gray sea roared in, all flecked with whitecaps, to crash on the coast below.

"It was from this tower," said Taggart, "that the Taran barons used to survey their broad domains."

"Ah! You know of the Tarans?"

"Of course. Why should we not—we who now occupy their ancient home? They were men of great power and vision, and their history is worthy of study. They might have ruled all England if they had not been too eager to show their hand. . . ."

Taggart stopped speaking—rather abruptly, Hamilton thought.
"De Taran is a very unusual name," said Hamilton. "I've never
run across it before."

"It is indeed. As a matter of fact, it was not the original name of
the founder of the line at all. Taran is the name of one of the oldest
gods to be worshipped in Europe, a god of lightning and thunder.
When Caesar's legions first marched into Gaul they found the inhabitants offering up human sacrifices to this god, and certain records
far more ancient than the Roman chronicles indicate that his origins
go far back indeed. Christianity suppressed the worship of Taran, of
course, but Baron Hugo later took up a furtive devotion to him for
reasons of his own, at which time his enemies all died off rather suddenly. His power grew swiftly after that, till finally, after amassing
great wealth in the Crusades, he openly styled himself Baron de
Taran, removed himself from public eyes and built this stronghold
here in the north of England. Since then, they say, the enemies of the
Taran line have had a tendency to die off early in life. Ridiculous, of
course, but fascinating legendry nevertheless, as I'm sure you'll
agree."

"I'd heard they were greatly feared. . . ."

Hamilton abruptly ceased speaking as a low, moaning howl
drifted up the shaft of the tower—a wild despairing, windy cry like
the sound he had heard near the cliff-base. Taggart, however, acted as
though he had heard nothing, and Hamilton wondered uneasily if
the sound might have been due merely to the wind howling amid the
shattered walls and battlements.

"I'm afraid there's little more to show you," said Taggart. "Come
on—let's get out of this cold wind." Then, as they made their way
down the tower stairs once more, he added: "I hope you have enjoyed
your visit as much as I've enjoyed having you come."

"I've enjoyed it immensely, thank you; but have you really shown
me everything? If I'm not being overly demanding, I'd very much like
to see the wine cellars and dungeons as well. . . ."

"I would willingly show them to you if it were possible," said
Taggart; "but, unfortunately, the cellars of the castle lie beneath the
ruined portion and were filled with rubble at the time of the destruction. They are quite inaccessible."

At this point they had arrived at the ground floor and had just re-entered the spacious, sparsely-furnished library, when suddenly, Hamilton heard again that faint, wailing howl of despair. This time it was clearer, and he could hardly doubt that it was the anguished cry of some living thing in dire torment. Before he could speculate further, however, a third man strode rapidly into the room and stopped abruptly upon seeing them. He was tall and lean, his pale face clean-shaven and scowling. He was dressed in the same manner as Taggart. Hamilton realized the man must be Pitts.

The newcomer's blue eyes glared with unconcealed hostility at Hamilton.

"Who is this?" he demanded of Taggart.

"A guest in our house." Taggart's voice was even yet emphatic. "This is Mr. Hamilton, an architect from Massachusetts, who is very interested in our ancient abode. Mr. Hamilton," he continued, "this is Mr. Jeremy Pitts, my friend and fellow scholar."

Pitts nodded slightly to Hamilton then turned to Taggart. "Come quickly," he muttered, then turned abruptly and strode out of the room, his dark cloak stirring the dust into whorls behind him.

"Excuse me," said Taggart, waving Hamilton to a chair. "I have some matters to attend to briefly. I'll only be a few minutes."

So saying, he strode rapidly away into the corridor, leaving Hamilton alone and puzzled. A moment later Hamilton thought he heard the strange howling once more, but it ceased abruptly following a heavy, grating sound as though a huge stone were being moved across the floor. After this, the castle grew utterly silent.

Some time passed, but Taggart did not return. As Hamilton waited he felt more and more uneasy. His memory of the strange howling, and the present atmosphere of silent gloom, were working upon him oppressively. He found himself impatient to be gone, yet a part of him insisted that he should not leave without thanking his host. Accordingly, he selected a book from the shelves and settled back to an easy chair, intending to read until Taggart's return.

The book was a large, black volume entitled: *The Complete Works of Edgar Allan Poe*. Its leaves fell easily and naturally open to a certain page, as though it had been opened at that page frequently, and Hamilton noticed several lines heavily underlined in dark pencil. The lines read:

A wrong is unredressed when retribution overtakes its re-dresser. It is equally unredressed when the avenger fails to make himself felt as such to him who has done the wrong.

The lines were from Poe's story "The Cask of Amontillado"—a tale of morbid and terrible revenge. Hamilton felt his spirits darken subtly, and he no longer wished to read. Laying the book aside, he began to pace restlessly about the room and, as he did so, he noticed on the table an aged tome of ponderous dimensions. Its yellowed pages were held open by a heavy paperweight; and, when out of mild curiosity he happened to glance at its title, Hamilton was slightly shocked to find that it was the mysterious *Necronomicon* which old Eric Scott had spoken of so hesitantly.

His curiosity aroused, Hamilton examined the book more closely. It was painstakingly hand-printed in archaic English by a certain Dr. Dee, evidently the translator rather than the author. Between the pages of this book several loose papers were thrust; some were ancient and brittle parchment covered with mystifying lines of Egyptian hieroglyphics and hieratic symbols as well as glyphs of languages Hamilton could not identify; the rest, apparently the translations, were written in English on modern typing paper. Hamilton glanced over these translations briefly, but did not read them; certain names which he glimpsed, such as "Taaran, God of Evil" and "Nyarlathotep, The Crawling Chaos," were vaguely disturbing.

The great book itself was obviously written during a time when the world was rife with the wildest sort of superstition; for the single page Hamilton glimpsed was probably but a sample of the fantastic ideas contained within the entire volume:

There are Ways in which the Mind of a Man is like unto an Eye, in that it can be used as a lens to focus the Powers that exist in the Spaces between the Worlds. Indeed, the Mind of any Man can be used, when severed from the confining ties of the Flesh and put into a state of Trance, as a Weapon of great Power. To the Sorcerer who brings such a Mind under his Control, nothing is impossible, for he will be able to see into the farthest Lands of the World by means of that Mind's Eye, and shall be able to inflict upon his Enemies a Vengeance of such Type as will leave no slightest Mark, but shall cause them to expire with Fear and great Terrors.

Before Hamilton could read further he heard once more the loud, grating sound, and hurriedly replaced the ancient book as he had found it. For some reason he was unwilling to have his host find him looking at the volume. He seated himself once more, and a moment later Taggart entered the room, apologizing for having left so suddenly but stating that it could not be helped. He did not explain the cause of his departure, however, and Hamilton, after exchanging a few final civilities with him, took his leave.

As he walked back along the wind-swept path by the sea, he was strangely troubled. Taggart, it was true, had shown him every courtesy, but his feeling that there was some concealed mystery had only increased. For one thing, Taggart had said there were no rooms left intact beneath the castle, yet, now that Hamilton thought of it, those weird howling sounds had seemed to come from below—or, rather, had somehow carried with them a sense of *depth*. . . .

And what, he wondered, could be the cause of the sound itself? The more he tried to recall it, the less likely it seemed that it could have been caused by the wind or any other inanimate agency. There had been a suggestion of agony and frustration in the sound, faint as it had been, and Hamilton grew angry at the thought of some hapless animal undergoing strange, painful experiments in some dark chamber beneath the castle. Was this why Taggart had been so hastily summoned—to aid in some such morbid experiment? Or was there an even darker reason? Certainly those ancient books he had glimpsed, though ridiculous and harmless in themselves, were not the sort of books to be taken seriously by rational men. Could the castle-dwellers be madmen who were performing magical rituals of sacrifice for secret purposes . . . ?

As Hamilton drove back to Duncaster, mulling over his impressions, he had to admit to himself that there was nothing on which he could put his finger. It troubled him that there were so many points of coincidence between the activities of the Americans and the accounts of the ancient Tarans. He no longer cared for the flavor of mystery which had at first seemed so colorful to him, nor did he like the thought of those old books he had seen, with their hints of

vengeance and strange powers. The afternoon had given him pleasure enough, but it had also left an unsavory aftertaste with him.

## IV

"You've far too great an imagination," said Mayfield as he and
Hamilton left the supper table to retire to the den. "You say you were
received very hospitably. What was it you didn't like about the men?"

Hamilton settled comfortably into a plush lounging-chair as
Mayfield poured the brandy. "I'm not sure, really. Maybe it was just
old Eric Scott's gossip that set my mind going. I must admit the
world seems more prosaic now, here in your cozy den . . . Thank
you." He accepted the glass of brandy from Mayfield, then added
thoughtfully: "It's just that there's such an intense air of mystery
about it all. . . ."

"Well, forget it." Mayfield handed him over a copy of the *London
Times* and pointed to an article. "This should interest you, considering your taste for mystery. Have you heard of the 'screaming deaths'?"

"No. I'd sworn off newspapers at the start of this vacation."

"Ah, but you devoured the account of the Loch Ness Monster last
week readily enough! You'll like this, too, I'm sure."

Hamilton sighed and began to scan the article. It seemed that
several Americans visiting England had, in the last month or so, been
afflicted with a strange disease which the newspapers, with typical
sensationalism, referred to as the "screaming death." Although only a
half-dozen people or so had so far succumbed to the disease, the
strange nature of these cases had caused considerable comment. Indeed, the term "disease" had been applied only for lack of a better
term. Doctors had referred to the deaths as "seizures," while psychia-
trists had called them "suicidal epilepsy" and other ridiculous names,
but none seemed to be able to point to any rational cause for the attacks. In fact, the police had gone so far as to consider them possibly
an ingenious form of murder, although they were at a loss for explaining the *modus operandi*.

Specifically, the cases were alike in that the disease always struck
suddenly and at night, usually in the early hours of the morning. It
was as swift as it was deadly, giving no symptoms or forewarning
whatsoever. The victims were invariably seized with great pain a few

minutes before their deaths, as was evident in their wild and terrible cries in the night, often waking people in neighboring houses. This agony was also doubtless responsible for the hideous, contorted expressions found on the faces of the deceased, the victims invariably being dead before anyone could arrive on the scene. And in every case their rooms were in chaotic disorder, suggesting that their deaths had been accompanied by violent physical spasms.

Those who advocated the murder theory pointed to this last fact as evidence of a struggle, while they also drew attention to the fact that each victim came from *the same city in the Midwestern United States*. Apparently, during the last month or two, each had decided—independently and rather impulsively—to vacation in England, despite the adverse weather conditions there during the winter season. Moreover, each had held a job in the fields of law practice or legal administration: one had been a petty judge, another a former police chief, while the rest had been either policemen or lawyers. Thus some sort of pattern seemed apparent, but one which pointed in no particular direction.

The murder theory was further weakened when autopsies revealed no marks of violence or evidence of poisoning in any of the deaths. Meanwhile doctors pointed out that the common origin of these unfortunate visitors was proof of *their* theory of strange disease or plague, and urged that American medics would do well to check out the possibility.

When Hamilton finished the article, his forehead was damp with sweat and his hands shook perceptibly. Mayfield, noticing his agitation, wondered if he felt ill, but this Hamilton denied hastily, saying that he was merely somewhat fatigued and that he wished to retire early. Accordingly, after bidding his host good night, he departed to the guest room.

Hamilton did not sleep that night, however. Too many coincidences kept turning up in his restless mind—coincidences that hinted at terrifying things beyond the threshold of sane reason.

All night he tossed and turned, trying to rationalize away his terrible imaginings. He could not. His mind held too many bits of information that fit together too well. What of the old Sheriff who, according to Eric Scott, had died in a way so similar to the visitors from the American Midwest; had he perhaps died because he suspected too much? And what of the fact that Taggart and Pitts were also midwesterners, as was evident from their accent?

The conclusions these ideas suggested were ones Hamilton's modern mind could not accept, yet the more he tried to shut them out of his mind the more they disturbed him. Most disturbing of all, perhaps, was the memory of that passage he had scanned in the pages of the forbidden and terrible *Necronomicon.*

At the first crack of dawn following a sleepless night, Hamilton stole silently out into the streets of Duncaster and made his way to the old bookshop of Eric Scott; his breath turned to fog before him in the cold, still air.

Scott was already puttering around the shop and, at Hamilton's insistent rapping, the old man permitted him to enter. He seemed surprised at the early visit, but his surprise changed to grave concern as Hamilton hesitantly began to tell his story.

The gossips of Duncaster never learned what was said that day behind the closed door of Scott's book-shop, though they knew that only a matter of great importance would have kept the mercenary old shopkeeper from answering his door or telephone. Probably it is just as well—things that tend to link unguessed realms of horror with the apparently commonplace world are often better left unsaid. It was guessed only that strange volumes were diligently perused, and that knowledge of a strange kind was doubtless gained and correlated with certain facts—but what this knowledge might have been, neither Scott nor Hamilton would ever say.

That evening Mayfield, on Hamilton's return, greeted his guest with curious questions. Hamilton, though polite, seemed strangely evasive. He was thoughtfully silent at supper that evening, and hardly spoke at all until Mayfield happened to mention a topic that quickly caught his attention.

"Remember the outlandish article I showed you last night?" he remarked. "The one about the so-called 'screaming deaths'?"

"Oh—yes, I recall it," replied Hamilton, who had thought of little else all day.

"Well, there was another story in this evening's paper. . . ."

Hamilton felt a pang of dread. Yet his voice was deliberately steady as he asked: "You mean there have been more deaths?"

"Yes—five, to be exact. This time an entire family was wiped out;

people by the name of Pearson or Parson—I don't remember exactly. But they were all from the same American city as the others. Isn't it the most puzzling thing you ever heard of? The local paper's full of it—they were staying at the Claibourne Inn at Burntshire, practically next door, you might say. If you and old Scott hadn't been so lost in the past all day, you'd have heard the whole town talking about it!"

Hamilton hoped his face showed none of his inward turmoil. He knew now that he and Eric Scott must soon take some sort of action. The law, he was certain, would never solve this mystery, nor would medical science ever find a cure. By some obscure twist of chance, Hamilton realized, the mad fiends of fate had chosen him and Scott to face alone the full import of this situation, and his soul seemed to shrink within him at the thought of the terrible responsibility that now rested upon his shoulders.

V

The wind whistled dismally among the rocks as Hamilton and Scott struggled up the steep footpath by the sea. Their uneasiness grew as the castle brooded ever more darkly and closely above them, and Hamilton wondered whether anyone had ever before spent a Christmas vacation more strangely.

"What shall they think of our visit?" asked Scott nervously. "They're sure to suspect."

"Just try to act natural. Tell them you're interested in seeing some of their old books I told you about. If they do suspect, well. . . ." He fingered the handle of the compact Smith and Wesson revolver that nestled in his coat pocket—an item he stubbornly risked carrying on all his travels whatever the local regulations might be.

As they reached the top of the cliff, a faint noise like rough pounding reached their ears. Hamilton gripped his pistol and led the way forward among the tumbled stones of the ruins. When they came to the end of the path they saw, to their surprise, that the oaken door of the castle hung open. It swung back and forth on its rusty hinges, causing the pounding noise as the wind banged it to and fro in its stone casement. The pair looked at one another questioningly.

"Could they have fled?" said Scott.

"We'll soon know. Come on."

They entered the castle. Fine wisps of drifted snow lay along the stone corridor. Without pausing, they hurried on until they came to the great library-room. It was as empty and cold as the corridor. The long drapes by the window stirred slightly in the draft. Most of the books, Hamilton noticed, were gone from the shelves, but a few lay scattered about on the floor. Scott began to examine these with interest, and was quickly absorbed in them. "Incredible!" he muttered as he glanced over a mildewed volume. "I thought this work had been lost a hundred years ago." And again, picking up another: "Surely the Church would not knowingly have suffered *this* one to exist. . . ."

Suddenly a long, low-pitched howl echoed dimly through the castle. Hamilton started as he recognized it.

"Stay here, Eric," he said. "I'm going to find out what that is, once and for all."

"I'll go with you," said the old man, but Hamilton waved him back.

"You're unarmed, and I don't know what we're up against. If I haven't returned to this room within thirty minutes, don't hang around—go back to town and bring the police."

Scott nodded and turned back to the books. Hamilton set out into the corridor. He had not walked more than a dozen paces before he heard the howling once more. Turning into a branch passage, he continued on toward the origin of the sound, uncertain that he was going in the right direction, however, so faint and echoing had been the cry. . . .

The passage was dim, and Hamilton produced a flashlight he had brought. As he flicked it on he heard the sound once more, this time louder and obviously ahead of him. Hurrying on, he reached the end of the passage and found it blocked by a massive stone door. This door was open about half a foot and looked like nothing but a huge slab cut from the wall. It would probably be undetectable when closed, Hamilton realized. He braced himself and tugged heavily at the door, and it came slowly open with a harsh, grating sound. A surge of dank air fouled his nostrils, and he glimpsed stone stairs leading down into an inky blackness.

So there *were* still underground regions of the castle, after all! Slowly Hamilton began to work his way down, careful not to slip on any loose stone or patch of moisture. He shivered slightly at the touch of the damp walls, and brushed away strands of clinging spider web with disgust.

The sound came again, welling up from the depths, and Hamilton stopped with a momentary pang of horror. There was now evident a distinctly *human* quality in the cry. Were the castle-dwellers actually engaged in the torture of some hapless fellow-being? Holding his pistol ready, Hamilton continued on.

After many windings under vaulted archways, the stair ended in a large subterranean chamber. Against the wall of this room stood several stone tables littered with great quantities of chemicals, flasks, electrical apparatus, tools and mildewed books. It suggested to Hamilton a combination of alchemist's laboratory and electrician's workshop. Much of the floor was scrawled with strange, smudged designs, and many half-melted candles stood upright. On one stone slab in the center of the room stood several empty wine bottles and two human skulls, and Hamilton noticed that the tops of these skulls were missing, having been cut off just above the eyes. On closer examination he was appalled to observe that the skulls had evidently been used as drinking vessels!

His speculations were cut short by the weird howl from the darkness, and he continued on across the great room and entered a narrow corridor on the far side. After only fifty feet or so he emerged into a still vaster space. This, he saw with surprise, was not man-made at all, being evidently a huge cavern hollowed within the rock by natural forces. A new sound came to his ears, and he realized it was the pounding of the sea. He knew now how he had first come to hear the howling from outside; there must be hidden fissures in the cliffside leading to this cavern.

Swiftly he crossed the stone-flagged floor, heading for a black opening on the far side. It was an artificial tunnel, obviously cut into the rock long ago. As Hamilton entered, he detected for the first time a sound that seemed quite out of place in these dim, archaic recesses. It was a soft, throbbing, pumping sound of machinery.

He advanced slowly down the narrow tunnel, keeping his flashlight partially covered so that its light would not shine out far ahead of him. The throbbing grew louder, mingled now with a rhythmic, wheezing sound which he could not identify. He clutched his revolver more tightly.

Suddenly he became aware of low mumbling that seemed to ripple softly along the slimy walls. Advancing cautiously, he saw that he was approaching an archway to a dark chamber at the tunnel's end. The mumbling resolved itself into muttered words, and as Hamilton caught their import, he froze in the grip of a strange horror.

"Holy Mary mother of God," muttered the voice, its tones conveying a hideous undercurrent of utter despair and madness; "pray for us sinners now and at the hour of our death Holy Mary mother of God pray for us. . . ."

As the voice repeated this phrase over and over, it grew steadily louder and shriller in pitch, until at last it lost all form and coherency and burst forth in a wailing, demonic howl of frustration and misery. Hamilton, feeling himself becoming unnerved, unveiled his flashlight and cried out:

"Who's there? Answer me!"

The voice grew silent, and only the sound of the throbbing machinery pulsed down the corridor.

"Who's there?" cried Hamilton again. "Come out of there—quickly. I've got a gun, and I'm not afraid to use it!"

A hollow laugh echoed from the dark chamber, and Hamilton felt his spine prickle strangely.

"Why should I fear death?" droned the voice; "I, to whom all in life is lost!"

"What do you mean? Who are you?"

"Men once called me Dunlap," the voice murmured, "but now they would call me—horror!"

"Dunlap! Then—you're the constable who disappeared several months ago . . . !"

"I was; but if you have come to rescue me, you are too late. . . ."

"But you're still alive . . ." began Hamilton, taking a step toward the black archway. A terrible shriek of warning from the voice made him stop short, trembling.

"No! Do not enter here if you value your sanity!" it cried.

"What . . . What do you want me to do?" said Hamilton. "I want to help you. Where are Pitts and Taggart?"

"They are gone," wailed the voice. "They left me here alive. They condemned me to linger on in these vaults—damn them!—and bade me remember all those I had ever aided in sending to prison while I languished here in the darkness. . . ."

The voice became more rapid and shrill as it raved on, and Hamilton listened in growing horror. "I was right about the boy—it *was* they who captured little Tom McCallister, and killed him in some strange way when they found his mind was not developed enough for their hideous purpose. Ha! ha! ha! But mine was—and when I came for them, they were waiting. . . ."

"What do you mean?" urged Hamilton, horrified at the rising madness in the voice. "What have they done to you?"

"They used me—ha! ha! They took me out to unformed spaces between the stars, and made me sign the black book of Azathoth, that my mind might be put to dark and terrible uses. Then they brought me down to this room and did terrible things . . . terrible things. . . ."

To Hamilton it was obvious the man was utterly mad, but he could not help listening with spellbound horror as the voice raved on:

"Then they looked into my eyes, and I could see into far places. There were strange and vast powers surging invisibly about me, and they forced me to use those powers in horrible ways. First it was to summon, summon, summon—and then to kill! God forgive me! It was not so bad when they made me kill the fat police chief, or the lawyers, or that senile, bloat-faced old judge; but that last time, over in Burntshire . . ." The voice broke in a desperate sob, then went on: "Perhaps the man *had* used his wealth for corrupt and cruel purposes and deserved to die as he did, but when they had me first slay his wife and young daughters before his very eyes—God help me! My soul shall burn forever in Hell for what I've taken part in—but, Heaven be merciful to a sinner! *Can even Hell hold agonies worse than these . . . ?*"

The voice had risen to a shriek and now dissolved into an anguished howl of despair. Getting a grip on himself, Hamilton strode forward, determined to give what aid he could to the demented sufferer, and shined his light into the room. The light revealed a wooden table and, beneath it, a complex tangle of wires, tubes and mechanical devices—obviously the source of the strange throbbing and wheezing. Upon the table was a single pallid object, vertically ovoid and set into an iron ring at its base. At first Hamilton's mind refused to recognize this object distinctly; but, as his light fell directly upon it and he could not avoid realizing what it was, all his courage vanished in an instant of electrifying terror.

"*Kill me!*" shrieked the voice madly. "*Kill me!*"

But Hamilton, his entire being shaken with horror, ran screaming and gibbering back down the dark tunnel and out into the vast cavern beyond. His wild yells reverberated in the awful blackness as he raced back the way he had come, stumbling blindly through the subterranean halls and rooms and up the dank, slimy stairway in a mad effort to escape those hideous black regions of utter horror. And all the while that terrible, mad howl of the voice rang in his ears, urging him on in his frantic flight from those nocturnal dungeons and the horror of what he had glimpsed therein. . . .

Hamilton remembered nothing of what followed during the next few moments; there are some experiences too utterly terror-charged for the human mind to retain. His next conscious sensation was that of the cold sea-wind against his face, and the realization that he was following stumblingly behind Eric Scott along the snow-swept footpath.

"I had to burn them," Scott was saying. "The knowledge contained in those evil books should never have been written down. I hope you will understand. . . ."

"I understand," muttered Hamilton. "God help me—I understand!"

"What was it you saw beneath the castle?" asked Scott, disturbed by his companion's shaken condition and odd pallor. "And what happened to Pitts and Taggart?"

"They are gone—don't ask me where. Perhaps they've hidden themselves amid the wild hills to the north, or have vanished to some far land, or—or somewhere else. Wherever they are, they've accomplished their terrible revenge, and I hope we'll see them no more.

"What did I see beneath the castle? I can never know for sure, for I only got a glimpse, and God knows how overwrought my mind was in that moment—but if my senses did not deceive me, then I must forever curse the weakness that kept me from doing that which was necessary and decent. The thing that was once Constable Dunlap should not have lived on in its condition, and was kept alive only by means unknown to medical science. No, Eric, the thing I glimpsed in that black, unholy chamber beneath the castle was not entirely a man; *it was only a living, breathing, hideously animated human head!*"

# The Horror on the Beach

## Alan Dean Foster

"**D**o you realize that this ranchero is over three hundred years old, Mr. Corfu? Three hundred years! One of the greatest old Spanish Dons lived here. This isn't a house, it's a piece of history!" The agent sidled closer. "Pardon my saying so, Dave, but you'll be sorry if you pass this up."

David Corfu ignored the unsubtle switch from "Mr. Corfu" to "Dave." All he saw was Julie, running her hands over the stonework, bringing imaginary azaleas and petunias to life in the empty planters. Well, the place was convenient to his office in Santa Barbara, near enough the Pacific Coast Highway, and the privacy was exceptional for beachfront property. Only one family near by . . . and the old beachcomber, who didn't count.

Julie was talking. "About neighbors, Mr. Bascomb? Naturally we like privacy, and all, but Flip is barely eight. A boy his age ought to have *some* companions apart from school-time."

"I quite agree, Mrs. Corfu. And I don't think you need worry on that account." He moved to stand by the front window. Big for the house, it was small by modern standards.

That window was a problem, Dave reflected. Oh well, they could have a larger one put in later. They'd damn well have to, because the thick wrought-iron bars behind it blocked out most of what light the ancient glass allowed in.

Bascomb gestured northward, up the beach. "As is specified in the deed, you share the beach and cove with just two other residences.

The Birch family has their place just over that big dune, there. They have two twin daughters (two or four, mused Dave) and as I recall they'd be about your son's age. Ought to get along fine. Down by the rocks, of course, there's old Joshua Whipple."

"That's the beachcomber we've heard about, right?" asked Julie. "Is he . . . I mean, Flip . . ."

The agent's hands fluttered nervously. "Oh, don't worry! Old Josh is probably the best neighbor you could ask for, Mrs. Corfu. Doesn't even come around to borrow the lawnmower."

"No grass," said Dave.

"Yes. Well he's a bit taciturn, but friendly enough."

"Oh, all right, we'll take it."

Julie's thank you kiss almost made him forget about the mortgage.

It didn't take Dave long to realize that he was attracting far more attention than an oil engineer in an ecology-conscious town ought to. Townsfolk favored him with brief, awkward glances. When he turned to stare at the whisperers, they became unnaturally cheerful or talkative to cover up their furtiveness. At first he ignored the attention, but it began to wear on his nerves. Even the men he worked with on the great platform out in the bay were not immune.

One afternoon he was sufficiently irritated to disregard etiquette and confront his watchers. Three drillers, their faces blackened with grease and crude oil so that they shone as if polished, stared back at him.

"Look, fellas, I'm getting sick of people talking at me instead of to me. Anything you have to say about me you can damn well say to my face."

They glanced at the steel floor, at the rig, anywhere but at Dave. If he hadn't been so upset he might have reflected on the oddity of three brawny, muscular bit-men reacting to the challenge of a slightly undersize engineer like so many kids caught snitching fudge.

One of the men licked his lips, fixed Dave with an uncertain stare.

"Sir, is it true that you live in the old house known as the Casa de Rodrigo de Lima? The one on the dirty sand beach in Cabrillo Cove?"

"Since everyone in Santa Barbara seems to know it already, not much use in my denying it. Why?"

"Then, sir, may God have mercy on your soul!" and the man turned back to his work.

Try, plead, threaten as he might, Dave could not get any of them to utter another word.

That night was the first time they became aware of the drums.

They'd returned from their regular Sunday-eve bridge match with the Birches. It was a friendship practically forced on the two couples, since their nearest other neighbors were several miles away among the more accessible portions of the wild Pacific coast. And it was not likely that old Whipple catered to bridge.

Julie noticed them first. She woke him gently. He turned to stare drowsily in her direction. But when he saw her face, he sat up fast.

"Hey, what gives, hon?"

She whispered, even though Flip was long asleep down the hall and there was no one but him to hear. "Shssh. Don't you hear it?"

"Hear what?" he answered inanely.

"Listen!"

He concentrated. There *did* seem to be a faint humming sound. He rose from the bed and raised the one window slightly. It let in the sound, along with a gust of salt-edged air that cut the sleep from his eyes. Yes, a slight drumming sound, not clear. It seemed to be accompanied by a modulated keening, as of many voices moaning or singing in unison.

"Odd. That's certainly not the ocean. Seems to be coming from the north, near the Point. Must be some kind of party or something."

"I don't like it," Julie said firmly. "It doesn't sound like any kind of party music *I* ever heard."

He yawned. "Well, it's harmless, whatever it is (why shouldn't it be? Why'd he think of that?). Probably a bunch of long-hairs from the University. Nothing worth losing sleep over."

The Birches had also heard the sounds . . . Martin Birch refused to call them "drummings." No, he didn't know what they were and yes, they'd heard them before. Although since the Corfus had arrived the nightly concerts had increased in frequency. Command performances for the new savior of the coast, Martin had grinningly suggested.

Dave grinned back. He was still grinning when he walked into Bascomb's office that afternoon.

"What I'd like to know, Bascomb, is why the townspeople give a hoot about the place I'm living in. At first I thought it was me, now I find out it's the house. Why? And why'd the last tenants move out, if it was such a great buy?"

Bascomb considered Dave through the steeple he'd formed of his fingers.

"Um. Well, the deed is ironclad, so I suppose you might as well know. Kindly do not laugh, Mr. Corfu, but people hereabouts have some funny notions where the de Lima residence is concerned. And some think they might have reason . . ."

"I'm home, honey!"

She was kissing him as he opened his briefcase, said "Big deal!" kissed him again, harder. He drew her over to the big couch.

"It seems there's quite a story behind our humble abode."

"You saw the agent?"

"I saw Bascomb. It seems that this was the de Lima's equivalent of a second home-cum-export plant. Hides and tallow from the de Lima herds were shipped from here to deep-water schooners. The shore drops off sharply out past the point and the big ships could maneuver in fairly close. Anyhow, it seems the first de Lima made a pact with the devil."

"The devil?"

"Uh-Uh. With a devil. The legend apparently is very specific on that point. Which particular devil no one seems to remember. In 1724 the de Lima ranchero was attacked by a whole tribe of Yani Indians. The family retreated from their central hacienda, near the old mission. Maybe they thought this place would be easier to defend with what they had left, since their retreat to Pueblo de Los Angeles was cut off. Maybe they hoped to signal a boat. Regardless, they were wiped out to the last man."

"The de Limas?"

"Nope. The Indians. Quite an accomplishment for three men, their wives, kids, a bunch of frightened servants, and old de Lima himself. He and the Indians never did get along, it seems. Which is funny in itself, because like most California tribes, the Yani were inclined towards being peaceable.

"After word got around, no one bothered the de Limas again. Not Indian, Spaniard, Mexican, or American, when they arrived. Something in the family reputation—or the family—got on people's nerves. So much so that the family eventually had to sell out and move to Brazil. Interesting?"

"In a gruesome sort of way, yes."

"And there's more. Know when the previous tenants vacated? 1889! Not a terribly popular piece of property, it seems."

"David, you stop that! Now, what about the funny music we heard last night, hmmm? What did he have to say about that?"

"Oh yeah." He frowned. "Funny, but Bascomb was willing to chat about the house all day, yet when I mentioned our 'music' to him he clammed right up tight. He insisted he didn't know what I was trying to 'pull.' You know, I met old Whipple on the road in and just on an off chance, I asked him. Turned positively *green*, he did. Now, I can get used to the noise—the Birches have—but I don't like this silence concerning it, either. I think I'll ask around town some more tomorrow."

But he didn't, because tomorrow was Tuesday, the day platform #2 started to leak. Despite frantic efforts of the platform's crew, the quantity of crude petroleum bubbling out of the ocean floor grew rapidly to critical proportions. Planes cruising over the area were the first to notice the phenomenon and were quick to radio the information to shore. So before the panicked oil company could get on top of the situation the news media were gleefully splashing it over every available line of communication.

"Oh, Dave! I heard on the radio . . . it's all true, about the oil?"

Dave flipped his briefcase onto the couch and collapsed in his favorite chair with a heartrending sigh.

" 'Fraid so, luv. We can't seem to cut the blasted thing off, it doesn't respond to normal shut down procedure . . . and it looks like we're shortly going to be on the receiving end of howls of outrage from down south. I'm glad I'm just an engineer and not the head of the public relations department!"

She sat down next to him and began massaging his neck muscles. He turned so that she could reach the tight spots more easily.

"Oh, I had a chance to talk with the local sheriff. They've heard of our nocturnal celebrants, but since no one's bothered to file a complaint, they've never interfered. They're definitely *not* college kids, though. Apparently it's some local nut cult that meets out on the Point."

"Like the Elks and those people?"

"Not quite." He chuckled, shifted on the couch. "The group seems to consist mostly of the poorer locals, with a sprinkling of more respectable types. As far as the sheriff could find out there aren't any criminal elements among them. The townsfolk don't care for them, but they've caused no trouble. They don't make much fuss, so I couldn't see swearing out a complaint."

Julie chewed on a lip, said, "I've talked with Sue Birch, and she says it's the rhythm that bothers you most."

"Well, we can get used to it too."

Julie sighed. "I guess so." She paused. "Dave, do you know some- times I couldn't help but . . . you'll think this is silly, and I don't blame you . . . but sometimes I wake up in the middle of the night and the house almost seems to . . . well, to be moving in sympathy with that drumming, or chanting, or whatever it is. There, I've said it! Now go ahead and laugh."

But he didn't.

Because the same thing had happened to him.


Polite hammering on bells far away swipe at them but they wouldn't leave dammit and how was a man . . .

Dave's eyes opened slowly. He looked around in that stupor of awkward awakening that people are prone to early in the morning. He stared at the phone which yammered back demandingly. Raising himself slowly to a sitting position, he glanced at the fluorescent dial of the night table clock. Now who the hell would be calling at four . . . no, *five* in the morning? Probably some crazy reporter, out for a can- did comment on the oil spill. He'd give him a candid comment!

He lifted the phone from the receiver.

What came over was not the voice of a reporter.

The words were distorted, high, shrill. They were all the more difficult to understand because of the sound of breaking wood which dominated the background. Despite the confusion and the unnatural timbre of the voice, he recognized the frightened, utterly terrified tones of Martin Birch.

"David . . . Dave, is that you? Listen Dave, you've got to get away! Take Julie and the boy and *get away!* My God, what an abomination!"

There was a pause, followed by what sounded like a series of muffled gunshots. More breaking sounds, louder now. Evelyn Birch could be heard shrieking in the background, along with a muted, whimpering voice which was probably one of the twins. And there was another sound, which Dave couldn't identify. The hair on his body tingled.

Martin's voice resumed, masked with long, heavy gasps for breath. "Hurry, man, hurry! There's nothing you can do here! Save yourselves! It's *all around us!* Don't come over here! It's coming in, my God, THE WINDOW . . . GREAT HEAV—!"

There was a crisp, shattering sound, and the line went dead with an abruptness that left Dave staring dumbly at the silent receiver. To his surprise he found he was soaking wet from sweat. Julie was standing by the open window. He hadn't even heard her get out of bed.

"Dave . . . I could hear sounds, from their direction. It sounded like things . . . breaking up. Oh D-d-dave. . . ."

She was in his arms then, shivering uncontrollably.

"Don't worry, hon, we're safe." He was aware of how hollow it sounded. Hollow.

"Well then, Mr. Corfu, what seems to be the problem?" The graying sergeant was gruffly courteous, but got it across he didn't like being called away from a warm station-house at daybreak on some damnfool nut call. "I understand you phoned in something about your neighbors. Been a bit rowdy, have they? That's natural, the night before . . ."

"That's not it at all, sergeant. I'm afraid they may have been victims of, well, vandals or something. Anyways, their phone line is dead."

"So you reported," said the younger cop.

"It's just over that dune," Dave added hastily. "Shorter than driving the long way 'round."

The sergeant grumbled, but followed Dave as he started up the sandy incline. The muttering and grumbling stopped the minute they cleared the last rise and got a clear view of the beach below.

The Birch home was a recent addition to the topography of the cove. Unlike Dave's, which had been there for hundreds of years, the wealthy Birch had had materials trucked in. The resultant ultra-modern structure had been an interesting contrast to the ancient abode of the de Lima ranch-house.

It had been flattened as though by a typhoon.

In somber silence, the three scrambled their way down the side of the dune, over low beach scrub and iceplant, sand-flies puffing in sooty clouds about their feet. No one said anything.

The poured concrete pillars that had supported the front section of the house had been shattered like matchwood. The shipped-in boulders which had formed the bulwark of the seawall were scattered haphazardly about the beach. Two-by-fours and wooden planking, even the resilient redwood, had been pulped to near-cardboard thin. Shattered glass sparkled everywhere amidst the destruction. Hardly a piece of furniture appeared to be intact.

Of the Birches themselves, there was no sign.

Almost as unsettling as the ruins was the condition of the beach. The Birch home had been set down almost on the high water line, while Dave's was much further inland. In a broad path all around the area of devastation the sand was gouged and compressed; no, *depressed*. The depression extended right down to . . . or up from, the watermark. It was as if something of considerable weight had been dragged up from the sea, around the house, and back down again. A storm-tossed boulder of great size could do that, Dave thought, but why in such a regular path?

Besides, there hadn't been any storm.

When he finally spoke, the sergeant's voice was muted, as if to fit the unnatural stillness of the air. Come to think of it, the normal raucousness of the gulls and sandpipers was missing this morning.

"I don't know what happened here, Mr. Corfu, but you better believe we'll check into this. I ain't never seen *nothing* the likes of this."

"Boy!" breathed the corporal. "Looks like someone did a job on this place with a big dozer. You say this guy gave you a call from *here* mister?"

"Yes. I could . . . I could hear the house coming down around them. He had a gun, too."

"Um," said the sergeant. He kicked at a mangled lampstand. "We'll have to get a crew out here soon . . . search for the bodies. I dunno. I just dunno." He shook his head as though it might help resolve an unresolvable situation.

Dave made no response. He was occupied in inspecting the depression, following it down to where it disappeared in the gentle ebb-flow of the sea.

"Honey, whatever happened over there this morning, and the sergeant had no more idea of what had than I . . . it took away a very strong man in Martin Birch. I don't want it happening to us!"

She looked at him thoughtfully. "You've got an idea then, but for reasons of your own you don't want to tell me what it is." He tried to protest, but she cut him off. "Never mind. Are you going to talk to the police again?"

"Uh-uh. I don't think they'd take kindly to my ideas. I'm going to have a talk with Pedro Armendariz."

"Who? Oh, that biochemist friend of yours at the University?"

"That's the one. If whatever happened to the Birches was caused by something that . . . that came out of the sea, then Pedro ought to know about it. Even if it was something 'out of the ordinary.' "

The big Ford grumbled crankily . . . sea air gets into everything, he thought . . . but it started quickly enough. He swung out of the driveway, scattering dirt and a few birds . . . at least the gulls had returned . . . and headed up the dirt access road.

It would have been hard to miss the tall, scraggly figure ambling along in the same direction, bowed under a large pack. He peered harder as the distance closed. Yes, it certainly looked like their ancient recluse, but what was old Whipple doing with a heavy pack?

"Say, Josh! Josh Whipple!"

Whipple obviously heard him, but hesitated before trudging over.

"Mornin' to ye, Mr. Corfu." He leaned closer and smiled slightly. "Ah, I kin see ye know whut happened over at th' Birch place, then."

"I do. Fact is, I'm going into town to see someone about it right now. The police have already been and gone."

"Huh!" snorted Whipple. "I kin imagin' whut *they* found. Nuth-in'!" He paused and stared sharply at Dave. Without knowing why, Dave squirmed as though under the eye of his superior.

"You listen to me, Mr. Corfu. Yer nice folks, ye are. The Birches wuz nice folks too, but it didn't do them no good a'tall. So I'm givin' ye a piece o' good advice. Take yer Missus and yer kid and leave this place, now. There's things takin' place that are way past ye, here, Mr. Corfu, and I'm suggestin' ye leave while ye got the chance.

"The Birches is dead."

The way he said it, with utter surety, left no room for argument. Dave thought furiously. He hadn't seen the oldster lately. Not that he'd been looking for him. He supposed it might have been possible for Whipple to visit the ruins before the police arrived. All of a sudden he was ashamed of what he'd been thinking. After seeing the wreck of the Birch home, Dave's evaluation of their probable fate hadn't been any more optimistic, although not so gruesomely positive.

"You know about that, then? Yes, obviously you do, although how you can be so sure, I don't know. They're missing, all right, but no bodies have been found as yet, and . . ."

For some reason Whipple found this very amusing. "Oh, they're dead enough. You kin bet on thet. Why, back whe . . ." He stopped suddenly and shouldered his pack, centering the load more precisely on his slender frame.

Dave eyed the bulky load, essayed a wild guess.

"You couldn't be leaving us, Josh?"

"I not only could, I am! I've things to do elsewhere, Mr. Corfu, things to do. 'Sides," and he chuckled drily, " 'taint safe around here for honest folks."

"Can I give you a lift into town, then?"

"No, thankee, I prefer to walk. 'Sides, I kin stay closer to the sea thetaways."

Dave was reluctant to let the garrulous old man depart. "I won-der what could have happened to them. Perhaps they left for reasons of their own. I know *I* wouldn't have stopped running yet."

Whipple chuckled again . . . man had a decidedly odd sense of humor, Dave thought.

"Ye want to know whut happened to 'em, do ye? Well, I told them they shouldn't ha' built thet big new place there. It didn't belong, ye know. I even offered to show old Birch the place in The Book, but he jest laughed at me . . . laughed! I warned him there wuz things goin' on he couldn't stop, and thet I couldn't control too well myself. *He* don't hanker to outsiders at this spot, Mr. Corfu!"

"*He?*"

"Call 'im what you will . . . sea-god, sea-devil, he's mor'n thet. Cthulhu, he . . ." He paused and gave a start, as though he'd been talking in a daze.

"Thet's all I'm saying to ye, Mr. Corfu. Ye be thankful fer thet. I could tell ye too much fer yer own good!"

Despite Dave's entreaties the old fellow set off at a steady pace over the low hills and was soon lost to sight . . . headed inland, he noticed.

Pedro Armendariz lived in one of the better sections of suburban Santa Barbara, on a hillside, commanding a sweeping view of the Pacific. Flowering iceplant and geranium covered the sloping grounds with a profusion of red and yellow blooms. Dave was enjoying the lethal poise of a garden spider, all yellow and black patience, when Armendariz opened the door. After mutual exchanges of hello and other small pleasures, they moved into the den which was the professor's inner sanctum.

Armendariz settled himself into a deep chair across from Dave and propped his feet up on the wrought iron table separating them.

It had been some time since Dave had had occasion to converse with his friend other than by phone. The black hair was graying a bit more at the temples, the olive skin showed a few more wrinkles, the nose seemed a bit more aquiline . . . but the same tiny, jet-black eyes peered inquisitively out from under almost feminine light brows. They regarded Dave with much the same interest that he regarded them.

"Well, David, it is too long since you have visited Rosa and me. And so I suspect this is not entirely a social visit, eh?"

"It's not about the oil spill, if that's what you're thinking."

"No? I had thought certainly that . . . but what is it, then?"

"Pedro, early this morning the house of my neighbor was completely destroyed, by what I don't know. Neither do the police. And the people themselves have not been seen since."

"*Que cosa.* Yet I am no detective, my friend. Vandalism, perhaps? An explosion?"

"No, Pedro. I mean *totally* destroyed. And there are other factors. . . ."

As well as he could, Dave related the occurrences at Cabrillo Cove, beginning from the day they moved in.

Armendariz remained characteristically unperturbed by the narrative, sometimes nodding his head as though to indicate agreement, now and then interrupting for clarification of this or that seemingly insignificant point.

"I see. And neither you nor the police have any idea as to the whereabouts of the people?"

"Only what our imaginations can supply. Only . . ." he paused. "We have . . . rather, we *had* a second, rather eccentric neighbor. Old guy named Whipple. Beachcomber, a likeable sort, if a bit of a recluse. I ran into him accidentally on my way to see you. Seems he was in the process of moving out. As much as suggested I do the same. He had some cock-and-bull story, said he knew what had been responsible for the destruction."

"Indeed?" said Armendariz politely. "And what did he offer as an explanation? Ghosts, perhaps? A petulant poltergeist?"

Dave smiled back. "No, he said it had been some sort of sea deity . . . Cit . . . Cthulhu, yes, that was it . . . I . . . say, are you all right, Pedro?"

A most extraordinary transformation had come over his friend's face. The normal complacent visage of the erudite sophisticate had dissolved to reveal the expression of a terrified savage. So brief was it that Dave wasn't sure what he'd seen. When at last the professor replied there was an undercurrent of seriousness and apprehension in his voice that was totally unlike him.

"What's that, what's that? *Cthulhu,* you say? That's *exactly* the name he used? It's not a common word. You're certain of it?"

"Pretty much so, yes," replied Dave. He was rather taken aback by his friend's abrupt change. "Why so curious? You mean it really means something? I know, it's a whale, or a large sea-turtle or something?"

A peculiar brightness was in Armendariz' eyes. "You are considering a large marine animal, my friend? No, I am afraid you could not quite call it an animal." His voice dropped and he spoke to himself in Spanish. Dave was fairly fluent, but only the rhythmic rise and fall of the professor's voice identified it as some kind of prayer.

He glanced up suddenly, startling Dave yet again. An air of unquestioning authority now permeated his questions.

"This elderly friend of yours, this beachcomber. Did he ever happen to mention his home to you? His place of birth?"

"Well, yes. We talked now and then. Someplace back East. Massachusetts, I believe."

This produced another unexpected reaction from Armendariz. He grinned. "Ah, Massachusetts, you say? What place?"

Dave was getting irritated. What did all this have to do with . . . ?

"Oh, I think it was somewhere on the coast. He liked the sea. I don't happen to recall the zip code!"

But the professor missed the sarcasm. He was deep in thoughts of his own. Dave knew the mood and politely refrained from breaking it. He was intensely curious, despite his irritation, to know the reason for his friend's remarkable behavior of the past few minutes. At length Armendariz rose and walked to a rear portal.

"Rosa!"

Rosa Armendariz was a plump but still vivacious little woman. She had to stand on tiptoe to hear what her husband had to whisper to her, even though he bent over. Dave couldn't make out what they were saying, but he noticed the way her eyes widened, and how she seemed momentarily transfixed the way her husband had a moment ago. She paused long enough to give Dave one unfathomable backwards glance before departing without as much as a hello.

"I suggest," began Armendariz, "that you send Julie and the boy up here to stay with us for awhile, and come yourself as soon as you are able. At least until I can determine what can be done about this. If even half of what I suspect is true, you cannot remain in that place a moment longer."

"Oh, come off it, Pedro! Stop trying to scare me with some crazy hocus-pocus! I hardly see the need for . . ."

Armendariz interrupted him with an almost bored fluttering of a hand. "Please, I have no time for arguing with you, David. I suggest this because I believe it is essential for your own welfare."

"But the police . . ."

"Can think what they like. Their suppositions are of no consequence in this, believe me."

"And yours are, I suppose?"

The professor was not upset. "Possibly. Possibly. If we are lucky. I must telephone some associates in Massachusetts . . . yes, that's right . . . Yale and Miskatonic, both. I must have some information from libraries there . . . it will take time, and I do not like doing such things by phone. . . ."

"Why not have the material photocopied and sent out?"

Armendariz smiled. "It would take too long, my friend, and besides, these materials do not 'photocopy.' I need also the advice of a certain enthusiastic antiquarian . . . I pray he is at home. . . ."

"Look, I really just came for some advice, Pedro. If this is going to put you to a whole lot of trouble. . . ."

"I do not do this for you alone anymore, David. I will expect you here with your family by tomorrow morning at the latest. Now please be good enough to leave me for awhile. I have much to do. And David?"

"Yes?"

"It is better than you know that you came to me. *Hasta la vista.*"

His last view of Armendariz showed the professor scribbling furiously at his desk, a tattered old book in one hand and a rapidly rising pile of notes at the other.


They were gathered around the fireplace in the living room. Dave was striving futilely for a way to plug a crack in the Pacific's floor. Julie was curled up on the couch transcribing recipes into her little card file. In the far hallway Flip was busy assaulting a coffee table with a large force of miniature dinosaurs.

There was a fourth personage present. General Lee, the mutated siamese, snuggled comfortably on a fat silk pillow between piles of geology texts.

Try as he would, Dave could not concentrate on engineering. Armendariz . . . why, he'd never *seen* Pedro act the way he had this afternoon! Ordinarily he was a pillar of calm, unruffled by the most outrageous happenings. Yet a few mild statements had upset him completely. At least he was interested, though. *Was* he! If he believed there might be something in all this talk of sea-monsters and such, well then . . .

His eyes wandered with his thoughts. They came to rest eventually on the light figure of General Lee. At which point Dave straightened in his chair, all thoughts of geosynclines and fault-prone strata gone.

The cat was no longer curled on its pillow. It stood instead before the heavy plank door. The hair on its back was stiff and erect, as was the peppered tail. Eyes abnormally wide, ears flattened back againt the sides of the head . . . everything in the animal's stance was suggestive of fear and terror.

Julie broke his concentration.

"Uh, Dave . . . is there someone out front, do you think?"

Not moving a muscle, straining his hearing, he listened. Nothing. No wait, wasn't that something, there? Yes, surely. A faint sucking sound, as of wet cloth being slapped lightly on cement. A mild, loathsome reverberation. It seemed perhaps to be . . . yes, it was clearly growing louder even as he listened.

Keeping his voice as level as possible so as not to startle Flip, he said to her, "Look at the cat."

She did, and stifled a gasp. Her eyes went as wide as the cat's.

A ponderous suction was now quite audible, carrying with it the suggestion of great weight. Every bristle on his body stiff as a quill, General Lee was slowly backing away from the door. The small fangs were bared and low sounds came from his throat that Dave would have thought impossible for a cat.

He stared likewise with dumb fascination at the solid oak door. It seemed to jiggle ever so slightly. His voice remained calm, almost divorced from the situation.

"Move quietly, Julie. Take Flip and try not to bump into anything, will you? We're going to go down into the old wine cellar, you understand? Okay, now . . . move."

She nodded and got up from the couch. The cards she had been laboring over slid to the floor. Dave walked to the center of the room and shifted aside the old throw rug to reveal a large square outline in the center of the floor, a single iron ring attached to one side of the outline. Flip mercifully kept quiet as Julie led him over. As lightly as possible, Dave lifted the ring. Below, a series of broad wooden steps appeared in the darkness. One day, Dave had planned to convert the old wine cellar into a playroom.

He cocked a nervous eye on the front door. It had begun to show an alarming bend inwards. He urged Julie and Flip down the old steps. The sliding, oozing sounds were now accompanied by a stench of stomach-turning intensity. He followed quickly, pausing only long enough to let a white streak, General Lee, dash down past him.

It was dark down in that cellar. One day he'd string electric lights. One day. Meanwhile the flashlight would have to do. Taking it from its convenient hook he switched it on. A small friendly path appeared in the blackness. After sweeping the entire room he settled on a small alcove behind a jumble of ancient shelving. A number of old burlap cement sacks showed there, brown against the mossy adobe. That was the side nearest the sea, and the stones dripped slightly. He gestured with the beam. Holding Flip tightly, Julie walked over and crawled back into the indicated recess. He then played his light over the spot but was unable to see her. Good. Giving the trap door a last glance he hurried over to join them. Damp as it was, the wall behind them was reassuring in its solidity. The heavy air, moist and thick as ink, closed around him like a straightjacket. Beside his left leg he could feel the shivering body of General Lee. Together the four of them stared at the place where the trap was.

There was a muffled snapping and rending, followed by a tremendous crash. Dull crunching sounds followed, along with a definite groaning of the ancient floor-beams. Loud snaps and cracklings could be heard, interspersed with a bumping and sliding that somehow managed to convey with it an almost audible wetness. That horrible stink filtered down into the cellar, and Dave recognized it in the cloying dark. It was an odor he'd encountered often out on exploratory rigs. The odor of the deep, deep sea bottom.

Slowly, he became aware of a pain in his left shoulder. He saw that Julie was digging her free hand into his arm with such force she was drawing blood.

His attention was diverted by a short, high-pitched squeal from Flip. His eyes widened in horror as they located the reason.

The trap was being slowly opened.

Not lifted, but bent *inwards,* forced down on its metal hinges by some incredible pressure. Light from the still intact living room fixtures filtered in around the edges.

From this point on Dave was later able to remember what happened only vaguely. The human mind can stand only a measured dose of horror before reflexive defense mechanisms take over to protect one's sanity.

A thing came slithering in over the splintered, tortured remains of the trap covering. It showed a dull green in the available light from the living room bulbs. A small thing, at first, shaped roughly like a paw . . . or was it a cable? A green cable. It moved down into the cellar with an obscene half-creeping, half-flowing motion. It was unmistakably searching for something. As it lengthened it grew until it filled the wide opening provided by the shattered door.

Dave never could give a coherent description of the thing. In color it was grayish-green, with here and there unhealthy-looking patches of some darker color. Impossibly, it gave the impression of being of variable consistency. Now it was like a syrup, now a gel, whether inside liquid or solid or some nauseating chemistry in-between he would never know.

It reached the bottom of the steps and seemed to hesitate. Dave reminded himself that this was only a *part* of whatever monstrosity rested on the floor above, fishing for them. Then, slowly, it began to move again. Towards their little hiding place, their last refuge of sanity. He prayed silently to the others, not daring to whisper. Don't scream. Whatever you do, think, feel, *don't scream.* As though she had read his thoughts he noticed that Julie had placed her other hand tightly over Flip's mouth. It wasn't necessary. The boy had fainted.

He dimly recalled the distant voice of Martin Birch, screaming over his phone. *"It's all around the house!"*

Staring with mesmerized revulsion at the horror he pressed himself against the moist wall, trying to become a part of the solid rock. The thing was poking among the burlap now, a large verdant worm. He knew with instant clarity that if the thing touched him he would start screaming at the top of his lungs. Scream and scream and never stop screaming, ever.

He was suddenly aware of a large black-and-white blur streaking past him. The strain had grown too much for General Lee. With a heart-rending yowl of desperation the poor animal took off like a shot for the one patch of clean visible light.

He never reached the second step. With whippet-like speed, the green thing enveloped the cat in mid-leap. It contracted, once. General Lee let out a shriek of such concentrated agony that Dave was forced to clap his hands to his ears. Julie fainted. The cat's eyes popped out like buttons on a fat man's vest. It hung limp in the green thing's grasp, something more than merely life crushed out of its small body. Apparently something had been sated, because the long length of protoplasm withdrew, leaving a trail of malodorous slime behind it.

He retained consciousness only long enough to catch a brief glimpse of the Thing that towered into the sky above the shattered trap, blotting out the evening stars. Then he, too, fainted.


When he awoke he awoke screaming, expecting to see that horror gloating down at him. But the broken trap was clear and filled with a square of pure, uncontaminated daylight. He was aware of the dampness of his clothes, not all of which was due to his prolonged contact with the adobe. He woke Julie, stifling the incipient scream with his hand, and gestured upwards. When she saw the empty opening and the brilliant daylight drifting down she collapsed completely in his arms. They rested like that for some time before he forced himself to move.

Cautiously he peered over the upper edge of the trap, ready to duck back instantly. All that was in view was the wreckage of their living room. Helping Julie with Flip, who was still asleep, they stepped out into the daylight. Daylight because a great portion of the roof was missing, torn away like paper. The daylight made him less cautious. The sky shone down on three scarred lives.

"Carry Flip out to the car. We'll come back later for what's left . . . maybe." She nodded numbly and guided the sleepy, now half-awake youngster out where the door had been. He seemed not to remember anything of the night past. Hopefully, his mind would never remind him.

Dave paused to examine the wreckage. The great wooden supportive beams were shattered like matchsticks. The huge black iron braces which had bound the door and windows to the thick adobe had been bent and peeled away like tinfoil. Some rubbing action had ground away much of the fronting adobe itself. On close inspection the rough section showed a clear, tacky slime. It smelled of bottom ooze.

In front of the house was a huge depression in the sand leading down towards the innocently curling surf. It was wholly familiar.

General Lee had gone the way of the Birches.


Dave had supposed his experience would be a surprise, not to mention a shock, to the professor. But when Pedro greeted him at his house that morning he only nodded knowingly and said, "You have seen."

After Rosa had gently guided Julie and a mercifully ignorant Flip to the guest cottage, Dave joined his friend in the peace and reality of the den. The events of the night previous seemed fantastic and unreal. There was proof enough, however, in the professor's face.

"Pedro, what in all the hells was it, and where did it come from?"

"Actually, David, I had intended not to tell you any more than you knew yesterday. People who become involved in such things are marked forever. But a little knowledge pales in comparison to the thing itself. I might tell you that it is also quite likely responsible for your errant oil. No, don't interrupt. Listen . . . remember.

"Whether you believe what I am about to tell you or not is of no real importance. Your belief or disbelief cannot alter the truth one iota."

"After last night there's not a hell of a lot I wouldn't believe. Go ahead."

"So. Long ago the universe was rocked by a titanic struggle between two groups of powerful entities, one more or less beneficent, the other decidedly evil. The evil ones were defeated and put into various forms of exile or restraint. But the Great Old Ones have been away a long time and the bonds restraining these evil ones grow weaker. Some say the time for the return of these is near. They require human . . . and non-human . . . servants to properly prepare the way for their return. Always they are trying to break the holds placed on them so long ago.

"I have reason to believe that by re-occupying the de Lima abode, at this particular time, you have unwittingly aided in a scheme to let loose upon the world perhaps the most monstrous of these beings. That is one reason why I have dissuaded you from involving the police any more than you already have. Such things are not subject to the normal laws of time and space."

"I see. Look, I'm not laughing. How did you find out about such, uh . . . things?"

"There are hints in certain forbidden and well-sequestered tomes, such as the *De Vermis Mysteriis* of Ludvig Prinn, and even worse, the *Necronomicon* of the mad Arab, Alhazred."

Dave brightened suddenly. "Then those cultists on the Point . . . is that what you meant by 'this particular time'?"

Armendariz nodded somberly. "For whatever reasons, they have been able to summon *him* from his house in great R'lyeh. I believe that this is in part responsible for the petroleum leakage that has stymied your best engineers. Though I fear its implications more than the fact."

Dave hadn't heard the last. "So that's what happened to our divers! We thought it was unstable currents on the sea-floor. Great Heavens, Pedro, we've got to notify the army, we . . . !"

He stopped. The professor was shaking his head slowly.

"You have not listened carefully. *He* is not subject to natural law, as we know it. We must try and fight this horror on its own terms. I have received what I can only hope will be sufficient information from my contacts at Miskatonic and Yale Universities. But first, you must tell me everything you can remember about the content of those strange chantings that disturbed you. . . ."

For hours Dave struggled to recall the odd words, the peculiar timbred phrases which had disrupted his sleep those first nights in the aged adobe. With a little hypnotic coaxing from Pedro he and

Julie were able to recall much more than they thought they'd heard. When the professor repeated the sounds back to him, Dave shivered. It was much like learning a language and then hearing it spoken by someone who knew the accent like a native.

"When do you want to . . . to do whatever it is you intend to do, Pedro?"

"As soon as possible. Time must not be wasted. With every night the chants grow stronger, the evil re-enforces itself. We must try to break the locks tonight, before the forging is complete."

Dave gestured at the phone. "I don't understand enough of this to offer any objections, Pedro, but don't you think we ought to have some *help?*"

Armendariz considered. "Yes. No, I still think the type of 'help' you have in mind would be worse than useless, but it occurs to me that the members of the cult may possess more earthy forms of argument. I have a friend at the missile base . . . a Major Gomez. He will not believe, but he will come. Tonight, then."


There was very little breeze to muffle the sounds of the leather on rock as Dave worked his way along the blocky promontory which bordered the north end of Cabrillo Cove. Despite the fact that it was too early for a pre-dawn fog, he felt damp. A glance to the left and right showed dim outlines of Gomez's troops, spread out along the rocks to cut off any possible line of retreat. Nearby, the major was muttering angrily to himself and to anyone who cared to listen, heedless of the fact that the glow from the cultists' fire was now quite visible.

"Damn foolishness! Pedro, if I didn't owe you this favor I'd haul you in for observation myself! 'Primal jelly' indeed! There'd better be *something* to this cock-and-bull story of yours. If this gets out I'll be the laughing stock of the base!"

"I can only hope," Armendariz replied softly, "that ridicule is the worst that confronts us."

Gomez snorted derisively, but said no more. They were close to a point where some caution was necessary. Here the sounds of that insidious chant sounded loud. They conveyed a perverse sensuality that invited rejection but refused it. Dave noticed that even the skeptical Gomez was swaying slightly to that suggestive rhythm. Only the professor seemed immune.

"That is the same wording you and Julie heard at nights? The same you at least repeated to me this afternoon?"

Dave could only nod mutely. The evil ululation, its throbbing subtleties, absorbed his complete attention. Below them, on a flat, open area of naked rock, the cultists swayed and danced in a jerking, writhing parody of something his deepest memories could but half guess at.

He stood, moving uncertainly to the insistence of that pulsating wail. Dimly, he perceived the others beginning to do likewise. A great feeling of loss mingled with exaltation came over him. He became aware that the professor was moving. With a great effort, he managed to turn his head.

Armendariz was carefully removing his clothing. As each item of apparel was removed the symbols and designs which had been painted on his body were revealed in the faint moonlight. Doubtless he'd drawn them himself, with Rosa filling in the areas he would be unable to reach. They seemed to merge into one another in a single swirling pattern of repellant appearance.

Completely devoid of anything to suggest he was a highly intelligent member of a high civilization, the professor stepped over the concealing rocks and walked out into full view of the cultists. Raising his eyes to the sky and spreading his arms like some impossibly tall wading bird, he began to declaim in a peculiarly artificial-sounding voice.

Staring in shock at the apparition which had shattered their chanting, the cultists stood frozen in place. Obviously they had been interrupted at a crucial point in their ritual. Only one among them, one who seemed faintly familiar to Dave, remained unaffected. He stood tall on the side of the fire. He was painted in a manner very similar to the professor, with the exception that the designs on his skin did not appear to have been painted on, but instead seemed to be *etched or burned into the flesh!*

It was the very first time Dave had seen Joshua Whipple with his clothes off.

The old man did not halt his sing-song, but the tone in which he chanted altered noticeably. Despite his ignorance of the strange-sounding syllables they forced Dave and the others to recoil in terror. The very modulation, the phrasing, was horrifying. That voice demanded all attention, dominating even the obscene green statue that stood to one side of the fire.

Undaunted, the professor instantly modified his own speech in response. Now it was the turn of the cultists to draw back in fear. They scrambled pathetically about the fire. A faint flicker of concern showed in old Whipple's eyes and he began to chant in deadly earnest.

Dave felt mildly dizzy. He tried to take a step backwards and found he couldn't move. He was tied to that chant and this spot until events played themselves out. Idly he noticed that both the cultists and Gomez' troops were in a similar state. Neither Armendariz nor Whipple seemed affected.

But what was this? It was far too early for the morning fog to be coming in, but a definite mist had gathered around the Point. It obscured vision for all but a short distance around. Perspective became terribly distorted and Dave found he could no longer properly judge distance. He couldn't even see the soldiers, who were lined up a short distance behind his position. His feet seemed divorced from the basalt beneath. This hardly seemed a normal fog. It had a peculiar tingle to it. Besides, it was almost black in color.

As the voices of Whipple and the professor rose yet higher, Dave thought he could begin to make out shapes again. Something there, in the fog, near the water . . .

He became aware of screaming all around him and realized in surprise that he was one of the screamers. Something began to giggle at the back of his skull. It wouldn't go away.

As Whipple's now quavering tone reached an impossible pitch, the object took on a definite form. It towered over the now vulnerable Point, its face . . . if such it could be called . . . a mass of writhing tentacles, its shape saurian with *translucid* wings flapping as it staggered forth trailing phosphorus in its wake. Dave recognized the smell . . . the same smell he'd breathed that awful night in the wine cellar. Maniacal laughter resounded in his skull as he clapped pale trembling hands upon his throbbing temples and screamed because he could not go mad.

A great claw hovered over the Point and the fire shrank away from it in terror. One cultist went mad on the spot. Another fell to his belly and began to make low, crooning sounds deep in his throat. Another uttered a series of high, yelping cries and threw himself over the side of the cliff to smash on the rocks below.

The great corruption-encrusted claw wavered uncertainly over the two vocal combatants, drifting uncertainly from one to the other. The professor's voice rose to the very limit of endurance and Whipple seemed to shrink in on himself as a thunderous, rolling cry of *"CTHULHU IA VGLNN!"* split the tension-charged mist.

The claw moved. It swayed and dipped and finally clutched . . . the scarred form of Whipple! An unhallowed shriek of damnation issued from Whipple's twisted lips as the claw wrung forth his soul while the great form slipped into the foaming ocean. A wall of water coursed over the Point nearly drowning Dave in its onslaught. The receding riptide sucked his heels from under him and left Dave shivering, drenched, prostrate and staring up into the stars now whirling, a midnight carousel in his consciousness converging, concentric, into oblivion's compassion.

Something refused to stop shaking him. Dimly, he tried to wish it away, but it refused to leave. Blinking painfully . . . his eyes seemed to ache . . . he rolled over, to stare into the haggard face of Major Gomez, framed in the delicious cream-blue of a Pacific sky. He sat up abruptly. How had he gotten such a terrific headache? Then he remembered, and wished he hadn't.

"Where's the professor?" he said suddenly.

Gomez jerked his head and Dave turned to see a pale bent form huddled under an army blanket. It was sitting by the edge of the southern cliff and staring out to sea. Dave turned back to the major.

"He's alive then. All right?"

"Yes to the first. As to the second," he shrugged. "Why not ask him yourself. I must see to my men and to the assembling of these . . . people."

Dave rose and walked over to the motionless figure. He noticed the soldiers were gathering up the remaining cultists and herding them down the slope towards waiting trucks. Rather urgently, too. The rough handling was partly the result of the soldiers' refusal to look where they were going. They showed a tendency to cast quick glances back at the peaceful ocean. The cult members themselves were far too dazed to offer even perfunctory resistance.

"Pedro?"

The professor turned his face to Dave. It was frighteningly pale. Dave sat down beside him. "Well, you did it."

"Yes, yes . . . whatever it was, I have done. I did not think I was strong enough, David. Knowing exactly the right words helped. Whipple was stronger, actually, but at the crucial moment he lost control."

They sat silently for some time, watching the waves roll in from Asia.

"I suppose this means the oil will stop leaking now?"

At this Armendariz smiled, then began to laugh. He laughed until the tears ran down his face and his side began to pain him, laughed so that Dave feared for his friend's sanity. But it was honest laughter.

"Forgive me, Dave. Your remark struck me as humorous. I needed the release badly. Yes, I do not doubt that your precious petroleum will be safe for now. Though I have heard disturbing things about what the Creoles have been doing down in the back country of Louisiana. And there is another thing. Look!"

Dave followed the pointing arm down, down to the floor of the little cove, down past the jack-straw rubble of the house of the unfortunate Martin Birch, over the low sand dunes, to see that where had stood the ranch home of Rodrigo de Lima there was now only a sparkling smooth expanse of white Pacific sand.

# The Whisperers

## Richard A. Lupoff

The so-called editorial office of Millbrook High School's student paper would never have been mistaken for the city room of the San Francisco *Chronicle,* or even, to stick closer to home . . . the Marin *Independent-Journal.* A cardboard sign with hand-lettered copy was taped to the frosted glass; it said "Millbrook Hi-Life," and inside the musty room, wrestled a decade ago from a protesting language teacher, half a dozen battered desks crowded into an area suitable for half that number.

Karen Robertson sat behind the biggest of those desks. On its battered composition top stood a plastic sign announcing Karen's position, *Editor-in-Chief,* and on a rolling table beside the desk a battle-fatigued electric typewriter, its once bright paint-job suffering severely from the chips and fades.

Mario Cipolla and Annie Epstein sat in straight-backed chairs opposite Karen. All three were seniors at Millbrook High; another half a year and they would have their diplomas and be off for a final carefree summer before they started college. They'd been friends and schoolmates for a long time, but fall would see them scattered to Cal across the bay in Berkeley, to the local College of Marin in nearby Kentfield, to USC nearly half a thousand miles due south.

But now, on this miserable Friday afternoon in January, with the northern California sky a sodden, depressing gray and a steady thrum of chilling rain descending, they clustered around Karen's desk discussing the assignment that Annie and Mario would head out on that evening.

"Nobody gets interviews with the Whisperers," Karen said. "Are you really sure you can get in there, Annie?"

Annie shook back her long, rust-red hair. "My father says it's all set. We'll go in for the soundcheck, then get our interview, and we have backstage passes for tonight's show."

Mario nodded his support of Annie. Almost unconsciously he dug a couple of fingers past the felt-tipped pen in his shirt pocket and reassured himself that the precious stage-door pass was still there. It was a small cloth square with two words, *The Whisperers,* in stylized lettering and the words *Winterland, San Francisco* and the date rubber-stamped beneath in special ink that would fluoresce beneath a special light.

He had an attache case with a miniature cassette recorder in it, along with his pad and pencils. Annie had her camera around her neck—he'd hardly ever seen her without it—and a gadget bag beside her chair, with extra lenses and film. He knew that flash equipment was *verboten* on-stage, and that Annie, like the professional rock photographers, had learned to use ultra-fast films and wide apertures to capture their images by available stage lighting.

"I *am* a little nervous about the interview," Mario said. "You know, the Whisperers have had those big hit singles, 'Daemonium' and 'Erich Zann,' and I've seen them on television and all, but—" he shrugged.

"I've met lots of musicians," Annie replied. "Daddy's always bringing them up to the house to use the swimming pool or taking me to shows and introducing me to them. Most of them are perfectly ordinary people, and very nice."

Neither Mario nor Karen responded.

"Well," Annie resumed, "some of them are a little bit odd."

"I'll bet." Mario smoothed his medium-long hair. "The stories about weird carrying on, and drugs, and breaking up hotel rooms." He paused. "And groupies. They must all be strange people."

Annie said "No, they're not. At least not most of them. Not the ones I've met, and I've met practically every artist on the Dagon label, and a lot of others, that Daddy's friends introduced me to— Elektra, London, Epic."

Mario began to pick up his case with the recorder. He got to his feet and headed for the corner of the newspaper office, reached for his quilted downie jacket and rain-hood.

"Yeah, well, let's get going. We'll be going against the traffic but it's still going to be rush hour, especially in the city."

"Good luck!" Karen called after them. "Get a good story. We'll scoop everybody."

Mario and Annie headed down the hall, toward the front door of the school. It was after four o'clock, and by this time of day—especially by this time of Friday—Millbrook High was pretty nearly deserted.

They signed the late-exit book at the front door, headed down the steps hand-in-hand and sprinted across the front yard toward the student parking lot where Annie left the little Volvo 1800E that her father had given her for her senior present. She and Mario weren't exactly sweethearts—they'd both had dates with plenty of other kids, and had never got into the heavy senior scene—at least with each other—but they'd gone to parties and dances and generally hung around together ever since junior high. That was a long time.

Annie unlocked the door on the driver's side of the 1800. She looked across its sleek, rain-beaded roof at Mario. "Would you rather drive us into the city?"

He grinned. "Really, I would. I always feel kind of—strange—when a girl drives. You know?"

Annie said. "That's pretty old-fashioned, Mario." But she walked around the car's long hood and handed him the keys, waiting for him to climb into the driver's seat and reach across to unlock the passenger door for her. She settled into the leather bucket seat, fumbled in her gadget bag and came up with a pair of phototropic Jerry Garcia glasses. She settled them on her nose. In the gloomy wet afternoon they were as clear as plain ground glass.

Mario clicked on the engine and eased the Volvo's floor-shift into its smooth and powerful lower gear. He rolled it out of the parking lot, braked for the stop sign at the street, then headed onto Sir Francis Drake Boulevard and upshifted, cruising through the light traffic and the steady rain toward the freeway.

Out of the corner of his eye he could see Annie doing something with her hands in the car's map compartment. "You looking for something?"

"Do you know the Whisperers' music?'

"Their singles."

"Well, here." Annie pulled a tape cartridge from the map drawer and slapped it into the Volvo's Bendix tape system. "This is their new album. It's called *Chthulhu*. Daddy brought it home for me. It's a promo advance copy; the album won't be out till next week. They're supposed to push it on this tour."

Mario shook his head and at the same time pulled around a big Oldsmobile station wagon that was filling a lane and a half of Sir Francis. "Grocery shopping," he grumbled to himself.

The sound of water softly lapping at—what, a pier, the prow of a small boat?—came from the car's quad mini-Bozak speakers. Slowly the sound rose, and rising with it and through it came the indescribable theremin-like wail of an Arp synthesizer, then a deep, bass throbbing. At first Mario thought it was a drum, but when it changed pitch he realized that it was a pounding Fender bass.

"That's—I know that," Mario said.

Now the vocal entered, the unearthly multi-tracked female voice that he had heard so often before.

"That's 'Styx River Boatman', " he said. "I've heard that plenty of times."

"Right. It's the lead track on *Chthulhu*. The single's been out for a month. Now they hit with the album and the tour. They ought to go gold on both of them. The single's already charted with a bullet and—"

"I don't know what you're talking about, Annie."

"Oh. It's music business shop talk. Daddy always talks about his work and most of our friends are in the business. What I mean is, the Whisperers are going to be the biggest group around by the end of the year."

Mario made a sound something like *hmmf*. He dropped the thread of conversation, let the music fill his ears while he kept his eyes carefully on his driving. He'd banged a fender on the family Apollo last fall and still hadn't heard the last of it. Most of the other kids in his class had cars of their own, or at least got to use their parents' cars, and here he was riding on buses or begging rides.

The boulevard curved around and he took a ramp that ran from it onto the freeway. He dropped the Volvo into third, then down into second when he saw the traffic on the freeway. There was a break between a Plymouth Duster and a blue-flecked wide-open dune buggy—must be somebody headed home from Stinson Beach—and Mario had the 1800 onto the freeway, across into the center lane and accelerating in the space of a quadrophonic synthesizer howl.

"Very nice," Annie applauded.

"Listen," Mario said, "we better do a good job on this. You're sure this is the only interview they're giving on this gig?"

"Yep."

He shook his head. "I'd just expect Wasserman to get it then, or Phil Elwood from the *Examiner*."

The freeway wound and swooped through the hills between Mill Valley and Sausalito, plunged through the twin tunnels and slanted down the long grade toward the Golden Gate Bridge. To their right, the green wintry hills were bathed in ghostly shreds of fog that had worked their way in from the Pacific and through the Marin valleys. To their left, the bay was a dismal sheet of water, its surface pocked with a million impacts a minute.

"They're only doing it as a favor to Daddy," Annie called him back from his revery. "I told you that."

"Oh—well. I'm just surprised, that's all. If they wouldn't do it for the dailies, you know, I thought they'd give an interview to somebody from *Rolling Stone*, you know. Ben Fong-Torres or somebody, and Jim Marshall would shoot it or Annie Liebovitz. Or they could have that guy from *Ramparts* and Michael Gazaris could shoot it. Did you see those shots he got of Jagger last time the Stones played?"

Mario missed Annie's answer as he braked for the toll plaza at the northern end of the bridge. He put the 1800 into first and pulled away from the gate, settled for a steady 45 as they cut through the raindrops. Not yet five o'clock, yet the sun was gone, the sky a gray approaching black, the bridge illuminated only by the ghostly glare of its pink-orange high-intensity lamps.

They crossed the bridge without further conversation, the only sounds those of the tape system working its way from track to track of the Whisperers' new album and of the car's progress through the frigid rain: the drops drumming on the hood and roof of the Volvo, the beat-swish, beat-swish of the wipers, the shush of the car's four new Pirelli radials on the wet asphalt of the roadway.

The Friday commuter traffic was heavier now, snarled and made more dense than normal by the steady rainfall. Mario swung the Volvo around the lazy curve from the bridge onto Doyle Drive, all but overwhelmed by the sheer massive numbers of the cars and commuter buses moving in the opposite direction. He made his way past the neo-corinthian Palace of Fine Arts, down ugly Lombard Street with its neon motels and grimy gasoline stations, and turned onto Fillmore.

A line of cars stopped him at the traffic light at Union Street. From the seat beside him Annie asked if he could see the dingy little store they'd just passed. Mario looked back. "What, that button shop?"

"Know what used to be there?"

Mario shook his head.

"That was the original Matrix. Daddy says that he took me there when I was a little girl. I can hardly remember it. All of the bands played there back in the beginning. The Airplane, the Doors, the Warlocks, the New Riders. That was back in Flower Power times."

"That little place?" Mario cast a last glance over his shoulder, then followed a Porsche 914 as it pulled across Union. The Porsche dived into a parking space and Mario gunned the 1800 uphill in second. "How could they make a living playing in a joint like that?"

"I could never understand that either. Daddy says they lived on peace and love and holiness."

"Yeah. Just like the Whisperers, right? Or do they have a different trip going?"

"They sure do. They're making plenty. Daddy says they got a recording advance from Dagon and they're cleaning up on their tours and TV gigs. There was no such thing as rock on TV back in the old days, Daddy says, unless you could get on Ed Sullivan's show like Elvis or the Beatles."

Mario said "Who's Ed Sullivan?"

Annie said "I think he was something like Dick Clark, I'm not sure."

"Yeah."

The Whisperers' new album *Chthulhu* wound up with a typically weird, heavy number with odd words about somebody called the Reanimator. Annie pulled the cartridge from the Bendix unit and replaced it with the Whisperers' first album, *Anubis.*

The classic white apartment buildings of Pacific Heights gradually gave way to crumbling tenements as Fillmore Street changed from a high-price, old-line neighborhood into a grimy ghetto street. "Places like this give me the creeps," Mario grumbled. He held the wheel with one hand and checked his door latch with the other.

Annie said nothing.

"Look," Mario went on nervously, "you really know so much more about the whole music business than I do, I'm not so sure about this interview, Annie."

She shook her head, her reddish hair swinging into the edge of Mario's field of vision. "You don't have enough confidence, Mario. I always read your stuff, and we've done stories together before. Don't worry, relax, you'll do fine."

He found a parking place next to a boarded-up, deserted church on Sutter Street, and backed the Volvo into it. "I hope the car'll be safe here," he said, reaching behind the bucket seats for his cassette recorder in its attache case.

"It'll be safe, Mario."

"I don't know. A nice car in a neighborhood like this, maybe we should put it in the Miyako."

Annie ignored the suggestion. She hoisted her gadget bag onto her shoulder and climbed out of the car.

They walked together past a row of Japanese restaurants catering to visiting Asian businessmen and tourists and people arriving early for the show at Winterland. Mario looked at his watch. "We can get some dinner after we do the interview, then go back for the show afterwards."

Annie agreed.

They walked up Post to Steiner Street, then continued past the corner to the stage door of the cavernous concert hall. Mario rapped on the door with a fifty-cent piece, the echo of the metallic clash sounding off the concrete walls and sidewalk. "Will your dad be here, Annie?"

"He said he might come over for the show," she answered, shaking her head, "but he was stuck in a meeting all day. At least he told me this morning that he expected to be. So we should just go ahead."

"Okay."

The stage door, a heavy sheet of iron rivetted onto creaking hinges, swung open slowly and a hostile face glowered out at them.

"Uh—the Whisperers are expecting us," Mario muttered.

"Show's sold out," the doorman growled.

"Um—no, uh. We—"

The doorman slammed the heavy iron door shut.

Mario looked at Annie forlornly, then remembered. He unzipped the front of his waterproof jacket, fished his backstage pass out and held it in front of him. Annie grinned and hefted her heavy gadget bag to show where she'd stuck her own pass to its side.

Mario rapped on the iron again. After a few seconds the door creaked open and the doorman's face, more hostile than ever, appeared once more. Mario shoved his pass forward so the doorman could see it.

The doorman stopped, gazed unimpressed at the backstage pass and said, "Show's not for four hours. That doesn't get you into the soundcheck." He started to close the door again but it stopped at Mario's heavy hiking boot—the kind that all the kids at Millbrook High were wearing this year. The doorman's expression turned from one of general hostility to personal rage. "Say—"

"The Whisperers are expecting us. It was all set up by Dagon Records. You'd better check on it. They'll be pretty upset when they find out, otherwise."

The doorman grumbled incoherently, then said "I'll go ask their manager Bart Starke about it. You better be straight with me or it's no backstage, I don't care about any passes. And take your foot out of my door before I cut it off."

Mario reluctantly withdrew his boot. The door slammed shut. Mario turned toward Annie. "Nice fellow. I wonder why he hates me?"

"He doesn't hate you." Annie smiled at him. Mario could see the rain beading up on her forehead and the edges of her hair that extended beyond the nylon hood of her jacket. In the ghastly light of a billboard lamp advertising the Whisperers' forthcoming album, the only light on this side of the Winterland auditorium, the rainwater puddled and ran like icy perspiration.

"He doesn't hate you," she repeated. "That's just old Gooley the doorman. He'd have a thousand gate-crashers or groupies or assorted rip-offs in here every night if he didn't come on a little bit heavy, Mario."

"Hmmph."

They stood in the chilling rain waiting for Gooley's return. After a while the iron door creaked open for the third time. Gooley looked a little less hostile and angry than he had before. He made a gesture with his hand and Annie and Mario stepped over a low iron bulkhead that separated the dingily painted floor inside the doorway from the littered gray cement outside.

"Starke says okay." Gooley gestured over his shoulder, toward a short narrow staircase that led up to a half-elevated platform level.

A heavyset middle-aged man was standing on the platform. His jowly face was ringed with a fringe of graying hair. He wore a rumpled gray tweed jacket and baggy brown flannel pants. He smiled thinly at Mario and Annie.

"You the kids from the school paper?"

"Yes sir."

"I'm Bart Starke. Hal Epstein from Dagon said you were all right."

"Mr. Epstein is my father," Annie said.

Starke repeated his smile, more thinly than ever. "Yeah. Look, my kids are just starting their soundcheck. You go make yourselves comfy and you can talk to Johnny and Olly after." He jerked a thumb toward a wooden door.

Mario and Annie crossed the room toward the new door. Mario leaned his head toward Annie's and hissed, "Johnny and Olly?"

"The Whisperers," she answered softly. "Johnny Kendrick and Olivia Oldham, didn't you do your homework, Mario?"

"Oh, okay." He put his hand on the tarnished brass knob and pushed the wooden panel ahead of them. "Sure. I just never thought of Olivia Oldham as Olly, that's all."

Inside the big auditorium they made their way to the first bank of ancient, patched seats that flanked the dance floor. Annie tossed a quick look around the cavernous room, studied the stage for a few seconds and then busied herself over her gadget bag. Mario put down his attache case and settled into a dust-soaked cushion, then turned his own gaze to the stage that rose as tall as a man at the end of the auditorium.

The Whisperers were already in their places while sound technicians and lighting crew scuttered around them, checking cables, setting monitor speakers, aligning spots. The workers to a man wore battered blue jeans and soiled tee shirts, unconscious parodies, Mario thought, of an ancient Marlon Brando screen image.

The only musical instrument visible on the stage was Johnny Kendrick's white Arp synthesizer; the synthesizer, and two mikes atop their chromium stands, a gigantic sound console at one side of the stage and a towering bank of Acoustic 12-inch and 18-inch speaker cabinets under Ampeg V6c amp tops.

"Hey, don't they work with a full band?" Mario asked Annie.

She shook her head, pulling her attention away from the camera gear she'd been assembling. "Just them. All the rest is on tape—all the other instruments and the effects." She turned back to the 135 mm lens she'd been screwing onto her Nikon F2 body for ultra-long closeups.

Mario said "But—isn't that—I don't know, not quite—uh, *ethical* or something? I mean, this isn't a discotheque."

"Perfectly normal. Pink Floyd travelled with taped effects for years. First artist ever to go all out was Todd Rundgren—"

"Uhg!"

"Well anyway, he did a whole set right in this room with a whole band on tape. Just Runt and a guitar and a deck."

"Hmph!"

The technicians sifted away from the stage. Mario saw Annie slip away from the plush seats, glide out onto the middle of the gymnasium-sized dance floor to take some long shots of the Whisperers; tonight she'd use her backstage pass to get into the wings or onto the edge of the stage itself for live shots.

Johnny Kendrick was standing behind the Arp keyboard, Olivia Oldham at her mike at center stage. They started playing and singing their newest single. Mario looked at Johnny for a moment: he was dressed in a black satin stage outfit with crimson flashing. A heavy textured gold chain hung around his neck, with a huge clear jewel flashing red beneath the spots.

His hair was long, hanging in straight, glossy black planes on either side of his dark, serious face. He wore a dark moustache. Omar Sharif, Mario thought, made up to look like a satanic priest. He reached instinctively to finger a set of rosary beads he'd thrown in a garbage pail five years earlier. He turned his gaze to Annie Epstein.

The auditorium was in nearly total darkness, the only light in the great room the reflection of the stage lights and the spots that blazed from the balcony lighting booth. The stage lighting cycled through dazzling white, orange, red, green, blue and back to white.

Annie was pointing her Minolta light meter at the Whisperers, barely visible expressions of annoyance and distraction chasing each other across her round, animated face with each alteration in the lighting. In her bulky quilted jacket and ragged jeans, with her wire-rimmed glasses and rain-frizzed hair she looked like the underground comic book hippie chick Pudge.

Mario left the dusty plush seats and moved out onto the big dance floor himself. He turned back to face the stage; from this distance the elevation of the platform mattered only a little, and he could see the Whisperers without the distortion that would annoy a front-row listener and watcher.

They'd cut their first number short—no need to run though all of it at a soundcheck—and Olivia had turned her back to the "audience," to walk to Johnny's Arp and lean over it, conferring with him. After a little while the two musicians nodded their heads in agreement on some point and Olivia walked away from the synthesizer and back to her microphone. She made a small gesture with her left hand and a low eerie sound began to filter through the giant speaker banks behind the stage. It was the unearthly lead-in to another Whisperers' number.

Mario watched Olivia Oldham: she was a complete contrast to Kendrick. Where his hair was like jet, hers was a glistening blonde that picked up each color in turn from the glaring lights; under the white glare it looked as pale as Johnny Winter's. Her face was thin and pale; when she smiled or sang Mario could see the play of every tendon and muscle in her face and her throat. When she gestured— she had a peculiar, fascinating way of holding her fingers as if she were grasping some invisible line for support—he could almost feel her touching him.

He shuddered and squeezed his eyes shut, then opened them again. The stage lights were off for the moment, and the Whisperers were bathed in separate spotlights: Johnny Kendrick in a deep blue that emphasized his satanic appearance; Olivia Oldham in an almost tangible deluge of red that made her platinum hair, her pale, thin face, her billowing white dress a montage of crimson textures.

Almost involuntarily, Mario sat down, cross-legged on the hard wooden floor.

He'd heard all of the Whisperers' music before: their singles on the radio for the past year and a half since they'd appeared out of dusty midwestern obscurity, their two released albums *Anubis* and *Nightshade* the past few nights at home as he prepared for the big interview, the new *Chthulhu* in the Volvo 1800 on the way to Winterland today. But he'd never heard them before like this.

He watched the Whisperers on the stage. Under those lights, he thought, and with the auditorium itself in almost total darkness, the Whisperers could hardly know there was anyone present beside their technical crew. Yet the way they moved, looked, and sang. . . .

It was almost as if Mario were being carried away on some sort of astral journey, carried away by two creatures of some sort of— preternatural essences, of darkness and of light, pure distillates of yin and of yang, elemental embodiments of the male and female principles of being.

The colors cycled, the dark Kendrick and the pale Olivia were transformed from orange to red to green to blue; the eerie sounds coming from the big Ampeg/Acoustic towers seemed to whisper to him personally. He could almost understand what the Whisperers were saying to him, almost feel Olivia Oldham's tremulous, *needing* touch—

"You're not on something are you, kid?"

Mario flinched away from the heavy hand that was shaking him roughly by one shoulder. He blinked his eyes and saw that Johnny

Kendrick and Olivia Oldham were gone from the stage; the house lights were on and half a dozen casually dressed technicians were rechecking every piece of equipment.

Turning, Mario saw the jowly face of Barton Starke peering into his face. Starke looked annoyed. He was chewing a fat brown cigar, or at least the last inch or so that remained of one. Mario blinked up at him and grunted in confusion. He pressed both his hands on the floor and started to stand up.

"I said, you *on* something, kid?"

Mario shook his head. "N-no sir. I was just, ah . . ."

"Yeah," Starke nodded. "You got carried away with the music. All right, I don't want nobody coming around here stoned out on anything, you know? The customers are bad enough, but that's not my problem. You want that interview, you better get backstage now and do it before my kids go take their nap before the show." He jerked his hand toward the door that led from the auditorium to the backstage area where they'd first entered the building.

Mario rubbed his hands over his own face, picked up his attache case with the cassette equipment in it and started for the door. He was starting to get back together now. He could see that Annie had picked up her gadget bag and was a few paces ahead of him. He caught up to her as they reached the door and stepped through it directly behind her, Starke following at his heels.

He stumbled through the door, through the cold, drab room he'd been in earlier, up the stairway where he'd first seen Barton Starke. There was still a slight ringing in Mario's ears—surely the after-effect of the overwhelming loudspeakers in the auditorium—and his eyes had apparently not returned altogether to normal after that odd visual experience.

Annie Epstein seemed to have gone off somewhere, maybe to change lenses or load a fresh roll of tri-X. Mario stopped at the top of the stairs and looked back but he didn't see anyone—not Starke, not the doorman Gooley, not any of the stage hands or technicians.

He put his hand on the doorknob and went through into another room. It was dimly lighted—he couldn't tell whether there were recessed electric bulbs somewhere or whether the light came entirely from the candles that stood on low shelves. The room seemed to be furnished in dark plush, ancient black velvet cushions and maroon drapes.

There was an odor in the air—something musty, yet somehow sweet. He turned to look back at the door but it seemed to have receded, or else Mario had unconsciously advanced to the middle of the room. He looked down and saw that he was standing in the center of a dark, heavily patterned carpet. He tried to follow the pattern with his eyes: it wove tortuously, seemed almost to present an objective picture of—something. But he couldn't quite make out what it was, not in the dimness, the wavering illumination of the dark room.

There was a sound of swishing draperies and he saw a pale figure standing beside one of the candles. It was Olivia Oldham; in the flickering candlelight she looked slimmer than ever, and far more pale. Her hair looked almost pure white, and to Mario she seemed, for an instant, not to be the very young woman she had seemed on the stage.

For the first time he could see her eyes clearly: they were pale, too, like everything else about her. He couldn't tell what color they were: a pale, pale blue, or perhaps a whitened golden tint that picked up flickers of candlelight and gleamed at him across the room.

Olivia Oldham said "Hi."

The single syllable, softly uttered, struck Mario like an electric shock. He hadn't expected her to speak, somehow: as absurd as that seemed even to him. She had seemed like a creature from some other plane of existence. To hear her commonplace greeting was more astounding than it would have been to see her slowly fade into invisibility.

She crossed the room toward him and put her hand out as if for him to take it.

"You're Mr. Cipolla? Please make yourself comfortable. Would you like anything? A cup of tea?" She gestured, and beside one of the candles where Mario could not imagine not noticing it, there was a plain tray with a pot and cups. He barely managed to croak an affirmative response.

Olivia's voice was—somehow soft and low like a whisper, yet plentifully clear to him. Mario found himself sitting on a plush velvet bench. He felt somehow clumsy and inadequate.

Olivia Oldham, unbelievably fragile-seeming, sat beside him, a cup in her hands. Mario looked into her eyes. They *were* golden. He realized suddenly that she was the most beautiful person he'd ever seen, that he was—he felt himself turning crimson and hot.

He fumbled for his notebook, his recorder. "Uh—there's—Annie said her father had—"

"Annie went with John Kendrick." Olivia sipped at her cup, raised her eyes to look up at him as she did. "To get some shots in better light. Brighter light, that is."

"Uh." Mario tried a sip of the tea himself. He'd heard stories of the strange backstage scenes at places like this, of the dangers and the temptations. He looked at Olivia. She seemed completely at home in this dim, plush room, her white gown almost floating about her like the soft wavering fins of some delicate tropical fish. Mario's head felt light, his body seemed to tingle. He took another sip of the hot orange tea.

Outside, he reminded himself, the world was going on. He was here to do an interview for his school paper, Olivia Oldham was a singer, half of the Whisperers, that was all. And not forty feet away, outside this place, San Francisco was going about its rainy Friday night routine: late commuters still heading for the bridge to Marin, tourists from Omaha and from Osaka riding up and down the city's hills on cable cars, freaks from Berkeley and what was left of Haight cueing up right now at the front door of Winterland—

He snapped his head up and looked at Olivia Oldham. "Uh— where's—uh—where did you start, um . . ." If only he could get the interview going, get back in control of the situation somehow. But Olivia seemed to be making that peculiar gesture with her fingers, and Mario found it harder and harder to move.

She took the cup from his hands, put it back on the shelf. She stood before him and drew him up to his feet.

"Uh, I meant to ask you . . ." he plowed doggedly on, trying to clear his head. If he could get some fresh air. It was so stuffy in this room, the peculiar odor in here. He looked at Olivia, and couldn't tell whether she was very tiny or whether she towered over him, whether the room itself was crowding in or retreating to monstrous dimensions.

"Oh," he tried once more, "the, ah, the Whisperers—"

She smiled at him and nodded encouragingly.

"Ah, you have unusual material. I mean, ah, why do you write songs about such, ah, morbid topics? Like, ah, your new album. What does *Chthulhu* mean? Doesn't it have something to do with ah, some old ah—?"

"Yes," she nodded, "it is an old tradition. Very old. You might even call it an old religion. Those who know of the Elder Gods. Those who would open the way once more."

"But why the Whisperers? I mean if it's a religion—"

"A religion that was suppressed a million years ago. A religion that existed only in secret places, only in isolated villages. A religion that was discovered and secretly attacked again and nearly wiped out fifty years ago. You can read of it, you can find it all in the works of the Providence writer."

"But—but—" Mario stammered.

"But now," Olivia went on, "now we have the way. Tonight you will see. Tonight you will see four thousand young people swaying and chanting with us, moving in the ritual steps, calling back the Elder Gods, worshipping, worshipping."

Her thin hand holding his seemed to be made of iron, strong and resistless; she seemed to tower above his head, her eyes gleaming; her white flowing dress seeming to flutter and whirl with a life of its own, as if it were not mere cloth, but a sentient thing.

"But why do you tell me this? Won't you be destroyed again? I'll write about you, we'll print it. Annie's photos—"

Her shrill laughter cut into his voice, and from behind him there came more laughter, deeper. He whirled and saw Johnny Kendrick standing, the candlelight reflecting from the black satin of his suit and the red of its flashing, of the great jewel that hung from its filigreed chain. Beside Kendrick stood Annie, her face blankly expressionless.

"Four thousand people," Kendrick said softly. "Four thousand young people, full of the vital energy needed to feed the beast, to summon the opener, to bring back the Elder Gods.

"We let you come so there *would* be a record of this great night. Use your best words, boy." He turned to Annie. "Use your best skill, girl. Tonight is a night that will live forever. And in coming days, as the mighty sounds of Chthulhu music drive from millions of speakers, drive through millions of brains, the mighty one will hear. He will rise. The Elder Gods will return."

Kendrick stepped to the door, opened it, snapped "Starke! Send that nuisance Gooley for some food for us. Get enough for our guests. We have to be considerate of the powers of the press!"

He laughed, and slammed the door shut.

# Lights! Camera! Shub-Niggurath!

## Richard A. Lupoff

One of the more glamorous towns in Starrett is called—now don't be surprised—Hollywood. You'll remember that there was the first Hollywoodland, later shortened to Hollywood, back on earth. Later came the famous Hollywood-on-the-moon, where they were able to get such fabulous scenic and lighting effects and where the light gravity made it easy to use heavy equipment.

In time the builders and managers of Starrett, that giant tincan world that plies its wares in the interstellar deeps, deemed it wise to carry on the tradition. Hence, Starrett's own Hollywood-between-the-Stars.

You've probably heard about Starrett, but just in case you haven't, here's how that artificial world survives. It's so big there's a complete eco-system (and a complete economy!) inside Starrett's massive shell. Thus, as Starrett travels from star to star and visits planet after planet, it functions something like a high-tech gypsy camp.

The space-folk who live in Starrett buy at this world and sell at that. They sometimes carry passengers between remote solar systems. They provide varied forms of entertainment for the mud-hoppers (a.k.a. rubes) who shuttle up from planetside for a special treat.

And they produce some of the biggest money-making shows in the known galaxy.

Even if you're thoroughly familiar with Starrett, it's less than likely that you've ever heard of Dinganzicht, another artificial space-habitat that didn't travel as widely as Starrett. Not by a long-shot. In fact, Dinganzicht hardly travelled at all, except in the somewhat diffuse astronomical sense. That is, Dinganzicht was associated with the trinary star system Fornax 1382. As Fornax 1382 moved relative to other nearby objects (and, in the ultimate view, as the universe continued to expand) Dinganzicht moved along with it. But that doesn't mean much on the local scale.

Fornax 1382 consisted of 1382 Alpha, a red giant star; 1382 Beta, a green dwarf; and 1382 Gamma, a medium-size, yellowish main-sequence star not very unlike Sol. These three stars were sometimes known as the cosmic traffic light, or as the sherbet triplets Cherry, Lime, and Lemon.

Dinganzicht was a large construct. It had been positioned to remain stationary in the gravitational nexus of Cherry, Lime, and Lemon. As the three stellar members of Fornax 1382 wove their complex orbital net around Dinganzicht, Dinganzichters could peer out through the viewports of their hollow metallic world and see an endlessly changing light-show. Cherry would rise and Lemon set, or Lemon would rise as Lime set, and so on. The combination of colored sunlights might produce a bright orange effect one day, a lurid chartreuse another, a truly glorious magenta another.

Dinganzicht was probably the worst place in the universe to live if you were color-blind. Not because you would suffer any particular harm from living there. Just because you'd miss so damned much natural spectacle.

Considering the number of inhabited worlds in the galaxy—and that number was increasing all the time, by the way—there was a limitless market for the wares peddled by Starrett and a number of similar interstellar gypsy camps. The space-folk might have just kept producing copies of existing productions and selling 'em to new customers, but that would have reduced their art to mere commerce. They insisted on continuing to turn out new productions all the time.

The three biggest studios in Hollywood-between-the-Stars were

30th Century-Bioid, Universal-Interdimensional, and Asahi-Kirin-Toyo. Running a distant fourth was an outfit modestly known as Colossal Galactic Productions, or Colicprods for short. Colicprods was headed by one Tarquin Armbruster IV, *nee* Isidore Stickplaster, a nervous, balding, cigar-chomping man of middle years, much given to stodgy, old-fashioned dress. For instance, when the current arbiters of Hollywood-between-the-Stars fashion dictated wing-collared shirts and striped cravats, dark jackets, bowlers and brollies—Tarquin Armbruster could be seen in fluorescent tights and turquoise helmet, a style that had disappeared from the studios and watering-holes of Hollywood hours and hours ago.

It didn't help Tarquin's jumpiness any that Colicprods was in bad financial trouble at the moment. The chief-of-production for the studio was a statuesque individual who had been born Pamela Rose Tremayne but who insisted on being known professionally as Golda Abromowitz. Golda differed from most Starretteers, who were almost unanimously of earth-human ancestry. Golda too was human, but was of Formalhautian origin. She had immigrated to Starrett when it was visiting her home world of Formalhaut VIII. But you could hardly tell her from a native Starretteer, except that she was seven feet tall and had brilliant metallic-green skin.

In an era of specialization, Dinganzicht was one of the most successful of specialized worlds. There were planets devoted largely or exclusively to agriculture. There were others that concentrated on heavy industry, fine manufacturing, artistic creation, or prayer. (Of the latter, Reverend Jimmy Joe Jeeter—that was the name of the planet, yes, Reverend Jimmy Joe Jeeter—was the best known example.)

Dinganzicht specialized in science and technology.

The whole world, with only minimal support systems to provide such necessities as food, was a complex of laboratories, research facilities, and testing grounds. There were a great many independent organizations in Dinganzicht, and each of them managed to earn its way by developing useful devices that the Dinganzichters could sell to the rest of the galaxy.

There was, for instance, the Edison/Tsiolkovsky Corporation, whose most successful product was the famous rollaway cat impellor. There was the Vieux Carre Cast-Iron Products Company A.G., from whose laboratory had emerged the hypospace drive that permitted Starrett and worlds like it to move from star to star in such short periods of time. There was Z. Z. Zachary and Associates, who had developed the matter duplicator, that invention that has caused such happiness and plenty—and such bizarre headaches!—for users throughout the galaxy.

And there was Macrotech Associates.

*Oy,* was there ever Macrotech Associates!

Macrotech Associates had some of the best minds in Dinganzicht—or any other world, for that matter!—at its disposal. Well, and it might have been simpler in the long run if it hadn't!

Right at this moment there was a terrible argument going on in Tarquin Armbruster's office, a modest little room patterned on the one-time private audience chamber of Tarquin's favorite historical figure, the Emperor Franz Josef of Austria-Hungary. Tarquin was hosting the meeting himself, lighting a series of fat black cigars imported from La Habana Otra Vez, pouring little glasses of Puerto Mas Rican rum for himself and his guests, and sweating up a storm despite the carefully controlled temperature and humidity.

Also present were Gort Swiggert, a representative of the studio comptroller's office, wearing his harlequin outfit of red and black; Golda Abromowitz, swathed as usual in a thick, bushy coverall of synthetic polar bear fur; and Martin van Buren MacTavish. MacTavish was a screenwriter, just about the best in the industry. He wore a highland kilt, tam o'shanter, and sporran. Perched on one hairy knee was his portable word-processor. It was slightly smaller than an immy, and if you don't know what an immy is you've never really played marbles.

Every time Gort Swiggert gave Tarquin Armbruster a bit of financial news, the red parallelograms on his outfit glowed. Armbruster sweated, lit or re-lit a cigar, and gulped rum. The financial picture was lousy.

Golda Abromowitz peered out of her furs and said, "I *know* this picture will be a box office boff. It'll save Colossal Galactic. But it has to be done right. There's no other way. We can't survive putting on shows for the Saturday night blast-in circuit. This has to be top quality."

Tarquin Armbruster wiped away a freshet of perspiration. "But a horror movie, Golda? A big-budget, risk-it-all-on-one-throw horror movie?"

Golda turned her head to the side. "Tell him, Martin."

Martin van Buren MacTavish had been concentrating on his word-processor. In addition to storing, revising, and outputting the text that was fed into it, the word-processor could function as a video game, a holotape playback unit, a music-synthesizer capable of piping out any composition in the known history of melody (or of composing new selections to MacTavish's specifications), or an emergency cook-stove.

"Huh?" Martin said.

"I want you to tell Tarkie about the project," Golda prompted.

"Oh." MacTavish fiddled with the word-processor a little more, then clicked it off and slipped it into his sporran. "We had the girls in market research get us up a few figures, *jefe,* and they say that a really hot horror holoflik could sell on no fewer than twenty-kay worlds. Maybe as many as thirty-kay. We—"

Armbruster cut him off. "What about it, Swiggert?" He pulled at his cigar, tossed back a swig of rum. "You seen their figures?"

Swiggert nodded. "They look pretty convincing." The red parallelograms on his outfit faded to dull ochre and the black ones glowed. The bright glow of black diamonds produced an eerie effect all its own.

"Huh," grunted Tarquin Armbruster IV. "And what do you have in mind? You going to bring back one of those lurching monsters from the old days?"

MacTavish slipped one hand inside his sporran and fumbled his word-processor back to life. The machine had a Braille output plate, and although MacTavish was not blind, he had taught himself to read Braille with one sensitive thumb.

"I want to do a story called *The Dunwich Horror,*" he said.

Even though the matter-duplicator had been invented in Dinganzicht, in the electrotechnology division of Macrotech Associates

Ell Tee Dee, there were no matter-duplicators allowed in Dinganzicht. There had been a bunch of them at first, and they had of course been hugely useful. But they'd made so much trouble that they had been banned.

Here's one small example.

Lurleen Luria was a religious fanatic, possibly the only one ever in Dinganzicht. She had invented a religion based on the notion that one should eat only pimentos and think only of the number eight. She had a tough time winning converts to her way of thinking. Yet, she was convinced that if everybody would just adopt her faith, her diet, and her pattern of thought, there would be universal brother- (and/or sister-) hood, happiness and tranquility in the world.

Well, Lurleen thought to herself, if I'm the only one who understands that my religion is the one key to salvation, there would be universal salvation if everybody were just like me.

She took to inviting people over to her place and walking them through a matter-duplicator input bin disguised as a hallway. She'd already set her matter-duplicator, using herself as the model specs, so the organs, cells, even molecules of her guests were broken down into separate atoms and reassembled into new Lurleen Lurias. Who did, naturally, agree with the original Lurleen's dietary, intellectual, and religious notions.

They finally tracked down Lurleen and put her out of business (but not before a dozen security troopers got turned into new Lurleen Lurias). They never did get all the new Lurleens turned back into their original selves, though. What a mess!

When they tried to round up and dismantle all the matter-duplicators in Dinganzicht, the argument was made that the sane, innocent, and responsible users of the machines were being punished along with the (relatively few) crazy, guilty, or irresponsible ones like Lurleen Luria. But nobody could figure out a way to keep matter-duplicators only in the "right" hands.

One of the problems of getting rid of the things was this: If somebody owned one, and a friend of his or hers also owned one, they could dismantle the second duper, run it through the first, and reassemble the sections. Then they'd have not two of the gadgets, but three. And shortly, if they chose, four, five, or any number.

Well, they got 'em rounded up finally, but it was a tough job. In a bigger place than Dinganzicht, or a less organized one, it would have proved impossible.

That was a while ago, however. The current problem at Macrotech Associates grew out of the current hot research project in the electrotechnology division, the same outfit that had ginned up the matter duplicator.

The current hot research project was the instant communicator.

This was an attempt to tackle a problem that had first appeared with the development of space travel. Back in the days when everybody had lived on one planet, radio-spectrum communication was plenty fast enough. At one time, in fact, folks had thought that light waves, radio waves and the like worked instantaneously. In time they found out that they did take time to propagate, but cripes, they could circle the planet in an eighth of a second, so who cared?

But when you got up to interplanetary distances, you were talking about minutes, then hours, to send "Hi, mom, we're number one," and get back "That's a good boy, don't forget to eat your supper."

And once you got up to the interstellar scale, it could take *years*.

So Macrotech Associates, electrotechnology division, had an important project to work on.

The brains that were working on the project were those of a bright young fellow named Alexander Ulianov and a brilliant young woman named Amy 2-3-4 Al-Khnemu.

Alex and Amy were making good progress, too. But the top brass at Macrotech Associates (as well as the general management of Dinganzicht) were keeping damned close watch over the project. They remembered matter-duplicators—did they ever!—and the whole Lurleen Luria fiasco.

In fact, there was a little colony of identical Lurleen Lurias still living. They had been sequestered. Nobody knew which was the original (guilty) Lurleen and which her innocent victims. They were kept comfortable in a little compound where they were growing old together, happily living on pimentos and thinking of the number eight, while scientists from the psychotechnology division of Macrotech Associates happily studied them.

No, nobody wanted another matter-duplicator fiasco, and there was a good deal of nervousness about the implications of Alexander Ulianov and Amy 2-3-4 Al-Khnemu's work.

Tarquin Armbruster IV was more inclined to do a swashbuckler about pirates on the Spanish Main, or maybe even a Biblical epic than a horror movie. Then again, he had a fondness for westerns, too. But Golda Abromowitz and Martin van Buren MacTavish had the support of Gort Swiggert, and what the comptroller had to say carried a lot of weight with Tark.

He told 'em to go ahead.

MacTavish had an easy time turning *The Dunwich Horror* into a screenplay. It was one of the best stories of an old New England author who had more often relied on atmosphere than events to make his stories work, but this one was unusual for him. It was graphic, full of plot and events, and it had a couple of scenes in it that were real sockdolligers.

There was a big shambling guy in it named Wilbur Whateley. Wilbur went around in a baggy overcoat, summer and winter, like a flasher. And about two-thirds of the way through the story Wilbur's overcoat gets opened and the audience sees what's inside, and is it ever something! Wow!

Wilbur has a brother, too, who isn't seen until the grand climax of the yarn, and if you think Wilbur was something to make strong men retch, wait 'til you see his twin!

In fact, that was the biggest problem that Golda Abromowitz had with *The Dunwich Horror.*

Marty MacTavish and his wonderful word-processor turned out a good script in record time. Casting went well, too. Golda was able to get Nefertiti Logan, current holder of the "this season's blonde" title, to play the exotic albino Lavinia Whateley. For contrast, she hired the raven-tressed, flashing-eyed Gaza de Lure II to portray Sally Sawyer.

The male lead, the role of Professor Henry Armitage, she gave to a piece of beefcake called Rock Quartz. Rock used to stand in front of mirrors most of the time when he wasn't actually on camera, and when he *was* on-camera, he treated the lens like a mirror, too. The effect on audiences was devastating.

Curtis Whateley—he of the undecayed branch of the Whateleys—was played by Roscoe Inelegante. Roscoe Inelegante wasn't exactly the actor's real name, but nobody quite knew what his real name was, and word had passed in Hollywood-between-the-Stars that it wasn't wise to try and find out.

But who would play the Whateley boys, Wilbur and his fraternal twin?

There didn't seem to be anyone in Hollywood quite capable of handling the roles.

Golda might get an actor to portray Wilbur-with-his-overcoat-on. Somebody like Karlos Karch who had already parlayed a set of grotesque features and a growling, animalistic manner into a substantial career as a holocinematic maniac, brute, and general heavy.

But even Karch (who was, off-screen, a sweet-natured and gentle man, faithful husband and doting father) couldn't handle Wilbur-with-his-coat-off.

Martin van Buren MacTavish had turned up the original text describing Wilbur, and it was a doozie! Tentacles, mouths, fur, rudimentary eyes set in pinkish, ciliated orbits, a trunk with purple annular markings, ridgy-veined pads. . . .

The beautiful Golda Abromowitz nearly lost her lunch when Marty showed her the text.

They tried outfitting Karlos Karch with a cyborged rubber suit. It worked fairly well, and was totally disgusting to the eye.

The strangest thing, though, was this: Nefertiti Logan, Gaza de Lure II, and even Golda Abromowitz herself, found Karlos Karch a total turn-on when he wore his Wilbur Whateley suit. They either couldn't or wouldn't tell any of the men associated with the project the reason.

Even Karlos wasn't sure, but he and Martin van Buren MacTavish spent a long session with a bottle of Puerto Mas Rican rum filched from Tarquin Armbruster's private stock, and devised a theory. Nefertiti, Gaza, and Golda were all fantasizing, they decided, as to what it might be like to have an experience with all of those weird squirming tentacles and mouths and eyes and hair and ridgy-veined pads.

Karlos and Marty asked Gaza on the set the next day, but she just smiled dreamily and said, "Karlos, why don't you put on your rubber suit and we'll try your theory out."

But Karlos didn't go for that, so nobody ever really knew.

Anyway, things were going kind of poorly on the set by now. The Wilbur Whateley suit was less than satisfactory, and as for the role of Wilbur's brother, that was a complete conundrum. Marty MacTavish had turned up the original specs for Wilbur's brother, given in the words of a character in the original story. The story, by the way, was long since out of copyright, which was one of the brighter points in the day of both Tarquin Armbruster and Gort Swiggert in his harlequin suit.

Wilbur's brother was "Bigger'n a barn . . . all made o' squirmin' ropes . . . great bulgin' eyes all over it . . . ten or twenty mouths or trunks a-stickin' aout all along the sides, all a-tossin' and openin' an' shuttin' . . . all grey, with kinder blue or purple rings . . . *an' Gawd in Heaven—that haff face on top!*"

Well, they tried computer animation and they got some very interesting effects but they didn't get Wilbur's brother.

And they tried miniature models but they didn't work.

And they tried a full-size mock-up but it looked more like Happy the Humbug than it did a monster cross-breed between human and giant alien.

Now it happened that just about at the point when *The Dunwich Horror* was in danger of winding up totally on the scrap-heap—and Tarquin Armbruster IV, Golda Abromowitz, and Colossal Galactic Productions along with it—Starrett was approaching the triple star Fornax 1382.

Tarquin Armbruster IV and Golda Abromowitz decided that their last hope was to get some help from the superscientific shizzes in Dinganzicht. After all, any world that can produce the rollaway cat impellor should be able to provide a big boost to Colossal Galactic Productions.

Tarquin and Golda climbed aboard the ultralite shuttle *Clare Winger Harris*. They could have left Starrett from a port near Hollywood, but they were in a hurry and it was quicker to zip across the hollow middle of Starrett and exit on the antipodal side. Quite near the island of Kaspak, as a matter of fact.

To reach Kaspak Portal, the *Harris* passed smack through the null-g point in the geometric center of Starrett.

The null-g point and the ultra-low-g zone surrounding it were the homes of a number of fascinating species of life, both animal and vegetable. There was null-g lichen, for instance. There were floating blobs of water that hosted perfectly globular fishes of various colors. There were several species of footless birds that spent their entire lives in the air, never coming to earth (as it were), not even to lay their eggs or to build nests (which they did in the null-g lichen.)

One interesting aspect of this null-g lichen was the complex, free-form network of neural-like filament that spread throughout the stuff. It had been theorized that consciousness and intelligence, rather than being a discrete attribute developed by any particular species as the result of an evolutionary imperative, was actually an inescapable concomitant of *any* signaling network of sufficient size and complexity.

And the null-g lichen that floated in the center of Starrett was big enough, and the network of signal-conducting, neural-like fibres it contained was complex enough, to come in well over the critical line.

It might not be altogether inaccurate to characterize Starrett's null-g lichen as . . . *smart moss!*

And here was the ultralite shuttle *Clare Winger Harris*, flittering upward from Hollywood, containing one fat, bald, sweaty-browed, cigar-chomping, rum-swigging studio head named Tarquin Armbruster IV; and one seven-foot-tall, elegant, metallic-green, polar-bear-fur-covered production chief called Golda Abromowitz.

And what did Tarquin and Golda have on their minds as their shuttle penetrated the wispy outer edges of the null-g lichen that drifted in the center of Starrett?

Why, nothing other than the peculiar physical attributes of the wonderful Whateley brothers. You know, all those tentacles and suckers and half-formed eyes and writhing ropes and stovepipe legs and Gawd in Heaven that half face on top!

Now meet P. H. "Biff" Connaught.

Biff Connaught was head of security for Macrotech Associates. A red-faced, gray-haired, middle-aged fellow, Biff had been up and down the corporate ladder in his day. He now held a responsible but not very glamorous position, the chief advantage of which was the chance it provided for Biff to live out his fantasies.

In his youth, Biff had wanted to be a policeman complete with uniform, badge and gun. He didn't know quite *why* that job appealed to him. If he'd been a more insightful person, he might have detected a certain flaw in his own psyche, a gnawing sense of inadequacy, of psychic impotence, which he could overcome by placing himself in a position of psychological dominance and authority.

By the time Biff was of age, he was able to live out his wishes by becoming a cop.

How he came to leave the official police force is another story. But having done so, he moved into private security work, rose by diligent application from uniformed rent-a-bull to plain-clothes, and ultimately to head of security for Macrotech. He had, by this time, realized that the power of the plainclothes chief of security was even greater than that of the uniformed harness bulls he commanded.

Besides, Biff was issued a most impressive badge that he kept in a pocket-case ready for flashing. And he carried an old-fashioned snubnose revolver under his armpit; the snubnose had been purchased in an antique shop on Mirzam Beta IV. Biff personally restored it to working order and hand-loaded ammunition for it.

Top management at Macrotech Associates was very worried about Alex Ulianov and Amy 2-3-4 Al-Khnemu's research project on instantaneous communication.

On the face of it, it should be a boon to interstellar civilization. After all, the hypospace drive developed by Macrotech's competitor Vieux Carre Cast-Iron Products A.G. had been a positive gift from heaven. Prior to the availability of hypospace, nobody had been able to travel any faster than the speed of light. In fact, travel had been limited to a pace asymptotically approaching light-speed. Four-plus years from Sol to Centaurus, four hundred thousand (except that nobody bothered to try it) from Centaurus to Yggdrasill.

Once the engineers at Vieux Carre developed hypospace drive, and the company's sales force marketed it, all of that changed. Little exploring ships—and later, big colonizing ships—and still later, roving traders and interstellar gypsy camps like Starrett, Weinbaum, and

Zealia Reed—could go anywhere in the galaxy in a tiny fraction of the time it would have taken at mere light-speed.

Hypospace wasn't exactly a *faster*-than-light drive. It didn't involve tachyons or anything like that. Nor did it involve the fourth dimension, or those famous (but, alas, apparently nonexistent) "wormholes" in space. What the Vieux Carre hypospace drive did, in effect, was let you cut across space-time vectors and re-emerge into normal space wherever you wanted. It still took time to make the trip, but it didn't take anywhere near as long as it would have in normal space.

Kind of like this. If you were sitting in a house on the surface of a planet—say, in the city of Xnmp'pr on Houdini III—and you could sort of anchor yourself to one spot while the globe spun beneath you at a thousand miles per hour or so, you'd get the effect of traveling at a thousand miles per hour without actually moving at all.

If you added all of the vectored motions going on around you— the rotation of Houdini III, the orbital motion of the planet around its sun, the movement of that sun within its local star-group, the motion of that group relative to the rest of the galaxy, the spin of the whole galactic disc, the motion of the galaxy within *its* local galactic cluster, and so on up the scale—you could accumulate a terrific amount of speed.

That's what the Vieux Carre drive did for you. And it yielded the effect, if not the literal actuality, of faster-than-light.

But it still wasn't instantaneous.

Now then, while hypospace drive had been a vast blessing, matter-duplicators had been, let's say, a *mixed* blessing at best.

The folks in the executive suite at Macrotech Associates wanted to make damned sure that instantaneous communication, if it ever happened, was put to only beneficial use.

They were also concerned that it bring a nice fat profit to Macrotech. Unlike the matter-duplicator, which had yielded a modest profit to Z. Z. Zachary and Associates, but quickly ceased to do so once people caught on to the trick of using matter duplicators to make more matter duplicators. It was sure as hell cheaper than buying 'em from Z. Z. Zachary.

So P. H. "Biff" Connaught was called to the executive suite of the Macrotech headquarters palace and presented with the problem of keeping Alex and Amy and their glittery project under control. Along with Biff, the top dogs also summoned Cyndora Vexmann, the head of Macrotech's psychotechnology division. They figured Cyndora might have some pretty good suggestions to make.


The little shuttle-ship *Clare Winger Harris* penetrated the null-g zone in the center of Starrett. As the ship moved through the region it pierced the cloudlike body of lichen that had mutated and evolved in the peculiar conditions that obtain in the very center of a hollow world.

The ship's passage through the lichen caused a wave-field to ripple through the lichen, making a sound, a barely audible sound. If you'd been there you might have described it as a kind of brushing, swishing, crackling noise. You might have reproduced it, at least approximately, by making a soft *ch'ch'ch'ch* sound with the middle of your tongue pressed against the roof of your mouth, the tip of your tongue pointed toward the backs of your top-front teeth, and your lips slightly pursed.

Try that and exhale through your mouth softly, and you'll get something close to the sound.

The lichen had never had a name, but if you want to call it something (other than "lichen," of course), you might as well call it "Ch-ch-ch."

Inside the *Clare Winger Harris*, Tarquin Armbruster IV was sitting at the pilot's post, chewing a black Nueva Cubana Magnifico and sweating bullets. Golda Abromowitz was bent over a copy of Martin van Buren MacTavish's script for *The Dunwich Horror*, trying to figure out a way to portray the Whateley brothers and save the production (and Colossal Galactic into the bargain).

Ch-ch-ch was minding its own business, keeping its resident birds, insects, ponds, fishes and small reptiles happy.

Suddenly Ch-ch-ch felt itself punctured. It was a hell of a shock, although it probably didn't exactly *hurt* Ch-ch-ch. Can you apply the concept of pain to a null-g lichen? Even to an intelligent one?

Probably not.

In a fleeting moment the *Harris* was gone. Ch-ch-ch, being fairly amorphous in composition, slowly drifted back together and resumed its commonplace little life.

But a chunk of Ch-ch-ch got itself hooked on the outer skin of the shuttle, and was carried away from its parent.

Responding to the local gravity of the shuttle this new body of lichen spread itself thinly over the skin of the ship.

Inside the *Harris*, Tarquin Armbruster IV chomped down on his Nueva Cubana Magnifico and grunted. To Golda Abromowitz he said, "Hey, I never noticed before, this little ship even has tinted glass in the viewplates. Not bad! Maybe we should try a space adventure."

"Too old hat. Forget it." Golda didn't even look up from Mac-Tavish's *Dunwich Horror* script.

The intelligent lichen spread almost invisibly thin over the shuttle was having all sorts of interesting new experiences. Gravity. Inertia. Weight. Kinesis. Thought.

Above all, thought.

Ch-ch-ch had been exposed to the mental activity, such as it was, of the many small creatures that lived within its spongelike channels and protuberances. But now, Ch-ch-ch Junior was picking up the mental emanations of Tarquin and Golda.

Junior was absolutely flabbergasted. Dazzled, amazed, strangely pleased by the sensation of thought and mental imagery. And flabbergasted.


"You understand why you can't know anything about your work," Cyndora Vexmann purred.

"No, we really don't," Amy 2-3-4 Al-Khnemu replied. She shot a glance at Al Ulianov; he nodded in response. She was to speak for the two of them.

Cyndora smiled. "Place yourselves in the company's shoes. The operative precedent—I was briefed by legal, of course—goes back to the old Disney versus Sony case. You remember that."

"No, we really don't," Amy replied.

Cyndora heaved a sigh. "It had to do with videotape recorders. I don't suppose you remember those, or even heard of them."

Al Ulianov said, "I think I remember learning something about them in a history course. I think they were phased out in favor of wax gramophone cylinders. Or was it the other way around?"

"What it had to do with," Cyndora said, "was providing the public with technology they could use to duplicate copyrighted tapes. Disney held a lot of valuable copyrights. Once people had video recorders, they could make copies of their own. Either capture broadcast material or duplicate existing tapes. Disney wanted to restrict the public to play-only technology."

"Huh! What happened?" Amy leaned forward in her chair. "I never heard of the case."

"What happened was, Disney won in court but it was too late to stop the recorder business. There were already millions of the things around. So they won the battle but lost the war."

Amy exchanged another glance with her partner. "What does all this have to do with us?"

"I'll tell you what, you little creeps!" That was Biff Connaught speaking, as you probably figured. Biff didn't purr. He growled sometimes, and roared occasionally, but he did not purr.

"I'll tell you what," Biff repeated. "We know what you're up to! Instantaneous communication!"

"Of course," Amy agreed. "It's in our reports. It's in our funding requests. You're some detective, Biff, to figure that out! Next you'll tell us that you've discovered what the P. H. in your name stands for."

"Never mind my name! Biff will do, you—" The last few syllables of Biff's speech trailed away. He glared at Amy. "Come to think of it, it's Captain Connaught to you. As head of security I'm equivalent to police captain in grade."

"Come on, Alex." Amy 2-3-4 Al-Khnemu placed her hand on Alex Ulianov's wrist. "We don't have to put up with this."

Cyndora Vexmann stopped them. "Dr. Al-Khnemu. Dr. Ulianov. Please accept my apology on behalf of Macrotech Associates. Captain Connaught here meant no harm. He's just an unlettered ruffian." She turned toward Connaught. "Please, Biff, either learn to treat people decently or limit yourself to dealing with trespassers and petty thieves."

Biff managed to flush beneath his walnut-colored complexion. "Uck! I guess I . . ." Again his words trailed away.

"What top management is concerned about," Cyndora turned

back toward Amy and Alex, "is that your work will get out of corporate control. And once the secret is out—well, you know how hard it is to enforce things like patents and copyrights over interstellar distances."

"Indeed. But—what do you have in mind?"

Cyndora smiled her most disarming smile. "We just can't afford to have information leaking out about your work. And, to be totally candid, we can't afford to have you know about your work, either. That goes back to the old video recorder case, too. Technicians were working for companies, trying to concoct security devices for broadcasters. Then they'd go home and design boxes to unscramble scrambled signals, crack the very codes they themselves had devised. Oh, it was really something!"

"You still haven't told us what you want to do. Or what you want us to do."

Cyndora shot a glance at Biff Connaught. She said, "Amy, Alex, all we want to do is lock up Macrotech's proprietary information. When you go home from work, we want you to leave everything behind you. Have a good time. Enjoy yourselves. Go null-g swimming, listen to good music, imbibe your favorite euphorics, do whatever you please.

"But we don't want you to do anything about instantaneous communication. Not talk or even think about it. *Not—even—know—about—it!*"

Amy laughed, a single, grunt-like laugh. "And how are we supposed to do that? It sounds like the famous club where the initiation test was to stand in the corner for five minutes and *not* think of a polar bear."

Cyndora stood up and walked a few steps, so that she stood before Amy and Alex, facing them, a broad window stretching horizontally behind her.

Through it, Amy could see the rolling, concave landscape of Dinganzicht. Linden trees, elms and willows dotted the green vista outside the Macrotech building compound. In the distance, before the rising hills faded into a misted vista, a narrow stream purled over a rocky course. Jumping fish splashed every now and then.

A small brown bear bent patiently at the edge of the water, waiting for dinner to make itself available.

Cyndora Vexmann said, "You'll just forget all about instantaneous communication when you leave work each evening, and remember it again when you come back in each morning."

"And how will we do that?"

"Ah, that's where Biff-o boy over there finally showed a little intelligence. He came to me. And I devised a simple little scheme. We just give you each a couple of key words. We set up a mental compartmentalization for the instant-com project, and we lock it off from the rest of your mind. When you come to work, we speak one key word, the lock opens, and you have complete access to the proprietary data. When it's time to go home after work, we just speak the other key word, and—*click!*—the door goes shut, the lock snaps closed, and you don't have to worry anything about your work until tomorrow. Isn't that wonderful?"

Amy and Alex exchanged glances.

"I'm not so sure it is," Amy said. "I don't like the idea of you or Biff-o or anybody else tampering with my mind. And I'm sure Alex feels the same way."

Alex nodded. "Sure do."

Cyndora shook her head slowly. "I don't blame you for feeling that way. I wouldn't want anybody tampering with my mind either. But this has been used time after time. It works perfectly, and it doesn't interfere with your free will or your recollections in any way."

She smiled winsomely.

Amy said, "Except?"

Cyndora shot a glance at Biff, then said, "Except what? What do you mean?"

"I mean, there has to be an *except*, or you wouldn't bother with all this."

"Oh." Cyndora gave Amy a very sincere look, turned and did the same to Alexander Ulianov. "Well, except you can't remember what you're working on. Actually, we usually give people a little cover story. People feel uncomfortable not knowing what they do all day, and if they're not allowed to know what it is, we give them something else to *think* they've been working on."

She shifted her position uncomfortably. "For instance, we might work out a little cover story for you two, for you and Alex here, that you were working on, say, a whole new generation of ultra-high-tech food processors. You see? You'd actually believe it yourselves, in your off-duty hours. You could tell that to your friends and they'd believe it. Only, when you got to work each morning, thinking you were going to work on the new food-processor line, why, Biff or I or someone else would be waiting, and we'd just say the key words, and you'd remember all about the instant com project."

Alex Ulianov said, "I wonder how many people are already working that way. Amy, you know Zipper Dornbauer down at the lab? He always says he's working on an advanced pastry wisk product. But Macrotech doesn't make pastry wisks. I've wondered about that. And Magda di Gazzioli in advanced projects says she's reformulating basic cold Crayola wax formulas. She's really enthusiastic about the project, always talks about it down at the corner saloon. But Macrotech doesn't make crayons."

Amy 2-3-4 Al-Khnemu had been paying close attention to Alex's words. Now she turned angrily back toward Biff and Cyndora. Before she could speak, Biff stood up.

The stupid, somewhat cloddish features on Biff Connaught's face assumed a more animated character than they usually showed. (Which, admittedly, was not very animated at that.)

Biff said, "Pope Innocent the Sixth."

Cyndora Vexmann took a step backward and stood beside Connaught. They watched with slitted eyes.

Alexander Ulianov rose from his chair. He seemed for a fleeting moment totally unaware of the presence of Biff and Cyndora, seemed almost unaware of his surroundings. He looked at Amy Al-Khnemu and said, "Hey, look at the hour! We'd better get to work or we'll be in bad trouble! Those new infravibratory food-processors have to hit the market in time for Escoffier's Birthday!"

Amy 2-3-4 Al-Khnemu looked at her wrist chrono-tempo-meter and gasped. "You're right! Let's go!" She looked around and raised one hand to her face in surprise. "Captain Connaught! Dr. Vexmann! What—?"

"Don't worry about anything, lady," Biff grunted. "You and your pal got to get to work on your instant commo gadget."

"Instant commo?" Puzzlement spread on Amy's face. "What are you talking about? We're assigned to the new food-processor line."

Connaught laughed. "Right. But listen to this." He chuckled, then almost whispered, "Vera Hruba Ralston!"

Amy 2-3-4 Al-Khnemu and Alexander Ulianov both looked stunned. But the shock lasted only for a moment. Each of them seemed to stagger, to regain control and then Ulianov said, "Hey, look at the hour! We'd better get to work or we'll be in bad trouble! Those new instantaneous communicators have to hit the market in time for Marconi's Birthday!"

Amy 2-3-4 Al-Khnemu looked at her wrist chrono-tempo-meter and gasped. "You're right! Let's go!" She looked around and raised one hand to her face in surprise. "Captain Connaught! Dr. Vexmann! What—?"

"Don't worry about anything, lady," Biff grunted. "You and your pal got to get to work on your new food processor."

"Food processor?" Puzzlement spread on Amy's face. "What are you talking about? We're assigned to the new instantaneous communicator line."

Connaught laughed. "That's right, I made a little mistake. Well, you two superbrains go about your superscientific work, hey? It's too much for me, I'm just a simple old cop trying to make a living. Ain't that right, Dr. Vexmann?"

Cyndora said, "That's right, Biff-o."

Amy and Alex left the office and headed for their lab. Almost before the door had hissed shut behind them, Biff Connaught's office sounded with the mingled laughter of a man and a woman.

While these events were transpiring in the offices and laboratories of the Macrotech Associates Ell Tee Dee complex in Dinganzicht, and while the little shuttle *Clare Winger Harris* was bearing studio head Tarquin Armbruster IV and production chief Golda Abramowitz toward the triple sun Fornax 1382, events were continuing to move within Starrett.

In the city of New Chicago, for example, trade was brisk at Olde Doctor Christmas's Booke & Brownie Shoppe. The proprietor, Will Lux, was having one of his best seasons ever.

In the Starrettian metropolis of Bombay VII on the western shore of the Muschelkalk Sea, Ponnemperuna's Pet Emporium had just closed for the day. Business in the pet trade was also excellent, and the Ponnemperuna family, Mohandis, Jitendra, and their beloved daughter Chitarhi, were preparing to sit down to a savoury dinner of dhal, curry, and ancient Bombay style bread.

In the state of Floridalso, it was spring training season for the baseball clubs from "up north" (whatever that term might mean in a tincan world like Starrett). The New St. Louis Browns were training in the village of Bahia Mar, and the sensation of the camp was a fabulously talented kid catcher. The kid was knocking the cover off the ball, he had a rifle for an arm, and the way he moved behind the plate, you'd think he had oiled machines for knees.

What was most remarkable about him was this. He wore his catcher's mask all the time, behind the plate, up at bat, in the locker room—everywhere! Nobody on the club had seen his face, and it was rumored that he had been hideously scarred in an accident, so nobody tried to peek. Who cared, as long as he could perform the way he did?

He wouldn't even give his name, but since they needed to call him *something*, he asked for a roster of long-retired New St. Louis Browns players. And since he was a catcher, the kid took the name of a mug who had once played in a single game for the club. "Joe Nieman Junior, that's my name," he told the manager. "You can just call me Joe."

The manager said, "Keep playing like that and I'll call you anything you like!"

And in Hollywood-between-the-Stars, they were still working on *The Dunwich Horror*, pending the return of Tarquin Armbruster and Golda Abramowitz with some new technology for the sequences involving the Whateley monsters.

One of the nice things about Starrett was its size—this was a *big* tincan world! Out at the Colossal Galactic property they had built a complete New England village to provide scenery and background and sets for *The Dunwich Horror*. There were already rolling hillsides and green farmlands; it was a perfect place to make the flik.

Martin van Buren MacTavish had left behind a final (or nearly final) script when he went with Tarquin Armbruster and Golda Abramowitz to the shuttleport. He saw them off on the *Clare Winger Harris*, then returned to "Dunwich" at Colossal Galactic.

Golda Abramowitz had appointed a director and the director had hired a special effects crew, a camera crew, a set-decoration crew, a costumer, and all of the rest of the people necessary for the production.

Gaza de Lure, Nefertiti Logan, Rock Quartz, Roscoe Inelegante and Karlos Koch were all rehearsed in their roles, and shooting had actually begun, under the careful supervision and control of the director Golda Abramowitz had left in charge. That was Josephine Anne Jones, whose directorial credits included such successes as *Pirates of the Plains*, *The Haunted Garage*, and one X-rated hit (she did this one under a pseudonym, and you will *please* not tell anyone!), *The Garden of Shamballah*.

She had even worked from a Martin MacTavish script before, Marty's early effort *Betelgeuse Beach Party*, a flik billed as "the universe's first outer-space surfer spectacular." The flik made money for years, selling over and over and over again wherever Starrett happened to visit.

At the very moment that Tarquin Armbruster and Golda Abramowitz, travelling in the *Clare Winger Harris*, hove into sight of Fornax 1382 and exclaimed with pleasure at the lighting effects that the triple glare of Lemon, Lime, and Cherry produced inside their shuttle ship . . . at this very moment, the day's shooting was about to begin on the set of *The Dunwich Horror*.

The scene they were shooting at Colossal Galactic that day was #237k on the master scene list. Josephine Anne Jones was present dressed in puttees, cravat, beret, and long cigarette holder. (She was a traditionalist; she even wore a monocle tied to the end of a ribbon, but never screwed it into her eye in public; she hadn't mastered that trick and it embarrassed her to make the effort and fail.)

Martin van Buren MacTavish was also present, script-book in hand. He had not been pleased with his relationship with Josephine during *Betelgeuse Beach Party* and he was not happy to have her as director for *The Dunwich Horror*.

They were shooting indoors. The scene took place inside the Miskatonic University library. Karlos Karch, as Wilbur Whateley, was decked out in fright-wig, putty nose, plenty of paint and distorters for his face, and even temporarily modified hands. He wore a slouch hat pulled down over his forehead. It was a triumph of costume and camera angle: it would give the illusion that Wilbur's face was hidden from view while actually affording the audience a thorough examination of Wilbur's frightening and distorted features.

And Wilbur, naturally, wore his customary ankle-length overcoat.

Gaza de Lure, as Sally Sawyer, had been written into a new task, that of managing librarian for Miskatonic U.

Gaza was a throwback to an old earth type of beauty. She was slim and fragile looking—she couldn't have weighed more than four kilograms and she was barely 1.6 meters tall. She had softly flowing, pale blonde hair and eyes of a deep yet brilliant emerald hue that were famous on a gross of planets.

One holoflik historian had traced through prints of ancient fliks and stills from even more ancient ones, and had found an amazing prototype or avatar of Gaza, an ancient toodee film actress named Veronica Lake. If you can't find a holo of Gaza de Lure, see if you can turn up a toodee print of Veronica Lake or one of her films (that's what they were called, films or sometimes ((I don't know why)) "moompichas") and you'll see what this is all about. Be prepared to fall in love.

Well, there they were on the set. Wilbur Whateley (Karlos Karch) shambled up to the checkout desk.

Sally Sawyer (Gaza de Lure) greeted him. Her face showed an amalgam of horror, fear and disgust.

Wilbur, in his strange, guttural tones, spoke to Sally. "There is a book I must have. It is a very rare, very old book."

Although Karlos in his natural speech was a most articulate and pleasant-spoken man, he adopted a very different voice as Wilbur Whateley. It was a combination gasp, hiss, and guttural groan.

"The author of the book is a mad arab named Abdul. Abdul al-Hazred."

The multisense receptors on the flik camera picked up a foetid odor of ancient alienness as Wilbur spoke.

"I know the book you mean, sir," Sally said. "I'm afraid it can't be taken out of the library. If you would like to use it here, we have a special room with armed guards, heavy locks, thickly armored walls, where you may be permitted to use the book for a limited period of tiktox."

"That will do," Wilbur hissed. "That will have to do. Please show me to the locked chamber. Please get the book for me at once."

The camera showed Wilbur's hairy, distorted hands writhing as with a life of their own.

Josephine Jones yelled, "Cut!"

The set-lights dimmed back, the camera ground to a halt. "That looks pretty good." Josephine gestured to the camera op. "Let's take a quick peek at what we've got."

Even before she could see the rush, Marty MacTavish was standing before her, jumping up and down. "It isn't right!" MacTavish yelled. "You changed the dialog! You're wrecking my script again, just like you did on *Betelgeuse Beach Party*!"

"I'm in charge here," Josephine Jones said. "Keep quiet or I'll bar you from the set, MacTavish."

"You can't do this to me! I'll talk to Golda about this! I'll talk to Tarquin! I'll blow the lid off *The Garden of—*"

"Shut up!" Josephine hissed. "Mention that topic once more and I swear, I'll get a contract and have you killed. I mean it, MacTavish. I'll do what I say."

Marty backed up a step. He burst into a cold sweat. "You would, too, wouldn't you?"

Josephine Jones merely nodded. She stood up and said, "Okay, everybody. Tea break, then 237b. Nobody leave the set please."

After tea they started on 237b. That was the scene of Wilbur trying to smuggle the book out of the Miskatonic library by concealing it under his overcoat. Being Wilbur Whateley, he'd have his hands free because he could hang onto the book with some of those tentacles and other bizarre appendages he possessed.

Josephine Jones settled in her director's chair, ordered the actors to their places, uttered the time-honored cry: "Lights! Camera! Action!"

Martin van Buren MacTavish, standing behind Josephine, danced up and down in anxiety, clutching his master copy of the script.

Karlos Karch came shambling out of the shadows, out of the dim corridor that led from the circulation desk to the locked and guarded rare book room.

As Karlos passed by the circulation desk, the voice of an extra came from off-camera. "Stop that man! He's stealing a book!"

Gaza de Lure hit a button and an iron gate (this was Marty's invention and he was proud of it) clanged into place, blocking Karlos' exit from the room.

Lemon and Lime were at the opposite ends of the sky, Lemon just rising and Lime just setting, with Cherry directly overhead as the *Clare Winger Harris* spiraled down toward a landing in Dinganzicht. The artificial world's landing portal was opened and the shuttle entered neatly.

Within a matter of minutes, Tarquin Armbruster IV and Golda Abramowitz were greeted by a marketing representative from Macrotech Associates, and within a matter of minutes after that a conference was taking place between Tarquin, Golda, and a team of Macrotech sales and engineering people, in a plush office within the Macrotech complex.

Back in a service hangar, the shuttle ship *Harris* had been racked and fueled and was being held for its owners' return.

Some of the service techs and space jockeys who worked in the hangar noticed that the *Harris* had a thin coating over most of its surface, a peculiarly textured greenish gunk that looked almost like an ultrathin layer of sponge. But, what the hey, the owners hadn't requested a scrub-up, just a top-off of the fuel tanks. And what they asked for was what they got.

Ch-ch-ch Junior was left pretty much to itself. It still had the thoughts that it had picked up from Tarquin and Golda to ponder, and although Junior had been alive for a fairly lengthy period of time— and although it was a remarkably intelligent bit of vegetation—Junior was still very new at this consciousness business, and was having quite a time for itself trying to deal with all of the perceptions and thoughts to which it had rather suddenly fallen heir.

So, since nobody had bothered it any—hey, nobody had much noticed it!—Junior just hung onto the *Clare Winger Harris* and pondered.

Golda and Tarquin, over at Macrotech, had pretty well sketched in their problem for the marketing and engineering folks. The Macrotech people invited them to have lunch in the executive dining room, but Golda, who was of somewhat proletarian attitudes, insisted on buying her own lunch in the employees' cafeteria.

Now you have to pay close attention at this point, because something very remarkable happened. Something that couldn't have been planned. It makes you wonder about the workings of chance, and whether they are altogether blind. Hmm.

Here's what happened.

Golda and Tarquin were seated with some Macrotech honchos at a small table, eating a cold salad.

Amy 2-3-4 Al-Khnemu and Alexander Ulianov were sitting nearby, also eating a cold salad.

Golda and Tarquin were talking about the movie business.

Amy and Alex were talking about high-tech food processors, having been "Pope Innocent the Sixthed" as they left their communications lab at lunch time.

At precisely the same moment during the meal, both Amy and Golda found it necessary to answer a call of nature. Both of them repaired to the facility. While there they struck up a casual conversation.

Amy told Golda that she was working with Dr. Ulianov on a new line of food-processors.

Golda expressed only polite interest.

Then Golda told Amy that she was working for Mr. Armbruster of Colossal Galactic Studios, that she was production chief and they were planning a big-budget horror movie.

Amy allowed as how she was interested in movies herself when she wasn't designing food processors. Especially old movies.

Golda allowed as how she shared that interest. She was, in fact, probably the greatest Formalhautian film historian alive.

Amy responded with enthusiasm, reeling off the names of her favorite old-time films, directors, writers, and actors.

Golda responded with her own favorites. Now, would you like to know the names of Golda Abramowitz's favorite real-old-time movie actresses? You would? Good! Here they come:

*Sara Algood.*
*Verree Teasdale.*
*Butterfly McQueen.*
*Anna May Wong.*
*Jane Darwell.*

*Dorothy Gish.*
*Lupe Velez.*
*Lynn Bari.*
*Carmen Miranda.*
*Vera Hruba Ralston.*

*Bingo!*

No sooner had Golda mentioned Vera Hruba Ralston, the star of such memorable fliks as *The Lady and the Monster, Storm Over Lisbon,* and *Murder in the Music Hall,* than Amy 2-3-4 Al-Khnemu underwent a sudden, slight but noticeable, transition. Her face seemed to sag for an instant, before resuming an expression almost—but not quite—exactly the same that it had shown before the mention of Vera Hruba Ralston.

Not for nothing was Golda Abramowitz regarded as one of the brightest talents in the entire flixbiz. She was knowledgeable, she was intelligent, she was talented, and she was perceptive. Wow, was she ever perceptive!

That fleeting change in Amy Al-Khnemu's expression, that momentary sag of the jaw muscles, that instant of disorientation in her eyes, would have gone unnoticed by almost anyone not carefully looking for such signs. But they didn't get past Golda Abramowitz. She took hold of Amy's hands.

"Are you all right?"

"Of course I am." Amy blushed. "Look, I've really enjoyed our little chat, I'm happy we met. Maybe we can get together for a mild intoxicant after work. But right now I have to get back to the instant commo project with Alex."

Did you catch that? Golda Abramowitz sure as hell did. "What instant commo project?"

Amy shook her head. She pulled her hands free of Golda's. "Look, I have to make a living. I'm working on an instant communicator for Macrotech." She checked the time. "I do have to get back to work."

"Now just hold on. There's something very strange here."

Amy might have been inclined to push past Golda and just stalk away, but she thought better of *that*. After all, Golda Abromowitz was a seven-foot-tall Formalhautian. You didn't just brush past her. No you did not.

Golda and Amy sat down on a cushioned sofa there in the ladies' lounge, and before coffee could cool back at their respective tables, they had unravelled the whole scheme that Biff Connaught and Cyndora Vexmann had so skillfully and ruthlessly woven.

The one thing that they could *not* unravel was the key word that set Alex and Amy up to think they were working on food processors. But even that part of the Macrotech scheme was shortly to fail—and in an equally unlikely and farfetched manner.

Dig it:

As Amy 2-3-4 Al-Khnemu and Golda Abramowitz sat in the lounge working out the details of the key word security scheme, Tarquin Armbruster IV and his hosts were still seated in the cafeteria, sipping coffee, smoking cigars, and carrying on a conversation consisting of just the type of small talk that such new business acquaintances would indulge in under the circumstances.

One of the Macrotech executives remarked on Tark's classical name.

Armbruster explained that he was descended from ancient old earth Roman nobility. He was one of a family that had produced Roman senators, Italian doges, and Catholic popes. Among his illustrious ancestors, Tarquin mentioned—yes, you guessed it!

And just as Tarquin Armbruster IV spoke those portentous words, *Pope Innocent the Sixth,* Golda and Amy hove into earshot.

Again Amy 2-3-4 Al-Khnemu's face sagged for the barest instant. Golda hissed, "Quick, Amy! What's your project?"

"Uh—high tech food processors. But—"

"Vera Hruba Ralston!"

"Instant communication."

"Amy, that's it! Grab your partner. You two and Tarkie and I have got to have a private conference, fast!"

Mere hours later, Tarquin Armbruster IV, Golda Abramowitz, Amy 2-3-4 Al-Khnemu, and Alexander Ulianov were aboard the *Clare Winger Harris* and that little ship was making its way from Dinganzicht back to Starrett and Hollywood-between-the-Stars.

It had taken some doing to hire Al-Khnemu and Ulianov away from Macrotech Associates. Basically, Tarquin Armbruster had offered them fat pay checks, full support for their research projects, and a major participation in any product they developed in behalf of Colossal Galactic.

Getting them away from Dinganzicht, physically, had been an equal challenge. Macrotech didn't want to let them go. There was no legal way the corporation could stop Amy and Alex from leaving, but they used every bit of moral suasion, economic arm twisting, and psychological pressure available.

Biff Connaught even tried pulling a gun, believe it or not. But when Amy threatened to blurt out the real meaning of the "P. H." in P. H. "Biff" Connaught with her dying breath, Biff subsided.

Cyndora Vexmann tried some of her hypnotic-conditioning type manipulation, but Amy and Alex were on their guard against that and Cyndora couldn't bring it off.

There was even a squabble at the Dinganzicht portal about customs and astrogation clearances, but Tarquin Armbruster had the right combination of nerve and smarts to get them through that.

So here was the *Clare Winger Harris* shussing merrily along, the yellow, cerise, and green of Fornax 1382 behind it, the metallic shape of Starrett looming in its radar-telescope, and its four occupants chatting in the cabin while the shuttle coasted along.

Amy and Alex mainly listened; for all their engineering know-how and scientific prowess, they felt themselves to be planetbound rubes in the presence of these members of the interstellar set.

"I don't really understand, Tarquin, why you're so interested in this instantaneous communication project. Are you planning to give up flix for the commo business?"

Tarquin peered through the space telescope at Starrett. He turned and relit a soggy, half-smoked Havana Perfecto. "Darling, let me tell you something. Golda dear, you are a wonderful production chief, you know all about old movies and all about new flix. You are terrific at your job plus having the prettiest green skin and white fur of anybody I know, Golda."

Golda flushed blue (that's how Formalhautians blush or flush). "We were going to Dinganzicht for some help with the special effects. With the Whateley twins. That isn't what we got."

"Darling," Tarquin said, "what we got here, I tell you, is worth thirty yukky monsters. No, thirty thousand."

"I know you really mean that, Tarquin. You always start sounding like a character out of Yiddish theater when you're sincere, which isn't often."

"Golda, you can say such a thing to me, to Tarquin Armbruster IV?"

"But what good will a super space telegraph do Colossal Galactic?"

"Golda sweetheart, listen to an old man what has seen it all, things that would make you blush like cobalt. Golda, when we make a show, like *Suicide Ranch*, starring Buck Longabaugh, may he rest in peace poor Buck. How many times did we sell *Suicide Ranch*, to how many planets, do you remember? And for how much *gelt?*"

"That one I know, Tark. We've sold it a hundred eleven times. The flik made production costs on the sixty-third sale, total nut on the ninety-sixth. Now it's a nice little money-maker."

Tarquin drew on his Perfecto, blew a perfect smoke ring, and winked in the direction of Amy and Alexander. "And by the time we finish selling *Suicide Ranch*, Golda sweetheart, how many times do you think we can sell it? A hundred fifty? Two hundred? Before it's too old and creaky and we got to put it on the art-house circuit which pays, may my worst enemies make only art-house fliks, practically nothing?"

"I guess about two hundred."

"But if we didn't have to wait for Starrett to visit each world? If we could send holo images like the old teewee pix, only instantly not at light speed, darling? If we could offer, say, *The Dunwich Horror* all at once to everybody while it's brand new? If we could make for it a galaxy-wide simultaneous premiere with spotlasers and celebrities on every civilized planet in the galaxy—how many times could we sell it then? Hah?"

Golda opened her lips to answer, but before she could get a syllable out, Tarquin continued.

"Don't interrupt your elders, darling. Think of me, an old man. Soon I'll be dead and gone, so let me talk please while I can. Thousands of planets we could sell to, thousands. What will we make from *The Dunwich Horror* I'll tell you, Golda, a fortune. A positive fortune. That's why I hired these two bigdomes, you should pardon my bluntness Dr. Al-Khnemu, Dr. Ulianov.

"So!" Tarquin leaned back in his chair and grinned. "What do you think of that, hey?"

Ch-ch-ch Junior found itself back inside Starrett and felt a pleasant sensation that it might have known as the warmth of homecoming, had it ever heard of such a thing. The little ship *Clare Winger Harris* entered Starrett via Kaspak Portal and then skimmed its way across the center of the tincan toward Hollywood-between-the-Stars.

En route, the shuttle zipped through the null-g zone and bits of Ch-ch-ch Junior were scraped off, reattaching themselves to Ch-ch-ch Senior, transferring their recollections with them. Simultaneously, bits of Ch-ch-ch Senior adhered to the rough surface of the *Harris* (said roughness consisting of Junior!) and remained with the ship as it dropped toward the wall of the world.

The *Harris* made berth at Hollywood-between-the-Stars, mid-way between Mix Mes and Lugosi Lagoon. Tarquin Armbruster IV and Golda Abramowitz, Amy 2-3-4 Al-Khnemu and Alexander Ulianov, set out for Tarquin's office to talk business. They didn't even look back as they moved away from the *Harris*. They didn't see the translucently thin, greenish coating slide from the shuttle and begin to slither across the ground.

They didn't see the greenish stuff, that initially resembled nothing more than a cloudlet of thin, blowing dust moving across a drought-parched swamp-bed.

Ch-ch-ch Junior felt itself picking up the mental emanations of the numerous carpenters and technicians, lighting operators and camerapersons, costumers, directors, assistant directors, makeup men and women, set movers, sound-effects operators, musicians, holo mixers, scent-and-taste sprayers, animal handlers, animals, actors, extras, and hangers-on who populated the Colossal Galactic lot.

Bits of what looked like dust, blowing in what seemed an otherwise unpredictable, even undetectable, breeze, moved here and there around the lot.

One wisp of dust swirled through the Miskatonic University library set, then swirled away and rejoined a larger cloudlet of the oddly greenish stuff.

On the set, Josephine Jones consulted her chronotempometer and yelled peremptorily, "Time! Places, please!"

Gaza de Lure as Sally Sawyer set herself behind the old-fashioned New England librarian's desk.

Karlos Karch, long overcoat hanging to his high-shoed ankles, took position at the cast-iron door. He faced back toward Gaza, a look of desperation on his distorted, almost acromegalous features.

Gaza threw her hands in the air and screamed.

Karlos lurched toward her.

Gaza screamed again and pointed toward Karch and the cast-iron gate.

Josephine Jones signaled directions.

Cameras rolled.

Gaza leaped across her desk and headed away from Karlos, toward the dark alcove that represented the opening to the library's vault. She disappeared through the alcove and out of camera range.

Karlos Karch halted in puzzlement.

Josephine Jones yelled, "Cut! Cut! What the hell's the matter with Gaza? What's her blocking? Doesn't anybody here know anything?"

Karch turned back to face Josephine. His eyes widened in horror. The sight that he beheld, moving toward the set, was one that had been seen before by the human imagination, first by the strange scrivener of College Hill in the city of Providence on old earth. It was a sight that had been reproduced in the imaginations of the generations of readers who perused the prose of that scrivener.

It was a vision that had challenged—and defied!—the pens, brushes, and hands of generations of illustrators and sculptors who had attempted to render in ink, oil, or clay the vision as the gaunt dreamer had described it.

It was Wilbur Whateley's unnamed fraternal twin, the twin who had resembled old Lavinia Whateley's alien mate more nearly than he did the pitiful albino Lavinia!

Karlos Karch's voice rang out. That voice which had chilled myriads of thrill-seekers, armies of audiences who had come, over the years, to associate the very name Karlos Karch with shuddering, chilling, paralyzing fear and revulsion.

But never, never in a career that had spanned both decades and light-years had Karch delivered a line the way he uttered these words:

"Oh, oh, my Gawd, that haff face—that haff face on top of it . . . that face with the red eyes an' crinkly albino hair, an no chin, like the Whateleys . . . an octopus, centipede, spider kind o' thing with a haff-shaped man's face on top of it, an' it looks like Wizard Whateley only it's yards and yards acrost . . . !"

And the thing, the nameless monstrosity that lurched and *oozed* through the bars of the cast-iron door, responded! "Ygnaiih . . . ygnaiih . . . thflthkh'ngha . . . Yog-Sothoth! Y'bthnk . . . h'ehye-n'grkdl'lh!"

The monster billowed and bulged, swelling to engulf almost the entire set. Karlos Karch, screaming hideously, was engulfed, disappearing utterly beneath the tentacles, claws, gullets, eyes, fangs, speckles, tympanum-like disks, and indescribably horrifying miscellaneous organs of Ch-ch-ch Junior.

Josephine Jones bolted from her director's chair, leaped to one camera operator after another, commanding each of them frantically to keep rolling, keep rolling, whatever might happen and at whatever cost to life, limb or expensive studio-owned equipment—*keep rolling!*

Only when the shooting was over and a degree of calm—a very small degree of calm, it should be noted—had returned to the set, were the cameras finally shut off.

There now assembled the cast and crew of *The Dunwich Horror*.

Karlos Karch, still in full Wilbur Whateley makeup and costume, sat as best he could in a prop library chair. Opposite him, quite indistinguishable except in size from its former horrifying appearance, sat Wilbur's twin brother, Ch-ch-ch Junior. Somehow, among Junior's apparently limitless powers of self-shaping and coloration, was the ability to expand or contract itself to any desired density or size. Junior was now precisely the same size (although not the same shape) as Karlos Karch.

Martin van Buren MacTavish, the copy of the *Dunwich Horror* script literally shredded in his hands, paced back and forth, unable to keep a seat. "It's great!" Martin kept repeating. "It's great! It's stupendous! It wasn't what I wrote, but we can work around it! It's the most gloriously gross and terrifying scene ever filmed, taped, crystalled or acted live! Oh, even the old boy himself would have loved it! He would have loved it!

"You splendid old monster, however the hell you managed that, I love you!"

And Martin van Buren MacTavish ran to the most hideous monster in the history of Colossal Galactic or any of the studios in any of the Hollywoods in history and gave it a mighty hug and a resounding kiss smack in the center of one of its most disgusting (but undescribable) organs.

Two weeks later (Starrett standard calendar) *The Dunwich Horror* was finished.

Two months later the Al-Khnemu/Ulianov Instantaneous Communicator was put on sale by Colossal Galactic Enterprises Unlimited, a wholly-owned subsidiary of Colossal Galactic Studios.

The first big promotion carried out through the new communications system was the initial release of the Colossal Galactic production of *The Dunwich Horror*, starring Karlos Karch, Gaza de Lure, Nefertiti Logan and, making its holofliks debut, the newest and greatest horror star in history, billed (for obvious reasons) as the protege of the veteran Karch—Ch-ch-ch Junior.

*The Dunwich Horror* opened simultaneously on 4,888 planets. It had the largest single-performance audience of any production in the history of the galaxy, and was the biggest money-maker as well.

There was a huge party of celebration on the Galactic lot. Junior, of course, was wildly lionized. Amy 2-3-4 Al-Khnemu and Alexander Ulianov floated about, bemused. Gaza de Lure made a pass at Karlos Karch who brushed her off and carried a plate of *hors d'oeuvres* to share with his wife of some twenty-six years.

There was hardly a lull in the course of the party, but at one point the noise level and frenetic activity did lessen a bit. It was at this point that Golda Abramowitz used her towering green-skinned presence to beat a path to the side of the cheerfully gloating Tarquin Armbruster IV.

"Tarquin," Golda asked sweetly, "now that *The Dunwich Horror* has made us one of the biggest fortunes in the history of the universe—"

"*Us?*" Tarquin interrupted her. "Us? What's this *us* business? I own Colossal Galactic, darling, don't forget."

"All right," Golda went on undaunted. "Now that *you* own one of the biggest fortunes in the history of the universe, scattered over some 4,888 planets . . . tell me, Tarkie, how are you going to collect it?"

Tarquin Armbruster IV blanched.

In fact, there was a way. But that was another matter, and the telling of it is another story.

# Saucers from Yaddith

## Robert M. Price

### I

Oh, I've little doubt that you will believe me, Mr. Turrow. And I suspect most of your readers will give my story credence as well. But to be perfectly frank, no reputable newspaper would listen to the first five words of my tale. Only a tabloid such as yours would even give it a second look. Now please do not misunderstand me, sir, I am no less grateful to you for this opportunity, but we are both adults, are we not? We both know how little commercial journalism need have to do with truth. So even if you do not believe me, it is all the same. I can scarcely believe it myself. Perhaps it will take on a greater air of reality if I speak of it and get it out in the air between us, eh Mr. Turrow? Discussing something always seems to . . . Well, yes, I will get on with it.

I suppose one must place the beginning of the affair back merely a few weeks ago. My circle, ever dedicated to the expansion of its horizons, had applied itself with diligence to the study of this and that field of arcane knowledge. How well I can recall how old Elkhart, the artist among us, had experimented with Tibetan Mandalas. His canvases were damnably suggestive of questions beyond mortal imagination to frame, much less to answer. Our prolonged meditation on these windows to deeper recesses of the mind finally served but to increase our Faustian thirst to know what lay *beyond*.

Preus, ever the religious seeker himself, suggested that our grail of ultimate knowledge was obtainable only through certain doctrines and rites suppressed over the centuries by church authorities. In fact it was for the discovery and exposition of such gnostical fantasies that Preus himself had been first expelled from divinity school, then actually excommunicated, many years before. But all of us had noticed only too readily the gleam one catches in the eye of the fanatic. It seemed an unspoken consensus that whatever hidden truths might lie down the paths Preus had trod, we would as soon pass them by. Expanding reality was one thing, after all, but leaving it behind was quite another.

If Preus' proposal was received with a distinct coolness, Barlow's urgings to follow him into what he called the "lefthanded path" of Tantric mysticism were dispatched with all the speed that politeness allowed. For none of us was willing to throw over his inherited moral codes for the questionable pursuits which seemed so completely to have enthralled our friend. Seeing our reluctance, he quickly added that of course he only knew of such practices from his reading.

Finally there was St. Joshua, whose philosophical views ran toward the mundane. An adherent of Russell, Ayer, and the positivists, he was merely tolerant of the rest of us, I suspect.

The group was, as you can see, heterogeneous, companions kept together by old school ties and overlapping interests here and there. All of us did share a thirst for knowledge, as well as an ache of frustration since none of us was any closer to our goal of enlightenment. At last I myself broached a suggestion.

I had of late taken keen interest in the mind-expanding potential of certain drugs. The writings of Huxley about mescaline had intrigued me no little, and it was this avenue down which I would have our group turn. All seemed willing at least to consider it, if yet concerned to know what precautions might be taken for safety's sake. Such concerns were, of course, my own as well, and I assured my companions that I would attempt, as far as I might, to chart our probable course before we embarked in earnest. The conversation soon turned down other avenues. It seemed to me that the others felt only mild interest in my proposal, certainly nothing to compare with the excitement that I had begun to feel. Eventually the meeting adjourned, and I hurried home, lost in thought.

I decided I had best seek the advice of physicians. But given the controversial nature of our envisioned experiment, I would have to take especial care in choosing doctors whose confidence I could trust. At length I obtained the names of two local authorities. Their contributions to the medical journals implied that they might be sympathetic to the kind of exercise we were considering. In fact, as I read between the lines, I saw, or imagined I saw, reason to believe that one doctor had already tried such experiments himself. His allusions were so vague, yet so suggestive! Alas, this man, a Dr. Martin Rhadamanthus, was currently traveling abroad. His offices at the medical college where he taught were somewhat evasive as to either the exact location or the duration of his sabbatical journeys. This I could well understand, however irksome the fact, since few professions are so harrowing and tiresome as his. He must need his solitude as much as he desired it.

The other specialist I had chosen was not a teacher but an active practitioner, Dr. Phineas Whitmore by name. At length I succeeded in making an appointment with him. It was to be a simple physical examination, on the pretext that I feared I was evidencing initial signs of a particular nervous condition in which the doctor was known to specialize. Given his wide reputation, it was not surprising that the first available opening was yet two weeks away. I was assured that two weeks was in truth an unusually brief time to wait, and that normally one waited months to see Dr. Whitmore. I was appropriately, and genuinely, expansive in my thanks and hung up. Two weeks! Short enough by any usual reckoning, to be sure. Yet the thirst for knowledge which possessed me was now so consuming—and all the more since now a concrete possibility for its satisfaction seemed within reach—that two weeks seemed like as many years!

Before one week was out, I was ready to act impetuously. I would take a modicum of the drug myself, come what may. After all, Huxley and others had tried it, and with what risk? Surely, I had been overcautious up to this point, and would be merely foolish, even cowardly, to delay further. The very night of these deliberations witnessed my first experiment with the drug. I was charged with a sense of expectancy and, I do not mind admitting, a good deal of anxious apprehension.

Having taken a small dose I settled myself in a well-stuffed armchair, placed so as to face the large picture-window. My thinking was that visual stimulation might serve as a catalyst for the perceptual transformation I expected. And I was not disappointed. As Huxley had predicted, ordinary objects soon began to take on a kind of extraordinary aspect. They seemed to gain new depth and then to shine forth in hues only distantly akin to their mundane colors—somehow more vivid and brilliant. At the same time, all seemed fairly translucent, as if made of precious stones. Though I had read several descriptions of this very experience, both in scientific journals and in the accounts of the mystics, none of my studies could have prepared me for the indescribable beauty of this panorama! How the most common things might be utterly transfigured!

Next I began to notice the auditory effects. Did I hear a subtle whistling or whirring? It sounded mechanical, yet musical. This sound was positively unearthly. In fact, it is puzzling that though I can recall it distinctly, I can in no wise imagine how to convey it by humming or whistling.

No sooner had the weird tones begun to sound than my attention was drawn to an indefinable disturbance of the air, just above the trees which divided my lot from the adjacent property. It was something like the sight of autumn leaves caught up for a few seconds in a whirlwind. Yet as far as I could see, nothing was being propelled in the wind. And, strictly speaking, there *was* no wind. As I said, it looked to be a disturbance, a spinning in the air itself. This motion centered about an expanse several yards across. I dimly recall wondering what natural phenomenon it might be that was so metamorphosized in my affected perception.

In less time than it has taken to describe my vague impressions, the spinning had commenced moving in my direction. I felt that I might be in danger, but that given my present mental disorientation, this might be simply another hallucination. Being now able to view the uncanny phenomenon more clearly, I observed that the spinning seemed confined to a ring. Though the motion seemed rapid, incredibly rapid, it was not particularly violent or forceful. What might it be like at the center, I wondered?

So help me, with the thought itself, my perspective changed so that for the briefest instant I seemed actually to occupy the center of the whirling. I could see my house, my window, even my chair, *but the chair was empty!* Yet all these observations occupied but a moment until the scene changed yet again. Now I seemed to be lying prone atop a platform of some material and design quite unknown to me. The haunting sound was still discernible, but much more faintly now, and muffled in tone. At first I saw nothing, yet I did not fear any harm had been done to my sight, for such misty radiance was apparent as one "sees" in a darkened room. It was not the absolute blackness of space, the dark and complete oblivion of the blind.

A few moments passed in this manner, and I began to wonder if perhaps my metabolism had somehow dampened the effect of the drug so that I would remain under the present, rather mundane, hallucination for the duration of the experiment. But I need have feared no such eventuality, for soon two shapes began to take form in the darkness, almost as if the dusk itself were gathering into a tangible aspect. As the outlines grew more and more distinct, my heart raced. For now, certainly, I was beginning to get what I had bargained for! Here were apparitions from beyond waking reality, albeit drug-conjured wraiths from the depths of my own mind. As tall as a man they were, the two creatures, yet anthropomorphic in no other respect at all. If I must employ the categories to which we are accustomed, let me say they were perhaps . . . insectoid. Even to designate them so is radically misleading, but let me not linger upon the point lest I rob my tale of whatever plausibility remains.

It was inevitably futile for me to try to discern the expressions that crossed faces of so alien a mien, but some intuition told me that the monsters were as startled by my appearance as I was by theirs. If anything, they seemed more agitated. As strange as it may sound, I did not feel particularly alarmed. After all, I reasoned, this is *my* hallucination. It seemed to me as if I were the host, and they, the figments of my supercharged imagination, were my guests.

For some period of indeterminable length, I passed into an all-but-oblivious state. During this time, I had but the faintest sensations of what went on around me, or better, *within* me. In retrospect I would compare it to reports I had read of how a man under the influence of some drugs will gain a heightened sensitivity to his own heart-rate and autonomic nerve functions. Yet that was not quite what I experienced in that pit of leaden torpor. Rather I felt that somehow I was being probed, even, yes, dissected and reconstructed; that parts of me were being removed and replaced, as one might adjust the parts of an automobile engine and replace its fuels and lubricants. Yet all these are but loose analogies that ill-approximate my sensations. I seem to remember reflecting through the clouds of near-unconsciousness whether this were what it felt like to die. Perhaps so, for just then I lapsed into thorough oblivion.

## II

When I came to myself, I noticed with a profound sense of relief that I was still in my chair, and had scarcely even shifted position. I was, I confess, a bit surprised that fully the whole night had passed. I had commenced my experiment an hour or two before sunset, and now the sun was just about to rise. Yet I had anticipated the possibility that my time perception might be affected, so I was not disturbed. I seemed otherwise to be quite unaffected. My only discomfort was my impatient and childish desire to tell someone, anyone, of my adventures of the night just past. The club would not meet again till the first of the month, and I had a week to wait before my appointment with Dr. Whitmore. How to contain my enthusiasm in the meantime? I was almost grateful to have the usual round of banal chores to occupy me for a few hours each day, and somehow I passed the week without exploding with my secret. How difficult it was, though, to pretend interest in the simpleminded matters I must discuss with my everyday acquaintances. How I wished to tell even them of my forbidden journeys into inner space, and of those weird denizens of my own subconscious! But I did not care to risk the odd stares and whispered remarks such words would prompt if spoken to the wrong people.

Finally the day came for me to call upon Dr. Whitmore. As I sat vacantly leafing through one of the old books left on the waiting room table, I wondered how well I would be able to maintain the pretense of a nervous ailment. Could I keep it up long enough to detect some hint on Dr. Whitmore's part of his openness to discuss my

hallucinatory experiences? The initial experiment had not been repeated, for the odd though illusory physical sensations I had undergone caused me to put off further attempts pending the physical
examination for which I was now waiting. Indeed, what had originally served simply as the pretext for my visit was now a matter of
real interest to me. I seemed in good, at least passable health, but
mightn't the drug have had unexpected side effects? I would soon
find out, as the door now opened, revealing the receptionist, dressed
in a uniform so crisply white it almost seemed to shine. Responding
to the call of my name, I rose and followed her down the hall to one
of the examination rooms, where I would wait (but a moment, she
assured me) for the doctor.

In surprisingly few moments, Dr. Whitmore himself arrived. He
was a man of medium height, somewhat stooped, and bearing a bit
of a paunch. Just past middle age, his hair and beard were well-
grayed, but the lines of his face seemed to reflect more care than age.
We exchanged a few pleasantries, and I began to lie as convincingly as
I could about my invented symptoms. I spoke in generalities, and
hoped I had the skill to phrase my data so it would sound more like
the description of personal experiences than a list of textbook symptoms. Fortunately, he seemed satisfied after only a few questions, and
began the tests. Some time later, I lay on the examination table waiting for him to return with a chart containing the results. Finally,
Whitmore returned, still scanning the sheet as he stepped into the
room. I sat up attentively and waited for him to show the mild puzzlement that all doctors evidence when their various probes yield
nothing to justify the patient's complaints.

Sure enough, nothing seemed wrong with me physically. I was
relieved at this news, but anxious, trying to hit upon a diplomatic
way to reveal the true concern of my visit, to procure his advice, perhaps even his supervision, for further experiments by myself and my
friends. But then he spoke again. It seemed that the only ailment here
was a typographical failure on my previous medical records. According to the files I had supplied him, my blood was listed as Type O,
whereas the bloodwork he himself had done on me showed it to be
Type A. Had I not noticed this error myself? If so, why had I not had
it corrected before now? It would certainly have caused some danger-

ous mischief had an accident rendered me unconscious and in need of a transfusion. But I was too overcome to answer him. I could only think back with frozen horror to the peculiar physical sensations of my . . . hallucination? For *until now my blood had been Type O!*

## III

It was with some puzzlement that Whitmore dismissed me, as might well be imagined, since my dumbfounded stupor seemed scarcely warranted by his mild rebuke. If I suffered further symptoms of my (pretended) malady, I was to let him know, but otherwise he could suggest nothing. How I longed more than ever to confide in the doctor—yet how impossible that had now become! Whatever his disposition regarding drug experimentation, Whitmore was after all an alienist and could hardly be expected to do other than take my fabulous tale as evidence of paranoid delusion on my part. And, indeed, might it *not* be? But, no, taking a moment to regain my composure after leaving the building, I satisfied myself that my memory and my sanity were alike intact. My blood type *had* formerly been as the records indicated, just as surely as it was now otherwise. Somehow the impossible had happened. Just how, I could not guess. Still less could I imagine what connection my hallucinatory experiment might have with the change, though certainly connection there was. And with this thought there rose anew in my soul the thrill of hope. Traumatic it had been, but was not the present mystery proof enough that somehow I had been right? Did I not hold at least the seeds that might yet blossom into that full occult knowledge that the club had sought, up till now, in vain? No doubt I did, and not even the instincts of foreboding caution which now stirred could make me pause.

With two weeks yet remaining before the next scheduled meeting of our circle, I considered two alternatives. It would be simple enough, of course, to call around and gather my colleagues for a special session. God, given what I might tell them, none of them would mind! Yet at this point there would actually be little to tell. There was but the bare experience itself, which still confounded me (though it had come to frighten me less since there seemed to be no damage to my health). My tale would cause no small stir, to be sure, but I felt I must be able to make it more intelligible, if I was to assure the circle that my course of investigation should be their own. I hoped I need not face further revelations alone.

And so I decided upon the second alternative; I would use the remaining days to research as best I could the physiological marvel which had befallen me. I had little enough knowledge of medicine, but research into obscure byways was nothing new to me, and my brief study of the medical journals preparatory to my meeting with Dr. Whitmore had acquainted me with at least a few of the major periodicals in the field. With luck, I hoped to find some precedent or parallel to my own case. Whether connected to hallucinatory trance-states or no, had there been any reported cases of . . . how would it be designated . . . ? "Organic transposition"?

The day following my decision, I betook myself to the nearby university library and sought the help of the reference librarian. The self-assured competence of this fellow, a bespectacled graduate student in his late twenties, gave me hope that my search might at least be comprehensive if not fruitful. Yet under the guidance of the young man, I soon realized just how formidable was the task I had set myself. Truly the literature was vast and I hardly knew where to begin. It was difficult to make the subject of my interest adequately understood, but at length the young scholar grasped that I was concerned neither with organic degeneration due to inbreeding nor with ordinary deformation. Once he had some idea as to the goal of my curiosity he was, he said, inclined to discontinue the search. He was as good as certain that his indices and files of abstracts contained nothing on so *outré* a subject. However, an acquaintance of his was presently enrolled in the university's medical school, and he would try to prevail upon him to make a few inquiries.

I was quite grateful for this kind gesture, doubtful though I was that aught could come of it. Still, I gave the student my address and 'phone so that I might be reached in the unlikely event that something should turn up. Needless to say, I was duly amazed when but a few days later the call came. My surprise, my shock, was increased a hundredfold as I recognized the name of my caller. The medical student had related my request to none other than the same Dr. Martin Rhadamanthus whom I had believed to be on sabbatical abroad. It seemed rather that he had stayed secluded in the area, isolated from most social and professional contacts, in order to pursue some special researches normally precluded by the demands of his teaching. Nonetheless, the student, some sort of teaching assistant or apprentice I gathered, had been able to approach him with my strange inquiry, and he had taken an interest in it.

I considered myself fortunate to have so aroused his curiosity on so idiosyncratic a matter, though at the time I simply credited it to the polite generosity of the true professional who feels bound to share what knowledge he has. Yet his very seclusion argued that such approachability was not his usual manner. If he had some personal interest in my case, I could not imagine its nature, nor did it then occur to me to do so.

At any rate, it seemed that Rhadamanthus's own research had once led him on a path of tangential cross-references which disclosed material relevant to what I had, he said, ingeniously named "organic transpositions." The account he had uncovered was contained in a seventeenth-century German work on, of all things, astronomy and astrology! It was entitled *Die Geschichte Den Planeten*, or *History of the Planets*, by a rather odd fellow named Eberhard Ketzer. He hailed from Schleswig-Holstein, and might have been a monk or perhaps a resident tutor in the Prussian court. No substantial biographical data had survived, save that derived from the book itself, to wit that Ketzer claimed, like Johannes Kepler, to have heard the "music of the spheres." Only, unlike the more famous though equally eccentric Kepler, he had not liked what he had heard. Instead of the celestial harmony imagined by Dante and described by Kepler, Ketzer had ranted of a crashing cacophony as mad spheres rolled blindly on collision courses, veering crazily through overlapping planes and dimensions. The time must come, he said, when all would hear the screeching din, and when this time came, Doomsday, the final collision, would be at hand.

What had this lunacy to do with my quest? Simply that Ketzer had set down any curious reports that reached him if they seemed to his deranged mind to abet his theory, and the sheer strangeness of a report was liable to make it qualify. The particular account to which Dr. Rhadamanthus had reference was the story of two brothers in Westphalen who claimed to have had an unusual "meeting" on their way back from Vespers one evening. They said they had been accosted on the path by shining "angels of God" who caused them to go to sleep, but a sleep filled with strange dreams. And when they awoke, they swore that they had shared one dream which seemed to have come true. The angels had removed and exchanged members of both brothers' bodies, so that each now possessed the hands and eyes of the other! They called on the village priest to bear witness that the odd change had in fact taken place. Their eyes, naturally, had been the same color from birth, so the hands must tell the story. Modern fingerprinting techniques would have made short work of the mystery, but an equally effective method was available. One brother was known to have lost a finger and the first joint of another in a recent woodworking mishap, yet this fellow's hands were newly whole, while his dismayed brother now *evidenced the other's mutilation!* The finger and joint were missing, with no sign of recent injury.

Of course, Rhadamanthus averred, the historical value of such tales was nil, the verification standards of oral folk tradition being what they always have been. If one cared to look for them, even more spectacular episodes were to be found in literature from the same period, ranging from rainfalls of blood to apparitions of the Virgin, and all were alike fanciful. But he mentioned this one since it did come closer than any actual medical case history to the sort of phenomenon which interested me. In fact, I might study the legend for myself if I wished, since he himself had run across it in the university library not very long ago.

I thanked the good doctor effulgently, hanging up only after the gross temerity (I admit) of asking whether I might contact him again. To my surprise he was most willing, should the need arise. Of course, I still had in mind my original motive of seeking his counsel on my drug research. I had by now concluded that Dr. Whitmore was quite innocent of the type of experience I had undergone. But fortune, I supposed, had guided me to the only remaining authority in this esoteric field.

Needless to say, I lost no time in returning to the library. The helpful fellow with whom I had previously spoken was not on duty, else I would have thanked him for his fruitful assistance. So I set to work locating the volume and securing a German to English dictionary. My study of the language lay many years in the past, and at any rate my merely conversational German would only get me started on what promised to be a difficult, rambling text.

Ketzer's work had been reprinted only a decade or so ago in a prestigious series on the history of science. Gratified at this convenience, still I mused how odd a choice for inclusion in the series this tome of superstition seemed. The text was left untranslated, though modern type-face made it considerably easier to read than the original heavy black letter script would have been. And topical subdivisions were indicated by the editor's italics. This device made it fairly easy to locate my passage. Once I had found it, it turned out not to be too difficult to decipher, since Rhadamanthus had already summarized its contents fairly closely over the 'phone. But I noticed here and there an interesting detail—obscurities that any casual reader would neglect, but which assumed singular importance to me.

It seemed that the two peasants had not described their supramundane visitors in any detail, perhaps because they could not. Rather they had called them "angels" because their arrival was signalled by the appearance of a *"halo in the air"!* I looked up the appropriate end note, but the annotator was at a loss to explain this detail. In the manner of all unimaginative commentators, he suggested textual corruption or a printing error in the original edition. I, however, knew differently, for had I not seen such a "halo," or spinning circle, myself? Here it was, then; the same invisible craft containing visitors from . . . where? Great mysteries remained; indeed, I had glimpsed, as it were, only the tip of the iceberg. Nonetheless, there was naught else to do now but break the news of my discoveries to the group, whose next meeting was only days away.

## IV

With old Elkhart's late arrival, our number was complete. Expectant faces all turned in my direction, my companions in esoterica sat about the spacious study: Barlow, Preus, St. Joshua, Elkhart. As was our custom, we rotated our place of meeting every month with the result that we now assembled in Barlow's home. Yet it was plain that I meant to take the lead this evening, and my demeanor gave me the aspect of host. Eagerly I recounted my experiment, my encounters with Drs. Whitmore and Rhadamanthus, and my research, occasionally doubling back to fill in a necessary detail or two. My friends were, as I had expected, quite astonished that things had proceeded so rapidly in the month gone by, when they had expected simply to hear whether I had secured any able supervisor, should any of us contemplate taking the drug. And here I had already taken it, without supervision, and with the most bizarre and unforeseen results! I half-suspected from the looks of one or two that they hardly knew whether to credit my strange tale.

Was I suggesting that the whole group embark on the voyage I had undertaken? Yes, I answered, I was, for did it not seem I had succeeded in making the first steps toward that goal of arcane knowledge that had so long eluded us? Further, I averred, I now felt sure that Rhadamanthus was our man, that he could be trusted to guide us and to take a scientific interest in our endeavors. With the group's permission I would approach him candidly with our proposal. With this suggestion all seemed in accord save the religious fanatic Preus, who was suddenly having second thoughts. For despite his wild flirtations with unorthodox mysticisms, he remained very much the Puritan in his behavior. And he could not, he said, countenance the use of drugs. Preus was obdurate in the face of our attempts to convince him, allowing himself at length to be won over by the reasoning of St. Joshua and myself. We pointed out that we would be using the drug in an almost medicinal manner, to reawaken dormant sense functions that evolution had atrophied. Henceforth Preus was willing, however reluctantly, to go along.

The next step was to be mine as I sought Rhadamanthus's help. We resolved to meet again the very next week, we hoped with the doctor added to our number. The rest of the evening seemed anticlimactic as we tried to discuss books read in the last month. And conversation would return again and again to my vision and its aftermath. Impatient expectancy had consumed us all: we were like children on Christmas Eve.

The following day I telephoned Dr. Rhadamanthus. Assuming I would reach only his answering service, I was unprepared to hear his own voice on the line. Incredibly, he was quite willing to interrupt his work for a visit that very afternoon. I could call on him at his home, a large brownstone adjacent to the university campus.

His residence was easily located, and I pressed upon the doorbell about 4 o'clock that afternoon. Rhadamanthus himself met me at the door, another surprise since I imagined he must leave such chores to servants in order to concentrate on his sabbatical studies. Once inside, I removed hat and coat, draping them on the bannister as my host indicated. I turned for my first good look at Dr. Rhadamanthus. He was a tall man, probably tending a bit to thinness, though his dressing gown obscured the details of his figure. His face, clean-shaven, had the almost fatherly aspect that serves doctors well in winning their patients' confidences. Indeed, his manner seemed a bit too paternal, almost patronizing, as he welcomed me and bade me follow him into his study.

The room was large and well-lit, with bookcases lining every wall, though not to a uniform height, since the cases did not match, having most likely been acquired and added one by one over the years as needed. But if the room lacked symmetry, still it was neat, every book in place, with papers and journals neatly stacked. If Dr. Rhadamanthus had been engaged in scholarly labors this afternoon, there was nothing to show it.

Seated behind his desk, he folded his hands in his lap and broke the silence. "What is it you want of me? And . . . oh, did you find the Ketzer volume?" I felt slightly embarrassed at his first words. I had interrupted him, one imposition already, and was making ready to ask yet another favor. My intention, then, was obvious, so I reasoned I had best be as frank as he had been.

"Yes, Doctor, I have read it, and with much interest—more than you might guess, as a matter of fact. And to tell the truth, that is why I've taken the liberty to impose on your time in this fashion. Again, forgive me, but. . . ."

"But you yourself have had such an experience as that described by the two peasants long ago, have you not?"

"Why, yes! Yes, indeed I *have*, Doctor . . ." I stammered, considerably shocked by his prescience.

"Tell me, how did you bring about the . . . hallucination? Or did you? Did the experience perhaps come upon you uninvited?"

I replied that I had invited *something* by my use of the drug, but that I did not, could not have, expected the amazing physical aftermath of the experiment. Was it possible for mescaline to effect such a change in the body? Surely nothing I had read would lead one to think so, and it was hard to imagine.

"No, no, you are quite right; no mere drug of whatever kind could cause the change you have undergone. I see by your line of questioning that you did not read quite far enough in Ketzer. Yet I can see how you would miss it. The old astrologer's work lacked much in the way of organization. What of the name 'Yaddith'?" My blank stare was sufficient reply, and he continued. "Ketzer wrote in rather veiled fashion of certain distant realms, whether of outer or inner space he did not say, and I am no longer sure there is any ultimate difference. One of these realms he named 'Yaddith,' all the more remarkably for the difficulty of rendering this word in German, where as you know our 'th' sound is lacking." I wondered momentarily how he would know how the word was pronounced. Had he independent information? "Such realms are sometimes opened to men, to those who can make themselves ready by various means."

"But Doctor Rhadamanthus, surely not all those who have taken mescaline have experienced what I have experienced. If mere drug-taking were the key . . ." He waved his hand as if to brush aside my words like a cobweb.

"But you have prepared the ground by your various occult researches over the years, as have your friends, from what you tell me."

Little more would he say, but he had said quite enough for me to puzzle over. If nothing else, it was obvious that from our first contact he had known far more than he told me. Indeed he seemed to know too much, about the mystery itself as well as my involvement with it. Perhaps this fact should have alarmed me, but instead it fueled the fire of my excitement. And with his last comment he had virtually asked my intended favor for me.

"Yes, Doctor, the members of the group have, as you say, prepared themselves, and now they are willing to join me in plumbing whatever truth may lie in this direction." I outlined our plan to him, and he readily assented to supervise us, to my great relief. Time and place were set, and I departed, scarcely able to assimilate all I had heard that afternoon.

## V

I had still not sorted things out completely when the six of us gathered at my home the next week. But I felt sure all would soon enough be clear to me—both the mystery of Rhadamanthus himself and the deeper truths I had spent so many years in pursuit of. As things turned out, I was right.

Our chairs were arranged in a circle in the very same room from which I had embarked on my strange pilgrimage only a month earlier. All of us were excited, Preus perhaps a bit more apprehensive than the rest, Barlow the more eager, but we were all ready to begin. Doctor Rhadamanthus had supplied each of us with our own dose of the drug, which we should all take together on signal, so to facilitate a collective and simultaneous experience. Rhadamanthus himself, of course, took no mescaline and sat outside the circle, his chair against one wall, where he had a clear view both of the group and of the picture window. This last was my suggestion. I reasoned that only so could we know how much of whatever transpired was internal and how much external reality. If someone who had not taken the drug saw any of the phenomena I had seen through that window, then we would know for certain whether the drug-induced mental state acted as "bait" for some beings more real than hallucinatory fantasies.

What I refrained from telling the doctor was that I, too, intended to observe what happened without benefit of the drug. I would but pretend to take it and see for myself what transpired. Would I still see what the others saw?

The moment came, and with it a flash of guilty panic. What might I have recklessly led my companions into? Well, no matter— they had taken the dose and I could only wait to see what followed. In a matter of minutes, perhaps a quarter of an hour, it began. The unearthly, sibilant whistling . . . did I see it? Yes! The very air began to spin in a huge ring, this time above our heads. Then it was no hallucination, whatever else it must be called. Would to God it had been! Dare I risk a glance over toward where Rhadamanthus was seated?

If he noticed, he would have to detect my subterfuge. Yet I supposed it did not really matter. I craned my neck to look, and . . . where but a moment before Rhadamanthus had sat in a posture of attentive concern, now there loomed one of the insectoid blasphemies I had seen in my vision last month! And this time I had taken no drug! God, I must rise and flee! But the strength had drained out of me, driven forth by the magnitude of my shock. As I felt myself fainting, I thought at least to turn back and catch a glimpse of my friends, but too late. Blackness swallowed me, this time the wholesome darkness of merciful unconsciousness.

When I came to myself, my first sight was of Rhadamanthus's now empty chair. Dreading what I should next see, I pulled myself to my knees and turned around to face a nightmare more hideous than any bred by fevered sleep. For amid scattered chairs and smears of blood stood abomination. To describe the indescribable the mind grasps wildly at the most improbable comparisons. What I saw resembled the cross-linked cage of a child's "jungle gym"; the revolting structure was a sagging composite of human limbs and trunks linked in a maze of insanity. Here a forearm ended at the wrist in another's chest, there a head sprouted from the small of a back; eyes stared out singly from shoulders or hands! Worse yet, no seam or breakage of skin was visible; the staggering castle of flesh looked as if it had grown as I now saw it! Dear Savior, if I could but tear from my memory the sight of the tortured faces of Elkhart, Preus, and the others, growing now from thighs and abdomens, staring blindly from empty sockets, screaming silently from mouths without vocal chords!

Reason fled my mind, as it must when reason has fled the world. All I knew was that this quivering miscegenation must outrage nature no longer. I half-ran, half-staggered from the room, down the stairs, and onto the porch where lay stacked wood for the fireplace, and . . . my axe! All I did, I did under instinct's dictates, pausing only later to contemplate my actions. Seizing the axe, I bounded back up into the room where the thing that had been my friends still tottered and flailed in agony. I determined that it should do so no longer. Poor Barlow, Preus, St. Joshua, Elkhart! They should have peace, even if the peace of everlasting oblivion! So I swung the axe, again and again, hewing and hacking with a fury I had not believed myself capable of. But of course it was the strength of the mad, for that is what I was in that moment. Screams filled the air, but I now realize they must have been mine.

(Sit down, Mr. Turrow! I assure you my bloodlust has quite spent itself! All I ask is that you listen to the rest.)

When I had finished, I and everything in the room were virtually afloat in blood. But at least nothing indicated that a short time before, the room had contained a structure of living flesh knitted somehow from four human bodies. Only pieces, small pieces, remained. Now I realize this to have been a mistake. For there is no longer any evidence of what really happened. One could prove no more than that a man went mad and butchered four men. But as I say, I was not thinking clearly then, not thinking at all. Nor was I when exhaustion bade me collapse on my bed in the next room.

The whole night I slumbered obliviously in the midst of that charnel house. When consciousness returned, so did the knowledge of what I had done. Perhaps all that saved me from final gibbering insanity was the detachment I felt, as if another had committed the atrocity, for as I have said, when I acted I was not myself. I sat up in bed and thought for quite some time. I resolved to complete two tasks that day, most likely to be my last day of freedom.

I dressed quickly, edged my way with tightly closed eyes through the next room, its air reeking of blood, and finally reached the door. Descending the stairs, I departed for the university library. I only hoped I might evade capture long enough to find some clue explaining the nightmare in which I now found myself.

Soon I had Ketzer's nefarious *History of the Planets* open before me once again. Sure enough, just as Rhadamanthus (or whatever he had been) told me, there was the mention of "Yaddith," and here was my answer, at least the beginning of it.

I replaced the book and left the campus, intent upon discharging my second errand, and that is when I came to see you, Mr. Turrow. My story must be aired, and from your paper's reputation I judged you the only one likely to air it. And I hope that you will. Now I have done all I may do, and can only await my fate. Perhaps the police will find me, but, more likely, *they* will. For you see, Mr. Turrow, this is what I read: that when a way had been opened to that other realm, contacts could be made, and truth sought and found. But openings might also be made *from the other side,* as presumably had happened in the case of the two German brothers. And in either case, those from Yaddith were just as curious as we. They, no less than we, were—are—inclined to . . . shall we say *experiment?* And now I, the seeker for truth, find myself in the position of a laboratory animal who through carelessness has escaped, and I believe they will not be long in finding me.

# Vastarien

## Thomas Ligotti

Within the blackness of his sleep a few lights began to glow like candles in a cloistered cell. Their illumination was unsteady and dim, issuing from no definite source. Nonetheless, he now discovered many shapes beneath the shadows: tall buildings whose rooftops nodded groundward, wide buildings whose facades seemed to follow the curve of a street, dark buildings whose windows and doorways tilted like badly hung paintings. And even if he found himself unable to fix his own location in this scene, he knew where his dreams had delivered him once more.

Even as the warped structures multiplied in his vision, crowding the lost distance, he possessed a sense of intimacy with each of them, a peculiar knowledge of the spaces within them and of the streets which coiled themselves around their mass. Once again he knew the depths of their foundations, where an obscure life seemed to establish itself, a secret civilization of echoes flourishing among groaning walls. Yet upon his probing more extensively into such interiors, certain difficulties presented themselves: stairways that wandered off-course into useless places; caged elevators that urged unwanted stops on their passengers; thin ladders ascending into a maze of shafts and conduits, the dark valves and arteries of a petrified and monstrous organism.

And he knew that every corner of this corroded world was prolific with choices, even if they had to be made blindly in a place where clear consequences and a hierarchy of possibilities were lacking. For there might be a room whose shabby and soundless decor exudes a desolate serenity which at first attracts the visitor, who then discovers certain figures enveloped in plush furniture, figures that do not move or speak but only stare; and, concluding that these weary mannikins have exercised a bizarre indulgence in repose, the visitor must ponder the alternatives: to linger or to leave?

Eluding the claustral enchantments of such rooms, his gaze now roamed the streets of this dream. He scanned the altitudes beyond the high sloping roofs: there the stars seemed to be no more than silvery cinders which showered up from the mouths of great chimneys and clung to something dark and dense looming above, something that closed in upon each black horizon. It appeared to him that certain high towers nearly breached this sagging blackness, stretching themselves nightward to attain the farthest possible remove from the world below. And toward the peak of one of the highest towers he spied vague silhouettes that moved hectically in a bright window, twisting and leaning upon the glass like shadow-puppets in the fever of some mad dispute.

Through the mazy streets his vision slowly glided, as if carried along by a sluggish draft. Darkened windows reflected the beams of stars and streetlamps; lighted windows, however dim their glow, betrayed strange scenes which were left behind long before their full mystery could overwhelm the dreaming traveller. He wandered into thoroughfares more remote, soaring past cluttered gardens and crooked gates, drifting alongside an expansive wall that seemed to border an abyss, and floating over bridges that arched above the black purling waters of canals.

Near a certain street corner, a place of supernatural clarity and stillness, he saw two figures standing beneath the crystalline glaze of a lamp ensconced high upon a wall of carved stone. Their shadows were perfect columns of blackness upon the livid pavement; their faces were a pair of faded masks concealing profound schemes. And they seemed to have lives of their own, with no awareness of *their* dreaming observer, who wished only to live with these specters and know their dreams, to remain in this place where everything was transfixed in the order of the unreal.

Never again, it seemed, could he be forced to abandon this realm of beautiful shadows.

Victor Keirion awoke with a brief convulsion of his limbs, as if he had been chaotically scrambling to break his fall from an imaginary height. For a moment he held his eyes closed, hoping to preserve the dissipating euphoria of the dream. Finally he blinked once or twice. Moonlight through a curtainless window allowed him the image of his outstretched arms and his somewhat twisted hands. Releasing his awkward hold on the edge of the sheeted mattress, he rolled onto his back. Then he groped around until his fingers found the cord dangling from the light above the bed. A small, barely furnished room appeared.

He pushed himself up and reached toward the painted metal nightstand. Through the spaces between his fingers he saw the pale gray binding of a book and some of the dark letters tooled upon its cover: V, S, R, N. Suddenly he withdrew his hand without touching the book, for the magical intoxication of the dream had died, and he feared that he would not be able to revive it.

Freeing himself from the coarse bedcovers, he sat at the edge of the mattress, elbows resting on his legs and hands loosely folded. His hair and eyes were pale, his complexion rather grayish, suggesting the color of certain clouds or that of long confinement. The single window in the room was only a few steps away, but he kept himself from approaching it, from even glancing in its direction. He knew exactly what he would see at that time of night: tall buildings, wide buildings, dark buildings, a scattering of stars and lights, and some lethargic movement in the streets below.

In so many ways the city outside the window was a semblance of that other place, which now seemed impossibly far off and inaccessible. But the likeness was evident only to his inner vision, only in the recollected images he formed when his eyes were closed or out of focus. It would be difficult to conceive of a creature for whom *this* world—its bare form seen with open eyes—represented a coveted paradise.

Now standing before the window, his hands tearing into the

pockets of a papery bathrobe, he saw that something was missing from the view, some crucial property that was denied to the stars above and the streets below, some unearthly essence needed to save them. The word *unearthly* reverberated in the room. In that place and at that hour, the paradoxical absence, the missing quality, became clear to him: it was the element of the unreal.

For Victor Keirion belonged to that wretched sect of souls who believe that the only value of this world lies in its power—at certain times—to suggest another world. Nevertheless, the place he now surveyed through the high window could never be anything but the most gauzy phantom of that other place, nothing save a shadowy mimic of the anatomy of that great dream. And although there were indeed times when one might be deceived, isolated moments when a gift for disguise triumphs, the impersonation could never be perfect or lasting. No true challenge to the rich unreality of Vastarien, where every shape suggested a thousand others, every sound disseminated everlasting echoes, every word founded a world. No horror, no joy was the equal of the abysmally vibrant sensations known in this place that was elsewhere, this spellbinding retreat where all experiences were interwoven to compose fantastic textures of feeling, a fine and dark tracery of limitless patterns. For everything in the unreal points to the infinite, and everything in Vastarien was unreal, unbounded by the tangible lie of existing. Even its most humble aspects proclaimed this truth: what door, he wondered, in any other world could imply the abundant and strange possibilities that belonged to the entrancing doors in the dream?

Then, as he focused his eyes upon a distant part of the city, he recalled a particular door, one of the least suggestive objects he had ever confronted, intimating little of what lay beyond.

It was a rectangle of smudged glass within another rectangle of scuffed wood, a battered thing lodged within a brick wall at the bottom of a stairway leading down from a crumbling street. And it pushed easily inward, merely a delicate formality between the underground shop and the outside world. Inside was an open room vaguely circular in shape, unusual in seeming more like the lobby of an old hotel than a bookstore. The circumference of the room was composed of crowded bookshelves whose separate sections were joined to one another to create an irregular polygon of eleven sides, with a long desk standing where a twelfth would have been. Beyond the desk stood a few more bookshelves arranged in aisles, their monotonous length leading into shadows. At the furthest point from this end of the shop, he began his circuit of the shelves, which appeared so promising in their array of old and ruddy bindings, like remnants of some fabulous autumn.

Very soon, however, the promise was betrayed and the mystique of the *Librairie de Grimoires*, in accord with his expectations, was stripped away to reveal, in his eyes, a side-show of charlatanry. For this disillusionment he had only himself to blame. Moreover, he could barely articulate the nature of the discrepancy between what he had hoped to find and what he actually found in such places. Aside from this hope, there was little basis for his belief that there existed some other arcana, one of a different kind altogether from that proffered by the books before him, all of which were sodden with an obscene reality, falsely hermetic ventures which consisted of circling the same absurd landscape. The other worlds portrayed in these books inevitably served as annexes of this one; they were impostors of the authentic unreality which was the only realm of redemption, however gruesome it might appear. And it was this *terminal* landscape that he sought, not those rituals of the "way" that never arrives, heavens or hells that are mere pretexts for circumnavigating the real and revelling in it. For he dreamed of strange volumes that turned away from all earthly light to become lost in their own nightmares, pages that preached a nocturnal salvation, a liturgy of shadows, a catechism of phantoms. His absolute: to dwell among the ruins of reality.

And it seemed to surpass all probability that there existed no precedent for this dream, no elaboration of this vision into a word, a delirious bible that would be the blight of all others—a scripture that would begin in apocalypse and lead its disciple to the wreck of all creation.

He had, in fact, come upon passages in certain books that approached this ideal, hinting to the reader—almost admonishing him—that the page before his eyes was about to offer a view from the abyss and cast a wavering light on desolate hallucinations. *To become the wind in the dead of winter,* so might begin an enticing verse of dreams. But soon the bemazed visionary would falter, retracting the promised scene of a shadow kingdom at the end of all entity, perhaps offering an apologetics for this lapse into the unreal. The work would then once more take up the universal theme, disclosing its true purpose in belaboring the most futile and profane of all ambitions: power, with knowledge as its drudge. The vision of a disastrous enlightenment, of a catastrophic illumination, was conjured up in passing and then cast aside. What remained was invariably a metaphysics as systematically trivial and debased as the physical laws it purported to transcend, a manual outlining the path to some hypothetical state of absolute glory. What remained *lost* was the revelation that nothing ever known has ended in glory; that all which ends does so in exhaustion, in confusion, and debris.

Nevertheless, a book that contained even a false gesture toward his truly eccentric absolute might indeed serve his purpose. Directing the attention of a bookseller to selected contents of such books, he would say: "I have an interest in a certain subject area, perhaps you will see . . . that is, I wonder, do you know of other, what should I say, *sources* that you would be able to recommend for my . . ."

Occasionally he was referred to another bookseller or to the owner of a private collection. And ultimately he would be forced to realize that he had been grotesquely misunderstood when he found himself on the fringe of a society devoted to some strictly demonic enterprise.

The very bookshop in which he was now browsing represented only the most recent digression in a search without progress. But he had learned to be cautious and would try to waste as little time as possible in discovering if there was anything hidden for him here. Certainly not on the shelves which presently surrounded him.

"Have you seen our friend?" asked a nearby voice, startling him somewhat. Victor Keirion turned to face the stranger. The man was rather small and wore a black overcoat; his hair was also black and fell loosely across his forehead. Besides his general appearance, there was also something about his presence that made one think of a crow, a scavenging creature in wait. "Has he come out of his hole?" the man asked, gesturing toward the empty desk and the dark area behind it.

"I'm sorry, I haven't seen anyone," Keirion replied. "I only now noticed you."

"I can't help being quiet. Look at these little feet," the man said, pointing to a highly polished pair of black shoes. Without thinking, Keirion looked down; then, feeling duped, he looked up again at the smiling stranger.

"You look very bored," said the human crow.

"I'm sorry?"

"Never mind. I can see that I'm bothering you." Then the man walked away, his coat flapping slightly, and began browsing some distant bookshelves. "I've never seen you in here before," he said from across the room.

"I've never been in here before," Keirion answered.

"Have you ever read this?" the stranger asked, pulling down a book and holding up its wordless black cover.

"Never," Keirion replied without so much as glancing at the book. Somehow this seemed the best action to take with this character, who appeared to be foreign in some indefinable way, intangibly alien.

"Well, you must be looking for something special," continued the other man, replacing the black book on its shelf. "And I know what that's like, when you're looking for something very special. Have you ever heard of a book, an extremely special book, that is not . . . yes, that is not *about* something, but actually *is* that something?"

For the first time the obnoxious stranger had managed to intrigue Keirion rather than annoy him. "That sounds . . ." he started to say, but then the other man exclaimed:

"There he is, there he is. Excuse me."

It seemed that the proprietor—that mutual friend—had finally made his appearance and was now standing behind the desk, looking toward his two customers. "My friend," said the crow-man as he stepped with outstretched hand over to the smoothly bald and softly fat gentleman. The two of them briefly shook hands; they whispered for a few moments. Then the crow-man was invited behind the desk, and—led by the heavy, unsmiling bookseller—made his way into the darkness at the back of the shop. In a distant corner of that darkness the brilliant rectangle of a doorway suddenly flashed into outline, admitting through its frame a large, twoheaded shadow.

Left alone among the worthless volumes of that shop, Victor Keirion felt the sad frustration of the uninvited, the abandoned. More than ever he had become infected with hopes and curiosities of an indeterminable kind. And he soon found it impossible to remain outside that radiant little room the other two had entered, and on whose threshold he presently stood in silence.

The room was a cramped bibliographic cubicle within which stood another cubicle formed by free-standing bookcases, creating four very narrow aisleways in the space between them. From the doorway he could not see how the inner cubicle might be entered, but he heard the voices of the others whispering within. Stepping quietly, he began making his way along the perimeter of the room, his eyes voraciously scanning a wealth of odd-looking volumes.

Immediately he sensed that something of a special nature awaited his discovery, and the evidence for this intuition began to build. Each book that he examined served as a clue in this delirious investigation, a cryptic sign which engaged his powers of interpretation and imparted the faith to proceed. Many of the works were written in foreign languages he did not read; some appeared to be composed in ciphers based on familiar characters and others seemed to be transcribed in a wholly artificial cryptography. But in every one of these books he found an oblique guidance, some feature of more or less indirect significance: a strangeness in the typeface, pages and bindings of uncommon texture, abstract diagrams suggesting no orthodox ritual or occult system. Even greater anticipation was inspired by certain illustrated plates, mysterious drawings and engravings that depicted scenes and situations unlike anything he could name. And such works as *Cynothoglys* or *The Noctuary of Tine* conveyed schemes so bizarre, so remote from known texts and treatises of the esoteric tradition, that he felt assured of the sense of his quest.

The whispering grew louder, though no more distinct, as he edged around a corner of that inner cubicle and anxiously noted the opening at its far end. At the same time he was distracted, for no apparent reason, by a small grayish volume leaning within a gap between larger and more garish tomes. The little book had been set upon the highest shelf, making it necessary for him to stretch himself, as if on an upright torture rack, to reach it. Trying not to give away his presence by the sounds of his pain, he finally secured the ashen-colored object—as pale as his own coloring—between the tips of his first two fingers. Mutely he strained to slide it quietly from its place; this act accomplished, he slowly shrunk down to his original stature and looked into the book's brittle pages.

It seemed to be a chronicle of strange dreams. Yet somehow the passages he examined were less a recollection of unruled visions than a tangible incarnation of them, not mere rhetoric but the thing itself. The use of language in the book was arrantly unnatural and the book's author unknown. Indeed, the text conveyed the impression of speaking for itself and speaking only to itself, the words flowing together like shadows that were cast by no forms outside the book. But although this volume appeared to be composed in a vernacular of mysteries, its words did inspire a sure understanding and created in their reader a visceral apprehension of the world they described, existing inseparable from it. Could this truly be the invocation of Vastarien, that improbable world to which those gnarled letters on the front of the book alluded? And was it a world at all? Rather the unreal essence of one, all natural elements purged by an occult process of extraction, all days distilled into dreams and nights into nightmares. Each passage he entered in the book both enchanted and appalled him with images and incidents so freakish and chaotic that his usual sense of these terms disintegrated along with everything else. Rampant oddity seemed to be the rule of the realm; imperfection became the source of the miraculous—wonders of deformity and marvels of miscreation. There was horror, undoubtedly. But it was a horror uncompromised by any feeling of lost joy or thwarted redemption; rather, it was a deliverance by damnation. And if Vastarien was a nightmare, it was a nightmare transformed in spirit by the utter absence of refuge: nightmare made normal.

"I'm sorry, I didn't see that you had drifted in here," said the bookseller in a high thin voice. He had just emerged from the inner chamber of the room and was standing with arms folded across his wide chest. "Please don't touch anything. And may I take that from you?" The right arm of the bookseller reached out, then returned to its former place when the man with the pale eyes did not relinquish the merchandise.

"I think I would like to purchase it," said Keirion. "I'm sure I would, if . . ."

"Of course, if the price is reasonable," finished the bookseller. "But who knows, you might not be able to understand how valuable these books can be. That one . . ." he said, removing a little pad and pencil from inside his jacket and scribbling briefly. He ripped off the top sheet and held it up for the would-be buyer to see, then confidently put away all writing materials, as if that would be the end of it.

"But there must be some latitude for bargaining," Keirion protested.

"I'm afraid not," answered the bookseller. "Not with something that is the only one of its kind, as are many of these volumes. Yet that one book you are holding, that single copy . . ."

A hand touched the bookseller's shoulder and seemed to switch off his voice. Then the crow-man stepped into the aisleway, his eyes fixed upon the object under discussion, and asked: "Don't you find that the book is somewhat . . . difficult?"

"Difficult," repeated Keirion. "I'm not sure. . . . If you mean that the language is strange, I would have to agree, but—"

"No," interjected the bookseller, "that's not what he means at all."

"Excuse us for a moment," said the crow-man.

Then both men went back into the inner room, where they whispered for some time. When the whispering ceased, the bookseller came forth and announced that there had been a mistake. The book, while something of a curiosity, was worth a good deal less than the price earlier quoted. The revised evaluation, while still costly, was nevertheless within the means of this particular buyer, who agreed at once to pay.

Thus began Victor Keirion's preoccupation with a certain book and a certain hallucinated world, though to make a distinction between these two phenomena ultimately seemed an error: the book, indeed, did not merely describe that strange world but, in some obscure fashion, was a true composition of the thing itself, its very form incarnate.

Each day thereafter he studied the hypnotic episodes of the little book; each night, as he dreamed, he carried out shapeless expeditions into its fantastic topography. To all appearances it seemed he had discovered the summit or abyss of the unreal, that paradise of exhaustion, confusion, and debris where reality ends and where one may dwell among its ruins. And it was not long before he found it necessary to revisit that twelve-sided shop, intending to question the obese bookseller on the subject of the book and unintentionally learning the truth of how it came to be sold.

When he arrived at the bookstore, sometime in the middle of a grayish afternoon, Victor Keirion was surprised to find that the door, which had opened so freely on his previous visit, was now firmly locked. It would not even rattle in its frame when he nervously pushed and pulled on the handle. Since the interior of the store was lighted, he took a coin from his pocket and began tapping on the glass. Finally, someone came forward from the shadows of the back room.

"Closed," the bookseller pantomimed on the other side of the glass.

"But . . ." Keirion argued, pointing to his wristwatch.

"Nevertheless," the wide man shouted. Then, after scrutinizing the disappointed patron, the bookseller unlocked the door and opened it far enough to carry on a brief conversation. "And what is it I can do for you? I'm closed, so you'll have to come some other time if—"

"I only wanted to ask you something. Do you remember the book that I bought from you not long ago, the one—"

"Yes, I remember," replied the bookseller, as if quite prepared for the question. "And let me say that I was quite impressed, as of course was . . . the other man."

"Impressed?" Keirion repeated.

"Flabbergasted is more the word in his case," continued the bookseller. "He said to me, 'The book has found its reader,' and what could I do but agree with him?"

"I'm afraid I don't understand," said Keirion.

The bookseller blinked and said nothing. After a few moments he reluctantly explained: "I was hoping that by now you would understand. He hasn't contacted you? The man who was in here that day?"

"No, why should he?"

The bookseller blinked again and said: "Well, I suppose there's no reason you need to stand out there. It's getting very cold, don't you feel it?" Then he closed the door and pulled Keirion a little to one side of it, whispering: "There's just one thing I would like to tell you. I made no mistake that day about the price of that book. And it was the price—in full—which was paid by the other man, don't ask me anything else about him. That price, of course, minus the small amount that you yourself contributed. I didn't cheat anyone, least of all *him*. He would have been happy to pay even more to get that book into your hands. And although I'm not exactly sure of his reasons, I think you should know that."

"But why didn't he simply purchase the book for himself?" asked Keirion.

The bookseller seemed confused. "It was of no use to him. Perhaps it would have been better if you hadn't given yourself away when he asked you about the book. How much you knew."

"But I don't know anything, apart from what I've read in the book itself. I came here to find—"

"—Nothing, I'm afraid. You're the one who should be telling me, very impressive. But I'm not asking, don't misunderstand. And there's nothing more I can tell you, since I've already violated every precept of discretion. This is such an exceptional case, though. Very impressive, if in fact you are the reader of that book."

Realizing that, at best, he had been led into a dialogue of mystification, and possibly one of lies, Victor Keirion had no regrets when the bookseller held the door open for him to leave.

But before very many days, and especially nights, had passed he learned why the bookseller had been so impressed with him, and why the crowlike stranger had been so generous: the bestower of the book who was blind to its mysteries. In the course of those days, those nights, he learned that the stranger had given only so that he might possess the thing he could gain in no other way, that he was reading the book with borrowed eyes and stealing its secrets from the soul of its rightful reader. At last it became clear what was happening to him throughout those strange nights of dreaming.

On each of those nights the shapes of Vastarien slowly pushed through the obscurity of his sleep, a vast landscape emerging from its own profound slumber and drifting forth from a place without name or dimension. And as the crooked monuments became manifest once again, they seemed to expand and soar high above him, drawing his vision toward them. Progressively the scene acquired nuance and articulation; steadily the creation became dense and intricate within its black womb: the streets were sinuous entrails winding through that dark body, and each edifice was the jutting bone of a skeleton hung with a thin musculature of shadows.

But just as his vision reached out to embrace fully the mysterious and jagged form of the dream, it all appeared to pull away, abandoning him on the edge of a dreamless void. The landscape was receding, shrinking into the distance. Now all he could see was a single street bordered by two converging rows of buildings. And at the opposite end of that street, rising up taller than the buildings themselves, stood a great figure in silhouette. This looming colossus made no movement or sound but firmly dominated the horizon where the single remaining street seemed to end. From this position the towering shadow was absorbing all other shapes into its own, which gradually was gaining in stature as the landscape withdrew and diminished. And the outline of this titanic figure appeared to be that of a man, yet it was also that of a dark and devouring bird.

Although for several nights Victor Keirion managed to awake before the scavenger had thoroughly consumed what was not its own, there was no assurance that he would always be able to do so and that the dream would not pass into the hands of another. Ultimately, he conceived and executed the act that was necessary to keep possession of the dream he had coveted for so long.

*Vastarien*, he whispered as he stood in the shadows and moonlight of that bare little room, where a massive metal door prevented his escape. Within that door a small square of thick glass was implanted so that he might be watched by day and by night. And there was an unbending web of heavy wire covering the window which overlooked the city that was *not* Vastarien. Never, chanted a voice which might have been his own. Then more insistently: *never, never, never. . . .*

When the door was opened and some men in uniforms entered the room, they found Victor Keirion screaming to the raucous limits of his voice and trying to scale the thick metal mesh veiling the window, as if he were dragging himself along some unlikely route of liberation. Of course, they pulled him to the floor; they stretched him out upon the bed, where his wrists and ankles were tightly strapped. Then through the doorway strode a nurse who carried a slender syringe crowned with a silvery needle.

During the injection he continued to scream words which everyone in the room had heard before, each outburst developing the theme of his unjust confinement: how the man he had murdered was using him in a horrible way, a way impossible to explain or make credible. The man could not read the book—there, *that* book—and was stealing the dreams which the book had spawned. *Stealing my dreams,* he mumbled softly as the drug began to take effect. *Stealing my . . .*

The group remained around the bed for a few moments, silently staring at its restrained occupant. Then one of them pointed to the book and initiated a conversation now familiar to them all.

"What should we do with it? It's been taken away enough times already, but then there's always another that appears."

"And there's no point to it. Look at these pages—nothing, nothing written anywhere."

"So why does he sit reading them for hours? He does nothing else."

"I think it's time we told someone in authority."

"Of course, we could do that, but what exactly would we say? That a certain inmate should be forbidden from reading a certain book? That he becomes violent?"

"And then they'll ask why we can't keep the book away from him or him from the book? What should we say to that?"

"There would be nothing we could say. Can you imagine what lunatics we would seem? As soon as we opened our mouths, that would be it for all of us."

"And when someone asks what the book means to him, or even what its name is . . . what would be our answer?"

As if in response to this question, a few shapeless groans arose from the criminally insane creature who was bound to the bed. But no one could understand the meaning of the word or words that he uttered, least of all himself. For he was now far from his own words, buried deep within the dreams of a place where everything was transfixed in the order of the unreal; and whence, it truly seemed, he would never return.

# The Madness out of Space

## Peter H. Cannon

### I

Friends and family have wondered at my abrupt return from college a full week before the beginning of the Easter vacation. Explanations of an unforeseen, early termination of school work I hope have satisfied them; for I dare not hint as yet as to the real cause. Eventually, I realize, I must tell them—and the world—of the fate of my roommate and closest friend, Howard Wentworth Anable, who disappeared in the early morning of March 15, 1929, into the densely forested, still winter-frozen hills that extended west of the university town of Arkham, Massachusetts—or so people believe. How much of the "truth" I will reveal remains for me to decide, as I run the risk of being declared mad as that singular individual whose bizarre and lamentable history I am here about to disclose. I admit that relations between us had been strained in those final months, an unhappy consequence of his physical and mental deterioration; but this in no way affected the underlying fondness and respect I had always held for him.

I fear that I have seen the last of my comrade; for certain evidence—certain damnably conclusive evidence, which for the sake of mankind's collective sanity I hesitate to reveal—indicates that he has ventured into terrible cosmic realms from which no mortal can ever return.

Duty required that I inform Anable's mother and grandmother, who live near the center of the old colonial town, of my gravest suspicions; but without giving away anything of the specific horror I had observed. The Anables had half-anticipated a climax of this sort, and bore their grief with admirable Yankee stoicism. There ensued a discreet investigation, which received no publicity other than a short notice in the *Arkham Advertiser*.

The police theorize that Anable was forcibly abducted, the broken window and the disordered furniture and books in his bedroom supporting this conclusion. Anable's relatives had known of his association with an undesirable band of cultists, who, camped out in the Arkham hills, may have taken revenge on the youth for some imagined transgression of their laws. Search parties discovered no trace of Anable or his suspected abductors (who, in any event, may have left the area months before), and after several days they abandoned their trampings through the woods.

Naturally the authorities questioned me closely, but I was able to demonstrate to their satisfaction that I knew little of Anable's dealings with any queer characters living in the hills. Through an extreme effort of will I managed to suppress my feelings of awful horror and show only normal shock and dismay. Indeed, until the last mind-shattering revelation I had dismissed Anable's ravings as nothing more than a lot of theosophical hocus-pocus. A rational man could easily have taken his strange pronouncement toward the end as the phantasies of a psychotic. But now I know otherwise; and because I do I may myself fall a victim to those same dread forces that claimed my friend. Therefore, for the written record, I am presently setting down, during these days of early New England spring, while events are still fresh and there is still time for me, an account of this frightful matter—of the madness out of space.

## II

I met Howard Anable our freshman year at Miskatonic University, which is not Harvard, nor is it even Ivy League, but whose unparalleled reputation as a freewheeling, "progressive," co-ed institution attracts unconventional and original minds who care little for prestige. It is located in the glamorous old, gambrel-roofed town of Arkham, renowned along the North Shore as a place especially sensitive to adumbrations of the paranormal. Both he and I enrolled in an advanced course in Colonial American literature. (Miskatonic's Pickman collection of early American documents is justly famous for its size and completeness—second only to that of the John Carter Hay Library at Brown University in Providence, Rhode Island.) I was immediately impressed, as were the other students and Professor Waggoner, by his profound and encyclopedic knowledge of the subject. Anable boasted that he had read Cotton Mather's *Magnalia Christi Americana* in its entirety, and would quote lengthy passages from memory to illustrate all sorts of nice points in class discussion. It appeared that he had done extensive research from his earliest years into the history, folklore, culture, and architecture of New England.

Physically unobtrusive on first sight, Anable really cut a remarkable figure the more one studied him. He had a frame so excessively spare that, although he stood an inch or two above average height, people usually took him to be much taller. A spectrally pale complexion, set off by strikingly deep, intelligent brown eyes and short-cropped, mousy brown hair, combined to give his face a perpetually startled expression. (That he was fair-haired and blue-eyed as a child Anable never tired of repeating when I knew him better.) He wore conservative clothing, a dark suit with a plain, dark knit tie being his preferred dress.

Although I frequently engaged in academic debate with Anable, I knew practically nothing about him outside the classroom, other than that he lived at his family's home on Valley Street. Fellow students remarked that they never noticed him at any of the usual campus haunts; rumor had it that he spent his free hours taking long, solitary walks beyond the town. His rapid stooping gait soon became his distinctive hallmark.

An independent figure, Anable ignored the voguish crowd of campus "sophisticates," who courted him as someone whose eccentricities and tastes would have made him immediately welcome among their select circles. Instead, his high-handed disdain of their "immature indulgences," as he put it, won only their resentment. I myself, being by nature more gregarious and eager to be accepted by the elite, was at first given to mixing with the "wild set" but by the Christmas holidays I had grown weary of their superficial pseudo-decadent thrill-seeking, and ceased associating with them altogether with the start of the second term in January.

I think Anable observed this shift in my social preferences. He began speaking to me on his own initiative after the honors American literature class, devoted to a thorough study of those classic if largely neglected authors—Cooper, Irving, and Charles Brockden Brown—of the early Republic, that we shared in the new term. A casual friendship developed between us that I was pleased to cultivate; for I appreciated in Anable his genuine erudition and sobriety of manner—indicative, I sensed, of a special understanding of things outside the ordinary in life.

We soon discovered that we held a good many common interests, as Anable's outward reticence gave way to a voluble stream of talk about himself and his ideas. I already knew him to be an enthusiastic student of the New England scene; now I learned the personal side.

Howard Wentworth Anable was descended from a line of well-to-do Arkham merchants who had flourished during the days of clipper ships and the China trade; the family since the turn of the century, however, having been reduced to the state politely known as "genteel poverty." As a boy of nine, soon after the death of his father, he had moved with his mother from his family's Anawan Avenue mansion, built in the 1820s by his great-grandfather, Captain Adoniram Anable, celebrated in Arkham history for his daring exploits in the South Seas, to the less than grand neighborhood of Valley Street. (The log of the *Miskatonic,* the vessel in which Captain Anable made his most successful voyages, is preserved in the archives of the Arkham Institute.) His first American ancestor, of Northumberland stock, had sailed on the *Arbella* in 1636, Anable proudly told me once; adding that his people were among the very earliest settlers of Cape Cod. Of his father Anable rarely spoke—and then merely to say that he had worked for the 'phone company.

I visited Anable at his home, a privilege granted to few, and was much impressed by the Chinese plates and vases, Polynesian wood-carvings, and scrimshaw still in the family's possession—surviving relics of a more prosperous age that seemed so sadly out of place in the undistinguished, Victorian frame house, divided into apartments, that now formed the Anable abode. With no brothers or sisters or congenial playmates to divert him with the usual childhood activities, Anable had grown up with only the memories and dust of the past to occupy his imagination. A voracious reader, he had mastered the family library with its shelves of mouldy Essex County histories and other quaint, antique volumes. Anable sometimes spoke wistfully to me of someday recovering the family mansion and restoring it to a semblance of that departed glory of his forebears. Alas, that shall never be!

Anable detested cats, and in his youth used to throw rocks at any feline so foolish as to prowl into the Anable backyard and wander within range. He also hated ice cream, amazing as it may seem that anyone could become nauseous at even the slightest taste of this universally loved treat. On the other hand, staunch New Englander that he was, Anable adored seafood—lobster, clams, fried or steamed, mussels with butter, cod, scrod, sole, flounder or haddock, chowder of the Boston variety, he relished them all.

In his devotion to this vision of a purer, happier past, he had, with the advent of his teens and less parental supervision, become increasingly drawn to the countryside beyond Arkham—to the pine, maple, and birch forest that covers the undulant, ravine-intersected hills as far as the sparsely populated regions of the upper Miskatonic valley. It had been on extended walks through the woods that Anable had felt his most exquisite and poignant sensations of wonder and adventurous expectancy—caught especially at sunset in the vista of golden roofs of the town laid out below.

That spring Anable took me to his favorite spot for viewing Arkham and its sunset effects—Satan's Ledge, an outcropping of sedimentary rock on one of the higher hillsides (part of a vast tract of public land), well-nigh inaccessible from the Arkham direction save for a difficult ascent up its steep slope through uncommonly thick vegetation. Believing me not up to the strenuous climb, Anable suggested that we ride the Bolton bus which drops off passengers during warm months at a roadside picnic area on the westward fringe of the hill, where the slope is considerably gentler. From this picnic area the ledge was but a walk of a half mile along a well-marked path.

Indeed a scenic viewpoint, Satan's Ledge formed a level surface of moderate extent, upon which rested granite boulders arranged in a disturbingly symmetrical pattern—one that no retreating ice sheet was likely to have left, in my opinion. Peculiar ideographs, most badly eroded, were graven on these imposing rocks—no doubt the work of the vanished Indians. Ethnographers had conjectured them to be of cabalistic or magical significance, Anable informed me, but who could say for sure with so few discernible details. Analogues are to be found on rocks in the remote mountain regions of Vermont and Maine and in the decadent hill country around Dunwich.

At the end of the school year in June, our friendship firmly fixed, Anable asked me if I cared to share lodgings with him for sophomore year.

"I've noticed, Winsor," he began, as we sat in the Ratty, the undergraduate refectory, over coffee (his heavily laden with sugar as was his custom), "that you're a fairly sensitive fellow. I think you're someone who understands, who sympathizes. Living with my mother and feeble old grandmother while going to college I've found 'restrictive,' to say the least. It's time I got out on my own, and I don't mean into one of the hideous dormitories with the herd. I'd like a companion— partly for financial reasons I admit—who'd be willing to go halves with me on a place.

"You see, Winsor, I feel I'm on the verge of making a 'rift in the horizon's wall,' so to speak—but just where or how I cannot begin to tell, let alone explain to you. It has something to do with the sense of adventurous expectancy that hits me on occasion whenever I view scenes of particular aesthetic appeal, such as old gardens, antique harbors, or Georgian steeples topped with gilded vanes." Anable's great brown eyes glowed, as if he were gazing at a Bullfinch cupola and not at a student cafeteria.

"I'm afraid that if I become too absorbed in my search I may lose all sense of proper proportion, act rashly. I may well need a friend close at hand, someone stable whose good judgement I can rely on— a pal such as you to point out to me when I'm going astray."

Flattered by his proposal, I was nonetheless taken aback by his last cryptic remarks. My uneasiness must have been obvious to Anable, for he suddenly shifted back to the main point.

"I've found decent furnished rooms at 973 Hale Street near the end of the trolley line at the north end of town. The location may be far from campus, but the trolley stop is just two blocks away. I've been there once, when I answered the ad in the *Advertiser*. The landlady, Mrs. Delisio, would provide meals. If you're free we can go take a look right now."

I could not help but be intrigued by Anable's offer; here was a unique opportunity to increase our intimacy. His baffling comments forgotten, I readily assented to examine the place. We drained our cups and headed out for the trolley stop in front of Miskatonic Hall.

The building at 973 Hale Street proved to be a small, eighteenth-century clapboard house, which retained much of its antique charm despite its overall dilapidation. I was particularly struck by the isolation of the address, right at the outskirts of Arkham proper. A stretch of dreary marsh land bordered the modest backyard.

The "upstairs suite"—two bedrooms separated by a common sitting room—was clean if bare and severe, containing the basic minimum of furniture. From the windows, which faced the rear, one could look out over the acres of marsh to where the wooded hillsides rose, brilliant with spring green—and to Satan's Ledge, which Anable pointed out to me, just visible as a gray protuberance.

The price Mrs. Delisio cited was only too reasonable, and we signed a year's lease on the spot. Mrs. Delisio, an elderly widow, seemed glad to have engaged two Yankee boys as lodgers. Anable announced his intention of taking up residence for the summer, agreeing to pay the whole rent until I joined him in the fall. He said that his mother would probably disapprove, but there was nothing she could do. Her policy had never been to oppose him when he was adamant enough in his wishes—within certain limits. Besides, he had recently secured a job stamping and addressing envelopes and doing other petty tasks for a local bookseller, and thus he figured he could almost cover this new expense with his summer earnings.

## III

After transferring my few belongings to our new quarters on Hale Street and helping Anable move his possessions there, I rode the B. & M. home to Boston, not expecting to return to Arkham until September. I lingered briefly at our residence on narrow, cobbled

Acorn Street, before repairing with my family to our house in West Chop, on the island of Martha's Vineyard, for the summer. After the academic rigors of the past year at Miskatonic, I looked forward to the idle months of sailboat racing, tennis playing, and sun bathing. A part-time volunteer job at the Dukes County Historical Society, conducting tours at the venerable Richard C. Norton "Reading Room," would form my excuse for useful employment. My father's harpsichord factory in Cambridge had thrived mightily in recent years, and he was in a position to spend the entire summer on the island, much to the delight of the rest of us, leaving his business to the care of junior partners.

As I settled into the pleasant routine of healthy athletic activities by day (when not at the museum) and gala social events by night (in particular the weekly dances at the Casino), I began sending Anable cheery postcards, urging him to come pay me a visit. His staying in that stuffy apartment all summer, pursuing his esoteric researches in the university library (in between stuffing envelopes and his usual rambles in the countryside), struck me in my agreeable environment as more and more dubious. A change of scene, a little "fun," would be good for my scholarly friend.

These accounts of my idyllic existence elicited a response from Anable that plainly revealed to what an advanced degree he had already become immersed in the offbeat historical lore he had made his special province. (Puzzled at first by the "1728" at the head of the letter, I eventually realized that Anable—antiquarian that he was—affected to date his correspondence two hundred years earlier.) Here is the complete text.

26 June 1728

My dear Winsor:—

How infinitely gratifying to hear from you of your tennis and dancing, and I do appreciate your invitation to come join you in said frivolous diversions. Quite frankly, however, in light of an exciting development here, I am afraid I haven't the time to indulge in such things. I think you'll understand when you absorb what I say below.

While you've been burning in the sun (by the way, I

don't care to tan), I've made an important discovery. You may remember I told you that I intended to read all the material available at the library on those queer Indian ideographs at Satan's Ledge? (Of course, I already knew the general background—but, I must confess, I was rather weak on the more recent history of the formation. Post-Civil War history has never really interested me.) Well, in the course of digging through the stacks, I came across a very curious monograph, "Satan and His Works in Latter-Day New England," printed privately in 1879 by one Thomas Hazard Clarke of Arkham, concerning an odd religious sect that had a settlement near Satan's Ledge in the latter part of the last century. Originally a Shaker splinter group, which Clarke belonged to, this motley assortment of pious fanatics came gradually to fall away from orthodox Christian practices. It seems the more lunatic of them began to assimilate elements of the pagan myths surrounding Satan's Ledge from the few surviving Indians in the region, and took to holding ceremonies at the ledge surreptitiously—"in which the Christian deity had no part." Many of the members, several dozen men of all ages, were dim, stupid folk, degenerate from generations of inbreeding. Clarke and others who continued in the pure faith were naturally alarmed by this ominous conversion among a sizeable portion of the community. The apostates grew in number, as it devolved that somehow their gods or "Old Ones," which they called by the exotic names of "Azathoth," "Nyarlathotep," "Yog-Sothoth," and "Cthulhu" ("agents of the devil" to Clarke), were more receptive to their worship than the aloof-from-the-petty-affairs-of-men traditional God. At last, with the defection of the chief minister, John G. Hartnett, to the new "Cthulhu cult," as it became known, they began to practice the blasphemous faith more openly, using the ideographs apparently to aid in "calling down from the sky" some mysterious entity which Clarke guardedly refers to as "the madness out of space." During certain times of secret worship at night among the degenerates, Clarke could detect a horribly foul odour emanating from the direction of the ledge, along with a muted white glow in the atmosphere above it—but he never tried to witness these repulsive ceremonies for himself. When finally the situation became intolerable, Clarke, as leader of the few members remaining true to the original faith, organized his followers into a campaign to suppress the heresy. Unfortunately, at this point in his hitherto detailed narrative, he becomes vague, hinting merely that after a "great trial," in which he and his men had to resort to means derived from the unclean rituals of the Cthulhuists—and with the assistance of selected Arkham town officials—they succeeded in eradicating the evil. He is specific about a "cataclysm of God" occurring on October 31, 1878, which utterly destroyed the Cthulhu cult—a fire that swept the settlement and burned to the ground every dwelling (tents and flimsy shacks). Most perished in the conflagration, including Hartnett, the few survivors scattering into oblivion. Clarke retired to Arkham, a badly shaken man, but his solid faith along with the help of an alienist, as he candidly admits, sustained him. He warns others of the dangers of deviation from Christianity, closing with a long, pedantic section extolling the virtues of the Congregational Church to which in the end he converted.

Clarke is reasonably precise about the location of the community, and I'm confident that I can find it somewhere to the west of Satan's Ledge when I go look for it tomorrow after work. That fire he speaks of must have thoroughly effaced the site, since undoubtedly I've passed over it in my exploration and not noticed any remains. In fifty years the forest can wholly reclaim a cleared area.

I'll let you know what my search turns up. Until we meet again, and wishing you luck in the forthcoming holiday races, I am

Yr. Humble Servt. HWA

My reaction to this incredible missive can scarcely be imagined. As I studied its substance the initial indignation I had felt at Anable's cavalier dismissal of my invitation and aspersions on my summer lifestyle gave way to an ambivalent sense of skepticism and wonder. This Cthulhu cult business was indeed an intriguing mystery, but evidently this Thomas Clarke was some kind of half-baked religious crank who had made up most—if not all—of this wild story. (Funny that Anable seemed to accept the narrative almost at face value.) Yet, even if the element of truth was small, here was a peculiar historical footnote of the sort to satisfy Anable's longing for the *outré*.

I did not have to wait a week before hearing the sequel.

1 July 1728

Winsor:—

Eureka! Success! Forgive this uncharacteristic outburst of elation, but truly marvel grows upon marvel. I've discovered what I believe is the former cult site. I'll concede my conclusion isn't based on any direct evidence, for I found no charred relics—rather in a part of the woods a quarter-mile northwest of Satan's Ledge, where the trees are relatively sparse, there stands a makeshift hovel, which could only have been erected within the last couple of weeks. I can tell someone is living in it from the rough mat and store of supplies inside. No, I haven't met its inhabitant. But I've caught glimpses of him, an elderly man in tattered, nondescript garments, in its vicinity and at Satan's Ledge—where I nearly surprised him in the act of carving *fresh* ideographs into the rocks, in an apparent effort to restore those obliterated by weather and time. These, when I examined them, proved, crude as they were, not to be mere copies or tourist *graffiti*—but new designs consistent with legible existing ones. I'd evidently interrupted him in the midst of his work, because when I returned the next day there were several more carved into the brittle granite. I've not come close to catching this individual since our near encounter at the ledge, try as I might—and lately I've been thinking that maybe it's a bit unwise for me to attempt it alone.

To speak plainly, would you mind coming up to Arkham to help me run this fellow to ground? If we could only talk to him I suspect he could tell us a fascinating story or two about the ledge and the ideographs and, who knows, perhaps the cult. Surely after the 4th celebrations Wednesday you could take some time off. Possibly this coming weekend? Anxiously awaiting your reply, I am

Yr. Servt. H.

I reacted to this second letter from Anable, received on the 3rd, with a great deal of confusion. Where before he had simply outlined a fanciful if disquieting story from a pamphlet in a library, now he had ventured into the physical reality of the Arkham woods and found a real mystery—an innocuous one on the surface to my mind and yet a touch sinister, if one could credit the Clarke monograph at all. Reluctant to miss the Fireman's Ball in Edgartown on Saturday night but eager to assist my friend, I wired him to say that he could expect me Thursday, with the condition that I had to be back on the island by the evening of the 7th. I departed the morning of the 5th, a successful Fourth of July race series behind me.

Upon my arrival Anable impatiently rushed through the civilities and described his plan to me. We would get up before dawn, the idea being that our chances of catching the inhabitant of the hovel were better the earlier we reached the site. An inveterate night owl whose natural tendency was to stay up to three or four in the morning and then sleep well past noon, Anable was grateful for my presence if only to ensure his waking up at the appointed hour. Accordingly, we set the alarm for 5 a.m. and retired. Anable was glad I had been exercising regularly, since we would be approaching the ledge by the steep route. As I was weary from traveling much of the day—by ferry, by motorcoach, and by train—I fell asleep instantly on the bed my chum had thoughtfully made up for me.

The next morning after a breakfast of coffee and crackers and cheese (standard fare for Anable), we stole silently from the house in the half-light of an already warmish day and going a block east hit Route 127, the main north-south road that follows the coast of the North Shore. At this point in its sinuous course, just north of Arkham, 127 swings to the west and runs through an unpopulated stretch of woods, bordered by salt marshes on its eastern fringes. (Though Satan's Ledge was only about a mile-and-a-half away as the crow flies from 973 Hale Street, these marshes prevented us from reaching it directly.)

Farms had prospered in this region as late as the early nineteenth century, but had gone into rapid decline during the War of 1812 and the succeeding period of economic stagnation. One could hardly believe that where white pine and birch now stood once waved fields of corn, beans, tomatoes, and carrots, acre after acre in the rocky New England soil. Stone walls, in want of mending or in places simply heaps of rubble, ran nowhere through the trees and brush, mute testimony to the old property lines.

We did not keep for long to this main thoroughfare, however, but shortly took a left turn onto one of the occasional dirt roads leading into the forest interior. We must have followed this for a couple of hundred yards before coming to a fork, where Anable selected the more overgrown path (for it no longer could be properly called a road). Though the branches of the trees we passed under blocked much of the little light there was, Anable never faltered and showed no hesitation in his choice of direction when we encountered other forks in the course of our journey. Midges and other flying insects pestered us, and we swatted at these without much effect. As the ground rose perceptibly, I started to perspire.

Finally we were picking our way along what was at best a faint animal trail in the thick of the woods. All at once a steep slope, more nearly accurately a cliff, emerged before us and we began the precipitous climb Anable had warned me about. Above loomed the gray eminence of Satan's Ledge.

After many minutes of toil we stood, panting on the flat surface of the ledge. The sun was above the horizon by this time, and we admired the view of Arkham below and the sea beyond shimmering in the dawn. A lovely sight, but nothing, averred Anable, like its appearance at sunset.

Before showing me the new ideographs and checking for any more recent carving, Anable pointed out in disgust the "signs" that other, undesirable types (certainly not our man) had left to advertise their visits. Debris littered the rock floor; cigarette butts, paper wrappers, a beer bottle or two, and—upon part of the ledge covered by a smooth layer of soft earth or humus—several flattened, translucent balloons with wide mouths, resembling the hydra or some other primitive marine animal. (I had noticed this same peculiar detritus washed in great numbers on Martin's Beach near Gloucester, where my family used to summer in the days prior to our acquiring the Vineyard house.)

We surveyed this sorry spectacle but for a moment before Anable directed my attention to what was of prime importance. On the great, most easterly boulder stood out four rows of bizarre figures—a sequence of alien hieroglyphics whose outlines vaguely suggested odd animal forms rather than abstract characters. These incised figures, each six inches or so in height, proved on closer inspection to be highlighted by a dullish red pigment ground into the contours. They ran roughly in horizontal lines, about a dozen to each line, as regularly as the irregular surface of the granite allowed. Anable calculated that they had been created over a period of two weeks, at the rate of three or four a day. Original, worn figures had been carved over to form a kind of palimpsest. Other boulders had many fewer inscribed markings, we noted.

Once I had satisfied myself with my first view of these astonishing glyphs, Anable led me deeper into the trees in a northwesterly direction. Nature was very much evident at this hour—a rabbit scampered out of sight ahead, squirrels and chipmunks chattered at us as they scurried along branches, and above the pine tops I spotted the distinctive, "flying cigar" forms of chimney swifts gliding soundlessly, along with a stray green heron aimed for the marshes behind and below us. Fallen tree trunks white with fungi oozed the odor of decay—a not unpleasant scent.

After a fifteen-minute trek the woods and undergrowth thinned and we came out into a clearing. Wild flowers grew in spectacular clumps here, covering any sign of former human habitation—for this, conjectured Anable, was where the religious colony had been planted almost fifty years ago.

We crossed the expanse of clearing to where the trees began to grow thick again by a stream, and there beneath a great pine bough was a lean-to, or more accurately perhaps, tee-pee about five feet high. Peering cautiously inside, we saw a tarpaulin and blankets, a small cupboard, an ax, and other camping gear. A pile of ashes and blackened wood circled by stones in front bespoke the remains of a fire. Nearby on the ground rested a chisel and mallet, plus a stick of red chalk.

"Hello, young fellers," cried a hearty voice. "Up kind of early, ain't you, for a nature walk?"

We both turned around at once to observe, coming out of a pine copse about fifteen yards to our right, a short, thickly built, elderly man—smiling at us and tugging at his pants. He wore what amounted to a suit of earth-colored rags, and more than a touch of redness rimmed his eyes, the only part of his face visible in the great, gray mass of hair and whiskers that covered his head. He reminded me of the sort of slovenly rustic one tried to avoid noticing loafing around the Arkham Trailways station. Despite his decrepit clothing, he appeared to have a robust physique, and showed none of the faltering slowness of the aged as he advanced a few steps toward us, then halted. If not for his cheerful tone of voice and ingratiating manner, I would have thought him a very threatening fellow.

"What business have you boys in this stretch of the woods?" he asked. Anable answered that he often took walks in the Arkham hills, and had done so most of his life. Shifting to the offensive, my friend asked in turn what he was doing camping in these parts, and whether he had a permit.

"Well, my lad, I must tell you I'm no newcomer to this beautiful country," said he, looking appreciatively about, "though it's been a good many years since I set foot here—long before you youngsters were toddling around nosing into your elder's affairs. I was camped on this land when a person didn't need a permit to set up a house. Least we didn't bother with one . . . Maybe that's why we had to leave all of a sudden." He chuckled, enjoying his private joke.

Anable asked if he had had anything to do with the "Shaker" community that used to be located at this site—and was he around at the time of the "cataclysm of God" that had destroyed it.

"Oh, you've heard of that, have you? Thought folks had hushed that up ages ago. Not something people in polite circles in Arkham would talk about, even at the time."

Anable said that he had studied the Clarke monograph, "Satan and His Works in Latter-Day New England," and persisted in his questioning.

"So you've read that packet of lies that parsimonious prig slandered our memory with. . . . Yeh, I guess I was a part of it. But before I say more, who be you? And who be your quiet friend?"

My comrade introduced himself as Howard Wentworth Anable of Arkham, Massachusetts, and me as his fellow Miskatonic student, E. Phillips Winsor. Did I detect a happy gleam in the old man's eye, an abrupt perking up, at the mention of Anable's name?

"Glad to meet you, Mr. Anable, Mr. Winsor," he said, nodding to each of us, with a certain mock deference. With an enthusiasm lacking before he said, "Harper is my name. Jay Harper." I was grateful to be at a distance, as I had no desire to shake the paw of this unkempt vagabond.

"Yeh, I did belong to the sect. I was a youth then, not much older than you boys. In '76 it was. My people, they come from far up the valley—of good sound stock, mind you. My governor practiced law when he wasn't running the general store—sent me to Yale College for a spell, but Yale and me didn't hit it off and so we parted company.

"I had a hankering to wander, and came to Arkham since I heard the mills needed strong, healthy chaps like me. But I guess I was too late, 'cause I couldn't find a job right away. In the meantime, I became friendly with some of the members of this religious community in the hills who said it was okay for me to make my home with them—not that I was ever a devout churchgoer but it was a lot cheaper than staying in lodgings in town. Later when I got a mill job I kept where I was. I had a wild streak then, and I came to see that what those folks were up to was kind of exciting . . . If that self-righteous blockhead Tim Clarke hadn't meddled in business he had no understanding of . . ." Harper glowered. "Satan's Ledge, huh! Clarke with all his Bible learning could only figure things in Christian terms. We called it by a more suitable name, of course."

Harper smiled wistfully, adding sadly, "Well, if you've read that stupid 'treatise' of his you know the upshot. Poor Hartnett, he meant no harm. I was lucky to get away from that burning mess alive. I went back to Dunwich, where I've worked ever since for Whateley's Tree Service. Never been back to Arkham till now."

Harper paused, casting his eyes down on the chisel and mallet waiting for use. Anable asked why he had returned—and why he was carving new ideographs—and what was their significance.

"Now, son, don't be overinquisitive—one question at a time. Let's just say that I'm indulging myself in a show of sentimental reminiscence. Preparing the stage the way we used to before performing the rituals. I'm carving them from memory for old time's sake, you understand. There's no harm in it—we weren't bothering anyone outside the cult. As for their meaning, I might tell you another time . . ." His throaty chuckle after this remark made me flinch.

"See here, lads, maybe . . . maybe you can help me out. If you do, I'll tell you some secrets about the old cult that few persons alive today could begin to guess at . . . I'm running low on supplies, and would be obliged to you if you would buy me some groceries. In my state I'm afraid I'd draw too much unkindly attention if I was to go into town myself." He pulled out an oily sheet from his jacket, along with some dollar bills more brown than green. "Here's my list of what I need, and to show you how much I trust you boys"—he was looking straight at Anable—"I'm giving you the money now, no collateral. Do this for me and come back here in a few days and I promise I'll tell you some tales I think you'd like to hear. . . ." So saying, he passed the bills to Anable, who nodded in apparent assent.

Jay Harper retrieved his chisel and mallet, along with his red chalk stick, and escorted us back to the ledge, explaining that he could only get his work done there at odd hours—when snoops like ourselves were not around to disturb him.

"Our mysterious character-carver should reveal a thing or two of real interest, I think," declared Anable as we clambered gingerly down the slope. "Doesn't seem to be a dangerous sort either—though I was glad to have you standing by, Winsor. My impulse is to help out the old geezer, buy him his groceries. Too bad you can't stay around to see for yourself what happens."

My reaction to our meeting with this queer hill person was somewhat less enthusiastic than my companion's. When I told him so, he simply laughed and dismissed me as an old maid.

At my departure for Arkham the next morning, Anable renewed his vow to apprise me of further developments. Making the right connections, I was back on the island in sufficient time to attend the Fireman's Ball.

## IV

A month passed before I heard from Anable again, a longer interval than I might have expected in view of his eager anticipation of revelations to come when I left him. Had the old ruffian disappeared on him? Or had Harper's tales turned out to be so disappointing that Anable was ashamed to report on them to me? In any event, this Harper character was clearly a demented fool who was not to be relied upon as far as I was concerned.

Anable's letter (dated normally for once) read as follows:

August 8, 1928

My dear W:—

Pardon the delay, but I've been so absorbed in matters here that I've not been able to concentrate long enough to write even the briefest note. Between the necessary drudgery of licking envelopes at Dawber & Pyne and my conferences with Harper, I've hardly had a moment to eat or sleep! Let me begin by assuring you that our forest friend has proved informative beyond my wildest imaginings.

I returned with the groceries two days after our initial encounter, taking the more roundabout but easier route from the picnic grounds in light of my load. A bottle of bootleg whiskey I'd included as a surprise did much to encourage Harper's natural garrulousness, and he spoke to me for hours about the cult while I listened in wonder. Gad, what this man knows! What he has experienced! Harper informed me that he had had vivid dreams, growing in persistency, that drove him back to the settlement site—and in those dreams a cultivated young man figured prominently. When I'd said my name that first meeting he'd known instantly that it was I he'd seen in his dreams! He interprets this as a sign that I can be of invaluable service to him. When he asked for my help (and not just in supplying him with groceries), I readily agreed. Forgive me for not being specific on the nature of his purposes—even I'm not really sure—but Harper has made it a condition of our "pact" that I confide in no one, not even you, dear fellow. Already I say too much. The potential reward for me is tremendous, and I trust you'll understand when I tell you I don't want to jeopardize my chances to earn it.

Suffice to say that now that Harper has finished engraving the glyphs (the ones he hadn't remembered from his youth came to him in visions), he requires the consultation of certain arcane books available in the locked stacks of the Miskatonic library. In particular he wishes me to transcribe passages from Abdul Alhazred's *Necronomicon*, perhaps the rarest and most marvelous tome in the collection. As a Miskatonic student, I of course would be granted access to this volume more readily than he. I applied to the head librarian, Dr. Henry Armitage, who permitted me—albeit reluctantly—to copy from it. Harper could only provide me from memory with approximate locations of the pertinent passages, with a vague outline of their content. (The cult's copy was lost in the flames of '78.) My Latin proved fair enough, however, for me to determine from the context which lines were relevant.

Harper was pleased with the material I collected, and wanted me to make a second trip to the library for further transcription. Unfortunately, the next time I went to continue my research, on the 3rd, I was disappointed. Dr. Armitage, who has gone into seclusion at his house and refuses to see a soul, has left instructions forbidding anyone to be shown the *Necronomicon*. Harper greeted this ill turn of fortune with dismay, but thinks what I managed to get copied down before may be sufficient. Our progress is delayed, yet other resources do exist.

Looking forward to catching up in person fall term, I remain

Yr. Servt. HWA

So, Anable had taken to humoring the old half-wit in his crazy pursuits. I was beginning to grow alarmed, recalling that the *Necronomicon* had been furtively discussed among the decadent circles I had spurned as a book of colossal, cosmic evil. For the first time it struck me that Anable might be losing sight of reality. His account of his servility to Harper served to confirm my distrust of that scruffy creature. When I wrote Anable back, I told him as politely as possible that I disapproved of Harper and that he ought to keep away from him. In reply I got a short note from Anable, pervaded by a wounded, defensive tone, saying that I was regarding the situation in the wrong way and would understand better when he could explain things to me face to face in the fall.

The remainder of the summer passed pleasantly for me. It culminated spectacularly in an all-night Labor Day weekend aboard our yawl, *Arethusa,* anchored off the West Chop light. With this fete fresh in my memory, I anticipated the return to Miskatonic and reunion with Anable in a gay, trouble-free mood, the very opposite of the one I had sunk into at the time of receiving his unsettling letter.

## V

To say that Anable had subtly changed by the time I arrived back in Arkham in mid-September would be an understatement. As I stepped off the B. & M. coach at the station, he greeted me with an energy and effusiveness that I was wholly unaccustomed to. His usually languid brown eyes were animated, almost mirthful. He exhibited none of the somber demeanor so characteristic of him, and his pace was quicker than ever.

"Great and wonderful things are in the offing, Winsor," exclaimed my buoyant buddy as we settled ourselves on the trolley. "I've gotten to know our friend Harper pretty well in a couple of months. He's really quite a respectable fellow—a decent, middle-class Yankee, and a college man to boot (at least he was for a while). A pity he's had hard luck. But with a few changes of clothing I've provided him—well, it's made a big difference, as you'll see. . . ."

Anable paused a moment slightly embarrassed. "I have to warn you, Winsor, that I've allowed Harper to use your room, to stay overnight from time to time during damp weather. But of course now that you're back, he'll return to the woods for good. Besides, he now has company."

I looked quizzical.

"Yes, others have joined our survivor. There're presently several of his former cult members living on the old site. They, too, have heard the call—in their dreams just as Harper did—and have gathered from disparate parts of the country. They've set up a regular small camp—nothing like on the scale of the original of course."

I watched the houses become sparser as we approached the end of the line, and for the first time regretted my decision to move out of the comparative civilization of the university dorms. I was not at ease as we tramped the short length of the front walk and marched up the stairs to the second floor of 973 Hale Street.

As we entered the sitting room, a gentleman arose from the sofa whom I did not immediately recognize as the bedraggled individual I had met in the woods in the summer. His shock of hair was combed, and his sturdy frame was decked out in a clean checked shirt, denim trousers, and brand new work boots. This time I shook hands with Jay Harper. Apparently he had been reading, for next to him on the end table and on the sofa itself were scattered a number of battered, dirty-looking books.

"Well, Howard, I thank you again for letting me read at your place. Fine titles these books are. It'd be a shame if I had to store them in the tee-pee where the moisture'd get at them. Good day to you both," said the old man, picking up his jacket and striding out the door.

I glanced down at one of the more modern volumes on the sofa and saw that it was the shocking *Goblin Tower* by Frank Belknap Long. A quick survey revealed that the rest were just as dismal— among them *Melmoth the Wanderer*, R. W. Chamber's *The King in Yellow*, Bierce's *In the Midst of Life*, and Lord Dunsany's *A Dreamer's Tales* in the Modern Library pocket edition.

Noting my look of distaste, Anable made a half-hearted effort to allay my worries.

"While working at Dawber & Pyne this summer," he began, "I had the chance to search through their stock of secondhand books. Amazing what they kept lying around in dusty cartons in the attic. Because of their poor condition I was able to pick them up for a steal. Harper made a few suggestions on what to keep my eye out for and choose. His knowledge of the literature in the field is truly profound. I discovered more interesting works than I thought existed. They've been a great help in filling in the gaps in the data we culled from the

*Necronomicon.* Just because an author writes 'fiction' doesn't mean he doesn't put some important truths into his books, whether intentionally or not.

"Don't be alarmed—we're not out to destroy the world," he said, smiling. "It's all simply a personal concern that doesn't affect anybody else."

I was not persuaded by these arguments to disarm me. I said nothing, and went into my bedroom to arrange my effects that had been shipped in advance of my arrival.

Despite his initial show of friendliness, Anable displayed little interest in me or my affairs in succeeding weeks. I resented this behavior, and now and then told him he was involved in a lot of rubbish—but he continued to ignore me. Harper came to the apartment twice in the next month for conferences with Anable, held in his room with the door shut. (Had there been a lock on it I have no doubt he would have used it.) My roommate made frequent trips to the vicinity of Satan's Ledge—or so I assumed, for he rarely bothered to tell me of his plans before going out. He never asked me to join him. When I ventured to mention my feelings of exclusion, Anable assured me that he would reveal what he and Harper were up to at the appropriate time. I must remain patient.

In any event, I had my course work to absorb me. "Eighteenth Century Gothick Taste in England," "Literature of the Restoration" (with an emphasis on Shadwell), "Differential Equations," and "American Transcendentalism" (taught by Professor Albert N. Wilmarth who started the class a week late owing, rumor had it, to an upsetting, overnight visit to Vermont shortly before the term began) kept me immersed in my books for long hours. Anable, on the other hand, scarcely opened a text, his dubious collection of the weird forming his chief reading material. He often cut classes, an evening course in "Medieval Metaphysics" being the only one he attended faithfully. In sum, he was no longer the conscientious student of the previous year. I feared for his scholarship status.

At the apartment Anable alternated between extremes of moods. Either he would shuffle about in a state of suppressed agitation, or else would lounge around the sitting room in his dressing gown, sunk in lassitude. In this latter condition he seemed to be daydreaming, utterly oblivious of me or his surroundings.

I felt compassion for him just once when he announced to me that his mother had had to sell two ornately carved, Jacobean chairs that had been in the family for generations in order to buy a new refrigerator. He moped for a week, and I was genuinely sorry for him.

## VI

When, out of kindness, I asked Anable if he cared to accompany me to a Halloween party the 31st, he shook his head.

"I appreciate your concern for my social life, Winsor," he answered, "but I'm afraid I'm going to be busy with Harper and his friends that night. You might say we have a party of our own to attend in observance of the Hallowmas. If it turns out as I have every expectation it will, I can assure you—at long last, my dear fellow—of a complete and satisfactory explanation."

Of what Anable did not specify—and I did not inquire further. The truth is, I had become intimidated by Anable's actions. I faced the painful fact that by now he was not in his right mind—he was already far gone in his involvement in these outlandish pursuits, and it would do no good to confront him head on. Recalling his injunction to me to help him retain his "sense of proportion," I resolved at that moment to go on Halloween to Satan's Ledge, where surely he and his unsavory companions would be congregating, and observe their goings-on in secret. This would be a risky business to be certain, but I felt given Anable's evasiveness that I had to obtain information firsthand, assess how dangerous this evidently revived cult was to him. I no longer had confidence in his promise of revelation.

During the week prior to the 31st, Anable spent more and more time away from 973 Hale Street, presumably with his comrades in the forest hills. When I returned to the apartment after classes, he would be gone. I would be in bed asleep before he came back, his closed door in the morning the only indication he had done so. I saw him once or twice, and then fleetingly.

The day before Halloween I noticed a brown bag on the sitting room desk. Anable must have brought it in earlier that afternoon. Thinking it contained groceries, I casually looked inside. To my surprise I found a curious assortment of chemicals in glass jars as might belong to a boy's chemistry set: uniodized salt, sulphur, iron filings, compounds of cobalt, magnesium, nickel, zinc, and mercury. Among his other solitary childhood pastimes, I remembered Anable once saying that he had been passionately devoted to chemistry. Was this evidence of a resurgence of interest in that hobby? Again, I hesitated to ask.

That Wednesday around 3 when I got back from Miskatonic, Anable was pacing about the sitting room, as intensely agitated as I had ever seen him. He scarcely acknowledged my entry. "The dreams, Winsor, the magnificent dreams," he exclaimed and rushed into his room.

An hour later Anable emerged dressed in his worn winter coat and carrying his sack of chemicals. "Please bear with me," he pleaded, his brown eyes begging my understanding, as he ran out. For a second I softened and forgot my annoyance with him, overcome by a surge of pity for the fellow. I should not really blame Anable for his deplorable state—Harper and his disreputable cultists were the ones responsible. They had taken in my unworldly friend with their elaborate Cthulhu mumbo-jumbo. If I could catch them this night causing him any harm, psychological or otherwise, I would blow the whistle on them in a minute and call in the Arkham authorities. I had already confided my fears to Mrs. Anable, who agreed that her son was under bad influences.

Leaving at dusk for my party, I drove the model J Duesenberg my father had given me for my birthday earlier in the month into Arkham center. A paper bag with cut-out eyes would serve me as a simple costume. I spent several agreeable hours drinking cider and bobbing for apples at the Zeta Psi house, then set out on the serious mission of my Halloween night.

Since it would be hopeless for me to try in the dark to follow the forest trail Anable had led me on in the summer, let alone scale the steep slope to the ledge, I decided to take the more roundabout route of my original visit there. Besides, now that I was in possession of a motorcar, distance was no obstacle. I headed inland out Miskatonic Avenue, which runs along the river, to where it hits the Bolton Road. The moon had risen, and the beams of my headlamps illuminated the autumn leaves swirling and eddying in the cold breeze. An exhilarating and magical air suffused the landscape. In high spirits from the quantity of cider I had imbibed, I approached this uncertain rendezvous free of any apprehension. It was almost a lark.

My watch showed a little past 11 by the time I parked at the picnic area. In the moonlight with foliage above thinner than in warmer months, I had no trouble locating the path to Satan's Ledge. I kept to this at first, but not wishing to encounter possible sentinels, I strayed to the left and began a cautious circling movement through the woods, which were dense enough to afford adequate concealment. I was able to make my way with a minimum of stumbling as I worked up to gradually higher ground.

I was acutely aware of the noises in the brush and trees—the rustle of swaying boughs, the trickle of a distant stream, an owl hoot, a jay's cry. But soon I heard another sound, an unfamiliar one, a soft, rhythmic moaning, as if the forest itself was breathing. Ahead of me I began to catch glimpses through the branches and undergrowth of flickering, bobbing points of light—but it was too late in the season for fireflies. They seemed to be receding at the same rate as I advanced. As I continued my slow, upward progress, I realized that these were flames—candle flames. As I approached nearer still, I could perceive that each candle was held by a dim human form. A half-dozen men were walking in Indian file towards Satan's Ledge—for now at last in the faint light of the moon and candles I could make out the rough, Cyclopean boulders on the ledge's inner rim. I lay down behind a fallen birch trunk about thirty yards away, not daring to go closer.

The group proceeded across the rock floor of the ledge and arranged itself very deliberately in a semi-circle in front of and facing the great easterly boulder with its graven ideographs. From my low vantage point I had an unobstructed view of this scene. All of those in this strange procession (though I could only see their backs) appeared to be elderly folk, except for one—from his hurried, stooping gait I could not mistake Anable. The air was curiously still on the ledge, the flames stirring hardly at all—and the surrounding woods now seemed unnaturally quiet, the continuous, monotonous chanting the only sound.

Abruptly the cultists crouched down, bowed before the rock. One figure remained standing—the mass of hair and beard marked him as Harper. He moved to the center of the semi-circle, set down his candle by the boulder's base, and drew from his jacket an object that I thought at first was the mallet—but it was a pipe, for he raised it to his mouth and blew three, low loathsome notes. The others ceased the moronic chanting instantly in response. Harper next pulled from his jacket a small, glittering container, and started methodically to march around behind the huddled group and scatter a powdery substance from it with his fingertips. Soon emptying its contents, he withdrew another and repeated the process, and so for several jars until he had covered the length of the semi-circle and enclosed the band from one edge of the great boulder to the other. Thus were the chemicals Anable had purchased put to use.

Done with this seemingly pointless ritual, Harper rejoined the congregants, squatting down with them at one end of their semi-circle. They then raised their heads in unison to the rock and commenced to pour out, as if reading the blasphemous glyphs, an uncouth string of syllables in a language that not only bore no relation to English but to no sane human tongue on this planet.

"Cthulhu fhtagn," they recited over and over.

With the cry of "Iä, Iä, Shub-Niggurath," an indescribably foetid odor swept down upon me from the direction of the ledge. I almost swooned as I closed my eyes in disgust. My nausea stemmed not only from the ghastly stench itself, but from the sudden remembrance of Anable's description of certain events outlined in Clarke's monograph. Here these crazed cultists—and my brash friend—were reenacting an unholy ceremony of the sort practiced fifty years ago on this spot! I trembled, no longer the bold spy of a short time before.

I had barely mastered my nausea, the vile odor having passed within moments, when I opened my eyes to see, atop the graven boulder, a shrouded human figure—who must have scaled the rock from behind and emerged in the instant I had them shut. A great wind had sprung up and whistled and howled around this apparition, blowing his immaculate white robe in billows and nearly extinguishing the flames of the candles of the worshippers clustered below him. Emanating a brilliant glow of purest white, this luminous, lithe-limbed being glided down the nearly vertical granite face to the ledge floor, while the hideous glyphs burned a dark red as if reflecting his radiance. I could clearly discern his dazzling features—he was smooth-faced, delicately boned, and boyish, with the almond eyes of an antique pharaoh. From his crown luxuriant, silken, gold hair flowed as if electrically charged. I was more in awe than frightened— indeed overcome by the unearthly beauty of this personage. I was transfixed.

One of the crouched celebrants rose—it was Anable—and approached this exquisite, god-like creature. Harper and the rest remained prostrate. Anable knelt before him and raised his face and clasped his hands in supplication. The gorgeous youth began to speak, to murmur to Anable, but the wind had built to such a frantic pitch that I could catch nothing, though I believe he was using English. After communing with Anable for what seemed like aeons, he bent over and embraced and enveloped my friend in his wavering folds. They blended into one writhing, amorphous mass, Anable invisible in the voluminous robe—then they almost poured back to the graven rock and began effortlessly to ascend its steep face.

At this point I could endure it no longer. I lurched forward from my hiding place and ran screaming, "Anable! Oh, Howard! Watch out!" Perhaps emboldened by my liquor, perhaps driven by some mad, selfless instinct, I hastened to try to save my chum. Damn the risk! What had I to fear after all from a half-dozen old people, whom I could fast outrun if need be? As for the fragile fellow who had swallowed up my friend, I was suddenly overwhelmed with rage and hatred for him. I didn't know whether to kiss it or kill it! All that mattered was rescuing my companion from his willowy clutches.

Incredibly, I succeeded in my immediate attempt to cause disruption. The celebrants turned around in bewilderment, then hurried to their feet, extinguishing their tapers, and raced off in panic into the woods as I charged them, brandishing a stout birch limb and wearing my paper bag mask for added effect. The white-robed youth hesitated, then lowered the inert form of my friend gently to the rock floor, finally mounting the boulder again and swiftly disappearing over its top edge—he would have a difficult climb down the steep slope beyond.

Only Harper of the fleeing cultists paused. "Curse you, boy," he bellowed. "You've spoiled his initiation. Woe be to you, my lad!" Then he slipped with the rest into the darkness.

Guided by the moonlight, I rushed to where Anable lay prone on the rock. He was stunned and babbling: "The Great Old Ones . . . Cthulhu's Ledge . . . I was so close . . . Azathoth." Sheer nonsense, of course.

Frightened that the Cthulhuists might regroup and come after us once recovering from their surprise, I hoisted Anable to his feet, first ascertaining that he was in no pain. To my relief I found him ambulatory and was able to lead him by the path quickly back to the picnic grounds and the safety of my Model J.

During the frenzied drive back to Arkham, Anable continued his wild mutterings. At first incoherent, he abruptly began to speak in lucid sentences, albeit rapidly and with a terrific intensity, his brown eyes glazed.

"Yes, Winsor, I have met the Old Ones' avatar . . . who told me of marvels beyond the galling limitations of time and space as we conceive of them. I learned where Henri Rousseau had obtained his models for the jungle creatures in that curious and unsettling painting of his, 'The Children of the Kingdom.' And the primitive tribes of Guatemala and the Dutch East Indies archipelago are not the only repositories of secrets that would drive the mass of mankind mad if they were known. The woods of New Jersey, just a few miles from the Pest Zone euphemistically called New York City, contain creeping, insidious, eldritch horror, which threatens at any moment to erupt and spew over the land (a result I wouldn't mind seeing if it meant the destruction of that hateful burg). Nor even are the Connecticut suburbs safe . . .

"I learned, too, of those dark and dangerous forces that flop and flounder at the galaxy's rim . . . This goes infinitely beyond man's feeble morality. We're no more significant than the least bacterial scum in the larger scheme of the universe. The Old Ones have spared us worthless wretches so far because we count for so little. They may appear 'malign' to certain self-blinded earth-gazers, but are in fact indifferent—except to the occasional exceptional individual, to whom They may give the opportunity for the realization of and *participation in* the awesome secrets of time and space. There is a chance for human transcendence. Many hear the call, but few will heed it and be chosen. *Iä! Iä! Shub-Niggurath*, the Goat with a Thousand Young!"

At this last burst of insanity Anable trailed off again into gibberish, only to cry a minute later: "Oh but, Winsor, you fool! So much more could I have found out, unimaginable wonders, if you hadn't interrupted. Damn you!" With this imprecation he lapsed into permanent silence, slumped down in the seat beside me. His lack of gratitude stung, but I could hardly judge him harshly in the circumstances. Surely now it was essential that he sever all ties with Harper and company, who had brought him to this woeful condition.

Barely conscious or able to walk, Anable with my help staggered up the stairs and into his room where I eased him onto his bed. Thank God our dreadful Halloween night was over.

## VII

Anable spent the next several weeks in a state of utter collapse. Naturally, the morning after our harrowing misadventure at Satan's Ledge, I notified Mrs. Anable that her son had taken seriously ill, sparing her the worst of the details. She arranged for the family doctor to come to examine him at the apartment as soon as possible. Dr. MacDonald could find no signs of physical injury, but in light of my guarded account concluded that Anable must have suffered some kind of severe nervous shock that had rendered him powerless. When after two days Anable did regain consciousness, he was too weak to speak or get about on his own. It was clear that he could no longer remain at 973 Hale Street. With the aid of stalwart Dr. MacDonald, I succeed in transferring Anable in my vehicle to his family's Valley Street home. Mrs. Delisio, tearfully watching the doctor and me carry the patient outside, remarked what a pity that such a polite, mannerly young man should be so grievously afflicted.

Mrs. Anable was reluctant to call in the authorities, but she worried about the cultists who had harmed her son lurking still in the woods, and requested that I and some friends scout around the Satan's Ledge area. A week after Halloween, I persuaded three classmates—Messrs. Hailblum, Sullivan, and Klein—to accompany me on a "bird walk" (such was my excuse) during the day to see if Harper and company were around or not. In the course of our bird sighting, I discovered no trace of human habitation other than the discarded garbage. Perhaps with the onset of colder weather they had dispersed, returning to their places of origin. Nevertheless, a clever woodsman like Harper could easily evade detection and survive the winter outdoors if he had to. Mrs. Anable was relieved to hear my report that they had apparently pulled up stakes and departed.

I visited Anable at least once a week during his confinement at home. Sitting by his bedside, I filled him in on campus news and the progress of my courses—careful not to mention the cult or Satan's Ledge or the disturbing doings Halloween night. Though capable of speaking for brief intervals (according to his mother), Anable chose to keep silent at these interviews. Indeed, he often closed his eyes, as if overcome by weariness, and turned his head to the wall away from me. When his luminous brown eyes were open, they seemed to stare at me, as if with—could it be?—resentment. I was generous not to take this as a personal slight, but rather attributed it to the grave mental strain he had undergone, perhaps coupled with a resumption of that natural reserve that shut out even his best friend.

Anable's physical health did improve steadily, however, and he regained sufficient strength to walk unassisted by the end of November. By early December he could leave the house on short trips. But, having a constitutional aversion to cold weather, aggravated by his present weakened condition, Anable could not remain outside for very long. This was one fortunate complication, for he had begun to express a desire to revisit the ledge, so Mrs. Anable confided to me. She did not wish him to return to the scene of his traumatic experience, and made me promise to do everything in my power to prevent him from doing so.

His mental state, alas, did not change much for the better. Anable continued to be withdrawn and apathetic—as if he had expended all the tremendous energy that had been building within him since summer in one shot that Halloween night, with none left to sustain him for the rest of the year. The dean of the university showed his understanding when he allowed Anable to take incompletes in his fall subjects, at no penalty to his scholarship status.

When I returned to Arkham following the Christmas vacation, I was pleased to find Anable had resumed residence in our Hale Street apartment. His greeting was effusive, yet somehow perfunctory, lacking the warmth of the previous reunions. At least he was displaying more liveliness.

"Ah, Winsor," he exclaimed, "trust you enjoyed the holidays. Happy 1929! Dr. MacDonald has judged me well enough to get back to my studies at Miskatonic—which I can tell you I'm eager to do. An invalid's existence is a terrific bore.

"As for the cult business, let me put your mind to rest on all that. You needn't feel anxious for me any more. I realize now I was fooling with forces that no person with his wits about him should ever get mixed up in. I'd become so immersed in arcane lore, shall we say, that I'd lost all perspective—just as I warned you I might. I have to admit you were correct to be suspicious of Harper. He was luring me into the midst of a sinister 'cosmic conspiracy'—but you showed up out of the blue and saved me in the nick of time. I'm through with it now for good, believe me. I'll not bring up the subject again—and I'll appreciate it if you won't say anything about it either. Let's forget about it. It's in the past."

So, instead of a truthful explanation of what he had been involved in, Anable gave me this assurance of his reform. Well, by this point I knew more than I cared to about this Cthulhu cult and was satisfied that it was all a lot of mysterious, mystical claptrap that had dazzled and misguided my friend. I was content to let the matter drop, hopeful that this was indeed the end of it.

Unsteady on his feet as he still was, Anable was nonetheless able to get to and from classes on his own via the trolley. He applied himself more dutifully to his studies than in the first term, yet I sensed his heart was not really in his work. On more than one occasion I caught him gazing out the sitting room window toward Satan's Ledge. And more than once, I suspect, he attempted to walk to the ledge by the direct, steep route—but the ice and snow must have thwarted him. When he asked me to drive him to the picnic area off the Bolton Road, I refused. He glared at me for a second, then subsided into a disappointed sulk. Unwilling, I suppose, to appear too keen on the idea of a return journey, he never brought it up again.

As the bleak winter term wore on, Anable made less and less of an effort to be sociable. Listless for long stretches, he also displayed at times a certain restlessness. He gave up all pretense of making conversation, except on the most mundane, essential topics. "Pass the salt" was about the most he would say to Mrs. Delisio or me. I forbore, more sorrowed than angered by his rude behavior. Obviously he had far to go mentally before complete recovery. Despite my protests, he continued to read those trashy, evil books by Chambers, Bierce, and others.

Then in February the dreams came. I began to hear him crying out unintelligibly in his sleep. After one particularly bad night he appeared looking extremely haggard—and yet oddly exhilarated, his eyes flashing with a light I had not seen since before his collapse. When I probed him, he admitted that "distressing" dreams had caused him to sleep fitfully, but his elated expression seemed to belie the notion that they had been in any way disturbing. He would not comment on the content of these dreams.

One night late in the month, after returning from a rush party at the Kappa Sig house, I could hear Anable through his bedroom door talking in his sleep. Pressing my ear to the door, I could make out the following snatches. "He promises to come again . . . Satan's Ledge too far . . . must try one more time . . . I cannot fail Him . . . He shall not fail me . . . chant the Dhol formula . . . Nyarlathotep. . . ."

I was profoundly alarmed to recognize the sorts of words and phrases he had not mouthed since our delirious ride back to Arkham on that Halloween night. At last I had to face the fact that Anable's derangement was more serious and lasting than I had guessed. A doctor who specialized in mental disorders would probably have to be consulted soon. But events moved too swiftly for me to act—and, in retrospect, I doubt if it would have affected the ultimate tragic outcome.

The unfortunate climax, when it came, did not catch me entirely off guard. Since Anable had abandoned even an outward show of normality, I was prepared to act forcefully if I had to.

It was a chilly winter evening, a Thursday, with no sign in the air of the forthcoming spring, that I sat on the sofa checking over my notes for a paper on Shadwell's use of irony. Vacation was only a week away. I was feeling quite relaxed after Mrs. Delisio's delicious spaghetti dinner. Anable had retired to his room from which shortly he emerged wearing his heavy overcoat.

"I'm going out, Winsor—into town, to my mother's," he announced.

I offered him a lift in my motor. He declined. I insisted on leaving with him, seeing him to the trolley stop. Grudgingly, he allowed me to accompany him outside. When we reached the street he turned the wrong way—north toward 127 and the woods. I hurried after him as he broke into a run on the slippery pavement. I easily overtook him in his semi-debilitated condition. When he ignored my command to halt, I had no recourse but to seize him and wrestle him gently into a drift at the side of the road.

"I must get out tonight . . . I must break through the Gate . . . I must merge with Him . . . leave me alone," he panted as we struggled.

When Anable realized the futility of further resistance, I let him up and he reluctantly returned with me to the house. We were both soaked from rolling around in the wet snow—it was lunacy to stay out any longer with the temperature falling sharply. Anable was wheezing, gasping for breath.

Ignoring his imprecations against me, I assured him that it was in his best interest not to go to the ledge considering his poor health in this weather at this time of night. Anable, furious, stormed into his room and slammed the door. I kept vigil in the sitting room to near midnight, then went to bed myself.

I did not know what time it was when I awoke (I could not see my alarm in the dark), but I soon realized what the cause of my waking up had been—a high wind that rattled the panes had blown over the trash cans in the yard beneath my window. The wind sounded louder than it should—as if its source were from within the building. I stumbled out into the sitting room to investigate. Judging by the great whistling noise coming from Anable's room I concluded that he had to have his window wide open.

Above the whine, which was like no natural wind I had ever heard, I could distinguish a high-pitched but forceful voice behind Anable's door that I knew could not be my roommate's.

"You know, Howard Anable, that the New England world you have loved and cherished from birth is only the sum of the marvelous sunset cities you have gazed upon (from a height) in your dreams. These have you yearned for with such keen frustration all your years. Ancient Arkham, insular Innsmouth, rumour-shadowed Kingsport, Boston and its ghoul-infested North End, Providence and its jeweller's conventions, these are but ephemeral transcriptions of the real places you have so far only dimly glimpsed—basalt-towered

Dylath-Leen, Kled with its perfumed jungles, The Plateau of Leng, Yith, Cyclopean and many-columned Y'ha-nthlei. Your longing for your great-great-grandfather's Greek Revival mansion with its widow's walk and Ionic pilasters is really a longing for a certain window-less, onyx pharos on nighted Yuggoth. When you wish to don small clothes and periwig you are in truth desiring to wear the unhuman trappings, the extravagant golden tiaras and armlets of the Deep Ones . . . Soon, Howard Anable, soon you can wander in the Vaults of Zin, and consort with ghasts and Gugs."

Someone—some madman—had plainly clambered up from the yard below into Anable's window! Had Harper or one of his cult co-horts returned? I switched on the lamp on the end table. Looking out the sitting room window I could see that Mrs. Delisio had turned on the light illuminating the back-yard.

"I am the Gate," continued the wailing voice. "The Gate that stands open, ready to receive you. Dare you enter? Come, come now. . . ."

I had had enough of listening to this mad drivel. I knocked on Anable's door, then tried to open it and found that some heavy object—possibly the bed—blocked it. I threw my shoulder repeat-edly against the door, but it budged not an inch. The wind had in-creased its daemonic scream—I could no longer make out that piping voice whose youthful owner I now knew, only the thuds of books and furniture striking the floor.

With a strength born of frantic frenzy, I burst through, dislodg-ing whatever was behind the door. I was immediately overwhelmed by a loathsome stench, which caused me to reel back in nausea—but not before I saw a large, white, flowing, viscous mass leap through and shatter the upper panes of the sash window. The flying shards of glass miraculously missed me, as I dashed forward into Anable's empty, suddenly odor-free room—to the damaged window. I looked down, expecting to see Anable and his abductor in a heap in the yard below. But the only person visible was Mrs. Delisio in her dressing gown and shawl, rushing out the back door at the sound of that final crash of glass and wood. Below the window, other than the toppled trash cans and debris, *there was nothing on the ground! In the next moment I looked up—looked up toward Satan's Ledge—looked up into*

*a winter's sky that was alive with motion in unimagined space filled
with transcendent whiteness. In utter stillness.*

## VIII

Understandably, I did not linger in that house of horror. I spent
the rest of that night and the next at Miskatonic in the dorm suite of
Messrs. Hailblum, Sullivan, and Klein. I remained in Arkham only
for as long as I had to, to calm Mrs. Delisio (who had apparently not
witnessed that last, soul-blasting vision in the sky), to speak with
Mrs. Anable and to the police suggesting the theory that Anable had
been spirited off by the cult members into the hills and possibly beyond. There was no keeping the authorities out of the matter this
time. As already stated, I withdrew to Boston for the remainder of the
term, arranging to take my exams after vacation. I spent the bulk of
my vacation time composing the above narrative.

There is one more thing. In April when I returned to Arkham, I
visited Mrs. Delisio to settle my affairs with her. She had already
agreed to terminating my lease short of the appointed year, and I
wished to pay her some fair compensation. (Insurance had covered
the damaged window.) After negotiations had been concluded as af-
fably as possible under the solemn circumstances, she gave me a
sealed envelope that she had found among Anable's effects before
their removal. It had my name on it, and contained a hastily scribbled note.

3/15/29

Winsor [it began]:
    By the time you read this I'll be far beyond your med-
dling reach. Despite your best efforts to interfere I should
soon be riding through the intergalactic void on the back
of a hypoencephalic centipede, frolicking with the night-
gaunts and ghouls—or some such. I regret you won't be
joining me here, as in fact you aren't worthy to transcend the
mundane human world—the mundane human world whose
economy within a few months, it's been my privilege to learn
from Him, is in for a difficult period. You and your kind are

going to suffer, and I can't say I feel very sorry for you. Enjoy what will probably prove to be your last summer on the island. Be forewarned that hard times lie ahead.

Yrs.—HWA

Thus read Howard Wentworth Anable's last—and certainly most unfathomable—communication to me and to the world; the final testament of a once noble mind stolen away from its rightful place among men by a cosmic evil that surely deserves, as I trust my pitiful account has demonstrated, the epithet, "the madness out of space."

# Aliah Warden

## Roger Johnson

Witchcraft is an ever-present theme in the history of the county of Essex. It is like a sinister drum-beat below the even tenor of life, often unheard but always felt. I was aware, of course, of the great witchcraft trials held in the sixteenth and seventeenth centuries and of the infamous career of Matthew Hopkins, the *soi-disant* "Witchfinder-General," but I little suspected that behind these painted devils there lurked something deeper, darker, and infinitely more terrible.

Late in the year of 1902 I was invited to call upon a Mr. Giles Chater, a Chelmsford solicitor, on a matter which has no relevance to my story. What is relevant is the fact that I accepted the invitation, for it was at Mr. Chater's office that I met for the first time Aliah Warden. My business was soon concluded, and Mr. Chater had just poured for me a glass of excellent Madeira wine—of which I was very fond—when his clerk entered the office and diffidently announced that there was a gentleman to see him, a Mr. Warden. "Aliah Warden?" cried my host. "Then show him in, by all means. He may care to join us in a glass of wine."

The elderly man who followed the clerk into the office was a very singular personage. To begin with, he was not, in fact, as old as he first appeared, though his hair was quite white above a wide face that was lined with wrinkles. He and Mr. Chater greeted each other cordially, and when I was introduced to him I took careful, but, I trust, unobtrusive, note of his curious appearance. His legs were thin, very thin, and gave the impression of being longer than they actually were, in sharp contrast to his squat, round torso. They were markedly bowed, however, and he carried his trunk bent forward at a sharp angle from his hips. This strange bodily configuration of curves and angles amounted quite to a deformity, and was largely responsible for the impression of age that hung about him. His hands and feet were large, flat and square—the hands in particular having one remarkable singularity: there were small but distinct flanges of loose skin between the bases of the fingers. The large, round head was placed directly upon the stocky torso, without any sign of a neck, and seemed to be almost split in two by the wide, flat-lipped mouth. The eyes bulged uncomfortably beneath the lashless lids, and the low forehead, the small ears and the back of the very large stiff collar were almost completely covered by the shock of white hair. This hair was in itself rather peculiar, for it was worn long, in the style of thirty or forty years ago; I perceived that it was of a rather coarse, thick texture and of a quite lifeless shade of white. Physically, at least, Mr. Warden was hardly a prepossessing figure.

Mr. Chater's voice interrupted my thoughts: "I am sure you will excuse us for a few minutes," he said. "Mr. Warden is shortly to retire from his practice over in Wrabley, and we have arranged that most of his business will be transferred to me. There are just a few papers to be signed now, and then the thing is done. Don't go, however, for I understand that you have certain interests in common, and I should like you to know each other better."

Mr. Warden pursed his wide lips and then smiled. "My practice is very small these days," he remarked. "The Law and the inhabitants of Wrabley have little to do with each other."

The interests that were shared by this strange little man and me centered upon the study of that misty region of learning where psychology, anthropology and comparative religion overlap. Before the cheerful fire in our good host's office, we drank Madeira wine and talked a good deal about witchcraft, devil worship and magic, while Mr. Chater smiled and puffed stolidly at his pipe. I recall Aliah Warden remarking at one stage, "Matthew Hopkins was a fraud, sir—a charlatan. In, that is to say, his capacity as a witch-finder. Ah, he was a cunning devil. What better mask could a fox assume than that of a hunter?"

I had barely time to consider this provocative question before the clock struck five, and I realized that I must be off to the railway station, and thence back to London, where I was to dine with some friends that evening. Before I left the solicitor's office, however, Mr. Warden extended to me an invitation to call upon him at some future time at his house in Wrabley, and made a remark—flattering, I fear— to the effect that he was always pleased to converse upon his favorite subject with one who was both intelligent and knowledgeable. I gladly accepted the invitation, for the strange old man had proved to be both charming and eloquent, and I suspected that his curious exterior masked a whimsical, if grim, sense of humor, which appealed to me. It was arranged that I should spend a weekend with him towards the end of January. "I have treasures in my house," he said as we shook hands. "Things that will surprise you." I did not doubt it.

When the appointed day arrived I packed my suitcase and set off for Liverpool Street Station. My feelings, as I boarded the train for Maldon, were distinctly cheerful, for my work of late had been prosaic to the extent of being boring, and I welcomed the thought of leaving the thronged and dirty streets of London for a few days. In Wrabley, the air would be clean, and miles of marshland would separate me from the metropolis. I looked forward, too, to the erudite conversation of Aliah Warden.

Long before my train reached Maldon, however, I began to feel that I had seen enough of the Essex Marshes. I had forgotten how very bleak and how very flat is this region which is not quite land and not quite sea. The glistening mud-flats seemed somehow sinister in their isolation, and the few lonely farms and decrepit clapboard houses only seemed to emphasize the loneliness. It was hard to realize that I was little more than thirty miles from the greatest city in the world.

Maldon is an enchanting little town, a small but busy port. There was a cheerfulness about the place that day that raised my spirits, and I felt that, after all, I had made no mistake in leaving London. Until, that is, I hailed a cab and instructed the driver to take me to Wrabley. His answer was not encouraging.

"I'll take you, sir," he said, "but I can't think why you would want to go there. 'Tis the most desolate hole."

I explained that I was visiting a friend there. At that, his manner brightened a little.

"Would that be Mr. Warden, sir? Ah, he's a nice gentleman—if a bit odd. But I won't hear a word against him. He always asks for me when he wants a cab from Maldon." The cabbie was silent for a moment, brooding, while the horses pawed irritably at the cobbles. "Still and all," he said, "I don't take back what I said about Wrabley. The place is run down something rotten, and so are the people. Huh. Rotten! Yes, I reckon that's the right word. Still—" (he gave a half-smile) "if you're visiting there I musn't put you off. Get in, sir, and I'll drive you there."

As we travelled along the north bank of the estuary, skirting the jagged reed-filled inlets, it seemed that the landscape became more desolate. The mere flatness of the land made it difficult to judge distances, and I was surprised when suddenly the driver pointed ahead with his whip at a low, jagged prominence and said, "There's Murrell Hill, sir. We'll be in the village shortly." I soon realized that the hill was covered in buildings—indeed, it was here that Aliah Warden had his house—and that it was this that gave it that curious rugged appearance.

The village, or rather town, had hardly spread at all on the landward side, but rather seemed to huddle about the little creek, where the weatherboarded buildings leaned precariously upon each other. We approached from the west, however, entering directly into the cobbled road that ran over the low hill. The houses were very large, suggesting considerable wealth, but it soon became evident that this wealth must have been spent long ago, for most of the buildings were in sadly poor repair. Only two or three houses survived in good condition—these and a solitary public building, a hall of some kind, whose doric portico bore the single word "Dagon," in discrete Roman letters.

The cab pulled up before one of the better houses, and the driver climbed down and opened the door for me. "This is the place, sir," he said. "Mr. Warden's house." As I paid him the agreed fare, I could not help observing that even here three windows of the eight in the not unhandsome frontage lacked curtains. With some misgivings, I lifted the heavy brass door-knocker.

My welcome, however, was as cordial as I could have wished.

Aliah Warden greeted me effusively, almost hopping along the hallway in his eagerness. This curious movement unlocked a door in my
mind, and I realized with a start what I had unconsciously recognized at our first meeting—that Aliah Warden, physically, bore a remarkable resemblance to a *frog*. I was strongly reminded of Tenniel's
depiction of the frog-gardner in *Through the Looking Glass*, and I was
unable to restrain a smile, which, fortunately, my host misinterpreted.
"Ah," he said, "you are looking forward to seeing my treasures? All in
good time, my dear fellow. First, I think, a glass of wine, and then
something to eat."

It appeared that Mr. Warden was his own cook and housekeeper,
and he suggested that while he prepared a meal for me I might care to
inspect his collection of books and various *objects d'art* which he had
accumulated during his delvings into what he called "the world's
most fascinating pastime."

Here were treasures indeed. One large room was almost entirely taken up by his library, and I soon realized that the man must
be possessed of learning far beyond anything I had suspected. I saw
Scot's *Discoverie of Witchcraft*, Stearne's *Confirmation and Discovery
of Witchcraft*, Mather's *Magnalia Christi Americana*, and others—
numerous others—with which I was familiar, but many of the books
were quite unknown to me, while others I had long believed to
be fabulous, having no existence outside the imaginations of certain
perverse cultists. There were handwritten volumes, bearing such
titles as *Cultes des Goules*, *Unaussprechlichen Kulten* and *De Vermis
Mysteriis*. Ah! And here was a title that I recognized, though I had
never thought that book actually existed. The volume was bound in
scarred and stained leather, and printed in tiny blackletter characters,
and on its spine was the one word *Necronomicon*. The title page gave
the information that this "treatise" was the work of one Abdul El-
Hazred, translated into English by John Dee, Doctor, in the Year
of Grace 1605. My host, it seemed, was a very surprising man indeed,
and one very learned in dark and mysterious matters. One particular name printed in fine gold characters on black leather, caught
my attention. I knew from my history lessons at school that Sir
Geoffrey de Lacy had fought beside the Conqueror at Hastings, and
that in the year 1067 he had been granted the manor and the earl-
dom of Ashton in Derbyshire, which manor became the city of

Ashton de Lacy. I knew nothing of any interest on the old warrior's part in matters of demonology, and yet here was his name above the Latin title: *De Potentiae Deorum Antiquorum.* Curious, I took the book from its shelf and glanced at the title page. This edition, it appeared, was revised and translated from the Latin in the year 1763 by one Thomas Dashwood Morley, who called himself *Frater Medramae*—a Brother of Medmenham. I began to peruse its contents.

I was gazing with some awe at one of the diabolical engravings which illustrated the book, when I became suddenly aware of Aliah Warden, standing behind me and peering over my shoulder. "Interesting, sir, is it not?" he said. There was a peculiar tone to his voice. "That is a rather fanciful representation of one of the Deep Ones, a creature that de Lacy claimed to have met and conversed with. The Deep Ones, you know, are the legendary servants of Dagon, the fish-god of the Philistines."

He paused, but before I could compose myself and put the question that was in my mind about the pillared Hall of Dagon that stood upon this very hill, he had turned over a few pages, and was speaking again. "This set of characters, sir, is a paean to the transcendental Kingdom of Voor. It is written in the letters of the Aklo, which are said to be a revelation from certain dark forces to their chosen apostles. Not many uninitiated have seen those letters. You are a privileged man, sir. Privileged." With that, he closed the book and motioned me into the next room where my meal awaited me. As I had half-suspected, it consisted principally of fish.

The picture of the Deep One had impressed me considerably, for the creature it depicted appeared some half-way between a man and a frog, having distinctly batrachian characteristics, but standing almost erect, like a man. Despite the fact that it was clad in a long, diaphanous robe, and was adorned with various primitive, if rich, accoutrements, the thing, in its overall appearance, reminded me more than anything of Aliah Warden.

"The marshlands," said my host, as I reclined comfortably in an armchair, with a post-prandial cigarette, "have long been the haunt of witches. They are so isolated, you see, and their people are accustomed to uncover the secrets both of the land and of the sea. They are, one might say, amphibious." He stopped short for a moment, and I half fancied that I saw a faint blush beneath the gray pallor of his wrinkled face.

"What of Wrabley, itself?" I asked. "The place seems so desolate, so decrepit."

"Hah! You may well ask! Half the houses are deserted—you have only to go down to the waterfront to see what I mean. The timbers are rotten, the walls are cracked, the windows are broken. And yet, people live here, though you would not see many of them, for they will have nothing to do with foreigners. Oh, yes, Wrabley is *in* England, but do not delude yourself that it is *of* England. The allegiance here is to something much older and far more powerful. Let me tell you of Dagon, for he is the true master here."

Again, the old man paused, and seemed somehow to be ill at ease. Then, bracing himself, he continued: "His minions, the Deep Ones, are mentioned in many texts, some of which may be found on these shelves. It becomes plainer the more one reads that it is the supreme test of these creatures, the duty for which they are born and bred, to do nothing less than precipitate the final Armageddon. And that, sir, is fact. Fact!" His voice was low and husky, and his expression arresting. I began to fear for the man's sanity. "When the stars are in their appointed places, then shall Dagon lead his servants to the living tomb of the One before whom even he is as nothing and less than nothing, and there they shall remove the seal that binds him, and he shall rise in all his majesty and terror, and open the cosmic gate to the unspeakable and unknowable things that lurk outside. Cthulhu! Great Cthulhu! See here, here! The words of Dashwood Morley, as he writes of the return of the terrible Priest-God."

I stared at the passage to which he pointed, one of Morley's "revisions" to old de Lacy's book. So startled was I that it was several seconds before I could comprehend the insane words.

He knows Them but dimly, yet His is the most urgent task of all, for when the stars shall be in their set places, and the times between be as the times that were, and are, and shall be, then shall He be awoken, and the prisoning Seal be lifted. Then the Deep Ones shall be as one with their Masters, and They outside shall be freed once more to possess Their especial Realm. After day comes night, and after night, day. Ia! Their day shall be your night. They sleep now, but where you are, They were, and where you are now, They shall be.

"For many untold aeons," said Warden, breathlessly, "Cthulhu has lain beneath the Seal of the Old Ones, far under the ocean, sleeping and dreaming foully, but the stars are approaching their proper positions, and the god is restless. The Deep Ones have not been idle in preparing his way. I give you warning!"

The old man gulped, and peered around him nervously. Then he steadied himself, but I could see that there was a twitch or tic affecting the lid of his protuberant left eye.

"Witchcraft, I said, and witches they are, but in Wrabley they worship a darker devil than ever that fool James could have imagined! The Deep Ones may, perhaps, be considered as a parallel development to mammalian life. For centuries, our sailors have told tales of intelligent life in the sea. Nonsense! said some. Mermaids, said others. Mermaids! Hah! If only they knew. . . .

"The Deep Ones, you see, have interbred with human beings."

"My dear sir!" I protested. "This is outlandish! Quite absurd. Mere superstition."

"No, no!" he replied, warmly. "It is truth, sir. Truth! Oh, it has happened in many places—in islands of the warm southern seas, and in the civilized world, too. In England, at Gate's Quay, and at Wyvern, and here. Hah! Yes, here, at Wrabley! Here!"

He was working himself up now, sweating profusely, and the twitch was more marked. Now that it was wet, his crusty skin seemed somehow curiously scaly, and his eyes bulged horribly. I was too taken aback to interrupt him, and he continued, stammering rather.

"Back—oh, hundreds of years back—in the early seventeenth century, the books say . . . The people here don't remember when, you see, but they remember *what!* The thing that Jabez Martyr brought back with him from beyond the Indies—the thing that he called his wife. Why were the sailor's children not seen again when they reached maturity? It was then, I tell you, then that the decline set in . . . Oh, yes, this town had been an important maritime centre; it was a borough, but where is its glory now? Gone with the coming of the outsiders! Fish, fish became the support of the people of the town. Fish, that the men of Maldon and Lowestoft could never match. But they didn't sell it, you see; they ate it. And they kept themselves to themselves. Hah! Do *you* know why the men of the marshes shun Wrabley, as they have done for centuries? And what goes on in that Hall of Dagon, while the church is empty? *I know. And why do the townsfolk look only half-human?"* The old man seemed near to collapsing with his insane exhaustion. I was alone with a madman in the darkness of a winter night, and I shuddered at the thought. He noticed, and smiled grimly. "Look at me!" he commanded. *"Look at me!* Am I not living proof of hell here on earth? Oh, Dagon! Why have you delayed so long? Why torment me, when whether I will or not I must soon go to join my brothers beneath the waters and prepare for the triumph that is to come?" He was racked suddenly by uncontrollable sobs; tears filled his huge eyes, and his narrow shoulders shuddered. The man was mad! Utterly, incurably mad!

Then he saw the expression on my face, and his own showed anger. "You don't believe!" he cried. "Hah! I'll show you! I had my pride once, and why do you think I have so much hair on this venerable head, when I could not grow a beard ever? See, see, unbeliever!"

Shockingly, inexorably, he demonstrated the very truth of the insanity of this world. We live our lives in a mist, and when it is lifted, be it only for a second, stark horror is revealed. When I saw what I saw, I fled in awe and disgust from that haunted house in that haunted town. I ran, stumbling and tottering from Wrabley, until I reached the outskirts of Maldon, and there I collapsed, exhausted, and lay under a hedge until daybreak, when I might catch the first train home to London, safety, and sanity. Even now, I can feel only fear and horror for the creature that I left, collapsed, twitching and moaning, as in a fit, in that house on Murrell Hill, for what I saw was this:

Aliah Warden put his hand, his webbed hand, to his head, and *lifted off* his benevolent mop of white hair. I hardly heard him as he muttered, "I had my pride, and I was human, once. . . ." For I saw, and realized horribly, that *the grey, bald skin of his head was closely covered with coarse, icthyic scales, while behind and below his little ears were two rudimentary growths that might or might not be gills.*

# The Last Supper

## Donald R. Burleson

The place had a hellish appearance on a night like this. My heart was quickened both by the phantasmal landscape and by the prospect of the awesomely significant and darkly appropriate deed which lay ahead. This was Prescott Village Burial Ground—one of those ancient and obscure New England graveyards of which no aesthetically sensitive ghoul could fail to be fond, lying as it did on a rutted and little-travelled road, with a weed-banked and sombre-looking river flowing sluggishly behind the backmost stone fence, and with nothing on either side save untenanted and dreary stretches of rocky terrain.

The graveyard itself was a ghoul's delight, extending a considerable distance back from the gate by the road, and from the rickety wooden shack used by the night watchman—back over sable undulations of sparsely grass-covered ground spotted at close intervals by tombstones which were at first the markers of relatively recent interments, but which became, as one progressed toward the back, older and more ill-preserved, until in a dark corner farthest removed from the road the stones became those black slate relics which marked, with their archaic inscriptions and ponderous carvings, the slumbering places of the town's early settlers.

This most ancient corner was to me artistically the most pleasing, especially with a hazy sky above the mound-hovering willows, and especially with a faintly soughing wind which stirred the trees into a slight but charming animation. But, quite apart from such aesthetic considerations, I must confess that the newer portions of this quaint necropolis were of more direct and practical meaning to me, because in the immemorial backmost graves whose slate markers bore inscriptions belonging to the eighteenth century, there was now nothing of which a questing ghoul could make a morsel. The nearer and more recent graves had indeed known defilement not only by me but by a number of my companions of kindred appetite.

It was because of the untimely death of one of those nocturnal practitioners of profanation, in fact, that my surviving friends and I had come here on this special night, had come for uncommon feastings. Ghouls we all were, with such an unholy kinship of sympathetic understanding that we had never even discussed the particular night on which we must gather in solemn conclave—we had simply known, and had come. We were unseen, but we were present.

The only visible motion in all this gloomy scene was the bobbing of the light as the venerable night watchman made his rounds, shuffling phlegmatically along the paths among the graves and taking copious pulls at the bottle which he kept, we well knew, close at hand. We watched in morbid and quiet amusement from our various dark hiding places—here behind a large gnarled oak, there behind an especially broad slab, there again in the shadow of a mound, everywhere concealment was offered. Drawing occasionally into deeper shadow as the light swung near, we watched the perambulating figure, watched even as he stepped past the very grave whose compelling interest had drawn us together.

This was the grave of Rowley Ames, whom we had all known and revered over many years of forbidden pleasure-taking: Rowley Ames, whose virtuosic command of the art of ghoulery my companions and I could only regard with profound respect and, in truth, genuine awe. He had been the Master, and a young person of necrophagous inclination could do no better than to study at the side of this inspiring and inspired nocturnal lurker, observing and imitating him as he deliberated upon the time and place of his conquest, exhumed some carefully chosen subject from the charnel earth, and spent the next hour immersed in unhallowed rending and chewing, as only a truly gifted artist might.

I had learned much from him myself, and I was here tonight, as were my colleagues, to pay grateful last respects—not the insipid memorials of his idiotically conventional funeral weeks before, but the one single, special tribute that we could best lavish upon him. We had all understood from the outset, naturally, that the unique tribute to be paid Rowley Ames must consist of our gathering at his grave for one wholly remarkable feast: the eating of his own long monstrously-nourished carcass.

Of course it would be a symbolic act; there were fully twelve of us, the remainder of a corpse-devouring coven minus its erstwhile leader, and for each of us his body, especially wasted as it was by his final illness, would provide only a token ingestion—but it would be enough, and it would be, we felt, the one way he would have wanted to be remembered. We had waited, by common tacit understanding, several weeks for a proper putrescence, and now it was time. "Only the man of intellect and judgment," the gastronomer Brillat-Savarin has reminded us, "knows how to eat."

I watched with some impatience from my point of concealment, as I knew the others were watching, while the shuffling lantern-bearer completed his rounds and returned to the decrepit shack near the front gate. Before long he had collapsed into the usual alcoholic stupor, and we emerged from the shadows to get on with our affair.

Under a pallid moon we gathered at the grave of Rowley Ames and exchanged silent but knowing glances. The grave was situated not, of course, in the backmost archaic corner which had so appealed to his sense of aesthetic charm, but rather in the newer section amidst actual former recipients of his nocturnal attentions. Indeed, it was ironic that the two graves flanking his own were graves which, as it happened, his hands and teeth had once defiled. And now it was his turn—we had come to pay him the ultimate tribute.

Words can scarcely convey the eagerness, the titillation, the sense of reverential awe with which we delved into the foul earth, turning an occasional furtive eye over the shoulder to see that we were un-observed, or indulging in an occasional appreciative glance at the wan moonlit sky forming, with the phantasmal willows overhanging mossy stones, so ghastly a setting for our anticipated deed. We fairly drooled in that anticipation, our mouths working and moving as if al-ready busy at delectable subterranean pleasures. As we worked fever-ishly to uncover his coffin, my uppermost thought was sometimes my respect for my old Master and sometimes simply the gustatory ecstasy that was to come with the devouring of one who himself had fed upon countless upheaved boxes of carrion delight. And in the midst of such musings I felt my hand reach a hard surface through the clammy soil, and knew that the feast was to commence forthwith.

Wheezing and panting with the exertion, we lifted the coffin up onto level ground and gathered about it in a circle of anxious faces. There in that charnel scene of spectral, sickly moon, morbid landscape, and sighing night wind, we were gathered, his faithful students in unspeakable arts, ready to behold his miasmal remains, to admire, to partake. We mouthed certain blasphemous litanies appropriate to the ceremoniousness of the occasion, and pried open the casket.

It took us a few seconds to understand what we were seeing. By what unthinkable process I do not know—but by some inconceivable organic process, he lived! He *lived*! Rowley Ames was animate, stirring—though flaggingly, as if he were now dying anew.

But it was not this fact, in itself, that sent us precipitately scattering in revulsion and dismay—not the mere fact of his odd reanimation or the hollow, sardonic laugh with which he greeted us as the coffin lid was raised. We might have been glad, on the contrary, to experience such unanticipated, unimaginable reunion with our Master—certainly our reaction would not normally have been to disperse headlong into the night and leave that scene at the grave site which a reporter would describe with so much disgust in the newspaper the following day.

No—what seemed insupportable to us, rather, was the fact that the consummate ghoul Rowley Ames lay there in his coffin with a hideously bloated belly but with most of the rest of the sinewy, wormy mass of his body loathsomely gnawed away. The wretch had waited, too, though not quite so long as we, and, writhing into queer animation in his coffin, *had eaten his own putrid flesh.*

# The Church at Garlock's Bend

## David Kaufman

Above Scranton, the Susquehanna is narrower and more wind-ing, and it is far more interesting as it switchbacks its way from the northwest out of New York than is the slower and more stately part of the river to the south. It flows through land that for a highly populated state is sometimes surprisingly primitive, and it is not too difficult, were you to travel its length through the hills of north cen-tral Pennsylvania, to come to one of a dozen or more small towns, towns with sometimes only twenty or so houses, with perhaps a store and a church—towns that time and progress seem to have ignored or forgotten. And the people who live in them or around them, while never overtly unfriendly, for reasons of their own keep to themselves and do not seem to care much for the rest of the world.

Above Skinner's Eddy, Garlock's Bend was such a town. I grew up on a farm just a few miles downstream, and my first memories of it are as lazy and slow as the summer heat in the green hills. It is a ghost town now, just a bunch of tired and worn out buildings, some of them leaning precariously—rotted wood on rotten foundations. But when I was young it was vital and as prosperous as such a small town so out of the way could possibly be.

It was the river that did it. It was the river and the thing that hap-pened in the river that took the spirit out of the town and caused its people to, I don't know, to just move away—one family, sometimes two families at a time. And then they were all gone. The town was abandoned.

Garlock's Bend was right *on* the river, or on a swell of it (we locals with typical Pennsylvania Dutch enthusiasm actually called it a lake, although it was only just a very wide, slow spot where the river came thrashing out of the tight hills, calming quickly, deepening, and widening), and the church was tight down against the water, shaded and cooled by a stand of large sycamore. They were things to look at from a piece downstream—the trees, the town, the church, and the high hills behind the whole of it. They were things that could make you love Garlock's Bend.

We were one of the first families to move away, and although I am sure we fussed about it, we children were never told why we left. There was some vague talk about my father getting a job down in Harrisburg, but I thought without ever saying it that there was some other reason. In the week or ten days before our departure my parents seemed quite agitated, especially so my father. Often they would stop talking if we came near them, or they would change the subject, talking a little too fast and a little too loudly. And we were in those last few days sternly forbidden to go anywhere near the river.

There was something so urgent in that command that we never questioned it.

Anyway, we left. I would have much preferred to stay in those familiar hills near the friends of all my youth, but I had the fickle inattentive mind of a youngster, and soon I had some new playmates down in Harrisburg. Bit by bit I came to realize that Garlock's Bend was not the only place in the world. Bit by bit I put it out of my mind.

Now I am a mathematician by profession. In certain narrow circles I am quite well known. And so it was not at all unusual for me to find myself invited to lecture this past summer session at Staunton, a small liberal arts college just a dozen or so miles down river from Garlock's Bend. I would once again, by lucky chance, visit the land of my youth. And while I might never have returned solely to visit my home town, I was happy to avail myself of the chance, now that it seemed so convenient.

Curiously, after I accepted the position, and starting almost at the *moment* I accepted, I began to feel a much stronger urge to return. I quickly came to the point that I could not get Garlock's Bend out of my mind. And as I remembered things long ago childishly dismissed, as I remembered the river, I had strange, concomitant feelings of uneasiness, of unbalance, of distaste even, begin to grow within me. It was, the whole of it, a curious mix of pleasure and displeasure, of delight and dread, and had I known what was in store for me, I would have yielded to these sudden mixed and mostly unhappy feelings and stayed away.

I wish I had.

When you visit Garlock's Bend you drive down out of extremely high hills to the valley below. As the descent begins, you come suddenly out of the thick green forest, and the whole of the valley then seems to open up. And you catch glimpses of the town now and again at overlooks as the narrow road curls downward, vaguely following the churning and thrashing of the rapidly falling river, into the valley far below.

I stopped at several of these overlooks the day I arrived, for pleasure at first because I had not even seen the town in some forty years, and *never* from that vantage point, and then I stopped because I felt myself drawn to the overlooks. It was as if I wanted to take in the whole of the town before I came to it. As if I wanted to revisit at once all of my lost past.

But nothing that I could see from the high hills told me anything but that the town was indeed deserted, decrepit, downfallen. I was overcome with sudden feelings of hopelessness, of sadness, of a strange kind of loneliness. And I was astonished at the intensity of these feelings.

When I had come down out of the hills, I dropped off the main highway onto the old dirt road that crawled along the river, past thick stands of hemlock and thin scraggly brush, until it came to Garlock's Bend, and then I made my way carefully down the only street of the silent little town. It was like driving backwards into time. I eased my car around the debris that was strewn about haphazardly. It looked as if no one had even *been on* Main Street for years. I parked just opposite the remains of Miller's, Garlock's Bend's only hardware store. The Saturday mornings I had spent there with my father! And now the roof of the front porch had fallen down, and the large picture window was broken. I could hardly see into the building, but it seemed probable to me that looters had taken all they possibly could, and then time and the dust had gotten the better of what was left.

I spent an hour or more just walking the length of that desolate town, peering into any window, any nook or cranny that I might, sudden little insights, like memories pricking at my consciousness, like long forgotten melodies. It was a bittersweet pastime.

Suddenly, there it was. Off ahead of me in the distance, down tight to the edge of the water, the church of all my youth. In every one of my fantasies concerning Garlock's Bend I always came again to the church. It had been the center of so much that I remembered with pleasure.

Soon I was standing down by the water, looking up through the trees at the double doors and the wooden cross just above them. The church somehow seemed new and clean. I remember noting how curious that was, and how small and timid the whole of it made me feel. The only notion I had of sound was the gentle lapping of the river. No other sound. Long years before I had climbed the few steps before the church dozens of times and more. Hundreds of times. And now circumstances had changed me so completely that I marveled at how like an interloper I felt myself to be.

Also, I had a curious sense of whimsy because of the poor condition of the steps. Odd, I thought, that I might go crashing through and break an arm or a leg. The thought made me doubly cautious because had such a thing happened it would have been dreadful—from all that I had seen I was certain there was no one around in all that desolation to rescue me.

I moved carefully through the old building, conscious of the dust, the ubiquitous dust, and the mordant smells of the past. It is curious how smells alone can pull lost memories back into our consciousness with a swiftness that astonishes. The smells of that old church took me quickly and completely.

I soon found myself sitting in the dusty pew that our family had used long ago, and I admit to being almost overcome with nostalgia. I do not know how long I sat there, lost in those memories of my youth. Some tens of minutes at least.

It was then so quiet I could hear the stillness of the place ringing in my ears. And it seemed to me, lost as I was in all that stillness, that if I really listened, if I really tried to hear, just vaguely and faraway I *could* hear, with pristine clarity, the voices of my folks and my friends of long ago, singing all the old songs. I wanted to weep, as do we all at such times I suspect, for my lost innocence.

How temporal life suddenly seemed to me.

I was brought round rather quickly. I *had* thought myself to be totally alone—in that silent church and in that forgotten town. I never would have dreamed it could be otherwise. But suddenly, from somewhere in the cellar of the church, just beneath me, I distinctly heard a low heavy thud, as if something of extreme weight had just fallen.

A few seconds of utter silence and then I heard the thing slam again, more clearly still. And then once more.

To say that I was startled by that knocking would be something of an understatement. But I remember that at the time I was only slightly frightened.

There are times in our lives when without reason we act foolishly, even irrationally. We do things we could not possibly later explain. *Now* I know how irrational was my next act; *then* it seemed to me to be the most natural thing in the world to do.

At the time my immediate and only thought was that I should go down into the cellar and find the source of the noise. Never mind the fact that I was alone and in a totally isolated place—a place where there could *be* no strange sounds, a place where there could not possibly be anything to *make* such noises.

I quickly found the door to the cellar. It was stuck from disuse, but with a series of impatient little jerks I managed to get it open just wide enough to squeak through. I could only imagine how foolish I must look, pulling and fretting at that crepitating door, flustering the dry dust that swirled in the little shafts of sunlight that came through the simple stained glass windows.

There was only silence now from below. Silence so loud as to almost ring in my ears.

The little wooden steps down into the cellar were narrow and badly rotted. I thought again of crashing through steps and there being no one who would ever know, no one who could ascribe an end to me. But the thought did not stay with me for long, so determined was I.

"Hello?" I called. "Hello? Is anyone down there?"

How *that* could be was something that did not occur to me to wonder about in my excitement. The floor above was covered with a thin layer of dry gray dust which only I had disturbed. All tracks were mine. I was indeed alone.

Now on the steps I noticed that the dust, which above was powdery and dry, was almost black and was oily or even waxy in texture, from the dampness and decay below the ground level, and the air was musty and stale, as if it had been bottled in for years.

I moved down the stairs carefully. The black dust was everywhere. It almost seemed slippery, and I had no wish to fall.

"Hello?" I called again, and then, as I began to realize how foolish the thought was that I might not be alone, sounds or no sounds, I smiled at my ingenuousness.

The only light in the cellar came from the two small windows at ground level. They were wretchedly dirty, but there was certainly light enough to see by, and quickly I was standing at the bottom of the wooden steps, in a state of excitement now about what I might find, and not a little impressed by my own daring.

The walls of the cellar were everywhere made of cut sandstone. Massive those walls, at least a foot thick (judging from the depth at the windows), and everywhere gray-red and covered with that same oily black patina. And sweating moisture and dankness and mildew until the whole of the cellar seemed a dismal wet dungeon.

The smell was awful. It was not the healthy acrid smell of age in the room above—this was the musty odor of rottenness and decay. And it seemed to me that the stench got worse and worse as I clambered down the fragile little steps, almost as if it were layered like thicknesses of slate and were denser at the bottom.

I looked carefully around the room, for what I did not know. I began to feel more than a bit uneasy now because of the stench and because I could see nothing that might have caused such knocking as I had heard.

I knew, as clearly as I know I am one day to die, that I had heard those noises. But there was nothing very unusual down there, nothing that was not covered with the dust of almost a half a century. Nor was there a sign of any disturbance. All was as time and neglect should have made it.

Across the room was just one little table that I could see. It was the only furniture in the whole of the cellar. But it was at least something, so I moved closer.

The table was ordinary and of little note, but beneath it, curiously, rested a wooden box that seemed half full of set mortar. A few small hand tools—a sledge, a trowel, a small claw hammer—lay carelessly strewn beside the box, everything long covered with the distasteful dust.

It was on the next wall, and it was the cause of everything.

It was the river wall, actually, fairly close to the table. On this was a clumsy bricked-in patch some four feet high by three feet in width. The sandstone blocks were patched in with a facing of ordinary red brick. The thing was quite visible, in spite of its coating of the loathsome dust, and so unusual that I felt a very real slash of fear. I flushed coldly when I saw it.

By this time I was sufficiently off balance from the horrible knocks and nauseated by the pungent smells that I was trembling. I stared at the patch for some time before deciding that I could bring myself to examine it.

I moved closer.

There were some loose bricks and a half empty bag of cement on the floor just to one side, and although the whole area was obscured by the heavy layer of oppressive dust, the patch gave every indication of being a jerry-built job. I could tell easily that the mortar between the bricks was not struck, the floor in the vicinity had apparently not been cleaned after the job was finished, and spilled little piles of mortar and the general cluttered look of the area suggested at best a slipshod piece of work, at worst a job frantically undertaken and frantically finished.

The bricks were recently bulged, as if the patch had almost been burst through, and where the bricks were loosened, the greasy dust was now darker, even more greasy looking, *wet* looking, and it was apparent to me that water was leaking through the bricks.

And then the thing happened that I shall never forget.

At first it was no more than an awareness that came to me, a feeling that something was amiss, that something was not right. I remember it caused me to stop all movement and listen. And then a slight whisper of a noise that grew and grew and became more real— a heavy gurgling sound it was, a kind of grinding or rushing, from behind the wall. It increased and increased in intensity until in terror I tumbled backwards, and then the next thing I knew I was frantically crayfishing away from the wall.

There was a deafening crash against the patch.

The patch seemed to *give*, several inches at least, in a sudden frightening bulge, the result of the awful smash it endured, and water spurted out from one side as if the whole of it was about to yield to the heavy force in the water. I lurched backwards crazily, convulsing, arching for air to breathe, until I slammed into the steps. I could not take my eyes from that hideous spurting water. In these few seconds enough had come through the wall to cover the floor. All I could think of was that it was about to burst its way completely through the weakened patch and engulf me. I was convinced in that second that I really was about to die.

I turned and scrambled up the oily black steps, thrust myself violently at the door and strained to be through it. My lungs and legs ached with pain. I raced the length of the church, almost vaulted the few little steps outside, and stopped, exhausted and nauseated, just short of the river. I grabbed at one of the trees and literally hugged it to keep from falling. I wept from relief. My clothing was covered with black slimy filth from the dust and water. My head was pounding, my flesh crawling.

For some long moments all I could manage was to cling to that tree and just gulp in deep delicious lungfuls of clean, fresh air. How good that was!

With benign indifference, a gust of wind made a deep swirl of a wave on the lake, and then was gone.

Still I clung to the tree. As I came round and began to breathe a bit more easily, I knew that somehow I was free of whatever it was that had made the great and terrible knocking I had heard, that I had heard and even *felt* the power of. I was outside the church, and I was free.

Essentially that is what happened to me the day I went into the church at Garlock's Bend. I have not shortened or embellished the details. All of it is truth. I saw nothing. There were no ghosties or ghoulies, no hairy antlered monstrosities from God alone knows where, trying to swallow me up or wrench away my immortal soul. I never saw anything.

But all the same I heard the noises. I endured that awful stench. And I saw the wall give.

Something was down there. *Some*thing.

Still holding onto the tree I began to calm. I grew less frightened. I looked up at the doors to the church, the cross above them, the motionless branches. All of it appeared so serene and so wholesome. And with the setting sun at the end of the valley and the absolute stillness of the lake, the ghost town of Garlock's Bend seemed to me to be almost innocent.

But I could never again believe that. I *knew*. I knew for certain.

Aching almost as if I had been physically beaten, I limped wearily up Main Street past all the abandoned businesses and homes, this time all but oblivious to the utter and complete desolation of the town. I sat for some minutes in my car, still in something of a daze. Now that I no longer needed adrenaline, it left me and I was suddenly completely exhausted.

And then, in awe of all that had happened, feeling very alone and very old, I eased the car into gear, pulled out onto the pathetic little debris-cluttered street, and left Garlock's Bend forever.

I did go to Staunton. I taught the summer seminar as I had intended. I saw no point in doing otherwise. When I was not teaching I thought a great deal about what had happened to me, about what had caused the awesome noises, about the terrors I felt so thoroughly. Those terrors were replaced with anger, and then in time with a kind of sad acceptance.

I decided to keep my story to myself. I was afraid, I suppose, that no one would believe me. And in the end I had no proof of anything.

Then one day, just a few days short of the end of the classes and my proposed return to Pittsburgh, I was sitting in the Oak Grove, enjoying my usual lunch of hard cheese and good bread.

Staunton is a fairly wealthy school, and so the gardens of the Oak Grove are well kept. It is not unusual to see a whole group of workers—pruning, weeding, planting—keeping to their tasks, laughing among themselves, but all the while inevitably working. It is the Pennsylvania Dutch ethic, and it is still typical of the area.

One of the oldest of the crew, however, I had been feeling for several noontimes, had been doing his best to keep his eyes off me, but with little success. Once or twice I caught him in a downright stare, and while he quickly looked away and avoided my glance, it was apparent that he had a deep interest in me. I was more intrigued than irritated.

On this present day he seemed as if he could avoid my company no longer, and at the lunch break he came and sat on the bench just opposite mine, unpacked his bucket very slowly and precisely, and stared at me while he chewed resolutely on what appeared to be a sandwich of Lebanon bologna.

I sensed his exquisite shyness and knew that the first move had to come from me. "Fine afternoon," I tried.

He nodded. And then, with a wry smile, "I think I know you," he said. "I think you must be Eugene Leventry's oldest boy."

I was stunned. "How in the world did you know that?" I cried. "And who are you anyhow?"

"Aach, you wouldn't remember me," he said, his voice thick Pennsylvania Dutch. He shook his head slowly. "You were just a little fella when you left here. You wouldn't know me at all. I'm Amos Myers. I knew your daddy."

"Of course," I cried. "Of *course* I remember you."

"I *knew* you was his boy," he said. He smiled broadly and came and sat by my side. His big paw of a hand almost crushed mine with enthusiasm as we greeted each other.

Then began a conversation that lasted for over an hour. The Pennsylvania Dutch are very orderly and very polite, and so we began by dealing with all the usual pleasantries. I asked of his history and he asked of mine. I learned that his nephew, Aaron Myers, had just frightened the whole family by having a heart attack. He was related by marriage to my second cousin on my father's side, over to Skinner's Eddy, and did I know that he had gone all through college and was an animal doctor? He was coming around, though, and going to live, thank the Good Lord. For my part I revealed to Amos, because he genuinely seemed to want to know, that my parents were both dead, that I was alone, that I had never married.

During all of that I was deciding to abandon my reticence and bring up the subject of Garlock's Bend. Somehow I came to feel as if I had to. Maybe because he knew my father.

"I've been teaching here all summer," I began. "I, uh, I went to Garlock's Bend when I first arrived." I hesitated for just a few moments and then added, "I visited the church."

He stopped working on the sandwich.

"There is something in that church," I said carefully, "that does not like people."

He was quiet for some moments. The muscles in his face seemed to tighten. He put down the sandwich. "You should not have gone there," he said quietly. "That place is shunned."

"I'm sorry," I said. "There is no way I could have known that. I've been away from Garlock's Bend for so many years."

And then it all came out. The whole of it. Soon I could not stop and did not want to stop. I told him about the awesome heavy knocking, about the hideous odors in that cellar, and I tried to describe for him the terror I felt when I was convinced I was about to die.

"But I never saw anything," I concluded, embarrassed, almost as if apologizing. "I never saw a thing."

The whole of Amos's body came round as he turned stiff-necked to stare at me for at least a minute. He looked very grave. "Never saw anything? No one ever saw anything," he said finally. "No one ever saw *nothing*."

He sat quietly. I could tell that he was deciding whether it was proper. I was essentially a stranger, and that made confiding in me a very large venture for him.

When he began, I thought at first that he sounded unconcerned, as if he were describing something that had affected him only from a distance. As if over the years it had become a sort of fairy tale. Something he took pleasure in telling to worthy strangers, like a soldier might rehearse a battle of little ultimate importance.

I was wrong.

When he had finished retelling it for me, he was weeping, weeping for his lost town and his lost friends, and for much more than that, and I knew that I had someone who understood, far better than I ever could, what was happening and what *had* happened so many years before at Garlock's Bend.

"We knew something was there, though," he began. "We knew it, right enough. Something unreal. We knew it when Joe Michaels was trapped in the lake just a little ways from Miller's Hardware. Suspended out there like something down under the water had him by the legs and wouldn't let go. He was waist deep in the water, out maybe fifteen feet from the shore, and just held there."

Amos was getting into the story now, easing into it as he might put on a glove, and telling it slowly and completely.

"And him yelling out crazy at first and then later babbling like a baby about how he was going to die. About what the thing was doing to him under the water. And why didn't we help him. Whatever it was kept a hold on him for a night and a morning. A Sunday morning." He turned his body again so that he could see me.

"It was mocking us, holding him like that. It was an unholy thing, and I'll never forget it. Old Joe was stuck out in the water, right in the floodlights we had put on him that night and all. He was just held there, like I said. All the men on shore, watching, feeling helpless because we couldn't do nothing. We couldn't save Joe. We tried, hard. We got nowhere. Then we got to just sitting there, waiting, not even moving hardly. Just staring at him in the water. And him motionless now. And off to the church the women had gone, and they were singing hymns. Singing hymns peaceful like. For Joe, you see. That was a lot of years ago, and I remember it just as clear."

It seemed to me that he was breathing heavier now, and sighing a lot. "Well," he said, and then stopped. He strained around to look at me again, "I don't suppose that your daddy told you any of this."

I shook my head.

"No, I didn't think so," he said. He was quiet for a long time. "Late in the morning the thing, whatever it was, started to pull him down, and one of the men killed old Joe. Just as it took him under."

His eyes were glistening now with the memory of it, his hands going in hopeless little circles, and I could not help but wonder how his life had been changed, to remember so deeply and mourn so deeply after so many years.

"With a shotgun."

"My God," I said.

"What could we do? Let it take him? It was his best friend that killed him. But any of us would of done it. None of us would of let it get him under the water alive." Amos shrugged. "And then there wasn't even nothing to show that old Joe was ever out there. The water was quiet, and he was gone."

"That's a horrible story," I managed, and somehow I felt more concern for Joe Michaels, gone nearly fifteen years, than for myself and my own tale. "It seems so unfair."

"It's true," he said. "It's a true story."

He was quiet for a few moments. "Well, that just sort of took the heart out of the town. Some people did leave, like I said." He paused.

"Your daddy took his family." He managed a smile and reached over and patted my leg gently. "Those who stayed shunned the river. Completely. And no one told anyone outside Garlock's Bend. That may seem foolish now, but it's the truth. It was sort of like a sickness or a disease we all shared, and didn't want anyone to hear of."

"I don't know what to say."

"Well, that ain't the whole of the story. Not for me anyway. Not by a long shot. Other things started to happen. And nobody can be sure, but it seemed like there were some, some tunnels sort of, and the . . . hell, I don't know, the *thing*. . . ."

"Ah, look," I said. "You . . ."

"No," he said. "No. I want to tell you. It just sounds so . . ." He took a long breath. Some minutes passed.

I had the curious feeling of being high in the air looking down at the two of us, sitting on that little bench in the sunlight, for all the world like two people in casual conversation. All round us in the Oak Grove students and teachers were walking, talking, full of their own pleasures and problems, oblivious to what we were saying.

"One of the tunnels was in that house up there," he said pointing, "up on Cedar Hill, and another was downstream in the valley. Bad things happened in those houses."

He pulled out a huge red handkerchief and wiped his eyes.

"Then . . . Then my wife and son Harold." He began to shake violently. "Ah-h, God," he wailed, "he was only four!" He wept for a few moments.

"Well," he said finally, "they come up missing, see, and I couldn't find them for a couple of days and I was just crazy over it." He was heaving now, heaving with the anguish of his story, and weeping openly, and wiping his eyes with those great gnarled hands.

"Bill Miller and Luther Ameigh, about three days after that even, found them."

I wanted so badly to say the right thing, but I could find no words.

"Found them by accident," he said, "down in the cellar of the church. By a big busted out place in the wall."

He paused once more.

Somehow when he began to speak again it was almost matter-offactly, almost as if he were denying that any of it had actually ever happened.

"They had gone down there for *some* reason, I don't know." He shrugged. "Why wouldn't they? And they were . . . They . . ." He shook his head again in that stiff way he had. "The men, they wouldn't let me down there."

Suddenly he was wringing his hands.

"I wanted to get them, I swear I did. They were my family. But they wouldn't let me." He had to stop again for a few moments.

"Aach, mister, listen," he said turning towards me. "I *wanted* to. I really . . . They was my . . . It was so . . . It . . ."

He was sobbing freely now. I found myself holding the hand of this stranger, weeping also. Weeping for him, weeping for his kin, weeping for the tears of things.

"Well," he said, summoning himself, "they got some guys to go down there, don't ask me how. They was just white with fear. But they went. And then they just pushed everything into the hole, the big blocks, some big rocks they brought down, the mud. *Everything.* Just pushed it all in. They put the sandstone blocks back. And then they bricked it all up. Fast."

He wiped his eyes again and stuffed his handkerchief back into his overall pocket. "Some grave," he said bitterly. He sat quietly for a few moments, and I did not speak.

"I really did try to go down there," he said coldly.

"I'm sure you did," I said.

I was stunned by what I had heard, hardly able to comprehend how he felt as he finished talking or must have felt so many years before. There was nothing I could say to him. I looked up, startled at the idle whistling of a passerby.

"Well," he said finally, "we figured to dam up the narrows down below town enough to flood at least the church tunnel. And I can't even say why. We spent most of one day doing that. Seems foolish now. It was something to do, I guess. You know how you get." Again he turned his body to face me. "More of it got out then. And people really up and left after that. I guess they figured enough was enough."

I listened to his story, hardly able to believe it and yet not able to disbelieve it. I heard him say something about locking doors to homes no one would ever enter again. And the town emptying for-ever without a word to anyone outside Garlock's Bend about the thing that was out in the lake.

But now I only vaguely heard what he was saying through his fi-nal tears. I was trying to deal, one last sad time, with all the memories that his story of so long ago brought back to me. I relived once again the awesome thumps, the crumpled patch, and the filthy smells of rot. Once again I clung in desperation to that tree outside the church, heaving for fresh air, awed by the bitter irony of the quiet lake and the green summer hills.

And I remembered that sudden deep swirl in the water. How in-nocent and how like a gust of air it had seemed to be.

# The Spheres Beyond Sound
## (Threnody)

### Mark Rainey

I never knew my father's father. My parents had been city dwellers since long before I was born, though before them, all our generations since the early eighteenth century were native to the Appalachian Mountains of Virginia. Grandfather lived in the old house atop Copper Peak, which my father's family had inhabited since its inception in this land. I had never been to the place before, though over the course of my life, the stories birthed there, the pictures, and my Dad's related memories had combined to create a mental image that I came to find was not far off the mark in reality.

Grandfather was dead and buried now. His house and property were destined to be sold, a fact that somehow did not settle to my liking. My parents' attitude that the place had outlasted any practical value seemed peculiar, as my Dad had lived there through his adolescence and generally reflected on those days with some degree of affection. Yet, even so, his reluctance to talk much about his family hinted at what I sometimes took to be shame. The reasons for this I never questioned; but I now found myself pondering what life in the mountains must have been like and what secrets the ancient dwelling must hide. Over two centuries of history had been seen from its windows.

Few people, even those that live among them, consider the Appalachian Mountains mysterious or oppressive. Unlike the Rockies, or the wilds of Canada, the Appalachians do not harbor many grave threats to man—there are few dangerous animals, the weather is usually moderate, and pockets of population are generally not too few or far between. However, as with all wild terrain, there are corners left that men seldom travel. Copper Peak lies in the western arm of Virginia, amid a range of treacherously steep, densely wooded ridges. The nearest town to our family place is twelve miles away, a little hamlet called Barren Creek that nestles in the valley between Copper Peak, Thunder Knob and Mount Signal. There is only one road on Copper Peak, which leads from the house to the highway into town; in the last ten years, it has fallen into disuse as my Grandfather's health precluded him traveling even those miles into Barren Creek. I have never quite understood how he existed; he did hire a man to deliver food and other necessities once a week, and to bring his mail from the Barren Creek Post Office, but I cannot imagine a man of his years and failing health subsisting in such an isolated environment. Nonetheless, he seemed to thrive there, and my father was never compelled to suggest his relocating.

After Grandfather's death, I took it to heart to visit the old house, knowing that if my parents sold it, my chance would probably be gone forever. I was due for a week's vacation from my business, so after minimal consideration, I decided that Copper Peak was where I would spend it.

I drove alone from my Washington, DC residence, with a set of maps and written directions provided by my father. The mountainous countryside along Interstate 81 filled my view through the better part of the trip; southwest of Roanoke, the road rose and the green mountains turned to steeper, rock-walled towers. When I turned off the Interstate onto the single lane highway into Barren Creek, I found myself entering a picturesque, quaint world of pastures and woods, occasional farmhouses, and rare drivers passing in the opposite direction. Barren Creek lay a few miles west of a small community called Aiken Mill, which I judged to be very wealthy by the size and style of most of the houses I passed. After the town, the road narrowed, and I found myself alone in a thickly wooded, rapidly rising countryside through which the road snaked and curled. Between Aiken Mill and Barren Creek, I did not encounter a single car going in either direction.

Barren Creek has a population of about two hundred people. The "town" consists of several small buildings on either side of the road, including a bank, a post office (a mobile home painted red, white and blue), a tiny grocery store, and a greasy-spoon diner. A few of the townsfolk were about, most of them old timers with missing teeth, wearing T-shirts and faded overalls. Several of them waved as I passed, to which I responded in kind. Then, a mile or so beyond this strip of urbanization, a gravel road turned to the right and disappeared into the woods high above me. Checking my directions to be sure, I slowed and turned in, realizing I had at last arrived at my destination.

The road was little more than an eroded rut down the mountainside that had been poured over with gravel. At places, the hill grew so steep that my tires spun and spat rock, and I began to think that I might not be able to take the car all the way to the top. But my Japanese coupe proved itself a sturdy little animal, and at last my ascent grew more shallow and less bumpy. Ahead of me, a patch of daylight marked a break in foliage. I passed over a rickety wooden bridge beneath which ran a spidery, shallow stream, identified by my father's directions as Barren Creek, whose source lay on this very mountain. And then, just beyond, I caught my first sight of the Asberry House, seat of my paternal lineage, home of my father's father's fathers.

At first I was surprised by how small it seemed. The few photographs I'd seen made it appear larger, or perhaps seeing it amid the rearing trees created a different sense of scale than did the tiny proportions of a picture. But the atmosphere of the place was much as I imagined it: somewhat dark beneath the sheltering branches, with an undefined but prominent smell of age about the place, carried on an early spring breeze. The weedy, unkempt grass that passed for a lawn disappeared into thick wiry brambles a few feet from the house in each direction, as if being consumed by an inevitable, creeping vegetation. The house's wooden siding was stained and speckled with lichen.

Still, the building appeared sound, and seemed like a natural part of the tranquil environment. I could imagine my Dad as a boy, playing in what would have been a well-trimmed yard, with smoke curling from the chimney and the aroma of some splendid meal being cooked drifting across the clearing. Again, I felt a pang of dismay that such a fundamental relic of our past would soon be either in the hands of others yet unknown, or more likely, demolished and replaced by some sterile piece of architecture as somebody's idea of a summer home. For a vain moment, I entertained the idea that I might buy the place; my profession as a graphic artist supported me adequately, but I could barely afford my single apartment in DC, much less an additional piece of property I would visit only infrequently. I would never be able to live here, for nowhere nearby could I secure employment suitable to my talents.

During that first afternoon, I began to familiarize myself not only with the house but with the surrounding land. After unpacking, I immediately set out walking, hoping to make the most of the remaining sunlight. I soon discovered several overgrown trails that must have been struck by my forefathers over the past two centuries. Following one of them, I came to find the small spring from which Barren Creek spouted, a short distance above the house. The stream wound down the mountainside, mostly parallel to the gravel road; I followed it for a time until I came to a sheer dropoff of at least a hundred feet, where the water leapt into space and plummeted into the valley below. In the summer, this stream all but dried up, hence its name which had been coined by some family member in the late 1700's. The scene was so quietly impressive, so stimulating to my city-numbed nerves, that I knew I *somehow* had to persuade my parents to retain the rights to this wonderful tract of land.

Upon returning to the house, I decided to begin a brief examination before I started thinking about dinner. My Dad had given me the keys, as he and Mom had been here shortly after Grandfather's death to remove a few valuables and generally straighten the place up. I had no idea what they had taken that might have been of interest to me, but happily, I found a wealth of interesting paraphernalia remaining, from old furniture, to books, to photographs, to a number of stringed musical instruments that appeared hand-made. Hanging in the little back room was a mandolin, a classical guitar, two violins and a dulcimer, all beautifully finished and in fine condition. I took this room to be a workshop, where my grandfather must have made these instruments himself. In the tiny den, I found some exceptionally old books, an antique radio, and a reel-to-reel audio tape machine that looked to be of early 1960's stock—apparently the most modern piece of electronics in the whole house. Fortunately, I did have electricity, running water (both hot and cold), and an indoor toilet, so life over the coming week would not prove a particular hardship.

Darkness fell early, and soon the woods came alive with the sounds of insects and nightbirds, something to which I was entirely unaccustomed. I sat down at about seven o'clock to a dinner that consisted of some sandwiches I had packed and a thermos of iced tea. The kitchen had been more or less cleaned out, and I figured that to-morrow I would visit the little store in Barren Creek and pick up a few necessary items. While I ate, I paged through some of the books I had found that looked interesting, including a couple of volumes on local history (courtesy the Aiken Mill Public Library—someone in my family had not been above stealing), an original 19th century copy of *The Abolitionist* by John Brown, which was probably worth a few dollars, and a book of music by one Maurice Zann entitled *The Spheres Beyond Sound*. I was not well-versed in musical theory, but this volume contained some oddly fabulous illustrations that imme-diately caught my interest.

I ate and read to a chorus of chirping and yowling from the dark-ness outside, which at first was distracting, but after a time faded to the background of my awareness. The pictures in the Zann book completely absorbed me, for they consisted of prints and drawings of imaginatively stylized subjects: lizards, birds, fish, skeletons (animal and human), and strange, monstrous-looking things one might ex-pect from a science-fiction movie. But when I began skimming the text, I discovered that this book was by no means a "normal" guide to music theory. Upon finding lines that read, ". . . vibrations of this ex-act frequency and volume are required to complete the summoning process . . ." and, ". . . by assimilating the perfect pitches and tones, the very essence of primal power may be achieved . . ." I decided to start reading the book from the beginning.

I soon found that the strange illustrations were perfectly com-plementary to the written contents. The author's basic premise was that music could open up gateways to other existences—not just in the mind, but in the physical world. Now for me, music is indeed a spiritual experience. It may be hypnotizing or violently stimulating. I

listen to and appreciate all kinds of music, from folk, to jazz, to classical, to hard core rock. When I was younger, nothing delighted me
more than to sit for hours wearing my headphones, carried away by
the power of music. Zann's contention was that certain combinations
of tones could actually alter space—that the correct modulation of
frequency could even reach into the realm of death . . . and beyond.
Needless to say, my first reaction was that I was reading pure fantasy,
but as I read further, the details became increasingly technical and
beyond my grasp, leading me to believe that these ideas were meant
to be regarded as factual. This book kept me occupied well into the
late hours of the evening. Even though there was much that I simply
could not comprehend, there was a certain sense of sobriety in the
writing that held my interest. I found myself almost shaking with excitement as I read this passage:

> . . . I have seen the power which the following strains will
> summon. The rhythm and cadence are extremely vital. The
> switch from 3/4 to 7/8 time signature followed by the 5/3 line
> illustrated below must be instantaneous, without hesita-
> tion or pause. The standard tuning E-A-D-G-B-E in perfect
> A must be changed to D flat-A sharp-E-B sharp-C-E flat to
> facilitate the playing of the proper notes. The range of vol-
> ume produced by each instrument must fall between 32
> and 35 decibels for the summons to be effected. Depending
> upon atmospheric conditions, results may be seen, if the
> process is completed flawlessly, from within three minutes to
> one hour.

Further in the text, there were passages relating to other types of
musical power, from hypnotizing human subjects to communicating
with the dead. But to me, the most astounding aspect of all was the
theory that certain musical arrangements could transcend the limits
of time and space to be heard by *things* existing in other universes.
The concepts of parallel or alternate dimensions have been explored
by both scientists and fantasists for years, I suppose, but never had I
seen such a lucid and calculated thesis on the subject as this. After a
time, I began to wonder why my grandfather would have owned such

a book and if he had given its contents any credence. I supposed the subject might have merely intrigued him, as it did me, especially given his apparent interest in music. Upon checking the front of the book, I learned it had been published by an independent firm in Providence, Rhode Island, copyright 1929 in a limited edition. Putting the book aside, I found that my imagination had been thrust into high gear, and being alone in this old house suddenly seemed a chilling prospect.

When I at last began to prepare myself for bed, I found my hearing to be unnaturally sensitive, such as instinctively happens when danger is present. My chair legs scraped the bare wooden floor with shocking volume, sending a harsh shiver up my spine. I stopped and held my breath for a moment, half expecting to hear . . . something . . . other than the cacophony of the night creatures in the woods. When I heard nothing further, I softly went to the bedroom, made the huge, oak-framed bed with fresh linens from the closet, slipped out of my clothes, and buried myself deep in the covers, leaving the living room light on and the door cracked so I wouldn't be engulfed by the total darkness of the mountain night.

I awoke early, to an absolutely brilliant morning, unable to remember when I had drifted off to sleep. I had slept heavily and peacefully, so it seemed, and I now felt refreshed, free of the odd anxiety which had gripped me during the evening. Morning birds chirped outside my window, in happy contrast to the eerie wails of the night creatures. In the daylight, the house took on a fresh new perspective, and some of my previous enthusiasm for the locale returned. I was hungry, and realizing I had next to nothing in the house to eat, left immediately for the general store in Barren Creek. The town was practically deserted at this hour, but the store was open. The proprietor, a Mr. Avery, greeted me cheerfully enough, asking me from whereabouts I came. When I told him I was the grandson of Timothy Asberry, he merely shrugged, and offered his condolences. Apparently, Grandfather wasn't a part of any close-knit group of locals; my family, like many of the back country dwellers, had valued its privacy and seldom gathered with neighbors.

When I returned to the house, I fixed a large breakfast of bacon, eggs and toast; after eating, I let my attention return to the weird volume of Maurice Zann. In the golden daylight, it no longer seemed a warped, dreadful recording of factual data, but a fanciful representation of some writer's bizarre imagination. I decided that, for the morning, I would forget it, explore some more of the mountain, and conduct a more thorough search of the house. There would still be a host of relics from my grandfather's day, and before, that would help me put together a more complete picture of my heritage.

About ten o'clock, I set out walking, heading north, in the direction opposite yesterday's expedition. I discovered a worn trail that led along the crest of Copper Peak, and I followed it, taking in the exhilarating view of the surrounding valleys and slopes. Off to the east, far below me, I could see a few tiny buildings, which I took to be Barren Creek. Further beyond lay Aiken Mill, a larger community, but still separated from "civilization" by a tall, knobby ridge.

About half a mile from the house, I came upon a flattened area beneath a canopy of limbs, and to my surprise, found it to be a small graveyard. There were maybe two dozen markers of varying shapes and sizes, all of them weathered with age, most of them nearly obscured by creeping flora. I strolled into their midst, noting the engraved names that were still legible: Nicholas Asberry, 1761–1834; Stuart Asberry (my namesake), 1820–1914; Suzette Asberry Washington, 1823–1902; James Druid Asberry, 1895–1938; Sarah Collins Asberry, 1811–1899. I found myself mildly excited, for here lay my direct ancestors, those whose names I might have heard only in passing over the years. Here, the past surrounded me, in the very earth which contained the blood of my progenitors.

My parents had not told me specifically where my grandfather was buried. "In our family plot, in the mountains," Dad merely had said. Now I wondered . . . I let my eyes rove among the stones, seeking. Then, in a far corner, standing alone . . . yes, a fresh marker above a patch of newly turned earth. I approached it, positive of what I would find.

I was correct. Timothy Cadden Asberry, my father's father, born in 1910. The remains of some flowers drooped next to the obelisk-like stone, probably those which my parents had placed here upon Grandfather's burial. Thin shoots of grass were just beginning to burst from the mound of earth, and brown spots of mold had broken out on the granite. I stood there for a time, not quite sure if I should grieve, or offer a prayer. Finally I murmured a low, "Rest in peace," finding nothing within myself worth conveying to the dead. Then I turned and left the graveyard, feeling vaguely disconcerted and a little confused. I didn't know why.

For a time, I wandered aimlessly, at last finding myself back at the waterfall I'd discovered the previous day. The air was quiet and still, and gazing at the tiny houses and green slopes in the distance, I came to realize that some odd strain of music seemed to be running through my head. It was low, harmonious and pleasant, but altogether unfamiliar. I am not a competent songwriter, and it seemed strange that something I was sure I'd never heard before would weave its way from my unconscious.

For a while longer, I stood musing, then started back for the house. I decided I would make a light snack and then sift through a couple of the closets I had seen. I had to admit to myself that suddenly I had become fascinated by the past; until recently, I had always been ambivalent about life before my time. Occasionally, when Dad would speak about his past, my curiosity would be slightly aroused, but immediately forgotten when I returned to my ordinary affairs. Here, I supposed, with little else to occupy my mind, the past loomed larger and more tantalizing.

By the time I reached the house, my enthusiasm for delving into its closets and cupboards had peaked. I built a substantial ham and cheese sandwich for lunch, chased it with a glass of iced tea, and then went to the bedroom to begin my foraging.

My parents had packed away most of the clothes and incidental personal items. But I soon came upon many neat little artifacts, such as an ancient shaving kit complete with brush and straight razor, a slightly rusted pocket watch, and a few bottles of age-old cologne, mostly still full. There were some more books stacked in a corner, including a Bible, a dictionary, something called *The Encyclopaedia for Boys*, and a world atlas, all at least forty years old. And then I spied some cartons that immediately caught my interest—a number of six-inch reel tapes for the machine I had seen in the other room. I pulled these from their corner, finding four in all, each labeled with faded black ink in crabbed script, which I assumed to be Grandfather's.

Two of them were sermons recorded at a local church, which Grand-father must have attended, one was a radio show from 1964, and the last was labelled "Zann," recorded in 1966.

I immediately took this one into the living room, found the tape machine in the corner, and proceeded to set it up for listening. I prayed the machine would work after however many years of dis-use. Upon plugging it in, I found that everything seemed to work well enough. The reels began turning, and I stood anxiously wait-ing as hissing and crackling sounded over the small speaker. Then, a voice began, which I knew immediately was my grandfather's: a slow, deep drawl with a pronounced southern Virginia accent, not unlike my Dad's. The voice sounded tentative and somewhat ner-vous, perhaps due to inexperience with talking to a machine. What he said was this:

> I am making this recording to test a few of the passages from the Zann text, on pages 121 through 128 of *The Spheres Be-yond Sound*. I am Tim Asberry, I live on Copper Peak outside of Barren Creek, Virginia, I am making this recording with the help of my neighbors, John Eubanks, Fred Wharton, Ray Philippe and Bill Miller. I am making this recording from my backyard, facing the crest of the mountain. Uh, we have practiced select verses, or uh, lines out of the book, but this will be the first complete performance of what Zann calls, uh, the summons. My neighbors and myself have all read the text, and we believe that if we follow the directions, as set down by the writer, we will actually experience the, uh, reve-lations he has foreseen.
>
> I have decided to record this activity on my recorder . . . we don't honestly know what to expect, but if we should be successful, then it is possible there may be some danger. Zann's text indicates that the, uh, existences, uh, on the other side are not necessarily malevolent, but they are destructive in nature, like a shark in the ocean. The means to send back the, uh, results of a summoning are printed on pages 135 through 137 of the text, and this part we have played in full at several practice meetings.

As I have said, I believe the writer of this book is sincere, for the simple reason that I have had proof. Two months ago, I took my fiddle up to the graveyard and played the piece on pages 39 and 40—the prelude to opening the barrier of death. As I played, as surely as I'm sitting here now, I saw the corrupted bodies of my relatives appear and stand around me, as solid as the earth under my feet. As I was so frightened, I quit playing, and they vanished, but on two occasions, I have gone back to the graveyard and heard weird music, though there was no one there to be playing it. I believe it was an answer of a kind to the invitation I played. But I haven't responded. And I don't go back to the graveyard anymore.

Now I felt a tremendous surge in my heart, a complete disbelief of what I was hearing. But I continued to listen, hypnotized by the fear in the low voice on the tape, not sure now if my grandfather were wholly of sound mind. I could sense that he was terrified of proceeding with this plan of his . . . yet the longing to unveil the mysteries of Maurice Zann's book so outweighed his fear that he was willing to risk unknowable consequences. There came a series of tonal pluckings and whinings as the group tuned their instruments—probably the very same ones that hung in the small workshop next to the living room. A couple of unfamiliar voices said something incomprehensible, and my grandfather spoke again:

It's getting dark now, and we're about to start. I will admit that all of us are pretty afraid, but we believe that the things we might learn are so incredible and so important that they warrant whatever risk. I think from what we've learned so far, we will be safe.

There was a pause and more background voices. Then, my grandfather's voice said, "So, you ready?" and after a moment, a sudden discordant jangle rattled from the speaker. Harsh plucking and flat strumming echoed through what must have been a still mountain night more than twenty-five years ago. The noise seemed to have no rhythm or melody. Insect-like chirps arpeggioed up and down unknown scales, bass thumps jumped from one time signature to another, without any pattern or structure . . . so it seemed. What I was hearing sounded more like a random banging of instruments by inexperienced hands than a complex latticework of music holding some deep-hidden power. But as I listened further, I caught strains of some unearthly harmony occasionally breaking through the chaotic dissonance. I began to hear tones that were not of stringed instruments, but of deep woodwinds or brassy pipes. The harmonic overtones of the mandolin, guitar, violin and dulcimer were producing sounds unlike any I had ever heard, even in the most radical of electronic fusion.

Beyond this cacophony, a definite melody seemed to come together, but at such distance as to be drowned by the brash orchestration. I turned the volume up on the machine, straining to catch the sequence of the evasive notes. I began to get distortion over the speaker, but I shut my ears to the pain, concentrating only on what lurked beneath. Yes . . . some sort of melody was forming, combining in arias of thin, reed-like whistles and lower, rich tones that could only be blown from a French horn.

And then, beyond that, another distinct tune, but so faint as to be lost in the crashing of insane strings. I sat there for a time, separated from my surroundings by a spell of mesmerizing power. My thoughts seemed to dissolve, and I allowed myself to be absorbed amid raw energy that explored every realm of ecstasy, tranquility, horror, and agony.

Suddenly, it was over. I sat facing the rear window of my Grandfather's house, peering toward the depths of the forest. There was a clatter from the speaker as the musicians lowered their instruments and simultaneously breathed exhausted sighs. For a full two minutes, nothing further issued except a soft sigh of breeze and a few crickets beginning their chorus for the evening. At last one of the background voices said, "What is it? Anything?"

My grandfather mumbled something low. Then, "No. Nothing." I waited again as silence returned, picturing the group of men looking about expectantly, probably with fear-widened eyes, their sweaty palms trembling. Then, Grandfather said, "Wind's picking up."

Sure enough, the drone of the breeze was growing stronger. It

rose and fell several times, whistling by the microphone that probably sat unprotected somewhere near the players. But still, nothing
more could be heard except for the increasing chatter from the forest.
Almost five minutes went by without a word from any of the men.

Then, Grandfather abruptly said:

> Well, looks like nothing is happening . . . so far. Guess we'll
> have to wait and see. The book said it could take a little
> while, I guess, if the weather is not conducive to picking up
> the message. I'd think these are optimum conditions . . .
> sky's clear, it's pretty cold . . . sound really carries. Wind's
> holding, I'd say between five and ten miles per hour. I sup-
> pose we could have done something incorrectly . . . damned
> piece of music ain't meant to be played by human hands . . .
> but it sure seemed like we did it.

Outside, here in my own time, the afternoon sun was well on its
way into the west. It would be dark within the hour. I felt a shiver run
up my spine. A gust of chill wind had swirled through the house.

> To save tape, I'll shut off for the moment and come back at
> the first sign of anything happening. Still damned peculiar . . .
> absolutely nothing. Nothing at all.

There was a click as the tape was shut off all those years ago. Another click followed as it was turned back on some indeterminate
time later.

> It's been thirty minutes now. No sign of anything unusual.
> The crickets are going nuts, as you can hear, but apart from
> that, everything seems normal. Pretty disappointing, but
> also kind of a relief. Maybe it's better if nothing happens. I
> guess it ain't right for Christian men to fool around with
> powers that only the Lord should know about. 'Course, I
> suppose there's a lot this family's done that ain't considered
> right and true. (Grandfather chuckled.) It's common knowl-
> edge that the Asberrys make the best whiskey outside
> Franklin County . . . but I reckon in the eyes of God that's

a small sin compared to messing around with the powers that be.

I frowned. I wondered if the Asberrys' "shady" side—moonshining—had been the source of my Dad's discomfort in sharing his family's past with me. My father was a decent and proud man, and I guess it would be like him to feel a sense of guilt coming from a background of less than upright standing. Having broken from his rural mold and successfully established himself in an urban environment, I could see how the simple—and illicit—life his family led might have developed into a sore point with him.

Now, though, I wondered if there might be other secrets my family had kept hidden . . . darker things . . . occult things. Perhaps the music of Maurice Zann was only one such example. Might this old family have been delving into unknown, forbidden lore since before they settled here from the Old World?

I have always considered myself rational and well-educated, reasonably wise in the ways of the world. Still, the purely intuitive side of my nature felt the stirrings of some primal dread; instinct had overridden reason, leaving me confused and uncomfortable. The woods and wilderness which I had found so charming and restful now seemed fraught with mysteries less than inviting.

Another couple of clicks came from the player. Then, my Grandfather's voice said:

Forty-five minutes now. Still nothing. The boys and me are starting to breathe a little easier now. John's gone inside to make coffee. We can sure use it after this. I guess it's better this way. Maybe we messed up, or maybe the Lord just said it ain't to be. Anyway, if nothing happens in the next few minutes, I think we'll all sleep much better tonight. After this, I reckon I'll be forgetting all about what happened before. I'll put that book away and never bother with it again. I should never have taken it from Daddy in the first place.

So, the book had been in the family even before my grandfather. Interesting.

Well, unless something happens tonight, I might as well give up on this recording. I'm pretty tired . . . all of us are right worn out, matter of fact. It's been hard work. So for now, I'll be ending all this up . . . uh, unless the need arises sometime later. So . . . signing off.

Grandfather ended on that uncertain note. There was nothing else on the tape, which disappointed me, as I had hoped for at least some explanation or commentary on the night's activities. Their attempt had surely been a failure, and I found nothing in the house to suggest any future effort to reproduce the experiment. And nothing mysterious seemed to have befallen my grandfather in the intervening years.

And what of this whole premise, I wondered to myself. Could I place any stock in the concepts my grandfather had sought—and failed—to prove? Surely not, I thought. There had indeed been some unusual, elusive depth to the music on the tape, but surely, nothing that could convince me of its mystical power.

My grandfather sounded like an intelligent man, with a modicum of formal education. I wondered just what his experience in the graveyard had been that encouraged him to seek the greater power revealed in Zann's text. Had he merely suffered some frightening manifestation of his own imagination? Frustration began to tear at me, for it seemed that this mystery was destined to die with no promise of resolve. Deciphering the technical concepts in *The Spheres Beyond Sound* was completely beyond my ability.

There had to be some other way of gathering information. Possibly, the neighbors that had aided my grandfather's performance—they could be of assistance if they were still alive and of sound memory.

Then I remembered the strange tune that had entered my head while I was walking from the graveyard. Had not Grandfather spoken of hearing supernatural music when he had gone there? Could I have shared such an experience here, more than twenty-five years after the fact? Suddenly, I realized I had to return to the woods to see if the same thing might happen again.

Late afternoon was creeping over the mountain, but I calculated

I could easily get to the cemetery and back before dark; and perhaps tomorrow, I could search for the men that had accompanied my grandfather on the tape. Maybe there was yet hope for this venture.

I disconnected the tape machine and returned the reel to its carton. Then I set out walking, carrying a flashlight just in case darkness fell upon me sooner than expected. The worst hazard would be the steep dropoff near the trail. Yet, it seemed that something about nature had been stirred up by the music on the tape. Since I was a child, I have seldom felt the thrill of fear, the sense of foreboding cast by the unknown. That feeling was upon me now, and though I was skeptical of it, I also held for it a certain amount of respect.

It didn't take me long to reach my destination. The graveyard was immersed in a pool of shadow as the sun dropped beyond the wall of trees; but I sensed something different, an atmosphere I had never felt before. Small whirlpools of wind were flitting among the gravestones, lifting earth and dead foliage into writhing dances in midair. Strange dark patches grew here and there that were not shadows. A low rumble issued from the ground, as if something huge were stirring from sleep. And from the air, my ears detected the faintest of tonal wails mixed with the whistle of the breeze. I listened carefully, finally managing to pick out a distinct, harmonious blending of tones from the background jumble of sounds.

None of these elements was spectacular or even blatant. They each combined to create a sense of awry atmosphere, a subtle *wrongness*. But my conscious mind now perceived that unnatural influences were at work here, for these phenomena could not possibly be ordinary acts of nature. I knew now that the music of Maurice Zann was, in fact, the source.

How? Why? The original attempt by my grandfather had failed. What conditions could have changed that allowed my thoughtless playing of the tape to summon whatever thing—or *things*—appeared to be struggling into existence? I had been so curious that I had never considered the possibility of the music having some mystical effect.

What the hell was going to happen?

I left the graveyard, running down the path that led to the waterfall. All I could think of now was getting away from this place.

Behind me, a weird, wild shriek suddenly tore into the forest; something animalistic, sub-human. It was joined by another, then another, like a ghastly choir of agonized voices. Something beneath my feet boomed deeply; then the ground shook so violently I was sure the surface had been rent and that now the denizens of the underworld would be crawling out of their blazing pits. More chilling cries from the graveyard sent me running even faster, down toward the house which I considered my only retreat.

Suddenly, before I realized it, I had reached the precipice where the stream pitched into space. I caught the trunk of a small tree just in time to save me hurtling over the edge, but nearly dislocating my shoulder in the process. A stab of pain halted me in my tracks.

Then, my eyes caught something moving in the valley below. The sun had just reached the horizon, and on this side of the mountain, facing east, only shadow filled the depths below. But in that darkness, something even darker, something gigantic, seemed to be crawling across the floor of the valley. My eyes riveted on that mass of blackness, its immensity mesmerizing me. My lungs stopped working, and for a moment, I felt I was falling; somehow, I was able to keep holding onto that tree. It was the only thing that saved me.

From the woods behind me, there now came a multitude of shufflings and scrapings, as of many bodies moving through the foliage. Gutteral groans and hoarse cries drifted through the dark woods toward me. A surge of panic sent me flying back from the edge and down the trail again, my way guided only by an instinctive urge to escape.

The woods had grown nearly pitch black, and I could not see the trail. Twice I slammed into hidden trees, luckily avoiding being impaled on broken branches. Reeling from the force of the impacts, I reached out to find support . . . and gripped a moist, muddy limb that seemed to hang too limply from something unseen. Then, to my horror, that limb moved of its own accord, and I felt something hard and firm take hold of my wrist. I jerked my arm back purely by reflex; and as I did, a shrill wail exploded from the shadowy form in front of me. I launched myself past it and began my flight anew down the treacherous path, blindly hoping to reach the house without killing myself.

Many times in nightmares I have found myself fleeing from some terrible threat. As often as not, my car is my refuge, for in mobility there is hope of safety. I was now living one of my nightmares, and my one goal was to get to my car and escape from this terrible mountain. And like in so many dreams, the darkness engulfed me, slowing me down, obscuring my path. I cannot count how many times I lost my footing or was snagged by grasping branches. Somehow, I at last reached the house, the kitchen light glowing invitingly. With profound but temporary relief, I pushed my way in through the back door, slamming it behind me, and leaning heavily against it.

I didn't care about the few belongings I had brought with me. My only concern now was to find my keys and get away from here with all possible haste. From outside, I could hear the restless chatter of the night creatures, more urgent than usual, and their chirps and buzzings spurred me on. I ran into the bedroom, found my keys on the bedside table. Grabbing them up, I turned and ran out the front door, not bothering to turn off the lights or lock the house.

The moment I shakily inserted the key into the car door, I heard a grating rumble from the woods just above the house. Looking up, I could see the tops of the dark trees shaking and pitching back and forth. The wailing sounds returned, drifting down from the darkness, drawing steadily nearer. A lump of terror rose in my throat, for it now seemed there was no way I could get down the mountain in time to escape whatever was coming.

I jerked the car door open with a burst of frenzied strength, slid into the seat and willed my hand to carefully insert the key into the ignition. I somehow accomplished this on the first attempt, fired up the engine, and flipped on the headlights.

The car faced the side of the house, and caught in the beams of the headlights stood a figure whose appearance nearly stopped my heart. It was a parody of a man, or had once been a man. It stood facing me on two spindly legs, its body a mass of dark, moss-covered earth. Two blackened eye pits gaped from its mud-encrusted skull, empty, but seemingly possessed of sight. For a long moment, it did not move, only stood there apparently regarding me. Then, at either corner of the house, two similar figures appeared, both facing me, but making no move in my direction.

Then, out of the empty air, I heard the mad strains of that mystical music, and to my shock and bewilderment, those corrupted bodies began to whirl and leap, spinning and pirouetting in a grotesque, fiery dance. And at that moment, above the roof of the house, a great mass of blackness rose into the night sky, blocking the glittering stars that had just begun to appear. The night fell utterly still; no wind cut across the mountaintop, no insect chirped. Only the notes of the supernatural music floated into the sky. The whirling figures ceased their dancing and dropped to their bony knees, prostrating themselves before the black shape that hovered over the house. I began to perceive at the far reaches of my senses the wistful notes of my grandfather's stringed cacophony.

As I sat there, the features of the huge thing before me gradually came into focus. I could see what appeared to be thick, arthropodic legs, dozens of meters long, and in the midst of the solid central mass, a myriad of tiny, flickering lights grouped in dense bunches. It was a gigantic spider-like thing with a thousand eyes which glared down at me as if ready to pounce. The worshipping corpses began a new wailing chorus.

As the glare of those thousand eyes bore down on me, I realized why my grandfather's original performance had failed to summon this entity, whereas the playing of the tape had succeeded: I had turned the volume on the machine up to catch the subtle undertones of the music. The lower, most subtle elements of the "live" performance on acoustic instruments had failed to reach the volume prescribed in the Zann text. Yet the very same music, played at a higher decibel level had been in the exact range to complete the summoning process.

Then another cold fear seized me—due to the failure of his attempt, Grandfather had not recorded the passage with which to return the extra-dimensional terror to its rightful place. There was no way to send the thing back!

Now, strange whispers, voices from somewhere beyond this plane of time and space began to swirl through the air around me like buzzing bees. Panic motivated my hand, and I slammed the gear lever into reverse and spun the steering wheel, turning my car down the road away from the house. In mad fury, the car screamed and bucked over the pot-holed road, several times nearly skidding into the woods on either side. I did not slow down though, for the fear of smashing myself into a tree was not nearly so real as the otherworldly threat I was leaving behind.

At last, I reached the bottom of the mountain and sent my car hurtling down the winding highway toward Barren Creek, not looking into the rearview mirror to see what might be following.

The music and whispering faded from my hearing, though my terror did not subside. Once, while speeding down a long, curving decline that allowed me a brief view of Copper Peak, I swore I saw a portion of the sky blocked out by a gigantic, spider-like shape resting on top of the mountain. But the road curved again, and Copper Peak slipped once and for all beyond my line of sight.

In Aiken Mill, I stopped to fill my gas tank, which had fallen dangerously close to empty. As I nervously pumped the gasoline into my car, my eyes darted repeatedly down the road whence I came, half-expecting to see some crawling, pitch-black silhouette advancing from the distance. But nothing appeared, and I paid the nervous-looking attendant who must have thought I had escaped from the nearby Catawba Sanatorium. By the time I reached Interstate 81 to head back home, I had seen nothing more, and the terror that consumed me slowly began to abate.

And yet for me, the real fear lies ahead. Whatever the music of Maurice Zann summoned must still lurk on the fringes of this world, somewhere in the mountains around Barren Creek. The only way to send it back is by playing the proper musical arrangements from *The Spheres Beyond Sound*, and the only copy of that book in existence seems to be at my old family house. Even if I could find the right passage, someone who could read music would have to play the piece. As it is, I have been unable to find that book, or any record of such a book at any library or bookstore, even those that I called in Providence. And I will never, never return to that place in the mountains, at any time, for any reason. I have urged my parents to sell the house, but to avoid going there at all costs. Of course, I discussed nothing about the events that had transpired there with my father, yet as irrational as I must have sounded, he seemed to accept my words without question—and with a strange appearance of understanding.

As I said, however, the real terror for me has yet to manifest itself. For surely, those animated corpses were those of my own relatives, their eternal souls somehow drawn back to their wasted bodies. Even now, they must dance and worship that black overlord of death which Zann's music called from beyond. Thus I have sealed my fate, for my own bloodline calls to me: at times, I can hear those demonic notes pounding in my ears, as if the long-dead Asberrys beckon me to join them. Whatever paradise might await others in the life after this, I know it is never meant for me; for as long as that black spider remains free in this world, the gate to the other side is blocked and guarded. Eventually, my time will come; I will then become one of those damned, dancing parodies that bewail their fate and bow to the demon master from the dimension beyond death.

Printed in the United States
by Baker & Taylor Publisher Services